# NO OTHER MAN

# NO OTHER MAN

NO OTHER

BOOK ONE

HEATHER GRAHAM

WOLFPACK
PUBLISHING
— EST 2013 —

**No Other Man**
Paperback Edition


Wolfpack Publishing
1707 E. Diana Street
Tampa, FL 33609

www.wolfpackpublishing.com



No Other Man was originally published 1995 by Heather Graham writing as Shannon Drake.

Paperback ISBN 979-8-89567-703-2
Ebook ISBN 979-8-89567-702-5

# NO OTHER MAN

# CHAPTER 1

*LATE SUMMER, 1875*

God was punishing her. It had to be that simple.

And that was awful.

As the stagecoach came to a jerking halt, Skylar wondered briefly if she deserved the kind of death that now threatened her. No. No one deserved the fate it seemed she was doomed to discover. Please, God, no one. And what she had done was surely not so very bad, not so horrible, not so...

Oh, God!

She had seen them coming. Seen the war-painted Braves on their speeding painted ponies, screeching out their hair-raising battle cries. She had prayed that the stagecoach might somehow outdistance them, but she had wondered even then if God would pay heed to her fevered cries after the deception she had so desperately carried out.

It seemed not.

The doors to the coach were suddenly wrenched open. Fear ran like an icy river throughout her limbs, clutching her heart and lungs. Suddenly sunlight poured in, somewhat blinding her, yet what she saw was enough to turn her fear into terror.

A massive shadow filling the doorway. Blocking out the sun. Huge, forbidding, terrifying...

It was Sioux country. She'd known there were Indians in the West. She'd known the United States Army was heavily in residence near here, battling the heathens on behalf of the settlers, more and more of whom had flowed into the Badlands area when gold had been discovered here. She'd heard tales about the savages. The eastern newspapers had been filled with reports of them, all of them, the Comanche, the Cheyenne, the Pawnee, the Crow, the Assiniboine...

The Sioux.

Indeed, she'd heard something about them. About the way they'd been moving steadily westward themselves, battling other tribes who vied for the same hunting grounds. They were what the soldiers called true "blanket and pony" Indians, hunting the buffalo on horseback, painting themselves garishly for warfare, finding the greatest honor in feats of daring in battle. She'd also heard there were good Indians—those who accepted the White ways and stayed on the reservations set aside for them. Then there were the "hostiles," those who refused to accept the boundaries of white treaties. Those who now raided white settlements and murdered whites whenever they could.

Those who attacked stagecoaches.

Oh, God, she had known that horrible things happened.

And she'd come here anyway.

She hadn't been able to allow herself to think about the Indian situation. She hadn't been able to allow herself to be afraid. Oh, God, she had been clutching at life, all right, grasping perhaps, and what she had done had been wrong.

She had taken just pains to escape the East, traveled a long, circuitous two-week route when the train might have taken her half the time. She had done everything to avoid danger in the east, and now, oh, God, she had been wrong, but surely, not so wrong as to deserve this.

She blinked furiously, trying to clear her vision. The dark, massive form in the doorway to the coach remained.

Impossibly tall, impossibly muscled and bronzed. His face was painted, half in red, half in black. Straight black hair fell past his shoulders. Buckskin leggings covered his thighs while beaded boots of a-like skin clung tightly to the heavy muscles of his calves. His chest, in all its muscled bronze glory, was bare except for designs painted in the same red and black shades that adorned his face. One look at him was enough to instill the very fear of God and the devil in her heart. She was well aware the Indians could be as merciless with women and children as they were with the soldiers.

Did they, perhaps, have a right to be so brutal? Hadn't she heard talk as well that the soldiers were terrible when they attacked Indian camps? Everyone had heard stories about the famous young brevet general, Custer, who had done such glorious deeds for the North during the War Between the States. In 1868, he'd attacked a Cheyenne camp on the Washita River. It was another "great victory" for the whites—articles from massacred settlers had been found in the camp—but there were those who had written about the number of Indian women and children who had been slaughtered during the attack.

But she hadn't slaughtered anyone!

Yet now, here, was this man, blocking the sun, threatening to make the earth flow crimson with her blood.

Split seconds passed as terror filled her.

But the hysterical scream she expected did not tear from her throat. Somehow, she swallowed it. If she was going to die anyway, she was going to do so fighting.

She'd heard enough about the Indians to know they'd enjoy her death even more if she begged for mercy while they granted not a whit of it.

Even as the brave at the door reached in to drag her out, she remembered the hatpin holding her mourning bonnet in place upon her head. She wrenched it out with a speed she found astonishing herself, grasped it firmly, and slammed it straight at the warrior's eye. Something deep, guttural, and furious spewed from his lips as he caught her hand with a half second to spare in which to preserve his eyesight. She cried out with pain as his grasp seemed about to break the fragile bones of her hand. His hold eased, but barely. Kicking and screaming, she found herself being dragged from the coach. Her wild gyrations sent both of them flying to the dry, dusty ground. She saw the knife sheathed at his hip and lunged for it, drawing it free and aiming it at his throat before he once more managed to salvage himself from her deadly intent, this time capturing her wrist and rolling to pin her beneath him. She cried out again in fury and fear as he slammed her wrist against the earth, causing her to give up her hold on the weapon. He straddled her then, catching both her wrists in his merciless grip, his thighs tight around her hips. She continued to struggle, swearing, praying that the swearing would help her. "Bastard, wretched pagan, savage, hideous demon from the fires of hell, get off of me!" Yet if he got off of her, what then? Three of his comrades watched just a few yards away from them, seated upon their painted ponies silently observing her desperate struggles. If she freed herself from this brave, the four of them would hunt her down, run her into the ground, rape her, take her scalp, and leave her carcass for the crows...

"Cowards!" she hissed, trying to spit, trying to claw, whimpering, screaming, twisting. As she fought against the weight and muscle pinning her to the ground, she realized that the buckskin leggings provided little covering for the savage atop her. They twisted with each of her wild, bucking movements, creating a wave of dread and horrific fascination within her as she noticed the man wore a scanty breechclout along with the leggings, and nothing more. "Cowards!" she cried again, twisting anew. "Attacking a lone woman! Slaying that poor old driver!" *Had they slain the man?* she wondered. They must have done so, for he was nowhere to be seen. He was not leaping to her defense. She had to be grateful that she couldn't see the driver's mutilated, dead body upon the ground. She started to cry out again, her fury all that kept her from pure hysteria.

"You are nothing but hideous beasts! I swear it! You will all die, you bastards. The cavalry will come. You'll die slowly, I promise, I..."

The cavalry would come? In time to save her? She doubted it. Still, her threats were keeping her alive. But to what purpose? If she stalled them this minute, they would slay her the next!

"God damn you. I will come back myself from heaven or hell!" she breathed, then inhaled, desperate for more breath to continue her tirade.

And in that second, she saw his eyes.

Strange eyes for an Indian brave. Green eyes. As deep and dark as the trees from which the Black Hills had drawn their name, yet distinctively and decidedly green.

Did it matter? Some white blood had ventured into this man's past, leaving behind a legacy of green eyes. Would that save her life now? She doubted it.

She sucked in more air, fighting the tears that stung her eyes. "Bastard!" she shrieked again. "Get off me—kill me or get off me!"

Oddly enough, in those seconds while she had stared, thoroughly startled, into his eyes, he had somewhat relaxed his grip upon her. With a wild, frantic effort, she freed her hands, managing to pummel his chest and swipe one set of nails across his cheek. A deep, rich, savage sound came from his lips, a sound so fierce it seemed to knife into her soul itself. He caught her hands again, this time leaping from her with swift agility and dragging her up along with him. She thought that she had found a new freedom with which to fight, but before she could begin a new onslaught in any way, she found herself thrown over his shoulder as he walked for his pony. The dusty remnants of her bonnet were left behind on the dry earth. Her hair, a very deep, rich honey blonde that fell past her waist in heavy waves—once a great pride to her but soon to adorn various teepees as trophies—fell free from the last of the hairpins that had held it regally in place just moments before. She gasped deeply as it tangled around her face. She twisted, freeing herself from the cloud of it, and struggled to rise against his back. As soon as she achieved enough balance to slam a fist against his back, she was lifted again and thrown belly down over his pony's flanks. And before she could rise from that position, he had scissored his legs over his mount's haunches and sat bareback astride the animal. Desperate, she struggled to rise against the pony's flanks, only to find him kicking the animal into motion while delivering a strike both painful and humiliating upon the region of her derriere, despite the black taffeta bustle that rested there.

Dirt spewed up from the earth. She coughed and choked, then

ridiculously found herself clinging to his knee in fear that the sudden speeding motion of the horse would send her hurtling down to the ground to be trampled. She didn't know how far they rode or for how long. Time and space lost all meaning during the reckless race they seemed to take against the wind. When he drew the horse to a halt at last, the daylight had waned. They had left the dust, flatlands, and rock behind and climbed into the hills. When he dismounted, dragging her numbed body from its precarious perch atop the haunches of the pony, a pale red glow of sunset was settling over a copse of trees and the small cabin that stood within that copse.

He set her upon the ground. For a moment she merely stared at the cabin and wondered when he had murdered the people who had once dwelled within it, for it had obviously been the small home of a white man, a trapper, perhaps. Maybe even that of a schoolmarm who had been dedicated to teaching the children of the scattered white homesteaders, miners, bankers, ranchers, and farmers. Some light glowed from within the cabin, as if a fire burned within a hearth, a fire to welcome home the weary.

She was free she realized. The Indian had led the pony into a small paddock that flanked the cabin, taking the bit and bridle from its head so that the trusty creature might munch freely on the hay that brimmed from a feeder.

The man's three comrades had ridden on elsewhere, she discovered with amazement.

She turned to run downhill, into the darkness, into the copse, into the night.

From there, where?

It didn't matter in the least. She had taken no more than three flying steps before she shrieked out with pain and stopped in her tracks as the Indian's fingers wound into her hair, dragging her back. "Damn you, damn you!" she cried out, trying to pummel him with her fists as he swept her up. She wound up face down over his shoulder again, swearing and fighting as he made his way to the cabin.

Once inside, he set her on her feet. She tried to run around him, determined to reach the door. But he caught her hair again and this time kept his grip within it, moving her deeper into the cabin where he forced her down upon a bed covered with a blanket of rich, warm fur. She grasped for his wrist, trying to claw his flesh, anything to force him to relinquish his hold on her hair. He did release her hair but only to pull a rawhide strip from his legging and bind her wrists together.

"No, no, no!" she told him, her voice rising as she struggled to keep from being bound.

It did no good. Down on one knee before her, he quickly and efficiently tied her wrists so that she could barely move her hands. Then he rose, leaving her seated there upon the bunk, moving to warm his own hands at the fire within the hearth.

"You must have murdered these poor people a while ago!" she cried out. Why was she taunting him? Wasn't she going to die an awful enough death as it was? Why was he waiting? He should kill her, have done with this torture! Yet as she lived, hope lived. She should keep silent. Humor him. Humor a savage who didn't understand a word that fell from her lips? No! Keep talking, keep fighting in spirit, pray that there would be one second when he would truly let down his guard!

"Quite comfortable here, aren't you, you goon?" she cried out. "Right at home!"

He didn't seem to hear her. He stared into the flames. She tossed her head, looking about the cabin. It was a one-room dwelling, and surprisingly, it appeared to be inhabited. Beneath the fur cover, she could see that the bunk was decked in cotton sheets as well. The pillow was covered with a clean matching case. There was a table before the hearth, and simple curtains hung at the four windows. A hip tub sat to the right of the table, near the hearth, and behind that, there was a wooden counter for food preparation, and within it, a pump that was surely attached to an outside well. There was a wardrobe against the wall behind the bunk, and a clothing trunk lay at the foot of it. A huge leg of ham and several pounds of cheese hung from pegs above the counter area, while shelves were filled with what appeared to be containers of preserves, bottles of wine, and even canned goods. It was a modest place, clean and neat. For one person or a young couple, it would make a cozy home.

Startled by the sound of water being poured, she looked quickly back at the Indian. He had taken a huge, steaming pot from atop the hearth and dumped the water from it into the hip tub. Her jaw dropped as she realized he was stripping down from his scant clothing to nothing at all. He stood naked, his back to her. Still stunned, inhaling a ragged breath, she seemed unable to do anything other than stare, her heart hammering fiercely. He was a very tall man, more imposing than she had realized in all her terrified struggling. Every inch of that height was savagely muscled. His shoulders were very broad, his back was long, his buttocks were as hard muscled as his sturdy, well-shaped legs. Even from the back, his arm muscles rippled.

She quickly averted her eyes, looking toward the cabin door as he stepped into the tub.

He lay back comfortably.

And sighed.

She stared at him at first, incredulous. She had read accounts of Indian captivity. Accounts of Sioux raids, encounters in which survivors were sometimes shot even as they assumed they were being taken hostage, encounters in which men, women, and children were taken for slave labor and used brutally.

But a savage warrior opting first for a bath did not quite seem to fit well with any previous account she had come across.

She couldn't see much more than the power of his shoulders and the sleek wet darkness of his hair as he sat in the tub, for he faced away from her. He seemed to be scrubbing himself furiously, removing his war paint. Why?

Would he paint himself differently to murder her? One set of colors for the capture, another for the kill?

Perhaps she was to be some kind of ritual sacrifice. Killed in a very specific way.

Oh, God!

She leaped up, lifting her bound hands before her, ready to throw herself against the door. What did she do once she was free with her bound hands? What if animals attacked in the night?

*How would that be different from the fate that awaited her here?* she shrieked silently to herself.

But again, it didn't matter. He may have seemed to be at ease bathing in the tub. But he could not have been so very relaxed, for he was out of the water even as she hurled her weight against the door.

"I will not stay here. You cannot keep me here!" she cried. He flung her around. She stared into his eyes, afraid to let her eyes wander down the length of him. "You think that you can keep me captive watching you mimic a murdered settler in his bath? I am the one who needs to bathe. I am the one who needs to wash away your touch! I—" She broke off. His wet hands were upon her arm, wrenching her back with such a force that she heard the delicate silk and lace of her black mourning gown rip and tear. She screamed, trying ridiculously to free herself from his hold. Both hands upon her shoulders, he shook her firmly. She gasped for breath and stared into his strange green eyes once again, and for the first time, saw his face. Really saw his face.

She couldn't ascertain his age, but she thought he was somewhere near thirty—not a very young man, certainly not an old one—one indisputably in the very prime of life and at the height of his strength and power. His skull was ruggedly sculpted, his jaw square, his cheekbones high, his forehead broad. His unusual eyes were large and bright against the bronze of his flesh, while his brows, as well as his hair, were blue black and cleanly arched. Were it not so fierce and menacing, it would have been a fascinating face. Compelling, intimidating, masculine, hard but so cleanly lined that among any race it would be considered handsome. His nose was long and straight, his mouth full, his lips oddly curled in a mocking smile that sent chills racing throughout her body once again. Skylar was quite certain then that many a beautiful young Indian maid had worn her heart upon her sleeve for this ruthless warrior, and yet there was something in the mocking eyes that made her wonder if there wasn't something dark and deadly in this savage's past that might make him deal as callously with one of his own as he dealt with her.

No. He'd not slay an Indian woman when he had finished with his taunting of her...

Taunting. He was naked now. Buck naked. Dripping upon her as he held her.

"Savage son of Satan! Bastard!" she shrieked. Hands tied, shoulders caught in his iron grip, she fought the only way she could, trying with all her remaining strength and energy to kick him. She caught a shin yet didn't draw so much as a grimace from him. A second passed while they stared at one another. Then she shrieked in real terror, for he plucked her up again and threw her down upon the bunk. As she struggled to inch away from him and rise, her fear began to escalate in leaps and bounds, for he caught her by one foot, and despite her thrashing and struggling, removed the black lady's boot from it.

"God, no. No!" she breathed, trying wildly to kick and fight, again to no avail. Both boots were stripped from her and thrown to the floor. She tried to slam her bound hands against him. Then she gasped, inhaling on a half sob when he plucked a wicked-looking Bowie knife from the floor beneath the bed, bringing it to her chest, straight against her heart. She stared at him in silence, wondering when the blade would find its way into her body, wondering what the pain would be like, how hard it would be to die. Oh, God...

"They'll kill you!" she lashed out, determined not to cry even as tears burned against her eyes. "The whites will come for you and slice you to ribbons, they'll disembowel you, they'll cut off your head—scalp you. Oh, yes, they'll scalp away all that black hair of yours and leave you bleeding until you die!"

She thought his lips twitched, but his eyes were unyielding. He moved his hand slightly, and she closed her eyes and screamed, waiting for the knife to pierce her flesh.

Instead...

She heard the methodical ripping of material.

Her eyes flew open, and she realized that he had rent the fabric of her mourning gown from throat to hem.

"No!" she cried out, shaking, trying to remind herself that it was better to bear torn clothing than torn flesh. She tried to use her bound hands as a weapon against him, only to find herself flung face down into the covers as he chopped away heedlessly at all the fabric covering her. While she shrieked and struggled, gasping for breath against the bed, he ripped and tore away the black silk and lace of her gown, chemise, and top petticoat, then the white cotton and linen of her corset and pantaloons, even the soft, pink-ribboned bows of her garters. With one hand he flipped her again so that she faced him, naked in the tattered remnants of her elegant apparel, and stared down at her.

"They'll cut out your heart!" she cried to him, still fighting tears and renewed terror. "Then you know what they'll do? They'll cut off your big, wretched, savage sex and feed it to the hogs, you bastard!" She was going to start crying or lose her mind to sheer hysteria. "I'll do it. I'll do it myself. Just you wait until I get my hands on a knife. You'll be so sorry, you'll—"

She shrieked because he was up and lifting her. She didn't know now in what form death would come.

And she was heartily startled when she found herself dropped into the tub.

He meant to drown her.

He was going for her hair again. He was going to use it to force her under...

But he merely lifted her hair from her back, letting it fall down the outside of the tub. He turned back to the hearth for the cauldron of water.

He was going to scald her to death.

But he poured the water so that it warmed the bath without burning her. He replaced the cauldron, throwing a bar of soap her way.

"You want me clean when you kill me?" she snapped out bitterly. "No—" She began to gasp again, for he had hunkered down by the tub. The knife was suddenly glittering in his hands again.

She shrieked again, closing her eyes.

But he merely used the knife to snap the rawhide binding her wrists. In panic, Skylar instantly took the soap and started to throw it at him. She cried out as he caught her wrist. His eyes were on hers then with such warning that she went dead still except for the furious pounding of her heart. "Fine!" she said, trying to keep her lips from trembling. "I'll scrub myself clean for that moment when you decide to murder me." She stared into his eyes. Crouched down beside her, he was more terrifying than ever. His own nakedness seemed not to bother him in the least, while she was ever more tormented by the nudity he had enforced upon them both. He was terrifyingly sexual, so perfectly honed and physically powerful, not to mention that he was surely exceptionally endowed, no matter the color of his flesh.

He let go of her and stood again, turning from her to move about the hearth. For the moment, she clutched the soap, suddenly glad of it. Time. She was buying time here. She furiously washed the trail dust and dirt and grime from her face. She scrubbed her arms, legs, torso, desperately thinking about how to escape.

She realized then that she smelled coffee.

The scent of it tantalizing, delicious...

There were no more sounds coming from the hearth. She turned to discover that he had decked himself out in a white man's long smoking jacket and that he was leaning against the wooden mantel over the hearth, his arms crossed over his chest, watching her, his green eyes as hard as emerald chips and giving away nothing of his thoughts.

Then she realized that he was actually studying her. A strange warmth seared through her. The oddest sensation of panic seized her, a panic she couldn't even understand because it wasn't simply a fear of him. Irrationally, she sprang from the tub, racing wet and naked for the door.

Naturally, she didn't make it. When he seized hold of her this time, lifting her into his arms, she half sobbed and half laughed, slamming her fists against him. The robe he wore came open. She was aware of his flesh, the warmth of it, the sleekness of it, the muscled strength that lay beneath it. He smelled of soap from the bath, and to her horror, though she was afraid, she was not as repelled as she should have been.

He laid her back down on the cot. He was entangled with her hair, she with his robe. Whether or not he'd intended to, he fell upon her, and she became more vividly aware of the structure of his anatomy and all the strengths and hungers within it. An awful breathlessness seized her, a fear, a fire. Desperate, she twisted and writhed, struggling to free herself from his weight. He caught her wrists, pinning them above her head, then cast a leg over the length of her, holding her immobile no matter what energy she set into her writhing and struggle. She was absolutely powerless against him and swiftly growing exhausted from her efforts to free herself. She spoke, staring at him with all the venom and courage she could muster.

"I will kill you, you know, you overgrown savage."

His green eyes narrowed. His fierce, rugged, oddly handsome features were very taut. He was furious with her. He might not understand her words, but he knew she was threatening him, she thought.

"Yes! I'll kill you!"

It was actually amazing that he hadn't already done her some irreversible harm. He stared at her still. With those green eyes.

A shudder swept through her. Green eyes. She felt a strange sense of familiarity as she looked into them. As if she'd seen them before.

There was something about them...

Yes! They were dangerous, menacing.

Deadly.

Again, she felt trembling and fire sweeping within her. She had to keep threatening and fighting. Until she died, she reminded herself. There was nothing else for her to do.

"I'll gouge your eyes out. I'll tear you to shreds, cut off your limbs one by one, beat every single oversized muscle into pure pulp. Skin you alive, feed your hands to the dogs, chop off your pen—"

She never finished her threat, for her captor decided to break his silence at last.

"Madam, make one more threat against my anatomy," he said suddenly in perfect English, "and I will feel forced to make good use of it before it exists no more!"

Completely stunned, Skylar lay dead still at last. "What?" she gasped, disbelieving.

"You heard me—and I do believe that I made myself perfectly clear."

He spoke English. Oh, God, he understood English.

She burned. She shook. She was still terrified.

But she was furious, too.

"You—you—despicable—"

"Take care!" he warned.

"Bastard!" she cried out heedlessly. "You bastard!" she repeated. "You speak English damned well, you—who the hell are you?"

Those strangely familiar eyes burned into her relentlessly. Undaunted. Merciless.

Deadly.

And he spoke again.

His voice deep, rich.

Its tone...

As deadly as the green fire in his eyes.

"The question, madam," he hissed furiously, "is just who the bloody hell are you?"

# CHAPTER 2

She was going to quit shaking. She was not going to die a coward.

Please, God, she was not going to do so...

"What difference does it make to you who I am!" Skylar cried, pressing her hands against him and finding him still immovable.

*Courage*! she reminded herself.

That lacking, bravado would do.

"You've murdered the stagecoach driver and abducted me. You'll surely hang no matter how good your English may be!" Perhaps threats were the wrong tact to take at this time. If he understood her, she could attempt to reason with him.

She began speaking quickly and breathlessly. "However, if you were just to let me go at this moment, I could speak in your defense. I could—"

"You're not listening to me. Who the hell are you!" he thundered.

She felt her limbs trembling despite her determination not to show fear.

"My name is Skylar Douglas."

"You're a liar!"

There was such rage and conviction in his voice that Skylar was startled into silence, staring up into his unusual green eyes. Desperate confusion filled her. What did her name matter to this Indian who might speak English amazingly well but was nonetheless a savage? Once again, she began to feel the physical discomfort of being naked and pressed to the bed by a powerfully muscled man whose rage was directed at her.

"Are you going to kill me?" she demanded suddenly.

His gaze slid over her face, down the length of her. She felt as if her flesh were being scorched by it. She willed herself not to tremble and shake, but she seemed to have no control over the chattering that seized her teeth, the way her blood seemed to race madly throughout her.

"I haven't quite decided yet. I want to know who you really are and what you think you're doing out here."

"Who the hell are you?" she flared, her temper briefly overriding her fear.

"A man ten times larger and stronger than you who is also in possession of a knife. Let that suffice for the moment. I'm the one asking the questions."

She closed her eyes, swallowing hard, still confused, frightened, trapped in anguish. She couldn't bear this any longer, feeling his flesh, the threat of his strength, the fury that created the staggering heat within him. This was worse than before. Somehow more intimate. Because he understood every word she said. And she clearly understood him.

"If you're going to kill me, get it over with," she forced herself to say with an even, calm voice.

"But I want an answer to my question."

"I've answered you!" she whispered.

He swore, then to her amazement and relief, suddenly rose, jerking his robe closed and retying it as he walked to the fireplace. Both hands on the mantel, he stared into the flames.

"You're not Lady Douglas," he said flatly.

"I am." Dear God, she thought, what difference did it make to him?

"You're not!"

"How can you be so sure?" she cried, starting to rise as well, then, recalling her nakedness, falling back and grappling for a pillow to hide behind. To her dismay and reawakened fear, he pushed away from the mantel, striding toward her again. She gasped, hopping up—with nothing—flattening herself against the wall on the opposite side of the bed.

Again, to her vast surprise and relief, though his green eyes did flick over the length of her, they bore nothing more than a glint of contempt.

And he didn't actually come near her.

He paused at the foot of the bed, threw open the trunk there, and tossed her a robe similar to his own. Shaking, she slipped into it, maintaining her position across the bed from him. He stared at her a moment, turned away, and walked back to the hearth. There he bent and poured the brewing coffee she had smelled earlier into two earthenware mugs. He set the mugs on the table, took a whiskey bottle from the shelf, and poured its contents liberally into both mugs. When he finished, he raised an arm, offering one of the mugs to her. She remained frozen to her spot.

"If I do decide to kill you, it won't be by poisoning," he informed her dryly.

She still couldn't move. She could barely swallow. She prayed that he could not see that, yet she was aware that the pulse at her throat was pounding.

He crooked a finger her way. "Can't use a drink? I surely can," he said pleasantly enough. But then the tone of his voice changed. "Get over here. I'm really not going to poison you, and I know damned well that you can really use a drink."

She bit her lower lip, feeling again a rise of temper that nearly vanquished her fear, and walked carefully around the bed and halfway across the room, keeping as far away from him as she could manage while accepting the cup at the same time. She took a sip. The coffee was hot and delicious with just enough whiskey in it to add a reassuring warmth to her system each time she swallowed. She swallowed more quickly. Closed her eyes. Drank it down.

The cup was taken from her fingers, and a moment later given back, full once again.

Coffee. It seemed a touch of normalcy in the midst of insanity.

Or maybe it was just that the whiskey in it was blurring the madness of her situation.

She felt him staring at her again, studying her intently. She backed away uneasily. She didn't really realize that she was doing so until her calves touched the edge of the bed. She didn't think she planned to sit. It was just that her knees wouldn't hold her upright anymore. She sank down, sitting on the edge of the bed as primly as possible. "I can't begin to understand what's going on here. I've done nothing to you! If you would just tell me who you are, explain—"

"I'm asking the questions, remember?" he said sharply.

"Then tell me what you are!" she cried. "You pretended to be an Indian, a complete savage—"

"Oh, I am an Indian. Sioux!" he interrupted, his tone deceptively soft. "And I suggest you not forget it. And as to being a complete savage...well, I have always found that some men are, by nature, savage, and some are not, race having no bearing on the issue whatsoever."

She swallowed another sip of coffee, amazed—unnerved. Not only did he speak English, he was also a damned philosopher. How in God's name had she fallen in his path?

"Perhaps you'd best change your behavior then," Skylar suggested sweetly. "For so far, it has been completely detestable, heathen, and savage."

"Really? I don't think I stated that I was among the men who weren't complete savages," he informed her with a sardonic smile. "I was merely making the point that 'savage' is often how the whites choose to view a society different from their own, when often white behavior is far crueler and more heinous. And frankly, I don't give a damn whether you consider me to be a savage or not. Now, back to basics. Who the hell are you, and why are you claiming to be Lady Douglas?"

Skylar warmed her hands around her mug, inhaling deeply. "I have told you the truth! I am Lady Skylar Douglas—"

"Married to—?"

"Lord Douglas, naturally."

"Naturally?" he grated.

She drained her coffee mug, grateful then for the riveting warmth that seemed to put some steel back into her own limbs. "Naturally. Well, actually, I am a widow now. Lord Douglas—died."

"After you married him?"

"Obviously," she heard herself snap. "That is the way one becomes a widow."

"When and where did you marry him?"

"That's none of your damned business," she informed him coolly.

But he started to take a step toward her, his green eyes sharply narrowed. "I ask you again, when and where were you married?" he demanded.

Skylar stiffened, afraid and indignant. She assured herself it didn't matter in the least if she did or didn't give him information that was actually public record.

"I married Lord Douglas a little more than two weeks ago in Maryland."

"And then he died. How damned convenient."

"How dare you—"

"Easily. Now, you married Lord Douglas—Lord who Douglas."

"What?"

"What was your husband's given name?"

"Andrew."

"You're certain."

"The name is on my wedding license."

"But your husband died."

"Yes."

"You're quite certain."

"I was there!"

"Ahhhh...!"

The drawn-out exclamation had a damning sound to it. As if he seemed to find it perfectly natural that Lord Douglas might have died—and that perhaps she might have had something to do with his death.

"Don't you dare look at me like that. Don't you dare sound like that!" she exploded, feeling pain welling up within her. "I was there with him, I was there—" she choked out.

"I'm sure you were!" he interrupted derisively.

"You heathen bastard!" she hissed. "How dare you—"

"No! How dare you!" he breathed back through clenched teeth.

She leaped up. "You've no right to accost me like this. You've no right to make any judgments about me. You want to talk about not caring? Well, I don't know who—or what!—you are anymore, but do you know what? I don't care! I'm an American citizen. I don't have to sit here and take this from you or anyone!"

She stood purposefully. She slammed her mug down on the table before the hearth, staring at him with daggers in her eyes. With her chin high and her heart hammering, only the whiskey giving her the courage she needed at the moment, she strode smoothly toward the door, determined that her manner alone would set her free.

But then she heard his voice. "Oh, Lady Douglas! I don't think so!" And even as she opened the door, his hand reached over her shoulder, slamming it shut again. She spun against the door, only to find herself blocked there, the imposing size and strength of his body before her, a hand on either side of her head, his bronzed arms caging her in.

She stared at him with all the cool authority she could muster. "I grow weary of this game!" she insisted.

"You think it a game?" he inquired softly.

"I think you need to let me out of here!"

"I think not!" His hand upon her arm drew her back into the room and sent her spinning toward the bed once again. She caught herself before she could fall against it. The robe was slipping off her. She drew it back together, drawing the belt tighter. She placed a hand against the poster at the foot of the bed for support.

"The army is in residence out here!" she cried. "And when they finally come, I swear I'll see to it that you are hanged!"

"They might just hang you."

"What?"

"For murder. The murder of Lord Douglas."

The night was insane. It was all insanity. Perhaps that's what caused her to snap and, in a moment of sheer madness, pit herself at him again. Instead of running, sensibly keeping her distance, she flew across the floor, raising a hand to slap him. When he caught her right hand, she was ready with her left. When she was deterred from his face, she did her best to beat against his chest. Sobs shook her body. She was only barely aware that she was lifted from the floor. Her head was spinning now. He must have poured half the bottle of whiskey into her cup the second time he filled it. It had given her courage and strength. Now she was paying for that false bravado.

"Stop it!"

She dimly heard his voice. No matter how rough the command, it didn't seem to penetrate to her mind. She couldn't stop fighting or sobbing, hysterically pummeling him with a strength born of raw fear and rage.

"Stop it!"

Her feet were off the ground. She was lifted, flying—and suddenly on the bed again. He was straddling her hips, pinning her wrists high above her head to keep her from hitting him. She inhaled raggedly, trying to get a grip on herself. She could barely breathe. Her robe had fallen open. So had his. The ridiculous intimacy of their situation fueled her hysteria.

"Please, please...!" she gasped out. She tossed and writhed, twisting against him, trying to throw him off her.

The fur bedcover and the sheets became tangled beneath her. His bare flesh pressed against her, as hers did against his. The pounding of her heart was growing louder and louder, along with the desperate sounds of struggling that escaped from her.

The pounding...it wasn't her heart. It was knocking at the cabin door.

The door...

It was suddenly thrown open.

"Hawk?" said a worried, masculine voice.

The man atop Skylar twisted at the sound of his name being called. Skylar stared past him to see that there were two men standing in the doorway.

Two men in uniform.

Uniform!

One was young with sandy hair and a clean-shaven face. The other man was older, with a graying set of whiskers, the mustache perfectly waxed and groomed.

Oh, God! The cavalry had come.

She let out a shriek.

"Oh, sweet Jesus, sorry, Hawk!" the older man said. He punched the other, his face turning beet red. "He's—occupied! With a lady."

Occupied...with a lady! The words echoed in her mind. Then the realization struck her. They thought that...

"No!" Skylar gasped, inhaling raggedly. He was still on top of her. He leaned down upon her. Close. His breath all but fanning her cheeks.

She couldn't get enough air to explain. She was mortified. She was more than half naked, his flesh was solidly pressed against hers. It did look like...

She stared with horror into those strange green eyes that now carried a wicked glint of pure amusement. Eyes so close to hers...

"Hush, hush!" he assured her, his voice mockingly tender. "My dear, the soldiers are gallant men, they'll say nothing."

"The soldiers will say nothing!" she exclaimed. "Dear God, they will certainly—" she began furiously, but a shift in his weight cut her off as what air she had managed to inhale was exhaled beneath his weight.

"Darling, please. You mustn't be so upset. It's really going to be all right. Shh..." came his whisper, his lips atop hers.

Then upon them. Forming perfectly over hers. His tongue demanding entry. She found her mouth parted with a startling force, the mercurial, hot thrust of his tongue. The taste of coffee and whiskey. She tried to twist away, but his fingers were threaded through her hair and brought close to her skull, holding her so taut she couldn't begin to resist. She couldn't breathe. The room was spinning...black stars burst before her...

"It's all right, my dear. Truly. You needn't be embarrassed."

He wasn't kissing her anymore. He was staring down at her, still looking amused while she desperately dragged in breath.

"Dammit!" she cried out.

"Sweet Jesus, I am sorry!" the older man protested. "Oh, ma'am, so sorry. Hawk, we'd no idea you had the company of a woman friend—"

The Indian interrupted, eloquent to a truly staggering degree.

"Captain, all apologies accepted. I should truly be embarrassed that I did not hear your arrival."

"Damn you all, wait!" Skylar lashed out again furiously.

"My dear! My dear! Don't you think these poor men are suffering enough as it is? I should have heard them—"

"That's what worried us," the older man said. "Why, Hawk, you can usually hear a pony snort a mile away."

"Ah, but then, I have been quite occupied, I admit," Hawk said.

The captain laughed. "The Sioux men may be darned right in their attitudes toward women, Hawk. Those boys know that being too close to a lady can cloud the mind and steal the senses!"

"Indeed, I'm humiliated."

"Hell, it proves you're human."

"Human!" Skylar managed to get in.

"Why thank you, Captain," the Indian stated, another shift of his weight making her gasp for breath again. "Perhaps I do have a respectable excuse. This is Lady Douglas, Captain."

All the while that he spoke, he stared down at her, still seeming to laugh down at her.

"Lady Douglas!" the captain said, gaping suddenly. "I didn't know that—"

"Yes!" Skylar managed to assert. They weren't going to get the better of her this time. She was going to make them understand. A feeling of triumph rising within her, she stared at the Indian with victorious eyes as she cried out, "Yes! Yes, damn you all, I am Lady Douglas." It was about time! She was going to make these men realize that she was desperate to be rescued, make them realize the situation. "Yes, my name is Skylar Douglas. Please, I—"

"Oh, ma'am, we just didn't know, hadn't heard... Please, please forgive us! Hawk, it's a matter of some importance, but I can find you within the next few days. I am sorry. We're leaving."

"Quite all right, my friend. Apology accepted. Of course, we would like to be alone again..."

The older cavalry officer pulled the younger man out, slamming the door hard.

"No!" Skylar shrieked. "No! We wouldn't like to be alone! No! Wait!" She slammed her fists against the Indian and tried to kick, jab.

Bite.

She got her teeth into his shoulder. He didn't blink an eye, but again, his fingers came threading into her hair. Pulling.

"Don't bite!" he warned icily.

"Then let me up!"

To her astonishment, he moved aside. She leaped from the bed, heedless that the robe barely covered her. She raced after the soldiers.

She threw herself against the door, fumbling then to find the latch to draw it open. "Wait! Wait!" she cried out. "Please, you're not listening to me. Won't anybody help me! My God, I swear to you that I am Lady Douglas. Please—" She finished the plea with a shriek because she suddenly found herself wrenched back into the room, away from the door, by the English-speaking Sioux they'd called Hawk.

Spun around, she stared into his eyes again. She looked down. His long bronze fingers held her wrist.

No.

The cavalry had come.

Help had been here!

"Help" had watched her on the bed with this man...

She looked wildly back to the door. "You have to let me by! They have to help me. They're the cavalry. You're an Indian. My God, what's going on with them? The entire world has gone insane!" She tried to shake free from his hold. She could not do so. She slammed her fists against his chest, half laughing, half crying. "Let me go! I've got to get to them. I've got to make them understand..."

She broke off, hearing the hoofbeats of the men's horses fading away.

The cavalry had come.

And gone.

"Let me go. Please, let me go!"

"For what?"

"So I can get them to help me!"

He released her, crossing his arms over his chest as he spoke to her next.

"They're not going to help you."

"They will when they know what's really happening. That you've abducted me, half—half—raped me! They'll save me from you—"

"They're not going to help you, and they're not going to save you from me, even if you are Lady Douglas. Especially if you are Lady Douglas."

She inhaled deeply, her spine suddenly very straight and stiff. "Why not, damn you?" she demanded. "Why won't they help me?"

He caught her upper arms, pulling her back close to him, and his eyes glittered now with both amusement and fury.

"Because, my lovely little gold digger, Andrew Douglas is not dead. I am Lord Andrew Douglas. Your dearly beloved husband."

"You're a liar! Lord Douglas is dead. And you can't be Lord anyone! You're an—an—"

"Indian?" he suggested.

"Yes! A savage, painted Indian!"

"That I am. But I do assure you, I am also Lord Douglas."

She stared into his eyes.

Green eyes.

Oh, God, yes. They were familiar.

"Damn you, know it! I am Lord Douglas!"

Green eyes. Eyes very similar to a pair she had seen before. Set into an older face.

Green eyes.

They faded to black.

# CHAPTER 3

Who the hell was she?

Staring at her, Andrew Douglas, called Hawk by both his Sioux kin and white friends, shook his head. She'd put up a hell of a fight—until his last words had struck home with her.

Then she'd passed out cold. Good thing. Now she lay against the bear-fur cover on the bed, a creature of ethereal—and, thank God, silent—beauty.

Deadly beauty, so it seemed, he thought bitterly. He still didn't understand the particulars, but it seemed apparent that his father had met this woman. She had coerced a marriage and had assumed she was marrying his father.

What had gone on?

And what truth could he ever really know? His father was dead.

She was going to tell him. Exactly what had happened to her.

It was difficult to keep his hands off her. He longed to shake her until he got the truth out of her.

But he managed to keep his distance and tried very hard to be analytical—something he had gotten fairly good at over the years, being a man split between two vastly different cultures. His years at

West Point hadn't hurt the development of his analytical abilities either.

So again. Who in God's name was she? Where had she come from?

Any feelings of tenderness that might have been touched in him by her beauty were stilled by the painful reminder that David, the late Lord Douglas, was dead.

Hawk had received word from Henry Pierpont, his father's beleaguered but ever-proper attorney, who had been informed by the president of their Maryland bank that David had died of apparent heart failure in Baltimore just two weeks ago. Henry hadn't mentioned anything then about a bride—for either his father or himself. It appeared that this woman did believe she was married to—or widowed by—his father. Yet she had said the name Andrew. His own.

Just what exactly had gone on between this absurdly young woman and his aging father? He couldn't begin to fathom it. David had always been dignified to the extreme, a proud man, a wise one. He had deeply loved only two women in his life, and he had married them both. He had been in reasonably good health when he had traveled east, in full control of all his faculties.

Then how...

The woman who lay before him must have been incredibly persuasive. And yet, though she seemed convinced that she was the widow of Lord Douglas, she apparently knew nothing about her late husband's life—or her late husband himself, for that matter. She hadn't even known that his name had been David, not Andrew.

All she'd needed to know, he figured, was that his father was titled with a British peerage and had obtained a land grant in the Black Hills, in one of the few areas not considered Sa Papa, or Holy Land, by the Sioux, where he had also discovered gold.

Again, he longed to shake her. How could anyone appear so fragile and innocent yet fight like a cougar and have the instincts of an alley cat! She lay there, still silent, her breath barely causing a slow but constant rise and fall of her breasts.

She would come around all right. He rubbed his chin, feeling his irritation grow along with an unbidden rise of desire within him. His robe was not adequate cover for her. Whatever had he been thinking to strip away her clothing and dunk her in the tub? It had been her insistence that she needed to bathe that had triggered his action. And perhaps he'd been goaded by her greed, which was so great that it had apparently led her into what was still—despite the ever-encroaching army and the wave of white immigrants—basically Sioux country where few men dared to tread. She'd come here, so she'd deserved to discover the perils that awaited the unwary. Whites were often waylaid, robbed, raped, abducted, murdered—scalped.

And he hadn't taken it so far as to scalp her.

Yet.

All right. He wasn't going to scalp her.

Yet no matter what his fury regarding his father, she disturbed him, and he suddenly wished he'd confronted her in a white man's court of law. Once he'd seen her, however, at Riley's, where he'd been with his cousins while her stagecoach was being repaired, his temper had taken control. There she'd been, claiming to be Lady Douglas, when he'd never seen her before, heard of her—or even imagined that a Lady Douglas could possibly exist. He'd been so damned determined to torment such an impostor, show her the dangers of the deceitful charade she played, force the truth from her. It seemed somewhat ironic now. Had he been so convinced that he could certainly not fall for the wiles of such a fortune hunter himself?

Wiles be damned. She was simply a well-built female, and the robe was falling open, allowing him far more of a view of her breasts than he wanted. His own fault, however...

He'd have to be dead not to be attracted to her himself.

He drew part of the robe over her breast. It fell back. Something within him quickened, and he muttered a sound of self-disgust, walking from the bedside to find the shreds of the black mourning dress she had been wearing. He searched the skirt for pockets and found one. It contained several gold coins, a small mirror, and a brush. He tossed those items impatiently at the foot of the bed, then searched the skirt again. In another pocket, he found what he sought.

Papers.

He drew them out, studying them with a fierce frown.

She carried a marriage license. It appeared to be a proper and fully legal document stating that Skylar Connor had been wed, by proxy, to Lord Andrew Douglas by the Right Honorable Magistrate Timothy Carone in Baltimore a little more than two weeks ago.

The exact date of his father's death.

He stared at the marriage license in his hand and then at the appendix behind it. His own signature was scrawled upon it. He frowned, reading further. The appendix was a proxy agreement. He didn't remember signing the paper—didn't even remember seeing it before—but it was indisputably his signature upon the paper.

But then he had been so impatient and irritable right before his father had started on his journey back east. When something pertained to the Scottish estates or Maryland property, Hawk had told David he must do as he saw fit because the property was his own. He was aware that his father had put many of his holdings into their joint ownership, determined there would never be any doubt that his Sioux son was now his legal heir. It was quite ironic. One of the first things his father had ever taught him was to read every word of a written contract.

He never read through a paper when his father asked for his signature. He'd still considered his father's property to be just that and had thought that David should manage it as he saw fit.

Too late, he realized now that such an attitude had actually been selfish on his part. He had cared when it came to the Black Hills or their home here on the Western frontier.

But he had not been able to see beyond the Black Hills and the surrounding countryside because the situation here had been growing more and more tense since the end of the war.

So did this mean that the wily vixen on the bed was indeed Lady Douglas? Had he—taken a wife?

Could it be legal?

He groaned softly. Lately his father had been urging him to marry again. Insisting he needed a wife. A white wife. Hawk had had long, passionate discussions with his father regarding the future of the native man in the West, but indisputably, no matter how passionately he had argued against his father's statements, he'd known they would eventually prove true—as true as the endless tide of white settlers and army who continued to come west in wave after land-hungry wave. David had not been without some influence in Washington, and even before his most recent trip, he had wearily assured his son that in the end the government would not honor any treaty. Whatever lands the Indians were given, the whites would take back. Americans considered it their "Manifest Destiny" to move from "sea to shining sea," to occupy the whole of the North American continent. If they could, they'd push back the Mexicans and the British in Canada. That might be difficult to do in light of world opinion. But to exterminate Indians...red men...

It was a damned frightening possibility. Coming closer and closer.

Hawk knew that it had been his father's love for him that had convinced his father he must marry a white woman. Live a white life. So what had David done? Pretended to a young gold digger that she was marrying a man on his last leg only to fall prey to her before bringing her west?

Because he hadn't wanted to see his son exterminated.

Except that David Douglas hadn't been on his last leg when he had gone east. He hadn't looked any different than he had looked all his life. A tall man, lean, white-haired, aging, still handsome with his extreme dignity, eyes that seemed to see and know everything and understand. He had been healthy all his life. He had constantly endured the rigors of travel. He had lived among the warriors of the Sioux nation, and he had withstood tests of endurance with the heartiest of them. Of course, that had been many years ago. But still, when he had left here, he had seemed fine.

*I should have gone with him!* Hawk thought, pain and guilt returning to tug upon his heart. *I couldn't have gone, not the way that matters, between the army and the Indians have been escalating here.*

But this...could it be real? Legal?

Hawk closed his eyes tightly. He'd been a brave warrior to the Sioux, a courageous soldier in the Union army in the recent War of the Southern Rebellion.

But he couldn't fight away the future.

He knew it. His father had known it.

For a moment, he saw a faraway time when the Black Hills had belonged to the Indians. The Sioux hadn't actually lived there then. The land had been sacred, a place to hunt, a holy place, and a shelter when it was needed. The Sioux were nomads, already pushed westward from the Mississippi by the flow of the white men. There were many Sioux: the Sans Arc, the Brule, the Oglala, the Two Kettles, the Hunkpapa, and the Blackfoot Sioux. And among those many Sioux, there were even more bands. Any warrior or family could break away as they chose. The Sioux were a free people, respected for the lives they must lead as individuals. It was a virtue among them.

And yet, as the whites encroached upon them, this independence became a danger as well. It made them divisible and vulnerable.

As a small boy, he had grown up in his mother's world. He had lain in his cradle board, seen the buffalo skins of the tipi as his first walls.

He had been loved. The Sioux valued their children. He was treated gently not only by his mother, but by Flying Sparrow, his mother's brothers, and his grandfather, the peace chief, Sitting Hawk. He was never struck. He called all men of the tribe "father," all women "mother." He was welcomed in any tipi. A Sioux boy must learn two things: to be a good hunter and to be a good warrior. Both meant life for his people.

Until his eleventh birthday, he knew very little of the white world. He knew now that until the Mexican-American War of 1846-1848, the Americans—who had gained the plains through the Louisiana Purchase—had considered them the Great American Desert, a permanent Indian border. But with the land gains made after the war, America's western boundary was thrown open to the Pacific. In 1851, he had gone with his mother's people, a small band of Oglala Sioux, to Fort Laramie, on the North Platte River. It was the largest gathering of Indians he had ever seen—many of the Sioux bands were present along with Cheyenne, Arapahoe, Shoshone, Crow, Assiniboine, Arikara, and others. It was agreed that the Indians were to be paid each year to make peace with the white immigrants—many traveling through to the new gold finds in California—and among themselves. The white men chose to call certain men "head chiefs." The Indians were told that they couldn't make war among themselves, but that was impossible because warring against one another was a way of life. The treaty was doomed from the time the whites first had their so-called head chiefs "touch the pen"—or put their hands upon it before white men signed their names for them in the white language.

From that day on, the whites began to come, but they didn't much influence his life. Yet.

He had been Little Sparrow then. He had remained Little Sparrow until a few months after his twelfth birthday. Then he had counted coup against one of his Crow enemies, slapping the warrior on the cheek before they engaged in hand-to-hand combat with their knives. Counting coup—striking an enemy face-to-face rather than killing him from a distance—granted a warrior honor.

It had weighed heavily on him that he had taken a life, even though he had fought the Crow with a deep-seated fury. A Crow warrior had led a war party into their Sioux village when their own warriors had been hunting. He had seized three young women, taken two for his own, and given one to a friend, Snake-in-the-Tree. Snake-in-the-Tree had abused his young captive so thoroughly that she had taken her own life. The young woman, Dancing Cloud, had been his grandfather's great-grandchild, and he had known that he must avenge her death to prove his worth.

At a victory dance that night, Little Sparrow had been given the name Thunder Hawk, for he had been as swift and strong as the bird of prey, as fierce as the thunder that could shake the plains.

Another year passed, and he danced the Sun Dance. The Sioux, the many factions and bands, met together once a year every year for the Sun Dance. It was the most important of the ceremonies prescribed to them by the White Buffalo Woman, who had come at the beginning to teach them their morality and their way of life. It took place in June, the month of the chokecherries, and lasted twelve days, requiring great strength of body and mind.

At nearly fourteen, Thunder Hawk was a tall boy, almost six feet, taller than many of the grown warriors, though his height was not that unusual, since he knew a Miniconjou Sioux, Touch-the-Clouds, who was nearly seven feet and truly towered over other men. Thunder Hawk wanted to be both a great warrior and a wise one. He wanted the guidance of Wakan Tanka, the Great Mystery, so he danced with skewers piercing his back muscles, praying for his people and for strength against all his enemies until he fell. He was honored among his people as a young warrior who showed promise of greatness.

Then his father had suddenly come back into his life.

He hadn't known the blond, green-eyed stranger who had come into their village, but he had known that something was different about him, and he had known that change was coming, and he had hated that change. He had feared it, but a boy who'd newly become a warrior with the name Thunder Hawk could not betray his fear.

The stranger who came to them was welcomed by the older warriors. He was an old friend who had lived among them before.

A white, who had danced the Sun Dance with the skewers through his chest, who had fought the Crow with them and counted coup.

He was still stunned to discover that the white man had come because his white wife had died—and because he wanted to make Flying Sparrow his wife now in his white world as well as in the Indian world. The Sioux did not think badly of him for having two wives—most Sioux warriors had more than one wife, though their wives were often sisters.

The man who came spoke the Sioux language very well. He was liked. He was called brother by the warriors. Thunder Hawk learned that the man had come here years before as a representative of the American government, as a man called a topographical engineer, a mapmaker. The Sioux had come upon him while scouting. He had fought bravely and been wounded. He had been taken captive, and Flying Sparrow had nursed him back to health. Then he had been the younger son of a wealthy British chief. Now he was no longer the younger son because illness had taken his brother. And now he wanted to make sure that his son by Flying Sparrow could be a legitimate heir to his vast estates. He had another son himself, an older son by his white wife. But that son did not mind having a brother.

Hawk minded. He didn't want to leave the band. He had many friends who were just becoming men, who had also counted coup, killed their first buffalo, and killed their first enemies. He had a kola, or best friend, Dark Mountain, who planned strategies for the hunt with him.

He had gone to the foot of the hills for his vision quest. For a Sioux boy, the vision quest was the center of his life. In his vision, a Sioux touched something sacred. He learned what road he must follow, what path he must take.

After three days without food or water, Hawk had collapsed and his vision had come to him. He had ridden a black pony between a herd of buffalo to his left and a flight of eagles to his right. The animals had cried out to him, tried to tell him something, yet he could not understand. He had to ride harder and harder. Then he was able to understand the eagles while the buffalo could not, and likewise, he was able to understand the buffalo while the eagles could not. A rain of arrows had come over him as he had ridden, but no matter how close they came, he knew that he had to keep riding. In the end, he saw the sun, and he kept riding toward the blinding golden light of the sun, reaching then into the sky to collect the arrows and keep them from falling.

His dream had disturbed him, but Mile-High-Man, a respected holy man, had told him that he was indeed intended to be a warrior, one who would be wise and able to communicate with others and lead well.

If such was to be his role in life, then how could he leave his band and join the household of a white man?

Perhaps he needed to go, Mile-High-Man suggested, to learn the ways to communicate with both the buffalo and the eagles.

A whimper from the bed suddenly distracted him from his thoughts. He came around, staring down at the beautiful blonde woman lying on the bed. Her arms suddenly rose as if she were warding off a blow. He frowned, almost reaching out to wake her then, but her arms fell. She shuddered and went still.

He wondered if she was still fighting him or if someone else was haunting her dreams. Now she lay so peacefully, her features delicate and exquisite, her hair a pool of gold to frame them.

He turned from her abruptly, walking away, staring into the fire.

He watched the flames. In time, he'd wake her. His fingers clenched his palms. Indeed. In time, he'd wake her all right.

# CHAPTER 4

Half a continent away, a young woman hurried along a hallway carrying a pile of bath sheets and two large bottles of liniment. She was of medium height, but she moved with such carriage and grace that she gave the impression of being taller. Her hair was a deep, dark brown, just touched with hints of henna that gave it a rich, sable appearance. Her eyes were a dark, vibrant blue green, almost turquoise. Until her mother's recent death, she might have claimed to have lived a happy life, despite the secrets of the past that had haunted them all.

But now...

In the last three weeks, she had faced far more than tragedy.

Horror itself had entered into her life. And surprisingly enough, she had discovered she had the strength to deal with it. Skylar had given her that strength. Skylar had always been there for her. She hoped that now...finally...they were managing to rescue one another.

Outside a doorway, she paused, squaring her shoulders. No matter what was said, she would play her part. Give nothing away. Nothing.

She pushed open the door. He sat there in his specially carved wheelchair, an afghan thrown over his useless legs. Still, he was somehow not a man to be pitied because when he gazed at her, the demons of cruelty and anger and...revenge...were in his eyes.

The doctor stood behind the chair. "Ah, there you are, my dear! The liniment, just as I've asked. Good. A number of towels, yes. Ah, there now, dear, fetch the brandy, a snifter for the senator...ah, yes, a good brandy relaxes the muscles, and the body—"

"Doctor," the senator said, shaking his head sadly. "Brandy, liniment. Relaxed muscles, tensed muscles! What does it matter, when I will never walk again?"

"Courage, now, Senator!" the doctor said. He was a bewhiskered old man. Sabrina thought he was doddering and wondered why the senator had chosen him for his treatments. Because the doctor wouldn't ask too many questions? She'd been surprised at first that the senator hadn't called in the police.

But then, if he'd thrown out accusations, he might have had a few accusations thrown back at him.

He was still staring at her. Smiling, a smile that conveyed no humor, no warmth. It was a chilling smile. One that warned, menaced...and promised as well. *I will have my revenge!* That smile seemed to vow. *In my own way, my own time. And don't doubt my power. God, no, girl, don't you go doubting my power.*

Perhaps, she told herself, determined not to respond to that smile in any way. If the doctor weren't there, she might be tempted to laugh, to taunt him in return. You can't hurt me now, you fool. You can't hurt me. Skylar stopped you when you tried!

He was a good-looking man. Handsome, dignified. He was always so careful to speak in low, well-modulated tones. His constituents knew him as a kind man, a benefactor to so many worthy organizations, a strong man, always willing to fight.

God, they didn't begin to know how willing he was to fight or to what levels he would stoop to win whatever it was he wanted. Whom he would hurt.

Whom he might have killed...

She handed him the brandy the doctor had ordered. She stared straight into his eyes as she did so. She didn't allow his fingers to touch hers as she gave him the snifter. She hoped that God would forgive her for praying that he would be a cripple even when this life ended and he rotted in hell.

She hoped as well that God would forgive her since it had occurred to her to poison him when he had first fallen. It was Skylar who had made her see that they could not. Not out of fear for the law or any hangman. But for their own souls. "No, my God, we can't. Don't you see, we can't become what he is, we can't. We need to beat him in life, don't you see?"

The doctor had turned to the table, sorting through towels and liniments. "We shall begin here momentarily!" he said with forced cheerfulness.

The senator kept smiling as his fingers curled around the snifter.

"What a good girl you are, Sabrina!" he mocked. "Such a comfort to me in my distress!"

"I hope you die!" she said in a calm, even whisper.

"But I won't," he promised her softly. "I'll live a long life. And I'll see to it that I carry out all the responsibilities I have regarding you, my dear. I'll care for you, I swear it. I do so enjoy caring for you!"

"You'll never even be able to attempt to touch me again, you bastard!"

"God takes care of the deserving."

"Yes, he does."

The senator started to laugh. The doctor turned. "Sabrina! Ah, doctor! She is, indeed, the delight of my discomfort." The doctor turned back to his work. The senator leaned toward Sabrina. She backed away a step. His face lost the convivial smile that had fooled so many. His eyes burned. "Now as to the other one...well, she will have her comeuppance. You think you're so clever. You little fools think that you're free...well, you're not. She's dead! That's what she is. No matter that you were there with your sweet, glib explanation of events..."

Sabrina took another step away from him. "I'll leave you to your patient and your work, Doctor," she said. She stared at the senator a moment longer, lowering her voice. "You'll never find her!" she promised very softly.

She turned and exited the room.

The senator watched her go, anger darkening his face. Then he started to laugh. And he looked down at his blanketed knees and then at his feet.

God bless America. Oh, Lord, yes. God bless America.

His toes were twitching. Twitching. Moving. Within a little more time, days...weeks...

He'd be walking again. But no one would know. No one. In fact, she just might be the first to share the joy of his recovery.

When she tried to run.

And he ran right after her.

---

THE FIRE FLICKERED WARMLY against Hawk's face. Ghosts of the past still seemed to dance within it, playing upon his memory.

When his father came for his mother, Flying Sparrow took on the Christian name of Kathryn. She was still very young herself and very beautiful. Many warriors had wanted her over the years, but she had chosen to remain with her father, and as a boy, Hawk realized that she had waited. That she had believed in her heart that her courageous white warrior would return for her. She had lived for that day and for her son.

She had been Thunder Hawk's support in all things. He loved her. She was leaving. He was old enough to make choices for himself, yet...

The white man had given him a Christian name as well. He was to be called Andrew David Douglas. The white man didn't try to influence him. He came to him and told him that he would love him always and welcome him always, just as he had made his place with the Sioux and knew that he could come to them.

Thunder Hawk was still not sure about the white man. But Mile-High-Man had reminded him that he must learn to listen to many languages. The message in his vision quest must be obeyed.

Both his grandfather and his mother begged him to give David Douglas a chance.

He sat with his grandfather one day, still torn and demanding to know why he should do so.

"David Douglas is a chief in his land. A lord, they call him. He is honored in Scotland, as his father before him."

"We are nowhere near Scotland. We have Americans encroaching on us always!"

His grandfather smiled, nodding his wise old head. "He came here like a warrior in his way, to make his own mark. Perhaps because the nomad's blood was in his veins. Because he had read of wide-open prairies, of endless vistas, of tall grasses that stretched forever. He read about people who were different. He came here to explore, and we seized him but did not kill him. Even faced with certain death, he was a friend who wanted to know us, rather than hate us. He sought knowledge, wisdom, those qualities we seek ourselves. He needed to learn our religion, our way."

"He left us."

"His father and brother died. His white wife was very sick. He loved both wives and did his duty to the woman he had taken first. When he could have lived a life of greatest comfort, he returned here. His place is in another land. His heart is here. Now he has arranged it that others care for the title and property that will go to his older son by the white way, yet he has come here with that son as well to live near the rivers where we place our villages. He knows your world. He learned it with his blood. He was our captive first, then our relative." He took a very deep breath, looking at Hawk. "One day, a tide of white men will come. I saw it many years ago, in my own vision."

"The tide already comes!"

His grandfather raised a hand in acknowledgment. "You have yet to see the wave! There will be blood before then. We will fill the prairie with our blood, nurture it, give to it. But we cannot stem the flow of white men. Therefore, some of us must befriend them. Some must fight, and some must die, and some must live. Else we have died and bled for nothing. Do you understand?"

"I understand I should fight!"

"The hardest fights are often those we wage within ourselves. Tell me, Thunder Hawk, when a Sioux brave has two ponies and his neighbor has none, what must the brave do?"

Thunder Hawk frowned. "Give his neighbor his second pony. We must always look after one another. We must always be generous. We are taught this from birth—"

"Then you must be generous with this man who is your father. You will always be Sioux. You will also always be white. You cannot be selfish with yourself. You must share your love with your mother, with your people—and with your white father."

His grandfather's words had heavily influenced him as had his vision and the words of the holy man.

But in the end, the main reason he had gone to live with Lord David Douglas was because he learned that Flying Sparrow—Kathryn—was ill. She lost weight daily. She could not sew the buffalo hides into a tipi, a garment, or a parfleche in which to carry things. She couldn't live where the smoke sometimes wafted back into the tipi in winter. Where there might be raids by whites or Crows or other enemies, where she might have to run in the cold and the snow. She needed the care that Andrew Douglas longed to give her. Hawk could begrudge David much, but he couldn't deny that the white man loved his mother. That love was apparent in every move that the man made.

So he came to discover just what the white blood in him meant.

Life was different. So different.

He found himself in a huge house with many rooms. He learned to sit on chairs rather than on the floor.

He met his white brother.

His brother was named David, like their father. He spent only part of his time in the United States, in the fine house Lord Douglas built near the Black Hills, because he was being groomed to become the next Lord Douglas, and he was being sent to school in England.

But no matter how hard Hawk tried to dislike his older brother, he could not do so. The younger David was too much like the older David, interested in everything and everyone around him, intrigued by different cultures rather than repulsed by them. He listened avidly to Hawk's boastful stories about counting coup and the Sioux ways of courage. He was eager to ride with Hawk when he went to visit his Sioux relations. He had a smile that could draw anger from the soul, melting it away.

As they grew older, they grew closer. When Kathryn died soon after Hawk's seventeenth birthday, his brother mourned with him, kneeling by her coffin throughout the night. For once, Hawk was glad to be part white, glad to have a reason to allow the tears to slide down his face.

His brother shed silent tears along with him.

In the years to come, they argued about the American Revolution and the War of 1812. They discussed American politics and British. David went to Oxford.

And ironically, Hawk was sent to West Point. Appointments were not easily acquired. But as a younger son of a British peer, David Douglas had spent a great deal of time in the employ of the United States Army. Hawk was half British and half American Indian, a most unusual candidate for the military academy, but one of David's very good friends, an aide-de-camp to none other than General Winfield Scott, saw to the appointment. David was greatly pleased by the honor for his son. Hawk, who had yet to realize that he loved his father, was anxious to please him. Also, for the benefit of his Sioux chief, he was determined to learn everything he could about the workings of the American army. Another factor influenced him. By this time, admittedly, he had gradually become just as white as he was Indian.

Neither he nor his father realized at the time why the appointment had come so easily.

The United States government had nothing against Indians battling Indians, Army patrols often used Crow scouts against the Sioux. "Civilized" Cherokee and Creek had been used against the Seminole in the Florida wars.

Such tactics could work both ways.

Hawk found himself at West Point. He was a natural student, and the world was opened to him in many ways.

At first, he was taunted for being Indian. Because of that, he went about scoring some of the best grades in his class and excelling in marksmanship, swordsmanship, and strategy. He made a number of very good friends. Just as he had learned to be a Sioux youth, he discovered the pranks that could be played by young white men. He went to dances, attended balls and luncheons. He engaged in his first affairs, all conducted with the proper chivalry of a future officer. He studied white women even as he studied the great military leaders of the past. In the end, he knew every campaign Napoleon had ever undertaken and how and why he'd met with his greatest defeat at Waterloo, the movements of Alexander the Great, and how Jackson had gone about winning the Battle of New Orleans. He also knew that white women could be very different from their Indian counterparts. Many were eager for possessions—they were not at all familiar with sharing. They were often determined at all costs to appear prim and innocent and beyond reproach, yet beneath such appearances, they could be complete mistresses of sensuality. Those young ladies who were most fervently—if secretively!—warned about his red blood were often the most eager to know him. Very early on he began to respond to such curiosity with a cool and courteous contempt. He was both careful and discreet himself, not averse to the charms of an entertaining widow, but always aware of his father's pride in him and determined he would disgrace neither his father nor his Indian heritage by bringing disgrace down upon himself.

He graduated with honors and couldn't wait to see David to taunt him with the fact.

He took his first trip to his father's estates in Scotland not a month after his graduation. He hadn't known until he arrived there just how dearly he had missed his brother or even the strength of the bond between them. For the first time in his life, he had really understood his father's family and his brother's place in a totally different society. He had been steeped in ancient traditions, ridden the vast boundaries of the Douglas lands, discovered that he belonged in a proud and ancient castle as well as in a tipi. "Learn to love it well, baby brother," David had told him gravely one day. "This is yours," Hawk had returned. "Your world."

"One day, you may be called upon to protect this world in the name of our family."

Hawk had told him, "I will be chief. You will be lord."

"Always, we will be brothers."

In America, the land was breaking apart. Lincoln had been elected president. South Carolina had seceded from the Union. Shots had been fired.

The war was begun over states' rights, but one of the rights the South sought was the right to keep slaves. Hawk had spent enough time among the great Northern political homes to learn American politics, and despite his concern for his own people and the never-ending battles on the plains, he felt that he had to fight a different war. In his heart, he knew that slavery was wrong.

There were Union troops in the West—fighting Indians. He didn't want to fight Indians. The Crow were his natural enemies, but only when he was fighting them as a Sioux. He didn't want to fight Indians as a white.

But he belonged in the war. He and his brother returned to America. David accepted an invitation from the Federal troops to train men, in order to remain close to his brother.

Hawk was one of the best horsemen to ever graduate from West Point. Numerous wealthy acquaintances asked him to take on command of militia companies with a higher rank than he might receive from the regular army. As a West Point graduate, he had earned a commission as a second lieutenant, but despite his youth, he was offered command of a cavalry company as a full lieutenant in the regular army. He accepted the commission, and he fought through all the long and arduous stages of the war along the eastern front. After four years of war, he had gained the rank of colonel and been brevetted as a brigadier general. With the war over, many of the volunteer officers were desperate for regular army commissions. Hawk no longer wanted his.

He would be sent west, he knew. To fight the Indians.

He resigned his commission. Worn and weary from the years of bloodshed, he went first with his brother to his father's ancestral home. But he was restless. David decided one day it was time to return to the raw Dakota territory, and they traveled together back to America. Hawk realized later that it had been his brother's way of sending him back, because David couldn't stay long. The Douglas lands in Scotland were a small empire. For Hawk, the mountains and wilderness were home. David belonged in the ancestral castle.

Hawk was glad to return to his father's Dakota house, where he could ride the open plains, the sacred Black Hills. He was glad to sit with his grandfather again and listen to his wisdom. He was glad to remember that he was Sioux. Many things had happened in the years of his absence. While he had been engaged in the eastern theater of war, Minnesota Sioux had gone on the warpath, killing settlers, destroying everything in their wake. The army had come after them, and the Minnesota Sioux had traveled west for help from their cousins. The army now said that the Indians must live on the reservations the whites had set aside for them.

Still, they refused to do so. As of yet, in the north, the army hadn't a strong enough presence to force its edicts upon the Indian populace. A brief time still remained with them.

But every day, more stakes were driven into the ground for the railroad to cross the country. More emigrants teemed west. The war in the East was over. The army was now free to fight the Indians.

Aside from his joy at being among his mother's people again, Hawk was happy to get to know his father. Proud to be his son. His father had created a cattle empire. Together they worked a vast estate. In turn, Hawk was able to see to his family, his band, and his tribe. When hunting was poor, Lord Douglas brought the family cattle. When the wars began to break out and escalate, Hawk found himself a mediator.

Then came word that his brother had been killed in a fire.

He had traveled with his father to Scotland, stared numbly at his brother's coffin, watched as it was set upon the slab within the ancient Douglas vault beside their grandfather's coffin. He had attended the inquest with his father. He had demanded full knowledge of his brother's demise. He had been the power and the fury when his father had not had the strength. All of his rage, however, could not change what had happened. The stables had caught fire. David had died. Lord Douglas had been too broken to remain in Scotland. The estates had been left in the care of Lord Douglas's distant kin, while father and remaining son had returned to Sioux lands.

Hawk had never imagined the grief that seized him at his brother's death. Yet, that did not seem to compare with his father's loss.

He had respected his father. His pride had made him determined to be a model son. He had even admired his father.

Yet now, finally, for the first time, he realized he loved him.

Watching his father grieve, Hawk thought that at last he truly understood the man who'd been a Scottish peer, yet had the courage to tell the world he had taken an Indian bride as his legal wife and would raise an Indian son along with a properly bred heir. And yet, in David's pain, he never grieved for his elder son as his properly bred heir—he grieved for him as his child, for flesh and blood, for laughter, for love. Lord David Douglas, for all his wealth, position—and white skin—was a good man. A father who deserved the love Hawk had withheld from him while giving it first to his mother, then his brother. In trying not to become too white, Hawk realized, he had betrayed all that his grandfather had told him was important about being Sioux. He had given up the generosity that was demanded by his Sioux heritage. No matter what a man had, he shared. Hawk had failed to share the emotion his father needed most. Now he learned to do so.

He fell in love. She eased the pain of his loss. Her name was Sea-of-Stars, and she was so named for her eyes, which were brilliantly blue and very beautiful. Her mother was a white woman who had been captured at a very young age. Her father was the war chief Burnt Arrow. Her brother was Black Eagle, an old friend and companion who helped explain to him everything that had happened between the whites and the Sioux and the other Indians in the time that he had been gone.

Hawk married Sea-of-Stars and divided his time between his father's home and his wife's. They had a child, a son, and the boy was the delight of his life. Little Hawk, the Indians called him. The future Lord Douglas, another Andrew, Hawk's father insisted with pleasure.

Hawk wondered about that future for his Indian son, and for himself as well.

But he didn't have to wonder long.

Smallpox killed Sea-of-Stars, his father-in-law, and his son before the boy had been a month old.

Again, Hawk grieved. The pain had been so great that he had been blind to all else, even his father's concern.

But he had been among his wife's people when word had come that the white army was about to attack the Indian village along the river.

That day, he had fought the soldiers. He had been numb and cold with his grief, ruled by fury, determined only that no one else in the village should die. He didn't care if he was killed in battle, and he was reckless in the extreme. The soldiers were turned back.

He collapsed. He had lost more blood than he had imagined. When he awoke, he was in his father's house. David had sat by his bed, nursing him, demanding to know. "My son, you have experienced the grief of a father for his child. How could you wish that pain upon me?"

David had been right. Hawk had healed, a wiser, graver man. He spent long hours with his father, learning to deal with the grief for his own wife and son. Time passed, never erasing Hawk's loss but easing his pain. Gold was discovered in the Black Hills, and one of David Douglas's expeditions claimed one of the most productive veins.

More settlers—miners, sutlers, shopkeepers, wives, dance-hall girls, and the assorted children of one and all—began to move into what had been Sioux country.

When the seriousness of the situation escalated, Hawk found himself in an extremely troubling position. Boyhood friends were among the most violent of the hostiles, men he knew well. As a boy, he had ridden with Crazy Horse, who was near his own age. He had listened to the wisdom of Sitting Bull, who was considered not just a great war chief but a very great holy man as well.

He knew them. He understood them.

Such had been the situation when his father had gone east.

David had not yet come home. His body was due soon. In fact, Hawk had gone to Riley's Trading Station early that afternoon with three of his Lakota cousins to find out when his father's body would be arriving for burial.

And that was when he had first seen her. The stagecoach should have been long gone with the first of morning's light, but a broken wheel had waylaid it.

He'd seen a vision of golden beauty and radiant youth bedecked in black and heard her claiming his inheritance.

She'd spent the night at the station, and she'd come downstairs into the kitchen when he'd been sitting at a back table with his cousins, talking with Riley about the army movements and the danger to hostiles that was forthcoming. He'd seen the coachman, Sam Haggerty, come in, heard him addressing her as Lady Douglas. Then she'd asked him how long it was going to take to reach Mayfair—the Douglas home in a valley off the Black Hills. And she'd very sweetly told him that she meant to keep the mine working, to live in the estate, to make it a home. And no, she wasn't afraid of Indians. Lord Douglas had told her that she wouldn't need to be afraid.

When old Riley himself would have stood and told her that she'd best be looking out for Lord Douglas, Hawk had dragged him down and hushed him.

One look at her, and he'd been determined to find out for himself just what trick she thought she played to call herself Lady Douglas.

And just what games she might have played upon his father. By God, she was young, a third of his father's age if that! He tried to tell himself that David Douglas had been no man's fool. Yet it plagued and goaded him that the elegantly beautiful young blonde woman might have seduced David into marriage and then...

Killed him.

Not with a gun or a knife but with those heavily lashed silver eyes. That perfect oval face, ruby lips, breathy laugh. Flashing smile. Perfectly rounded breasts. Supple, graceful, seductive movements.

She might well have caused him to have a heart attack. God knew, the mere sight of her could cause a heart to beat way too hard, cause a man's breath to catch, the whole of him to harden like quickening steel off a blacksmith's fire.

If she'd been about to claim to be his stepmother, he was damned determined she'd have other thoughts. And if she had somehow hastened David to his death, then...

God help her. She had to be either an impostor—or a murderess!

It had been easy enough for him and his cousins to slip away, change to breechclouts and leggings, paint their bodies and their ponies—and go after her.

What better way to challenge a white woman on the frontier than stage an Indian attack?

He'd even bribed old Sam Haggerty, the stagecoach driver, who hadn't been happy about them frightening a "sweet young thing" like his passenger, but then, he'd been just as puzzled by her claim to be Lady Douglas as anybody else might be.

So Sam had helped them stage the attack. It was easy...

Except, of course, that he'd expected something more of a desperate surrender from his elegant blonde captive. She'd managed to give him a few good wallops, and with his own knife, she'd nearly managed to make herself a widow in truth. And he could still feel her teeth marks in his shoulder. Whatever else she might be, the woman was a fighter.

Which might stand her well out here, he thought grudgingly.

But then he wondered again what her relationship had been with his father, and his heart grew cold.

He didn't know what had happened, but he was going to find out. David Douglas was dead, and she had made claim to the Douglas name, title, and property.

Well, fine. But she would find he meant to mete out his own justice —for every little clump of earth, for every single blade of grass and speck of gold dust she had come to take.

He left the fire behind and came around to stand beside her again. He'd left her in peace before, but he could no longer do so.

In fact, she continued to rest too damned long and too damned peacefully. He tapped her cheek lightly with the back of his hand. She didn't move. He went for the whiskey, pouring a shot into a mug, sitting again, and lifting her head to force some of the liquor between her lips. She sputtered, choked, coughed, and opened her eyes.

She opened her mouth and shrieked at the sight of him, terrified, fighting him instantly with flying fists and limbs.

"Dammit!" he swore, wrangling her down to the bed again. "I warn you, I am growing weary of this!"

She blinked, staring at him. He realized that she had been completely out, that in waking her, he had made her think she was under attack again.

She went dead still, not fighting him, staring up at him with her eyes cool and crystal clear. "I still don't believe you're Lord Douglas," she said. But she did know, he thought. She was staring into his eyes, which bore a strong resemblance to his father's.

"You're lying. You know damned well that I am exactly who I say I am, while you...well, we still have to decide about you, right? Where did you get that paper?" he demanded.

"What paper?"

"The wedding license."

"You went through my things—" she began indignantly.

"Damned right. Where did you get it?"

"Baltimore," she snapped.

"When you married Lord Douglas?"

She gritted her teeth together, staring at him. "Yes, when I married Lord Douglas."

"You really went through a ceremony?"

She hesitated just a second. "Yes."

"But you married by proxy? While Lord Douglas was there?"

"He—Lord Douglas—said he was not feeling well. Mr. Pike, the owner of Pike's Inn, stood in as the groom. The magistrate informed me that it was perfectly legal, that the signature of Andrew Douglas on the paper made the ceremony binding once I had agreed to the marriage vows and signed the paper as well." She flushed. "Lord Douglas insisted that the wedding take place that way. I could only agree to accompany him as a married woman—"

"So you admit! You bribed and seduced him!" Hawk said softly.

Bitingly.

Her eyes glittered like silver blades. "You go to hell. I seduced no one, and you weren't there, and you don't know—"

"I know that you thought that you married an old man who died of a heart attack on the same day you thought you'd married him."

She jerked up, heedless of his stare and of his words, grasping the robe to her as she leaned against the headboard. "I repeat. Go to hell."

He rose, plucking up the fallen license. "It looks legal."

"It is legal! But—"

"You thought you married an old man. Right?"

Her eyes rose to his. Her lashes fluttered. "I—"

"Yes?"

"Yes, damn you! But if—"

"My father's name was David."

"Those men called you Hawk."

"Yes, they did. It is what I'm called, but my Christian name is Andrew."

She stared at him as if he weren't just an Indian but perhaps the devil himself. As if he had sprouted horns and a tail.

He laughed softly, feeling a strange sense of bitter justice. "My dear, dear Lady Douglas! You sought to take advantage of an old man. Charm, coerce, seduce, marry. Excite him to death, play the lovely, grieving widow and take over all his vast holdings! Well, it appears my father played a trick on you instead. You're not a wealthy widow. You're the wife of a savage. A savage who is very much alive. And in full possession of all that you came out here to acquire."

"You are an incredibly self-righteous and arrogant ass!" she hissed. "I didn't attempt to do anything to anyone. I agreed to the marriage—"

"You didn't come to acquire Mayfair? To take over the mines? I see—you agreed to the marriage because you were in love with Lord Douglas?" he demanded skeptically.

"Damn you! I cared for him!" she cried.

"Umm. For all of an hour, perhaps, before you catapulted him into an early grave?"

"You son of a bi—"

"You should watch it. If this paper is legal as you claim, you're not a widow but a wife," he interrupted harshly. With a taunting smile, he returned to her side, sitting at the edge of the bed, not touching her, but close. "Remember, the wife of a savage, if you will, who wants no part of you."

Very regally, she moved back against the bedpost, drawing all the distance between them she possibly could. She remained pale, but her lashes rose, and her eyes focused on his. She had tremendous pride. And nerve—he'd hand her that.

"You needn't fear, Lord Douglas. Andrew Douglas. I promise, I want no part of you, either."

"Really?"

"Really!"

He itched to slap her. How dare she look so outraged with him after what she had done? He wanted to shake her, touch her.

Get away from her. It was too easy to see how his father had fallen...

Died.

"Well," he murmured very softly, bracing one arm over her hips and leaning closer to her. "I'm afraid that's your misfortune because I do want something from you, my dear wife. I want you to pay for what you did to my father."

He could hear her grating down on her teeth. She was trying to keep silent, avoid the argument he was baiting. She could not do so. "Get away from me!" she commanded.

He smiled. "I don't think so. I've just acquired a wife."

"I'm not an acquisition."

"According to that paper, you are."

"According to that paper, I am not an acquisition. I am legally wed—"

"To me."

"Well, that was a mistake. I did not mean for it to be so."

"But you've done it so. And I'm naturally...curious."

"Don't be!"

"How can I not be? You were intent upon marriage, Lady Douglas. Conquering new lands, heading out west for adventure—and profit. Well, madam, perhaps you will profit. But in the name of my father, my dear wife, you'll pay as well. I guarantee it."

# CHAPTER 5

"Don't you threaten me!" Skylar cried out. It was all that she could do. In a second, he'd have her so intimidated that she'd be pleading like an idiot for mercy when there seemed to be no reason within this man whatsoever.

She ducked beneath his arms and managed to slide from the side of the bed, rise, and stare back at him. There was a wry smile slightly twisting his lips.

"Oh, Lady Douglas. I intend to do much more than threaten."

Yet when he finished with those words, he made no move toward her. He stood as well, staring at her from across the bed and continuing, "I suggest you use some good sense after I leave and do not try to find your way out of here before I get back. You'll be safe enough as long as you stay here. Inside."

"You're—leaving?" she said, both stunned and hopeful.

"But I'll be back."

"Why? Where are you going?"

He arched a brow. "My business is none of your concern."

"But you've dragged me here. You've abducted me—"

"Do you claim this license to be valid?"

"Yes, but—"

"Then you've just been welcomed to your new home by your lawfully wedded husband."

"Really? And what of the stagecoach driver?"

"Old Sam?"

"Mr. Haggerty."

"I assume Mr. Haggerty has driven the stagecoach along on schedule back to Riley's."

"You—ass!" she hissed.

His eyes narrowed. "Well, ma'am, it's just not that often that I hear a complete stranger introducing herself to others as Lady Douglas while she announces she's on her way to take over my property."

"You might have introduced yourself and asked a few questions."

"The fact that my father apparently met you and died soon thereafter certainly influenced my choice of behavior. Let me warn you again. There are all manner of wild creatures outside. Bears, wolves—hostile Indians."

"You can't imagine that you can just leave me here and expect that I'll stay put—"

"Oh, but I do imagine."

"I want to go—"

"To Mayfair? You were on your way to the estate, right?"

"At the moment I simply want to return to civilization!"

"There is no real 'civilization' here, Lady Douglas."

"Civilization could simply be where you are not!" Skylar flared.

He offered her one of his mocking smiles. "You were on your way to Lord Douglas's property. You are on Douglas property. This hunting lodge is mine. Since I will not be here for a while, you may consider yourself in civilization—and at the end of your journey. Enjoy civilization—as I've said, I'll be back."

She stood where she was, staring at him with her jaw locked until he drew more clothing from the trunk at the foot of the bed. She burned with a raw fury unlike anything she had known before. He'd made a fool out of her. He didn't know her, didn't know anything about her or what had happened, and he'd labeled her an adventuress—and worse. A murderess. He'd faked a savage attack on her. He'd taken it as far as he possibly might have gone. She hated him. Loathed him.

Wanted to shoot an arrow between his eyes and take up scalping herself.

Not glancing her way, heedless that she remained in the robe, he shed his own robe and donned buckskin trousers. She felt her cheeks go afire, and she quickly turned away, her shoulders squared. She tried very hard to control her seething temper. "How long am I to wait here?"

"Until I find out from an attorney if this marriage license is legal."

"Oh, it is legal," she grated, keeping her back turned to him. "But—"

"We'll see what is and isn't legal. There's food here. You've the coffee—and the whiskey. I'll call Wolf to watch over you—"

"Wolf? Another of your cohorts in the stagecoach holdup?" she demanded, swinging around to look at him again. He was in dark buckskin trousers, high black boots, and a fringed buckskin shirt. His hair was plaited back. He was extremely tall and well built, striking in his appearance, and still entirely forbidding. He might have appeared white, except...that he didn't. There was something far too savage remaining in the glint of his stare upon her.

"Wolf is my dog. And yes, he is part wolf, thus the name. He'll protect you—or chew you to ribbons if you choose to leave the lodge. Perhaps you should get some sleep. I'll be back tomorrow before evening." He turned, about to leave her. "Do make yourself at home. As I've said, it is Douglas property that you're on now."

"Wait—" she began, but he was gone. The door was closed behind him. She clutched the robe to her, biting into her lower lip, and raced after him, ready to throw open the door.

But she heard him say, "Good boy, stay! Keep an eye on her, now. She's dangerous!" Then excited barking. She stepped back. It didn't seem prudent to open the door.

She leaned against the door, staring straight ahead, seeing nothing. She started shaking again.

She wasn't going to be murdered and scalped by an Indian. At least she didn't think so. He had a horrible temper and didn't seem to be afraid of the consequences for any of his actions, but he wasn't a complete savage.

She sank down against the door, shaking her head. She'd never meant to trick anyone. She hadn't married Lord Douglas for gain.

Apparently, she hadn't married the man she'd met at all. She'd married his son.

The trick had been on her.

She buried her face in her hands, trembling, then stared up at the ceiling, as if she could see God.

"Why?" she whispered, glad that the green-eyed savage wasn't around to hear the whimpering sound of her voice. She didn't deserve this.

She'd married to escape.

What in God's name was she going to do now? What kind of cruel hoax had they all played upon one another? Just when she had thought that life had finally given her a way...

She shouldn't have done it.

She had never meant any harm. Pike's place had always been her escape. It was a small inn, but it had been in business since Revolutionary times, established by Pike's great-grandfather. The present Pike had been her father's very good friend. A number of Baltimore matrons and their daughters came to Pike's for an occasional luncheon, and since it was considered such a respectable establishment, she's had little trouble claiming to her mother that she went to Pike's to meet friends. Lord Douglas had been a visitor over the years—it was quite the fashionable place for wealthy out-of-towners to frequent as well. Pike had pointed him out to her before as an eccentric Englishman living on the frontier who came east on occasion to see to his banking concerns. She had spoken with him politely in the past. But this time she had been there when he had so nearly collapsed. She had been the one to catch him, to insist on calling the doctor. And she would never forget the way that he had told her after he'd seen the doctor that there was little that could be done for him. But it was their secret, please.

He'd been so gentle, kind, dignified, fascinating. She'd realized she was the only one in the world who was aware of how ill he had become. She'd begun to open up to him in turn, telling him things she had never told anyone before. In a matter of days, she'd felt as if he'd been her best friend all of her life. He'd understood the gravity of her situation, the trickiness of it, and had suggested that she come with him. But she couldn't just leave. She didn't dare.

Then had come the night when she hadn't dared go home.

And he had offered her a way out. She had needed the help so badly…

Skylar leaped to her feet and began pacing the floor.

An annulment. She had to get an annulment. If she really was wed to this hateful creature.

She would just go back. Go back east.

Was she insane? She couldn't go back!

That thought racked her over and over again. No, she couldn't go back. And she hadn't married for gain, but she did need money. Desperately.

The fire was dying in the hearth. The cabin was darkening. It was probably very late. She was alone in the wilderness with nothing but a wretched, bloodthirsty dog nearby. She hoped. There could be worse creatures of the night beyond the door…

She couldn't be afraid, she told herself. Thankfully, she was too exhausted to feel much of anything.

She sat on the bed, then stretched out upon it. The thought remained with her, growing duller and duller. She couldn't go back.

So what did she do now?

She laid her head on the pillow.

What if he didn't come back? Who would die first, her or the wolf-dog?

She felt like laughing again. She was so tired. She closed her eyes and felt herself dozing. It felt good. So good. Her body eased down more comfortably into the mattress. And her sleep deepened.

---

GOLD TOWN, a small mining settlement that had grown up quickly in the last few years since gold had been discovered in the Black Hills, was rustic—and prosperous. Henry Pierpont did a decent enough business to keep a large office on Main Street, fully furnished from the East with handsome leather chairs and sofas and cherrywood bookcases. He had a secretary, Jim Higgins, a young man who'd originally come for the gold, then turned in his miner's equipment for pen and ink. The moment Hawk burst into the law office, Jim was on his feet. "Hawk. Er, Lord Douglas. Henry's been expecting you, Lord Douglas."

Hawk nodded, heading toward the inner office. He paused. "Jim."

"Yes, sir, Lord Douglas."

"My father was born in England. Lord Douglas suited him, don't you think? Hawk suits me."

Jim flashed him a weak smile. "Yeah, thanks. It's much more comfortable."

Hawk nodded again, then went on into Henry's office. Painfully thin with wire-rimmed spectacles and a prematurely balding head, Henry Pierpont leaped to his feet. He knocked over the coffee cup in front of him and started mopping up the coffee with his handkerchief. "Hawk. Your father's body is due at Riley's by tonight. It's come as far as it could by train, but the railroad had a little bit of a problem getting a proper conveyance to bring it on up. We're still really in the wilds out here, you know. But there's a matter that's come to my attention by the most recent post—" He broke off, shaking his head, miserable and very nervous.

Hawk threw the wedding license on Henry's desk and sat in the chair in front of it.

"Could this matter have something to do with a woman claiming to be Lady Douglas?" he demanded.

Henry went dead still, then nodded. He sank back into his own chair. "You must understand, your father was my client."

Hawk arched a brow.

Henry held a pencil. It cracked between his fingers. "I warned him that he shouldn't be carrying around proxy papers, that it just wasn't right."

"You drew up proxy papers?"

"Yes, I drew them up."

"Henry, damn you—"

"Hawk, I drew them up, but, well, you did sign them."

"Because I've never been interested in taking control of my father's estates! He managed his own properties! He was sound of mind. He was in good health—"

"He was aging," Henry interrupted quietly. "I wanted to contact you and let you know that he was quite determined that you should marry, but again, your father was my client, until his death. Of course, now you're Lord Douglas, my client."

Hawk felt completely at a loss. He lifted his hands. "Did my father know this woman before he left here?"

Henry shook his head. "No. I don't know where he found the young woman—" He broke off, puzzled. "How do you know about this? I just received your father's last letters to me with copies of the documents. The young lady hasn't arrived yet—"

"Oh, but she has!" Hawk murmured. He leaned forward, staring at Henry. "Just tell me—is this marriage legal?"

"Well, of course, you could apply for an annulment, if both parties were willing—"

"Is the marriage legal?" he demanded.

"It—er—yes," Henry said.

Hawk expelled a long breath. "I can't believe my father did this!"

Henry cleared his throat. "It—gets a little worse."

Hawk arched a brow at him.

"A little worse?"

Henry's Adam's apple moved up and down beneath the collar of his formal white shirt. He cleared his throat again. "If she chooses to force the issue of attempting to negate the marriage, she will be disinherited except for a small stipend she is to receive, even if she returns home. If she remains here as your wife, naturally, the house becomes half hers." Henry loosened his collar.

"Go on."

"If you choose to attempt to negate it—"

Hawk stood, incredulous. "My father disinherited me?"

"No, not completely. Only the Mayfair estate lands."

Thousands of Black Hills acres. Land David owned through land grants and claims, but Sioux land. Land he never developed because it had belonged to his wife's people, his son's people. Land he had to keep.

He'd been raised Sioux. Raised to believe that a man of honor shared everything, did not need riches. But he needed those lands. Especially with the confrontations that promised to come.

He sank back into the chair, shaking his head. His father had known him, known how to manipulate him. Known he didn't give a damn about Scottish estates or eastern property. He would have gladly rid himself of an unwanted wife by giving up those properties. But the Sioux lands...

The hot fire of pain spread throughout his chest. "I loved him," he said simply, lifting his hands, at a loss.

"He—he loved you, too. I truly believe that he did what he did for your benefit. Of course, he must also have been quite charmed by this young woman when he met her to have stipulated that she must be in his will as well."

"Yes, he must have been charmed."

"Well, you've met your, er, wife, is that right?"

"Yes. I met her stagecoach. Rather by accident. I'd gone to Riley's to see if my father's body had arrived."

"Well, then, is she—satisfactory?"

"Satisfactory?"

Henry was becoming increasingly more nervous and ill at ease. "I mean...is she, er...well, dammit all, Hawk, is she attractive? Is she—oh, lord—is she unattractive? Is there something wrong with her?"

Hawk smiled without amusement. "She's just—charming. Tell me—you're absolutely sure the marriage is legal. It's a proxy marriage—"

"Half the marriages in half the mining towns throughout the West are legal by proxy," Henry said wearily. "How do you think these fellows get wives out here? What proper young woman is going to come this distance without being a man's lawful wedded wife?"

"What proper young woman..." Hawk murmured.

"You know that I'm willing to be of service to you in any way," Henry said. "But your father was of sound mind when he made his arrangements. My hands are tied."

Hawk leaned forward. It was on the tip of his tongue to ask, "And what if she seduced, coerced, and killed the old man?" He didn't say the words. He could probably never prove that she'd had anything to do with his father's death. He might not even be able to convince Henry that Skylar Connor had thought herself married to his father—and a widow now. A widow ready to take possession of his property.

"Whatever you decide to do..." Henry said.

"She won't be getting my land. You can damned well bet on that!" Hawk said. Rising, he exited the office, so filled with fury once again that he could have knocked the door from its hinges.

He went straight for his horse, but before he could mount, he heard his name called. Black Feather, an old Hunkpapa friend who traded furs in town despite all the government edicts, strode toward him. He was a tall, well-built man with weather-leathered features and a slow, easy, thoughtful way about him. Hawk cooled his temper, grasping arms with his old friend.

"How are you, Black Feather? Your hunting goes well?"

"Hunting goes badly. The whites have shot the buffalo herds, killing hundreds, perhaps thousands, from their train windows. They slaughter game." He shrugged. "I'm a good hunter. Trading furs for gunpowder." He lowered his voice. "Come to your grandfather's village soon. Many friends, who cannot or will not come this close to white settlements, will be moving north and would like to bid you farewell."

"Joining Sitting Bull?" Hawk asked.

Black Feather nodded gravely. "We have but two choices. Become fenced in like white cattle or fight for our ways. You cannot argue this."

"I wouldn't attempt to argue it. I will come very soon."

"Your grandfather will be glad." Black Feather hesitated. "We have heard of your father's passing. My heart is heavy with yours. He was a great man."

Hawk nodded. "Thank you."

"He will be missed by us all."

"Deeply."

Hawk mounted his horse, lifting a hand in farewell. As he rode hard from the fledgling settlement, he felt as if he had been buffeted by storms with wildly opposing winds. He was angry with his father, in pain for his father, and he could never talk to him again to try to understand what he had done. And he hurt for David, wondering what pain had racked him in the end that he should have become so dependent and enamored of Skylar Connor that she could have manipulated him so. And now, in the midst of this personal tragedy and confusion, the country was continuing to trundle down a road of cruelty and injustice against his people.

The longer he rode toward the lodge on the far eastern border of his property, the more heated his temper grew.

He was ready to do battle.

---

DREAMS of the distant past had haunted her most of her life. Not continually. Just upon occasion.

The dreams always began the same way. She saw the gray swirls rising before her eyes once again.

Just as they had before. Long ago.

The night air had been thick with a low-hanging fog. Footsteps could be heard falling upon the streets, but no forms could be seen. It was a perfect night for clandestine meetings. For secrets in the darkness.

Maryland had been full of secrets.

A border state, it had teemed with spies and conspiracy. There were those who were openly Southern sympathizers and those who were vociferously pro-Union. There were those who pretended to be Southern sympathizers but spied for the Union. There were those who publicly supported the Union who were really Southern spies.

And there were those who were just caught in between.

Robert Connor had lived down in Williamsburg. Before the war, he'd taken a job as a young attorney there, and when the war had broken out, he'd wound up in the army.

And after Gettysburg, he'd wound up in a Union prison in DC. Only he'd managed to escape. And he'd managed to get a message to his brother, Richard, that he needed help.

Richard Connor lived with his wife, Jill, and their two daughters, Skylar and Sabrina, in a fine house in Baltimore. He'd spent the war years in torment himself, having been wounded early in '62 and sent home with a limp that would never go away. He'd been glad to come home. He'd believed in the sanctity of the Union, but he'd never believed in killing his Southern brethren. And when his brother had called him for help, he'd immediately given it.

So, Robert had come. And he'd played with the girls while he lay hidden in their attic, and Skylar had come to love him nearly as much as her own father. But word finally came that he was to be met by plainclothes Southern spies and spirited back to the Confederacy, where he would be safe.

And the fog and the mist had come

Skylar had been sent to bed, but she'd known what was going on that night. Her father and his best friend, Brad Dillman, were to take Robert to meet the Southerners. They'd all act like drunks down by the docks, then Robert would be spirited away, and Richard and Brad would stumble back to the house, apologizing profusely to Jill and the girls and promising to mend their ways.

Skylar never knew what possessed her to sneak out of bed that night, dress up in shirt and trousers, and follow the men out. Maybe it was the excitement.

Maybe it was some strange trace of fear within her.

She hastily raced behind them, a scarf pulled around her throat and lower face, a cap pulled down low on her head. She twisted through the streets by the water. She followed the men into an alley and down the docks where a small ship waited.

She heard conversation.

The mist settled down more heavily.

Suddenly, she heard someone crying out. She realized that the ship was slipping slowly from its berth in the harbor. She raced down the dock, not seeing any of the men.

She tripped and nearly stumbled over a body lying on the dock. She fell down beside it and realized who it was. "Father?" she whispered. "Father!" She tried to wake him, turn him. She touched his back and drew her hand away, shrieking when she discovered that it was covered with blood.

"Father—"

"Skylar!" It was a broken whisper, hissed out sibilantly. She didn't care. She tried to hold him, turn him, help him, stanch the flow of blood. He looked at her, but she didn't think that he saw her. But she felt the warmth of his bloody touch on her fingers, squeezing in turn. "Love you, careful, baby, careful, be a good soldier. I—betray—"

"I'll never betray you!"

"No, I was—"

"Father, shh, I'll get help, I promise, don't die, don't you leave me—"

His hand fell from hers. Richard was staring up at her, eyes wide open but unseeing. And she realized that he was dead, and she started to scream.

She was found by a Union soldier on patrol, who took her to an army office, where men plied her with questions despite the fact her heart was broken, and she felt as if she had shed her life's blood upon that dock as well. They kept demanding to know what had happened. Be a good soldier, he had told her. She'd never betray him, never...

They kept her all night. In the morning, her mother arrived, ashen gray with her grief, yet demanding her eleven-year-old daughter's immediate return. There was no proof that Richard Connor had ever been a Southern spy, and Jill Connor created such an uproar that the officers were forced to let Skylar go without finding out what had really happened.

That night, when her father's body had been set out in the parlor for the wake, Skylar listened dully to the conversations in the kitchen. Brad Dillman trembling, his voice broken as he told her mother how the filthy Rebs had repaid Richard's kindness with bloody murder. She had listened to her mother sob.

A heavy mist lay close to the ground again. Deep, dense fog, rising, flowing. She needed to be back outside again, away. So she ran through it. Ran and ran. And finally, when she could run no more, she ran toward home again. But she didn't want to see any more people. She still wanted to be alone.

It was by pure accident that she ran from the mist and into the stables to discover Brad Dillman, tall, handsome, with the well-built shoulders her mother had so recently cried upon, secretively wiping blood from a twelve-inch cavalry knife he had drawn from a sheath at his ankle.

Dunhill looked up from the bloody knife and saw her. "Skylar. Sweet, sweet little Skylar..."

He reached for her...

---

WHEN FINGERS TOUCHED HER CHEEK, Skylar shrieked, bolting up in the bed, fighting instinctively.

The lodge was cast in shadow. The fire had burned down to embers. She could scarcely see in the gloom of the cabin, but she was aware of the imposing figure first standing over her, then straddling her as he captured her arms and pinned them down, staring down at her.

"Is it just me? Or do you scream and attempt to pummel everyone who comes near you, Lady Douglas?"

It was him. The Indian was back. Atop her again. Mocking her again.

Perhaps even more bitterly now...

"You startled me," she said.

"Oh, not quite as much as you've startled me!" he murmured.

"You're—crushing me."

"Am I?"

"Please..."

He released her and rose. He turned away from her, a large dark shadow moving in the hazy light of the lodge. It was morning, Skylar thought. Or else it was early evening once again. She had slept long and deeply, and still she was tired.

He stoked the fire with a poker and added a log. Sparks flew. The fire once again began to blaze.

He didn't bother with the leftover coffee. He took the whiskey bottle from the shelf and leaned an arm upon the mantel, staring at her for a moment, then gulping down large swallows of amber liquid from the bottle, then staring at her again.

"You are my wife!" he grated out, emphasizing the last word as if it were a loathsome thing.

Skylar sat up, trying to smooth down her hair, trying to hold her robe together with dignity.

"I'm—sorry," she murmured coolly. She lowered her eyes, realizing the truth of her predicament. Yet, surely, there was some way out of it.

Except, she realized suddenly, if there were, she couldn't take it! She didn't dare accept any way out—and back east. No matter what, she had to stay here in the Dakota territory. She had to remain Lady Douglas. For the time being, at least.

He sauntered toward her, the whiskey bottle still in his hand. He paused before the bed, then hunkered down before her, his green eyes riveted on hers.

Apparently, he was having different thoughts.

"Something could be done about this. If you were to ask for an annulment, I could see to it that you were escorted back east as quickly as possible with—"

"No!"

"What?" he demanded.

He was too close. Almost touching her knees. He was dressed now, but she still wore only the robe. She leaped up, skirting around him, around the table. He stood, turning, watching her, his hands on his hips. She faced him from across the table. "I—can't ask for an annulment."

He arched a brow.

"Don't you understand?" he demanded angrily. "You're not a widow. You haven't"—he hesitated— "you haven't just inherited my father's estates. I have been to his attorney, who was astonished I hadn't given greater interest to papers when I put my name upon them. My father was actually out looking for a bride for me when he stumbled upon you. So, yes, you are Lady Douglas, but you don't have to be. You can file for an annulment. You can go home with money in your pocket—"

"No."

"Dammit, what do you mean, no?" he demanded bitingly.

"No. I'm not going back," Skylar repeated.

He just stood, staring at her. "I don't want a wife," he grated out.

The way that he had taunted her, half scaring her to death earlier, suddenly seemed possible to avenge in some small way.

"That's your misfortune," she said sweetly. Then she almost backed into the fireplace, she was so certain that he was going to come and do her bodily harm.

He did not, turning instead to slam a fist against the wall with such fervor that it seemed the entire place shook. "You intend to stay?" he roared.

"I have to stay!" she told him determinedly. He continued to stare at her with such leashed fury that she found herself hurriedly going on. "I will stay. I've come out here. I must stay. I won't get in your way, I promise. I—"

"How do you know?"

"How do I know what?"

"That you won't get in my way?"

"Because I won't. I—"

He strode toward the table, slamming the whiskey bottle upon it as he leaned toward her. "What if there are women I choose to have in my life?"

"Then—" She faltered, her eyes falling. She raised them, meeting his cleanly. "Then you must keep them in your life."

He crossed his arms over his chest, looking as if he liked her all the less the more she spoke.

"If you'd been about to take a wife, surely your father wouldn't have married you to me," she said hastily. "And as to anyone else...I'll stay out of your way."

"Really?"

"Completely."

He took a long swig from the whiskey bottle and leaned against the table again. This time his eyes looked as if they were on fire. "What if I wanted you in my way."

"What?" she whispered.

"What if I wanted you to be a wife to me?"

"I—I..."

"I believe I could get either an annulment or a divorce on the grounds that you were denying me conjugal rights."

The fire was hot behind her, but she knew that she flushed a crimson that was hotter than the blaze. He started to smile. He was trying to unnerve her. A strange trembling did seize her. Not because she was afraid. But because of something that was compelling about him. The way he moved, perhaps. The subtle scent of him, the hot gaze of his green eyes. *Don't give an inch!* she thought. For he would not. She lifted her chin. Then she allowed her eyes to sweep over him in cold assessment. She shrugged.

"If you want a wife, you've got one," she said evenly.

He was silent for a moment, watching her. He drew the whiskey bottle to his lips once again, his eyes never leaving hers. He lowered the bottle, placing it on the table, his hands on his hips.

"Lady," he said very quietly, "you really are one gold-digging little whore!"

The words seemed to lash out at her with greater violence than any of the actions he had taken against her. No matter how the force of them hit her, she willed herself to remain perfectly still, returning his stare. She weighed her reply carefully, speaking in an equally soft tone, "And you are a selfish, self-righteous, judgmental ass with all the manners of a sniveling piglet. You've no right—"

"You're giving me every right in the world, aren't you, Lady Douglas?"

She narrowed her eyes on the whiskey bottle. "You're drunk and insulting."

"I'm trying very hard to get drunk, and I'm calling a spade a spade. Besides, I would think 'drunk and insulting' an improvement over what you considered my previous potential for being murderous and scalp-taking."

Skylar knew she tread upon very thin ice. His temper was explosive —and he was convinced she had hastened his father's death.

She wondered if anything she could ever say would change his conviction.

There had to be a way to fight him. A place to strike.

"If I'm not mistaken," she murmured, meeting his eyes once again, "hasn't whiskey led to the downfall of a number of Indian tribes?"

He stared at her, smiled slowly, and came forward.

"Yes, it has. But I'm not a tribe. Just one Indian. Who also happens to be the son of a misguided English lord who discovered himself in love with a landscape and a people. Who also happens not to want a wife! Ah, but it seems that I have one, right? Drink with me then, my dear. Let's celebrate making each other's acquaintance!"

Suddenly he was in motion again, coming around the table. Skylar quickly circled away from him. The table wasn't big enough. She wasn't fast enough. His fingers caught her wrist, and he drew her around to crash against his body.

"Baltimore, eh? Tell me, Lady Douglas, do you come from a family deeply Southern at heart? Have I come upon a belle who wouldn't dream of swilling whiskey straight? I don't believe so. I think you're tough as nails. Have a swallow."

She closed her eyes briefly. She could be done with this. She could agree to his annulment, give him no more reason to taunt her.

She took the bottle from him. Took a sip. She wasn't used to straight liquor. She coughed and wheezed but quickly gained control of herself and slammed the bottle back into his chest. "We've celebrated," she said coolly.

"Have we?" He set the bottle on the table. His hands were suddenly upon her cheek and throat, his long fingers splayed along her chin, lifting it. His breath just fanned her lips, then his mouth touched down upon hers, forcing a full, open-mouthed kiss, his tongue plunging deeply into her, liquid fire, decadent in the extreme. His fingers slipped beneath the robe, touching her collarbone and throat. She was drawn inexorably nearer. His hand slipping down to cup her breast, his palm moving over her nipple. She was startled by the lightning rip of sensation that tore into her from the touch. Such shocking warmth, so mercurial, so sweeping, touching where he touched, touching where he did not.

She brought her hands between them to protest, to push away. But his lips had moved just a breath away from hers.

His fingers then threaded through her hair, and his whisper was soft and taunting against her ear.

"What if I wanted a wife, eh, Lady Douglas? Then I'd have a wife, so you say."

She went still, her heart pounding, hating him, hating herself. She wanted so badly to pull away.

Because she was so appalled by the feelings that engulfed her. At the simmering warmth that filled her. At the way she felt when he touched her, brushed her nipple, forced his tongue into her mouth, stroking with a strange insinuation that seemed to leap inside her as well as without...oh, God, she needed to be free from him!

But she didn't need to pull away. He suddenly thrust her from him.

"You are for sale to the highest bidder, aren't you, Lady Douglas?" he demanded.

She stared at him, shaking, realizing her robe hung open. She raised her fingers to her damp, swollen lips, drew the robe more tightly against her.

"You have his eyes but nothing else," she said. "There is nothing else of your father about you at all," she told him heatedly.

"Don't you tell me about my father," he warned her.

"I might have known him better than you."

"One has the feeling you've known many men. But now that we are wed, thanks to my father's efforts on my behalf," he said sardonically, "the only man you'll know is me."

"You bastard!" she hissed.

But he didn't hear her. He had turned away and slammed out of the lodge.

And once again, she was alone.

# CHAPTER 6

Wolf was an extraordinary dog.

He was the best guard dog in the world, ready to rip to shreds any enemy who might come near his master. Yet when Hawk came outside the lodge, slamming the door in his wake only to sink down and sit on the wooden porch, Wolf was beside him instantly, whining softly, sticking his wet nose next to Hawk's face.

"Hey, dog, good dog," Hawk said softly, rubbing his pet's fur strenuously. Wolf settled down beside Hawk, his nose on his master's knee. Hawk patted him absently. He leaned his head back against the lodge wall. He had swigged down way too much whiskey.

He didn't appreciate her informing him of the fact. Nor reminding him that yes, the Indians had been made fools of time and again over liquor.

He didn't, in fact, appreciate her very existence.

A dull pain struck him again. What had his father been thinking when he'd married him to this woman? He had known that David Douglas had been deeply concerned about US policy in the West because he was convinced that generals were running the government. Grant was president and therefore commander-in-chief of the Army. Sherman and Sheridan, who had done their share of devastating the South in order to win the war, had been turned loose on the American West for some time now. Each year, the conflicts increased the determination of the whites to open the West. Indians were to live where they were told or be considered hostiles. But there was nothing good about reservation living. The whites wanted the best lands. The buffalo were being hunted to extinction. When the Indians couldn't hunt enough game, they starved. Unless they could grow enough food. But the Plains Indians survived mostly off their hunting. And if they had been natural farmers, it wouldn't have mattered because any time the land was good, the whites eventually wanted it. On the reservations, far too often, the men grew lazy and indolent. They drank...

Until their pride drove them from the reservations. And then they became hostiles. And hostiles were to be exterminated.

David had warned his son of this frequently. Just as he had often enough urged his son to marry again, to heal the breach in his heart. Marry a white woman. One who would not be a sister or a daughter of a hostile. One who would not bring him more heartache.

He wished he hadn't left the whiskey inside.

He wished his head wasn't pounding.

He wished...

It was his cabin. What was he doing slumped down with his dog on the porch while she resided comfortably inside? Especially after he'd ridden through half the night to reach Gold Town and had spent a good part of today riding back.

Why wouldn't she go back home? Perhaps she knew the terms of his father's will. Knew that she had far more to gain if she remained here as his...

Wife. The woman was his wife. He almost laughed aloud, remembering how Henry had asked if there was something wrong with her. No, there was nothing wrong with her. Her eyes were almost pure silver. Her hair was almost pure gold. To touch her was to feel a stroke of silk.

To lie against her was to feel the greatest sensual pleasure. To...

His thoughts broke off as he realized that the pounding that had been in his head seemed to have filled the length of him. His groin was hot and hard. He could remember the taste and feel of her lips, the full curve of her breast.

Too damned bad she was his wife.

Bought and paid for, so it seemed. There was no returning her.

Even if she was his father's used goods.

Even if she'd brought about David's death.

He swore out loud. Dusk was already falling again. He'd been gone from Mayfair far longer than he'd intended, and he needed to travel out again to the river country beyond the hills where he knew he'd find his grandfather's band.

But not tonight. Tonight...

He'd always been sparing in most things. His eating habits, his use of alcohol.

Not tonight. Tonight, he wanted to get rip-roaring drunk. Toast the old man.

Toast the new woman.

Fall into a deep, drunken sleep and dream that time could move backward and the plains could be big enough for the red men, the white men, and the buffalo.

He gave Wolf a last pat on the head and pushed himself back up to his feet. He opened the door, stepping back into the cabin.

She stood pensively before the fire, then looked at him warily as he entered. Her robe was drawn tight. She'd drawn her fingers through the long strands of her golden hair to somewhat righten it. She appeared calm, dignified, her eyes touching his with that regal look she could manage. He noted again that she had been endowed with an almost startling beauty. The silver of her eyes was so intense, the gold of her hair so vivid, the sculpture of her oval face so defined, delicate, elegant, arresting. As he watched her, he realized that a tempting aroma was filling the cabin. She'd set a kettle atop the fire, and the hunger-rousing scent was wafting from it.

"It's soup," she murmured defensively. "You told me to make my myself at home. I found onions and potatoes to go with the ham. And some shell peas."

"Ah. What a good wife," he mocked. "She cooks."

"What a good husband," she retorted. "He drinks."

"Cheers!" He found the whiskey bottle on the table and lifted it to her, smiling grimly as he spoke. "He drinks—and he's a Sioux. Tell me, even if you're absolutely determined to remain here—and I'll grant you that Mayfair is a fine enough place to live—doesn't it disturb you in the least that my skin is red? I am an Indian. A Sioux—considered by many whites to be among the most savage beasts on the plains. You were hardly enamored with me when we met."

"You were attacking my stagecoach when we met."

"It's what Indians do."

She ignored that, walking to the fire. "If you'd like to try this, I'll get you a bowl."

"Indeed, yes. I'm ravenous. Do so."

She placed the soup before him. He pulled a chair from the table and tasted the soup, never taking his eyes from her.

"Well. Is it edible?"

"Not poisoned, right?"

"Not poisoned."

"It's quite adequate."

"How kind," she murmured coolly.

He caught her wrist, smiling up at her. "Perhaps it should have been poisoned. I'm a young man. It's unlikely that you'll induce me to expire from a heart attack."

She wrenched her wrist free, rubbing it. "Enjoy your adequate soup. The next meal you get from me you'll wear over your head before you ever get a chance to eat it."

She poured herself a bowl, joining him at the opposite end of the table. He tore his eyes from her at last, finishing his bowl of soup quickly. He sat back, stared at the whiskey bottle, drank long and deeply once again.

"A vice you indulge in often?"

"Every time I acquire an unwanted bride."

"Is that often?"

"Thankfully, no."

"You've never married be—"

"Yes. I was married before."

"Your wife—"

"Is dead."

"I'm sorry."

He shook his head. "Are you? Not nearly as damned sorry as I, Lady Douglas."

She stood abruptly. "Perhaps you should go ahead, then, and dwell in your self-pity and bitterness." She came around the table, lifting the whiskey bottle, slamming it back down right in front of him. "Why don't you just go ahead and drink yourself into a stupor? I'll enjoy the quiet."

She turned away from him with a dismissive contempt that seemed to light the short fuse of his temper. To his astonishment he found himself on his feet, wrenching her back by a corner of her robe. The robe fell from her shoulder, exposing one of her full young breasts. He'd seen it before, he reminded himself. No need to feel such a heated lust growing...

Yes, he'd seen her before. Familiarity was breeding desire.

"Madam, I could drink all night—and not fall into a stupor. And remember, you have chosen to be here. I've offered you a way out. You refuse to take it."

"You are hardly in a proper frame of mind in which to talk this matter through. You—"

"Talk!"

She tried to jerk free from him and spin away, gain distance from him. But his fingers remained taut on her robe, and when she left him, she left behind her covering as well.

When she turned to face him, silver eyes wide, she was naked, and at last, somewhat unnerved.

She blinked, moistening her lips, staring at him without moving. She lifted a hand toward him, indicating the robe that had fallen by his feet. "If you'd be so good as to hand that back..." she murmured.

He picked up the robe, still meeting her gaze. Then he opened his clenched fingers, allowing the robe to fall back to the floor.

"Maybe not. Maybe it's time you get to know me better than you knew my father."

He was taking two long, swift strides toward her before she seemed to realize her danger. She turned to bolt just when he reached her, his hands around her waist, lifting her, throwing her down upon the furs on the bed. She seemed stunned when she first fell, all that golden hair softly glittering in the subdued firelight, splaying out like tendrils of the sun. Again, she seemed to regain her breath and attempted to rise for an escape, but he was quickly down upon her, his weight pushing her deeper down into the furs.

She came to life then, twisting beneath him as she strained to throw him from her. She fought like a wildcat, trying to strike, kick, punch him.

"Lady Douglas," he mocked, avoiding the blows she was attempting to dole out. "I have no desire for a wife, remember? I need but your word that you'll go home—"

She lay still for a second beneath him, her breasts heaving, her silver eyes on his.

"We need to talk!"

"There's nothing to say. It will be one way or the other. We are man and wife, or we are not."

"You're in no frame of mind to straighten this out—"

"Shall we get an annulment then?"

"You're drunk—"

"Ah, but alas! I've fallen into no stupor. And, as you can see, I'm not on the verge of a heart attack, either."

"You'll wind up stabbed in the heart!" she cried, slamming against him again.

"Some men are easier to kill than others."

He straddled her, his fingers sliding along the length of her bare arms to her wrists, capturing them.

He leaned close to her face. "We're husband and wife, or we are not," he told her. "The choice is yours. Say the word, and I will let you up."

But she didn't speak. Her eyes glittered with a fury that matched any he had seen in the face of the most savage Crow warrior. She was dead still, staring at him, challenging him. At last she whispered fiercely, "I am not going back."

He didn't know what he had expected from her. He didn't even know exactly what he wanted.

Yes, he did.

He tried to tell himself that it was the whiskey in him, that he was drunk. But he had drunk to dull the sensations in him, the pain for his father, the desire for this woman. Hating her, doubting her, indeed, still wondering what part she had played in his father's death.

But it didn't matter.

He wanted her. Wanted her in a way that defied all reason. It was like a blinding pulse within him, a pulse that quickened its beat with each second that went by. It seemed like the force of a storm, like that of a hundred ponies tearing over the plain. More powerful than thought and reason and even pain. He was seduced as well. She had sold herself to the highest bidder. No matter how he challenged her, she wouldn't say the words that would force him to set her free now no matter what rage of raw lust had taken root within his loins.

"Again!" he exclaimed harshly, "I ask you—"

"I will be a wife!" she cried out furiously.

She was trembling, but he didn't care. He shifted his weight, shoving apart her thighs with the force of his knees, adjusting his buckskin trousers. The painful swell of his sex lay against the softness of her flesh when he noted her eyes again. They had closed. Her lips were slightly parted. Her breasts rose and fell as she gasped for every breath she drew. He watched her, drawing a hand down the length of her hip and thigh, firmly stroking the smooth dip of her abdomen, then running his palm over the golden thatch of her mound before sliding firmly between her legs to part the tender lips of her sex. She shuddered fiercely again, her lips moving, no sound coming from them. He thrust her thighs further apart and felt again the fierce shuddering seize her. He leaned closer against her, pausing to catch her face in his hand, as he leaned down taut upon her. "Open your eyes!" he commanded.

She did so. Swallowing as she faced him. That silver fire still with her. But her eyes seemed huge once again. Luminous. She moistened her lips, wetting them furiously with the tip of her tongue. She writhed as if to combat the threat of him between her thighs. Yet she stopped quickly, meeting his gaze, her lashes falling then.

"You said something," he whispered to her.

She shook her head.

"You spoke. What did you say?"

Her eyes opened again. "I said..."

"Yes?"

"Please."

"Please what?"

She shook her head, closing her eyes. "Please, just don't..."

He ground down on his teeth. Defied the savage hunger in himself.

"You can still be free."

"I...no."

"Then please..."

She shook her head again. She shifted. The hard, wildly-aroused length of his sex rubbed against her inner thigh. "Please, don't..."

He frowned. "Hurt you?" he whispered.

She tried to turn away, forcing the tip of his sex intimately against the portals of her own. She froze, and he felt her body shaking again, rubbing against him, now driving him near to insanity. But he placed his palm against her cheek, brushing his thumb over her lips. "I'll not hurt you," he heard himself promise huskily. "I'll do my damnedest not to hurt you."

He pressed his mouth to her slightly parted lips, opening them further, filling them with the force of his tongue, tasting, stroking, coercing, moving slowly, leisurely at first, lulling...until he was certain that she responded. He kept his lips upon hers while he allowed his hands the exquisite freedom to roam over her body. Touching. Fingertips light upon the flesh of her inner arms, his palms barely touching the tips of her breasts. Holding, caressing, cradling the weight of them, arousing the peaks once more with a stroke of his palm, the manipulation of his thumb and fingers. His lips rose from her at last. Trailed along her throat. Took root upon a swollen, crested nipple. Played long, slowly, suckling, teasing, his tongue darting against her flesh. Thunder played havoc in his mind. His body tensed into magnificent knots. He feared that he would implode with the hunger building inside of him...

She didn't move. Didn't protest. She trembled. At times, little sounds seemed to escape from her, gasps and moans. Only when he dipped lower against her, his lips skimming her abdomen as he moved his head in a horizontal pattern down the length of her, did her fingers suddenly clench his hair, then release it...and another sound escaped from her throat. He moved his hand down her inner thigh, his fingers stroking with a featherlight touch. With his fingertip, he drew a line that he touched then with the heat of his lips and tongue, feeling the rigid tautness of his own muscles, the straining within him, the desire spiraling with each taste of her. His fingers burned. His body seemed a roaring inferno. He brought the line of his touch, and the damp stroke of his kiss behind it, ever higher. He stroked the soft V of golden blonde hair, parted the outer flesh there, pressed intimately within her. She stiffened, muscles taut, her body shaking despite her efforts to keep still. He teased, invaded with a liquid caress, then rose, his fingers still touching her intimately, watching her curiously as he seared within. Her eyes remained closed. Her fingers were dug into the bed furs with such force that she might have torn the hair from the pelt. Enough. The thunder within him might well cause his heart to cease to beat within seconds. He rose again above her. Thrust apart her thighs, which she had instinctively brought together again. Thrust heedlessly, hungrily within her. Deep, deep within her, being encompassed, the relief of just being inside of her so great that he was both appeased and more wildly aroused and...

He went dead still, his body both burning and frozen, the pounding within his head now something that raged, denying all reason. Denying her innocence.

But he couldn't deny the physical evidence his own rough force had brought home to him.

Whatever else she might have done, she hadn't seduced his father into bed. Or at least not this far. Nor had she made her way through life sleeping with any man.

She didn't cry out. The same reckless courage that had brought her this far kept her silent now. Her fingers clenched the furs so tightly that her knuckles were white. Her eyes were fixed on the ceiling above. She had bit into her lower lip with such fierce determination that a tiny drop of blood rested there now...

His muscles knotted, eased, tensed, contorted again. Reason

demanded he withdraw, sanity demanded that he not. He caught her ashen face between his fingers, forcing her to look at him.

He should have whispered something reassuring, said something tender, gentle. He'd taken a virgin before, a virgin wife at that, and the night had been one filled with laughter and sweet, erotic pleasure for them both. But they'd both known what they wanted, what they were doing. They'd known one another...

"Damn you!" he whispered.

So much for tender words. But he could not withdraw, would not withdraw. They had come this far. She had insisted on being a wife.

He'd said he wouldn't hurt her. He hadn't realized...

"Damn you!" he whispered once again. But he drew her fingers from the fur, threading them through his own, holding her hands rightly, very slowly beginning to move. He kissed her lips, forcing open her mouth. As slowly as he moved with the thrust of his sex, he coerced and teased with his kiss against her lips, with the tip of his tongue upon her mouth, throat, breasts. Until finally her fingers were no longer entwined with his but braced upon his shoulders, his back, moving. Until it seemed that her lips parted to his demand, that her body arched, her nipples hardened again, her breasts swelled, the length of her form...

Undulated.

Arched. Moved to his.

Caution was lost. The thunder was like a hammer blow, driving him to a relentless, furious, shuddering rhythm. Heat built within like the rage of a firestorm. It spiraled throughout him, into her. Her fingers dug into his flesh, sounds tore from her throat. Her teeth grazed his shoulder, her head arched back. He grasped her knees, parting her further. A gasp ripped from her throat, the supple perfection of her form locked around his, rocked, writhed, undulated, moved with and against his...

That supple movement forced him to the explosive brink of climax. He strained to hold himself back, force her ever higher, force from her...

A cry, strangled back, so quickly swallowed. Yet not so easily hidden in the rigidity of her form before it went limp, the dampness that closed so warmly around his sex, driving him the last few seconds into an explosive, staggering climax, one that brought him thundering into her again and again and once again, his body constricted to a taut line, spilling out the firestorm that had raged and swept within him. It racked his body, shook it, tensed it, eased it, tensed it...

And then, it was over.

He braced over her, his flesh soaked beneath the clothing he had never found the time to shed. He couldn't remember the last time he had known such hunger or such fulfillment, such wanting, and such a volatile climax. He was unbelievably sated, yet thinking of her alone could trigger the sparks of something deep inside him again, ignite anew the subtle growth of such a wild hunger again. He stared down at her.

She didn't open her eyes. She had to inhale several times before she could manage to speak, and even then, her words were barely a whisper. "Could you...get off me now?"

He held still for a moment, chagrined, both his temper and a sense of shame he told himself he didn't have to feel growing. He couldn't say how many women he had known, Indian, white, respectable, experienced, just beyond the bounds of innocence. But he'd never had an encounter end like this, with the woman politely asking him to remove himself from her person.

But then again, he'd never been so incensed as to come to something so very close to force as this. It didn't seem to matter that he'd offered her every possible way out.

"No, I don't think so," he told her.

Her eyes opened. In them he thought he saw confusion, pain, and astonishment as if she'd just gained some startling new knowledge. Which he supposed she had.

"You could have told me you hadn't engaged in intimate relations before."

"Intimate relations!" she choked out. "Oh, God, coming from you that sounds so strange." Fire filled her silver orbs once again. "You have everything set in your mind. Why in God's name would I tell you anything? What you want to know, you can just find out on your own every damned time!" she promised him vehemently.

She had a way about her. A way of creating a wicked, unbearable rise in his temper and his blood.

He smiled grimly. He smoothed back a tangled lock of her hair, then rose, shedding his tangled clothing at last.

She'd created such a knot within him that he hit the mantle with one boot, the door with the other, the ground with his trousers and shirt. When he turned back to her, she was seated against the bedpost, furs drawn around her, her arms wrapped protectively around her knees, her eyes wide with alarm at last. Her silver eyes slid over the length of him. She trembled, flicking her eyes back to his.

"I've been a wife, right?" she demanded. "I'm so very tired—"

"You can sleep soon enough. But for the moment..."

"What?"

"Well, I'm curious. I think I want to find out just how long it will take me to arouse you a second time."

"Arouse me? Oh, you are a conceited and arrogant man. I never—" she began indignantly.

He smiled wickedly. "You liar. You did."

"No!"

She let out a shriek when he caught hold of her ankles, dragging her down the length of the bed. She brought her fists flying against his chest when he laid his body over hers.

But when he forced his kiss upon her, her arms stole around his neck.

And he was convinced that there was no pain.

Only pleasure.

# CHAPTER 7

Waking was painful.

She'd been right. He'd drunk far too much. It had been a downfall of his people before.

And last night...

He didn't think, in the whole of his life, that he'd ever felt more ashamed of himself. He groaned, wishing that his eyes didn't burn, his head didn't hurt, and he didn't feel such complete and utter self-disgust.

Dawn had become day. Light fell into the room, causing a riotous dance of dust motes. He could see them falling from the ceiling, playing in the air above her naked shoulder. A shoulder that lay against his chest. His arm encircled her, drawing her against him. Her silky blonde hair was tangled beneath his nose. Her back was curved to him, her buttocks against his groin, her legs entangled with his. His hand, dark copper against the pale ivory of her flesh, lay upon her abdomen. They slept like a long-married couple.

Married.

Indeed, he'd done it now. It was unlikely he could entice her into filing for an annulment at this point.

Did he really want an annulment? Didn't he feel, just on awakening, on feeling the softness of her against him, that she was not so bad a creature to possess?

He quickly disentangled himself from her, determined that his actions would not be ruled by his anatomy again. Naked, his head pounding, he stumbled to the tub by the fire, glad to use the now icy cold water to sluice his face and body and give him a truly rude awakening. He toweled himself dry quickly, eschewed the clothing he had scattered over the floor, found a pair of Mr. Levi's button-fly jeans and a cotton shirt in his trunk, and dressed quickly. He kept his eyes from the still-sleeping woman all the while, until he had started coffee perking, and drew up a chair at the table to wait until it had brewed.

Then he found himself staring at her once again. She was really exceptionally beautiful.

*With the devil's own temper*, he thought wryly.

And now...

She was his. He still didn't know a damned thing about her. He didn't know what had happened between her and David. Of course, he did know that she hadn't slept with his father.

Maybe she'd been willing to do so, just as she had been willing last night. But maybe David had expired before they'd gotten to the point where they'd gotten last night.

And maybe, just maybe, she hadn't caused David's heart attack at all.

Skylar opened her eyes to see the white of the sheets. She started to move, but even as she did so, she became aware that she was sore from head to toe. She winced, shifting just slightly, then met the steady green eyes staring at her from across the room. She went still, watching him in turn, unnerved by the intensity of his gaze.

He was up and dressed, hair queued back. He wore a white cotton shirt, just slightly open at the throat, and blue pants that hugged his muscled form. A form that she now knew very well. Broad, uncompromising shoulders, powerful arms and chest. The copper flesh of his chest marked by several unusual scars. Waist lean and taut as a drum. Trim hips...

She stopped, her breath catching. She didn't want to think about the rest of him. It brought too much color to her face. Made her remember. Not that he had pinned her to the bed. Not that he had forced her to choose. Not that he had insisted on their playing their roles as man and wife.

Rather it made her remember the way he had made her feel, the hunger she had found in turn. The longing to touch his body in turn, explore it, taste it. Move with it...

Indians were supposed to do nothing more than couple, like wild animals. She had heard it said among cavalry wives, whose husbands had said that it was so.

This Indian was an extraordinary lover. As wild as any creature on the plain, but adept as well, she was certain. Yet David Douglas had told her that Indians were just as human as white men, and all men, red, white, and black, were the same when taught the same things. David had actually taught her quite a bit about the Plains Indians. He had simply neglected to tell her that he had a son who happened to be one. Or that he was really marrying her to that son.

He'd neglected to tell his son as well. And so he was now studying her, watching her with those deep, fire-green eyes that seemed to promise he'd have much preferred slitting her throat and scalping her to taking her as a wife. No matter what expertise he had brought to the undertaking.

"You're awake. Good. Get up. Get dressed. We need to move on," he told her, rising from his chair and going to the fire. "I'm afraid I slept late myself, but we've things to do, and we're going to reach Mayfair tonight, no matter how late."

She gazed at the floor. It remained strewn with clothing, her robe where it had so fatefully fallen the night before. He'd made coffee again, this coffee straight, she was quite certain. This morning, he was all business and impatience. Not that he had been anything but brusque, even at the height of passion. The best he had offered her was his skill at taking a woman. No tenderness had entered into it.

Yet, she knew...

She hadn't allowed herself to be tender, either. Nor would she ever allow it when she knew what he thought of her.

Tears suddenly sprang to her eyes unbidden. She blinked furiously, knowing that she'd soon be under his scrutiny once again. He would probably find them amusing, part of the payment she must make for being a gold digger.

She rolled away from him, realizing he was turning back from the fire.

"I said to get dressed."

"I don't give a damn what you said," she replied. "I'll get up—"

She broke off because his hand was on her arm, pulling her around. Both their gazes fell upon the tangle of bedsheets that gave credence to her innocence and to the night they had spent together. Skylar pulled free from his touch, her cheeks on fire. God, don't let him say anything! she prayed. Don't let him—

But he wasn't about to apologize for what had happened.

"I want to get back to Riley's. My father's body should have arrived by now. You can go with me or stay here, but I'll be gone in twenty minutes."

"I can't get dressed!" she hissed at him.

"Why not?"

"You ripped up the only clothes I had!"

"So I did," he responded. Again, there was no hint of apology in his tone whatsoever. He walked around to the foot of the bed to the trunk and looked through it. She drew the furs around her, watching him. His features were burnished a true copper. They were so cleanly defined, the cheekbones broad, his nose strong and straight. She bit her lips, intrigued at the combination of heritages that had created his face. He looked both white and Indian. The Sioux in him was clearly apparent in his ink-dark hair. But his eyes were indeed his father's. It seemed amazing now that she hadn't recognized his eyes immediately.

When he looked up at her, she flushed, unnerved that he had caught her studying him so intently.

"I hope that these will do," he said, handing her a pile of clothing. "I'm not quite sure what exactly is required of women's fashion these days but...your trunk will be back at Riley's, and you can change there if you desire."

Skylar looked at the clothing on the bed: pantalettes, chemise, shirt, skirt. She couldn't help but wonder where the clothing had come from and whom it had belonged to. The style of the shirt was that of the simple frontier clothing sold in many stores in the East for those planning to take on the hazardous journey west. It had remained the same for many years.

She looked up at him.

"I do suppose your gown was much grander. You are, after all, Lady Douglas."

"This will do just fine. In fact, it's absolutely lovely, and I would have adored it had you given me this to wear rather than that robe."

He smiled slightly. "If you are determined to stay, what difference does it make that your marriage was consummated last night? You were given a choice. You couldn't have assumed that you would remain any man's wife and not shared his bed."

Her eyes fell. "It just..."

"What?" he demanded. He lowered himself before her, his face angry, his voice completely hostile once again. "Do you think that things will change? You are an interloper in my life. You came here thinking that you could take everything. Well, you cannot do so, and I will not suddenly forget that you came here to claim my father's estates. You wished to take on a role. You've taken it on. What's done is over. We are both spared the discomfort of discovery again. Now, if you are coming with me, get dressed."

"You are not just despicable. You are mean. You are cruel!" she hissed at him.

"Yes, well, you have made your bargain with the devil, haven't you?" he demanded.

So she had. She turned her back on him, rising and dressing as quickly as possible. She longed for a bath. To soak in hot water until...

Until she could wash away the past. How many years could she wash away?

That wasn't really the question. How much time did she have left to save Sabrina? No matter how horrid Hawk might be to her, he could not be as bad as what had nearly ensnared her. They were, after all, a married couple.

As soon as she'd donned the clothes, she turned. The skirt was a little short, a tiny bit loose. Otherwise, it fit well.

Hawk was back at the table, finishing his coffee. She ignored him, searching through the remnants of her clothing for her stockings. She was startled when he joined in her search, offering the stockings to her. She snatched them from his hands.

"Tell me, Lord Douglas, had I not proven to be your wife, had my marriage license not been legal, would I have walked freely from this place?"

He arched a brow at her. "Are you asking if I would have raped you? Slain you—scalped you?"

"You ripped my clothes to shreds. Would I have walked out of here naked?"

He merely shrugged. "You'd have walked out dressed as you are now. I'd have seen that you received whatever sum was necessary to replace your clothing and get you home. Generous, had you been an impostor other than a gold digger."

"Generous!" Skylar exploded. "Well, then, had it been that way, I'd have sued the pants off you. I'd have prosecuted. I'd have taken you to court for kidnapping and rape. I'd have—"

"You did inform me of all the torture you'd have dealt out had you been able. Get your stockings and shoes on. Have coffee if you wish. I'll saddle Tor and call Wolf."

He left the cabin. She stood there, shaking, enraged with her own impotence to act against him.

But she couldn't go back...

She finished dressing, then discovered that the black coffee was delicious, that it raced warmly into her system, and she was grateful for it. He had cleared the soup dishes from the night before. She had taken the coffee pot, ready to discard the grounds, when he came back in. He broke up the fire in the grate. He turned to her. "Ready?"

"I—should I dump these? And the water...in the tub will grow stagnant."

"Someone will be out to look after it all," he said briefly. "Let's go." He took the coffee pot from her hands, indicating the door. She walked on outside.

A bark greeted her. She jumped back alarmed, but the dog, Wolf, was wagging his tail furiously. He was huge, half her own size, Skylar thought, and looked as if he could shred her into numerous pieces. But even as her heart seemed to stop and she hung back, he came close to her, shoving his wet nose against her hand.

"He just wants attention," Hawk said, coming out and closing the door behind him. He hunkered down on the balls of his feet, petting the dog. "Good boy. Let's ride, eh? Let's get Tor."

Wolf barked and leaped on ahead. Skylar hurried down the steps, realizing the copse where they'd come was very pretty. High oaks shaded a trail down to a clearing where Tor waited. Wildflowers grew at the base of the trees. There were pines as well as the oaks, lending a sweet fragrance to the air and a soft carpeting to the earth.

Skylar reached the horse and came to a halt. He was saddled and bridled, though she hadn't seen a saddle on him the other day when she'd first taken a wild ride across his haunches. She glanced at Hawk, who read her thoughts. "Stable is right back there," he said, pointing down a path that led toward the right of the cabin. She nodded. He leaped up on his horse, reaching a hand down for her. She hesitated, wondering if she could manage such a leap, but she needn't have given her own abilities any thought. He reached down impatiently, grasped her arm, and easily swung her up in front of him. His horse instantly began a trot that sent her slamming against his chest time and again.

A few moments later, it was worse. They were racing across open plains. The breakneck speed terrified her, while it seemed that Hawk barely held her, barely kept her from flying from the mount. She grasped the horse's mane, clinging for dear life.

If she died, he'd be free again. The thought was not a comforting one. Yet even as Tor slowed his gait, she felt Hawk's hand against her waist, the rock wall of his chest behind her. She had been safe the entire time. He didn't intend to kill her. Not yet, at any rate.

When they reached Riley's, Riley and Sam were sitting on the long bench in front of the inn and stagecoach stop. Sam, his white whiskers twitching, his face red, rose quickly, coming forward to help Skylar down from Hawk's horse. "Afternoon, Lady Douglas. I'm glad to see you, I am—"

"You should be!" Skylar told him.

He stood duly chastised as Hawk leaped down to stand behind her. Wolf barked, wagging his tail, and Sam quickly patted him on the head in welcome while addressing Skylar. "Ma'am, I've got to admit, none of us here had an idea of who ye might really be—"

"Turns out she is Lady Douglas," Hawk said.

Sam's big blue eyes went moon wide. "You were married up with David—"

"No, she's married up with me," Hawk informed him. "Seems my father made the arrangements, just forgot to tell me. Sam, did you bring my father in yet?" he asked quietly.

Riley had come by then to stare at him and Skylar. "Your pa is in the parlor, Hawk. I sent word out to Mayfair. Guess you weren't there. I'm expecting someone back with a wagon so your pa can be laid out right at his home." He spoke to Hawk. He stared at Skylar, then scratched his head. "So—you're married?" he said in astonishment to Hawk.

Hawk tethered Tor in front of the inn. "Seems so. I'm going to see to my father. Have you anything good on the menu today, Riley? I'm starving."

"Some of the best damned venison you'll find either side of the hills!" Riley said proudly. "Fresh bread, apple pie—"

"We'll take the lot," he said. Without glancing in Skylar's direction, he walked into the inn.

Sam turned to Skylar then. "Lady Douglas." He spoke quickly. "I'm rightly sorry, miss, I am. Taking part in—what do you call it—sub-terfuge."

"Downright trickery," Riley said sadly.

"But you got to forgive us. Hawk didn't know who you were no how, and it just seemed as if you had to be playing some kind of that trickery on the lot of us. Do you understand?" Sam asked anxiously.

"Do you forgive us?" Riley demanded. "Wait a minute, now, I didn't really have a part in it—"

"As much as me!" Sam insisted stubbornly.

"Ain't much company out here," Riley warned. "What speaks English, anyway. You need to forgive us, really."

"You were both horrible," she assured them. "I thought that I was being attacked, that I was going to be murdered."

"But you've had your chance to explain yourself instead!" Riley said happily. He shook his head. "And turns out you two are man and wife. Don't that just beat all?"

"Oh, it does!" Skylar agreed.

"Rich folks! They wind up married and don't even know it. I say again, don't that beat all, Sam? Don't that just beat all?"

Sam shrugged. "Lady Douglas, you come on in and sit, and we'll get you some cool water, a cup of coffee, a glass of wine, whatever might warm your toes, eh?"

"Water would be lovely at the moment."

"Coming right up. Wolf, you go on out to the kitchen. Lem's in there cooking, and he'll find a bone for you."

Wolf barked and ran off, seemingly having understood every word Riley had said to him. Then Skylar was escorted inside by the two graybeards.

A young mixed-race Indian woman worked for Riley. She had coffee poured when they entered the public room, offering Skylar a cup before she was seated. Skylar thanked her, recognizing her as the girl who had brought her to her room when she had spent her one night here on her way west before the stagecoach incident. The girl was very pretty, she realized, and though she had been pleasant enough before, today she seemed to resent Skylar. Skylar didn't know why but determined that she would ignore the girl's coldness. Riley asked the girl to bring Skylar water as well as the coffee. The girl did as bidden but left them as quickly as possible.

"Been to Mayfair yet, Lady Douglas?" Riley asked.

"Into Gold Town?" Sam queried before she could answer the first.

She shook her head. "I've not seen much yet."

"They're newlyweds of a sort, Sam," Riley advised sagely.

"Well, you'd think he'd take her on to Mayfair," Sam said with a humph. "It's a fine house, a very fine house. You'll be pleased as punch when you see it."

"I'm sure," Skylar murmured. She sipped her coffee but then rose. "Where is the parlor, gentlemen?"

Sam indicated a hallway. She thanked him and walked along it until she entered a room somewhat smaller than the public room but more tastefully furnished. In the center of it, set upon a long table, was the coffin she'd purchased for David Douglas in Baltimore. It was fine wood, handsomely carved, cushioned inside with red velvet. She could see that because the man standing in front of it had thrown aside the top, heedless of the fact that the man inside had been dead many days now. Thank God the weather had been cool. Still, the scent of death permeated the parlor.

As Skylar paused, wondering if she could take another step forward without being sick, she saw Riley's Indian girl approach Hawk from another doorway. The girl easily slipped an arm around his waist, said something softly about the corpse, and leaned her head against Hawk's arm. Hawk made no protest, replying to the girl in an Indian tongue.

Skylar straightened her spine and turned quickly to return to the public room. She paused again because another man had come into the inn, one she recognized.

Like Hawk, he was dressed today in a cloth shirt and trousers. He had long, ink-black hair, worn straight down his back, a darkly bronzed face, and strong, handsome features. He appeared to be civilized, but she knew he had been one of the three Indians who had accompanied Hawk the other day, shrieking out their bloody war cries. She stared at him, and he returned her gaze but said nothing to her. She wondered if he spoke English, but then she heard Hawk's voice, uncomfortably close behind her.

"Willow. You've brought the wagon in?"

He nodded gravely, still staring at Skylar. He arched a brow at Hawk.

"Seems she is Lady Douglas."

"Oh?"

"My wife."

"Ah." He stared at Skylar, still offering no apology or explanation. "Sam, do you have the lady's trunk? Tell me where, and I'll fetch it while Hawk and his, er, wife have their meal."

"I'll help you with my father later," Hawk said. Skylar felt his hands on her shoulders, propelling her back toward the table. The Indian girl appeared again with heavy wooden bowls of venison swimming in gravy. She set them down without comment and disappeared to return with a platter of fresh-baked bread. Her eyes were on

Hawk, but he was apparently very hungry. He ate, heedless of her regard.

Skylar didn't think that she could manage anything after having inhaled the scent of the corpse. But she'd eaten almost nothing in two days, and when she took a bite of the venison, she found it delicious and realized that she was starving herself.

"When you going to have a proper service for his Lordship?" Riley asked Hawk.

"Tomorrow night."

"I heard as how some suggested he should be buried in some big family vault in Scotland," Sam said.

"His wishes were always clear. He wanted to be buried at Mayfair, next to my mother," Hawk said. "He'll have what he wanted. I'll get the Reverend Mathews out tomorrow around dusk to say the words. You all ride on out if you wish."

"Be fittin'," Riley said.

"He was one fine man."

"He was."

Riley was suddenly staring at Skylar. "Did you know him well, Miss —Lady Douglas?" he asked politely.

Hawk had suddenly ceased to eat. He was watching her, just as politely, his coffee cup in his hands. "Did you know him well, my dear?"

"I knew him well enough to know that he was aware he was ill, though he had told no one else," she said, returning Hawk's challenging stare.

His eyes darkened. He lifted his cup to her. "What a deep and binding friendship," he murmured, and only she, Skylar was certain, could hear the biting sarcasm in the comment. "I can't wait for you to tell me all about it," he continued politely. "Which I'm sure you'll be doing very soon."

"It's difficult these days to be too sure about anything, isn't it?" she inquired pleasantly.

He smiled. Sipped his coffee. "There are some things of which I am very sure," he said softly.

"But you're determined to find out things on your own," she reminded him.

"You've suggested I do so."

"From experience I know that you do so."

"Sometimes it's easier when I'm given a little information."

"Pity is that you don't seem to like to accept information when you're given it," she said very sweetly, very aware that both Riley and Sam had grown very silent, their eyes darting nervously from her to Hawk and from Hawk back to her again.

Hawk stared at her hard, setting down his cup. "You're right. What I have to find out, I will," he said simply. Then he stood abruptly. "Riley, you are managing to have food here good enough to attract a crowd. We're trying to keep the population down around here, remember?"

"There's gold here, Hawk. Ain't much chance of that."

"Reckon you're right. I'm going to give Willow a hand with the coffin, then we'll be on our way. Thanks for taking Pa in, Riley."

"There's nothing I wouldn't have done for him," Riley said sadly.

Hawk nodded, acknowledging the compliment. His eyes suddenly riveted on Skylar. "We'll be on our way in a matter of minutes. Be ready."

She resented his tone and didn't reply. It didn't matter. He didn't expect a reply. He went down the hallway. It didn't seem that a full minute had passed before she could see him and Willow through the doorway, carrying the coffin out to the wagon.

"So his attacking 'Indians' all speak excellent English as well!" Skylar murmured aloud.

"Now, young lady, that's not quite true," Sam said. "Lots of his kin learned some of the language from David, and some Indians as of late have been learning what they can of the white man's tongue in self-defense, but don't you go assuming anything around here. Willow lives not far from Mayfair. He's got the prettiest little mixed-race baby girl you'd ever want to see. But the other two Oglala with Hawk the other day are just about ready to turn their backs on all that's white, period, plain and simple. Then, you gotta remember this—many Sioux don't think a thing about trading with a white man one day and declaring war on him the next. These are dangerous times. You remember to take care out here, young lady. Great care!"

Skylar nodded. “Thanks for the warning. I’ll do that.”

“We’d best be getting you out there,” Riley said anxiously. “Looks like Hawk’s about ready.”

“And Hawk can’t wait a minute like anybody else, hmm?” Skylar asked him.

Riley stared at her, shaking his grizzled head. “Why, ma’am, I guess he’s just ready to get his father back home again.”

She nodded, sorry to upset these two. Despite the roles they had played in the charade, she liked them. They were comforting old fellows, two peas in a pod. And she might find friends few and far between out here.

“Then I’d best be going,” she said, striding by them out to the wagon. The coffin and her trunk lay in back. Wolf was in the back bed of the wagon as well, his muzzle set mournfully on the coffin.

Willow held the wagon reins in his hand while Hawk waited impatiently by the single step to the open front seat. Before Skylar had quite reached him, he lifted her up, setting her down next to Willow. “I’ll be riding ahead,” he told her flatly. “It’s only a couple of hours to Mayfair. The weather should hold.” He looked at Willow. “All set?”

“Yep, all set.”

“See you at home then.”

He stepped back, slapping the backside of one of the two heavy draft horses pulling the wagon. Willow lifted the reins, and the wagon wheels began to turn. They headed out from the flat expanse of rocky lawn in front of the inn to the road. Skylar looked ahead as they jounced out onto it. Then she turned back.

Hawk had mounted, but he hadn’t yet left the inn. The Indian girl stood by his side, her hands on his foot where it rested in his stirrup. He looked down at her, speaking with her.

Skylar turned her eyes back to the road ahead. The man, Willow, at her side drove in silence, his eyes ahead as well.

“I don’t suppose you’re going to apologize for your part in that pathetic act the other day?” she inquired pleasantly.

A slight smile curved his mouth, but he didn’t glance her way. “Act? He says that you are Lady Douglas, so you are. But that was no act, ma’am. We are all Sioux warriors; we have all raided, seized wagons, stolen horses...women." He shrugged. At last he turned to her, looking her up and down. "He needed to know who you were. It was the way he chose to find out. Apparently, he did. And you're still here. You haven't run. So we didn't frighten you so badly after all."

"You scared me half to death," she told him. "But I don't run easily."

He smiled again, looking ahead at the horses. "Then maybe you'll survive the Badlands," he told her, adding softly, "and the times to come."

"And your friends," Skylar added beneath her breath. She wondered if he heard her. Perhaps he did because he laughed quietly.

The sun was just beginning to set. Burned into dark pastels, it sank into a mauve splendor that edged the hills in the distance.

From somewhere, a wolf howled.

And against the shadow-draped sky, the moon rose even as the sun sank. The air became chill and sharp. Flatlands stretched ahead until the abrupt rise of the hills. The night was suddenly silent.

But then she started as she heard the sound of horse's hooves bearing down upon her.

She turned. Hawk rode at her side, looking down at her, his face as shadowed and dark and forbidding as the landscape.

"You've crossed onto Douglas property again," he told her. "Mayfair lies ahead. As do the rivers, the hills—and true Sioux country."

"So which is home?" she asked him.

"All of it," he told her flatly. "But Mayfair is all you need to concern yourself with. I'll be waiting there. Just what was your exact comment last night? What you want to know, you can just find out on your own? Ah, yes, that was it. There's a damned lot I still want to know. I'll be waiting to find out on my own."

She spoke softly, very aware of Willow at her side. "If you're expecting something from me, you'll be waiting until hell freezes over."

"We'll see," he warned her. "We'll see." He nudged Tor. The stallion suddenly took flight in the night. A dark, soaring shadow, horse and rider disappeared across the plains.

But she knew well that Hawk hadn't gone that far.

And that as he had promised, he'd be waiting.

# CHAPTER 8

Across the hills along the Powder River, Indian lodges stretched out along the horizon. There were perhaps a hundred lodges here, where close to three hundred warriors lived with their women and children.

When they reached the lodges, Blade and Ice Raven went to their sister's tipi. Pretty Bird was a young widow who had recently lost her husband during a raid against the Crow. She now lived alone with her four young children and was glad that her brothers had come to stay with her. She lived with the Crazy Horse people, not because they were one band or family but because she and her husband had chosen to do so. Still, life for a woman with young children could be difficult, no matter how seriously the rest of the group might take its Sioux responsibility for generosity.

Yet they had barely greeted Pretty Bird and had a chance to eat and slake their thirst from the ride when a warrior arrived, asking them to come see Crazy Horse. Both men were glad to do so.

Crazy Horse was a warrior who commanded respect. He had never suggested to others that they must follow him or become hostile. He led by example and was respected because his deeds in battle had always been so extraordinary. Crazy Horse refused to leave his injured braves behind after a fight. He was quick to lead and equally as quick to risk himself. He was brave without being reckless of the lives of others, a brave man who could think as well.

Crazy Horse had been a Shirt Wearer when the practice had been revived among the Sioux, one of a very few honored men among the people who had the power and authority to keep the young braves together in a hunt or a fight.

There had been one period in Crazy Horse's life when he had been reckless. He had been in love.

Black Shawl was a beautiful woman. Coveted by many men. He had once courted her in the way many braves had courted her, coming to her family home with his blanket and using his blanket as a screen while they enjoyed a few brief moments of private conversation. But when he had been away on a raid against the Crows, Black Shawl had married No Water. Crazy Horse tried to respect that marriage. He traveled, spending time with other bands, enjoying visits among the Northern Cheyenne. But in time, he came to see Black Shawl again, and his heart swayed both his mind and his conscience.

He ran away with Black Shawl.

Wife-stealing did occur among the Sioux. Sometimes, it was a simple matter. When the wife of a highly respected man ran away from him, pride dictated that he take it lightly, that he should, perhaps, expect a few ponies in exchange for her. But No Water let the matter strike his heart. He came after Crazy Horse and Black Shawl, shooting Crazy Horse. The shot shattered his jaw. No Water thought that he had killed Crazy Horse. But Crazy Horse hadn't died. He recovered in his uncle's care.

Wife-stealing was considered fairly minor. Shooting, nearly killing a fellow warrior, was serious. There might have been tremendous bloodshed. There could have been irreconcilable breaks among the bands. But cool heads prevailed. Crazy Horse was going to survive with a scar across his lower face. His uncle accepted ponies from No Water. Crazy Horse said the matter was done, so long as Black Shawl received no ill treatment because of the affair. Men received little chastisement for adultery, but though it was rare, women could have their noses slashed, among other mutilations.

The matter was settled. Black Shawl returned to No Water. Crazy

Horse endured his disgrace and went on again to prove himself a mighty warrior.

Now he sat alone in his tipi, cross-legged before his fire, smoking his pipe when Blade and Ice Raven arrived. Despite the scar that marred his jaw, he was a striking man, tightly muscled, with dark eyes and strong features.

"Welcome," he told them both.

They greeted him in return, sitting comfortably with him before the fire. He asked them if they were hungry, but they told him they had eaten. Then he asked them about the events taking place in the white world. "How is my white-striped brother?" he teased, referring to their cousin, Hawk.

"Mourning his father."

Crazy Horse nodded. David Douglas had been admired and liked among the Sioux. He had never betrayed a promise—a rare thing for a white man.

"We talked a long time," Blade told Crazy Horse. "He does not like what he sees coming in the future."

Crazy Horse waved a hand in the air. "That the whites now blanket the Black Hills?"

Ice Raven shrugged. "What bothers Hawk is deeper than that."

"He thinks that we should not be hostiles?"

Ice Raven shook his head strenuously. "No. He is Sioux. He knows each man follows his own vision. But he believes that the whites now see us as an obstruction which must be entirely removed. That they will want to kill us all, decimate our numbers, as they have decimated the buffalo."

"They have decimated our numbers as well," Crazy Horse murmured. Thousands of the Sioux were living on agency grounds now. They tried to influence their hostile friends and relations, telling them that the White Father, President Grant, saw to it that they were given cows for the warriors to hunt down and the squaws to butcher.

Crazy Horse did not want to hunt cows. And he was well aware from the many Sioux of different bands and groups who had left the agencies to join him that the stories of abundance were lies. Most often, grain rations were filled with worms. There were very few skinny cows, and those were often diseased. There was tremendous corruption in the agencies, and even many of those army men the Indians knew—some of them actually friends and some of them leaders who had spoken with the Sioux seeking peace—often admitted the corruption.

Crazy Horse wanted no part of it.

Now Red Cloud, who had once been a very fierce warrior, dealt with the white men. Crazy Horse did not resent Red Cloud for his choice. He simply didn't agree with it.

The whites wanted Red Cloud to sell them the Black Hills. Red Cloud couldn't do so. He needed the majority of the Sioux leaders to agree to sell the land. Crazy Horse was already aware that the agency Indians were planning to bring many of the Sioux together so that they could talk about the Black Hills. The people were divided. Some hostiles wanted to sell the hills, some did not. Some agency Indians wanted to sell the hills, some did not. No one agreed on what the price should be.

Crazy Horse didn't care.

They could invite him from now until the sun went down forever. He would not go to any meeting.

Thunder Hawk had left the Sioux. He had embraced many of the white ways, but his heart had remained Sioux. He always did his best to explain what the whites said—and what they meant. He could explain all the words used and translate true meanings. He warned the Sioux when he expected danger. He told his friends and family when he thought it might be best to bend and when not. He always remembered that he could advise, and that in the end, each man followed his own vision, just as he did himself.

"They will send out men from the agencies to ask you to come in and talk. And the army will ask Hawk to come to us."

Crazy Horse nodded in agreement. He smiled.

"He will come," he said with assurance.

Blade said, "Yes," in agreement. "Sloan—Cougar-in-the-Night—will come for him, and they will ride out together, most certainly. We were beginning to discuss this, but then he heard the woman."

"The woman?"

Ice Raven nodded gravely. "A white woman, young, very beautiful. As we talked at old Riley's stagecoach stop, she came in to eat. We could hear her. She claimed to be Lady Douglas. Hawk was upset."

Blade chuckled softly. "We played out an attack upon her stagecoach."

"She fought with more spirit than many a Crow!" Ice Raven laughed.

Crazy Horse arched a brow. Their traditional Crow enemies were certainly brave, though naturally they mocked their enemies. But the woman must have been interesting.

"Since his father has died," Crazy Horse said, "and Hawk is one with the white world, then he is Lord Douglas, as his father was called."

Blade nodded.

"So who was the woman?"

Ice Raven looked at Blade and shrugged. "We rode with him and Willow to seize the stagecoach, but from there, he wished to handle the matter himself. He took her away on his horse, and we parted company with our brother Willow and returned here."

"They're sending his father's body here from across the land. When it comes, they will bury David Douglas in the ground at Mayfair, as is the white way."

"I will wait for Hawk to come here to tell him we all honored David," Crazy Horse said. "I will not go near the whites."

"He knows what is happening. He will not expect you," Blade said.

"Perhaps his good childhood friend, Dark Mountain, will go," Ice Raven said.

Crazy Horse smiled. "Good. I am anxious to hear about this woman. Although..." He was silent a minute, then shrugged. "Men must be careful where women are concerned."

"He was angry, nothing more," Ice Raven assured Crazy Horse.

"She was very beautiful?" Crazy Horse asked.

"A man must like pale skin and blonde hair. If he does, then, yes, she was very beautiful. Eyes like silver. A fine, young, firm body."

"If she was very beautiful, and he was very angry, ah, well, then, it might well be dangerous," Crazy Horse said with a hint of humor. "I hope that Dark Mountain chooses to go to see Hawk to help give his father's body up to his god. Dark Mountain will be able to tell us about the woman."

"Well, if she is Lady Douglas, perhaps Hawk will be bringing her here."

"What white woman will come here?" Crazy Horse demanded.

Blade shrugged, grinning at his brother. "She has already been attacked by Indians."

"Perhaps he will bring her. I would like to see a blonde woman who can fight like a Crow," Crazy Horse said.

He passed his pipe then, speaking about their need to be close to Wakan Tanka, to keep in deep association with the White Buffalo Woman who had taught them all things. Soon after, Blade and Ice Raven left him again, to return to the home of their sister. They had agreed to form a hunting party the following day.

When they were gone, Crazy Horse stood outside his tipi. He looked to the east and the west, the north and the south.

As far as he could see right now, the world was his. The river, the earth, the night sky, dotted with stars. It was a beautiful time of year. The nights were growing cooler. Fall would come, then winter. Winter was hard and harsh. Even then, he loved the landscape when he looked forever, and all that he saw was Sioux.

What he saw, he knew, was a lie. For just within the hills, the white men lived. They'd come so quickly! They were madmen over gold!

Custer, he thought with aggravation. Custer had opened the way through the hills, Sa Papa. Custer, who fought the Indians. Who made Indians his scouts, mocked them, used them. Custer knew the Indians well. Knew that traditional enemies could be induced to prey upon one another.

So many army men in the West! When the white man had fought him, they had been weak. By the white way of war, the brave, wise men were kept in the East to fight one another. There were few men in the West who fought well then, who could be respected.

But the white war was long over now. More and more men came with the army to protect the settlers. They came, like a wave of giant white worms, covering the plain.

He closed his eyes. He would ride against them. Fight them. He would not give up.

But for a moment, he felt a curious shudder. He was not afraid. He was not a coward. He knew Death, he had seen it many times. He would never die afraid.

He wasn't afraid for himself, he realized.

He was afraid for the land. For the little children he could hear crying softly from various tipis. For something he could not see that stretched ahead of him.

He was not the only man to lead others against the whites. No Indian sat with greater determination against them than Sitting Bull of the Hunkpapa. He was older than Crazy Horse. A renowned warrior, a holy man. Crazy Horse listened when Sitting Bull spoke. Together with the others who shared their hearts, they would make a stand.

And still, he felt the shudder.

The whites were coming. Blanketing them.

He shook the feeling away and entered his tipi, focused on more cheerful thoughts. Like those of a half-white blood brother he called friend. He sighed, stirring his fire to heighten it. He lay down to sleep. "Ah, Hawk, my friend! Trust me as one who knows. Women are trouble!"

# CHAPTER 9

"My God!" Skylar breathed.

Mayfair. The house was magnificent. It was nestled in a valley surrounded by undulating land, with the Black Hills rising in the distance. Even by the moonlight in which they arrived, the lawn surrounding the fine house seemed teeming with color, softened by shadows brought about by dozens of different kinds of wildflowers. Mayfair itself was a large, whitewashed structure with massive white columns that framed a large porch filled with rockers and other chairs. A barn stood to the far right of the house and slightly behind it. Aside from those two structures, nothing broke the flow of the natural beauty of the land. The house seemed almost like a castle in the midst of a flowery Eden.

"It's so very elegant—in the middle of nowhere," Skylar murmured.

She felt Willow looking at her. She turned to him. "It's very beautiful."

Willow watched her, nodding. "The mine is some distance from here. Not quite in the Black Hills, the disputed land now, Sa Papa. Lord Douglas came here many years ago. When he built his white man's house, he would not do so on Sioux holy ground. Not even his gold mine rests on holy land. He had too much respect for the beliefs of the people. But now..."

"Now?" Skylar asked.

Willow shrugged.

"Now the people are divided in factions. Red Cloud was once a fierce warrior. Now he lives in the agency and tries to coerce more food from the whites. Many of the Indians live in the agencies, taking the government stipends. Even there, some wish to sell the Black Hills, while others refuse to do so. Some say that war with the whites has all but decimated other tribes and that we must learn the white ways in order to survive. And if we do so, we might indeed survive, but at what price? Others..."

"Others?"

"Others join with Sitting Bull to our west and the north. All that remains of our hunting territory. Men such as Crazy Horse and Sitting Bull will not even come in to speak at the agencies. They feel we must draw the line now and can surrender no more. Red Cloud went to Washington in the summer." He smiled with a shrug. "Red Cloud sees the strength and the might and the numbers of the white men and their government. He enjoys trips to see the Great White Father, your president. But on this matter, even Red Cloud despairs. Red Cloud went to ask that the Indian agents quit cheating. That they buy good cattle instead of rotten meat. Give us grain that is not laden with worms. No one would discuss the problems that plague us. All they want is the gold in the hills."

"There's been a depression for several years now," Skylar told him. She wondered if she could try to explain the confusion of economics when she barely understood it herself. "It's very bad for the white men now, too. A few summer ago, there were grasshoppers destroying the crops. So many, they say, that they darkened the sky and were several feet thick when they landed on the crops. Food became very expensive. The president was afraid of having too much money out that wasn't backed by gold, while the farmers thought that we needed more paper currency to keep them going. In the big cities, people were out of work." She hesitated. "After the great war when the Americans fought the Americans, many came west for a new life. Now they need to come west again to try to survive. Gold is to us what the buffalo is to the Indians. White men think they need it to survive." I need it at the moment, rather desperately, she thought.

Willow was studying her. He nodded with a grudging smile. "Once, it was a great crime for any Sioux to even mention to a white that there might be gold in the hills. They have known that the whites become madmen over gold dust."

"Well, men do go mad over gold!" Skylar agreed. She stared at the house, shaking her head again. "Lord Douglas came here, years ago, and lived undisturbed by the Sioux?"

"He lived among the Oglala, then returned to England. When he came back here, he built Mayfair. Undisturbed." He lifted a hand, seeking a way to explain. "Among my people, a man is expected to follow his own path through life. Crazy Horse keeps his distance from all things white. Young-Man-Afraid had been among his best friends, but they shook hands and parted when Young-Man-Afraid became an agency Indian. Young-Man-Afraid is now among the Indian police at the Red Cloud agency. Each man takes his own path."

"Young-Man-Afraid," Skylar murmured. "Interesting name. Is he—easily frightened?"

"Young-Man-Afraid-of-His-Horses," Willow told her.

"He's afraid of horses?"

Willow laughed. "No. His enemies are afraid, just of the sound of his horses."

"Ah!"

Willow was still smiling. He shrugged. "I live in a log house by the mining camp. My brothers went west to ride with Crazy Horse. We have parted but are still blood."

"It must be very difficult," Skylar said.

"A tide has come. Like a great wave. Just since I was a boy. By the time many more years have passed, everything I knew then will have changed. But—"

"Yes?"

"Well, it's not over yet. Many have seen the future in their dreams. There's blood shed ahead for us all—" He looked at her again, then seemed to feel that he had spoken too freely and said the wrong things. "I'll bring you into the house. Hawk will be waiting."

Willow lifted her down from the wagon. Wolf, aware that he had arrived home, jumped from the back as well, barking excitedly. Even as Skylar's feet touched the ground, three men appeared in the shadows, coming toward the wagon. "Lady Douglas," Willow said, pointing to each man as he spoke, "Jack Logan, who runs the cattle herd." Jack was a tall, wiry white, quick to tip his hat to her. "Rabbit works with Jack." Rabbit was nearly as tall but heavily muscled and pure Indian. "And this here small fellow with the gaping grin is Two Feathers." Two Feathers, as well, was Indian. He was a boy of about twelve, and he did have a wonderful, friendly smile. Skylar returned it. "Hello," she said to them all.

"We weren't expecting no bride out here," Jack Logan told her awkwardly, "just his Lordship back," he added, sorrowfully inclining his head toward the coffin. "But anything you need, Lady Douglas, you come to any of us."

"Thank you."

"You go on up to the house now, ma'am. We'll be bringing in his Lordship."

Willow held her arm, escorting her up the steps to the porch and then to the huge wooden doors that opened to the foyer of the house. She just stared at the doors, at their size and obvious weight.

"He had 'em brought over from Scotland. Things came by steamship, by railroad, then overland on wagons through hostile territory. Quite a feat."

Skylar agreed but said nothing because the doors had opened.

"Do come in."

It was Hawk's voice that greeted her. As she stepped into the grand foyer, newly amazed by the pure beauty of the house, she wondered how long he had been at the mansion. He had changed into a white shirt with slightly frilled sleeves, a black frock coat, and pants. He seemed every inch the absolute master of his domain, guiding her into the entry where her attention was drawn from him to Mayfair itself. The entry floor was marble, surrounded by highly polished hard wood. A curving staircase also made of marble led to the second floor, while double doors on either side of the entry led to other rooms. It was immense. It might have been opulent, but everything that might have been overdone was subdued instead, giving the place a feel of both elegance and comfort.

"The master bedroom is that second door off the main hallway leading from the staircase," Hawk said to her, looking past her to the coffin being borne to the house by the men. "Sandra!" he called. An exotic young woman in a simple calico frock and apron came from the left doorway, drying her hands on her apron, and looking curiously at Skylar. Skylar was certain she returned the scrutiny, for she didn't think she'd ever seen a woman quite as different—or beautiful—as this one. There was Oriental blood in her as well as white and Indian. Her eyes slanted slightly upward, their color unbelievably dark. Her hair was loose, hanging down past her shoulders in blue-black strands that glowed in the dimmest light. Her face was a gamine's, heart-shaped, intriguing as it was lovely.

"Sandra, Lady Douglas has arrived. If you would be so good as to show her to her room..."

Sandra ceased staring at Skylar to make a small bow toward her. "Lady, if you will..."

"Your trunk will be brought up," Hawk told her. "Sandra will see to anything you need. When you're settled, someone will bring you back down."

"As you wish," she murmured.

"No, my dear, as you wish," he said, mockery tinging the polite words. She felt him watching her as she followed Sandra up the stairway.

"This way, Lady Douglas," the girl told her, opening the door to the room for her. Skylar stepped into it, amazed once again at the old-world elegance that had found its way into a hostile land.

The bedroom was huge, with double doors leading to a porch. A huge four-poster bed with dragon claws and wings was the centerpiece of the room, which also contained a dressing table and two heavy bureaus. The brocade bedcover was crimson and forest green, showing hunting scenes. The pattern was repeated in the drapes. The hardwood floor was clean and polished but mostly covered with a Persian carpet that picked up the crimson colors in the bedding and draperies. An Oriental dressing screen stood in the far-left corner of the room next to a cherry wood washstand. Against the wall opposite the bed was a large fireplace with a marble and gilded mantle, bronze wall sconces on either side of it to light the room. A copper bath was in front of the fireplace, steam rising from it, while a rack with heavy linen bath sheets had been set close enough to it for the fire to warm the sheets. She could scarcely believe that she was at the very edge of the civilized world.

"Is everything satisfactory?" Sandra inquired politely.

Skylar nodded, awed. "Very."

There was a tap at the door. Two Feathers had arrived, carrying her heavy traveling trunk. "Where would you like this, Lady Douglas?"

"Down!" she said, laughing. "It must be very heavy."

"It is not so heavy," the boy said indignantly, but setting the trunk down as he had been bidden. He looked at Sandra, then back to Skylar. "We didn't know you were coming. We could have—done more."

"Everything seems fine."

"Hawk didn't know you were coming."

"Things have been very—confused."

She thought that Sandra sniffed derisively, but when she turned to stare at the exotic woman, she had taken hold of young Two Feathers's arm and was leading him out of the room. "There is a bellpull by the bed, Lady Douglas." She said the last words as if they caused her great pain. "You may call when you wish to go down."

"Thank you," Skylar told her, watching her curiously. What role did the girl play in the household?

The two left the room, closing the door behind them. For a moment, she simply stared around the room again, awed. She walked toward the fire, suddenly needing to warm her hands, then she spun around to stare at the room again. She closed her eyes, remembering how she had sat with Lord Douglas at his table at the inn in Baltimore. She had needed to move fast, really fast, and she had known it. But after the friendship they had shared, she couldn't just desert him and disappear. She hadn't even wanted to sit, she had been so anxious and so nervous, so very aware that she had to flee. But he had insisted that he had to understand her, understand what had happened. Then he had been grave. "I've suggested you come with me before—"

"I can't do that. It wouldn't be right. And if someone were to waylay me along the path, you might be implicated. I—"

"I'll take that chance. I am not without my own influence, young lady. I'm Lord Douglas, and even if you Americans did win the Revolution, most are still impressed with British titles. Ah, Skylar, you're so accustomed to crime and corruption on the part of your fellow man that you can't trust an honest offer. My health fails me. I need help—you know that. Nothing other than your kindness will be expected of you in return. Change your name, change your life. You've no choice anymore. It's the perfect answer. We must conduct a marriage service. You must come with me. Don't be afraid."

She could remember smiling and reminding him, "I'm not afraid. But, Lord Douglas, it is dangerous territory. It's Indian country—"

"Umm," he said lightly, "so there are a few Indians around. You'll grow accustomed to them." He winked.

"You may even like them. If the greedy Petes in Washington would hold to a single treaty, there could even be peace among them. Skylar, you've no choice now. Where else will you run? Where will you go? You will love the house, Mayfair. It's airy, comfortable, solid. My home. I love it dearly. You will, too. I will not be with you long—"

"Please don't say that."

"My heart is all but gone. I've known it, I've accepted it. The doctors have told me so time and again. I came east for a miracle, but there's no miracle to be had. You've been such a strength to me so far. Please don't look at me with those tears in your eyes. You've added the greatest happiness to my last days. To know that you would go directly to Mayfair with or without me would ease my days and delight me. That I may somehow be of service to you when your kindness and tenderness have so belied the travesty you lived! Come what may, you will love Mayfair. No matter what dangers you face, there you will be safe. I swear, it will be your home."

It will be your home...

Those words now seemed to repeat themselves, as if she could really hear him again, as if they ricocheted against the walls.

"I do love Mayfair!" she whispered aloud then, biting lightly into her lower lip. She smiled, feeling wistful tears touch her eyes all the while. "You scoundrel!" she said softly, addressing the spirit of the late Lord Douglas that seemed to be haunting her now. "You tricked me wickedly. Indeed, there are a few Indians around! An honest proposal."

Actually, he'd never told her a lie. He'd simply failed to tell her who she was being married to in the hasty proxy ceremony. And that he, one of the Indians, would be waiting, mad as a hornet.

Unwilling to reason or be reasonable in the least.

Her eyes fell upon the bath. She had longed that morning to soak in a tub. The opportunity awaited her—along with a trunkful of her own clothing.

She looked around the room again. This was the master bedroom. It was elegant—but it gave no sign of actual habitation. If Hawk slept here, nothing of his remained in the room. No pictures of friends or relatives, red or white, deceased or living. No hat, no shaving utensils, no brush upon the dressing table.

No arrows, scalps, or feathers decorating the walls.

He didn't sleep here, she thought. But it was where he would put his wife. A wife he'd have as a wife when and if the whim struck him. A wife he'd forget when he chose to. A wife he'd clearly stated he didn't want.

Well, it wasn't what she had imagined either! Mayfair. She had expected to arrive here nearly two days ago. She certainly hadn't imagined anything so grand.

But then, she'd assumed that when she did arrive, she'd be her own mistress...

How abruptly life changed. What wretched tricks it played upon the unwary! It seemed she was to be little more than a prisoner to a man who led his own life and intended to command hers. A man with a fierce ability to manipulate and seduce.

She trembled for a moment, not wanting to remember last night, seeing it flash before her whether she willed it or not. The choice had been hers. She could have run if she had desired. He didn't understand that there was no turning back for her.

No. To him she'd been for sale to the highest bidder— and he'd unknowingly paid the price. And the damnedest thing was not that he'd forced her to yield. What galled her was that he demanded so much more, managing somehow to steal a part of her very will, her soul. He hadn't just forced her hand. He'd forced her to respond. He'd proven that he couldn't just take what he wanted, but that he'd have it how he wanted just as well.

"Not again!" she whispered aloud. "If you don't want a wife, you're not getting a willing one."

She turned around, hurrying to the door to assure herself she could bolt it. She did so, then stripped off her clothing and sank into the scalding water. For the longest time she feared that he would somehow come bursting in upon her there.

He did not.

She leaned back, feeling the water steam and somewhat ease her. Her body remained just slightly sore. Memories of the past night brought hot flashes racing through her once again. Memories of him. The sleek copper skin, the scars on his chest and back. The ripple of his muscles against her. She'd been so terrified of an Indian attack. Of —rape. She nearly laughed aloud, it was so ironic. The same Indian who had seized her, scared half the life from her, trying to urge her to escape him by seeking an annulment...

Why didn't he go for his own damned annulment? Could he still do so now? Would he?

She wasn't going back. He'd have to understand that. She couldn't allow herself to be afraid of him. But she was afraid. Of what? Failure? She couldn't fail, wouldn't fail. She'd come this far. But now she had to have }...

Money.

Money to wire back east.

She shivered suddenly.

"Oh, God!" she prayed suddenly, vigorously. "Let everything be all right back home!"

The water grew cold. She rose, dried herself vigorously with the warmed towel, then opened her trunk. The clothing within it was new, purchased in St. Louis once she'd reached that gateway westward. She bit lightly into her lower lip, reflecting upon David Douglas. He'd insisted she carry with her a certain amount of cash—necessary if she was to help him, so he had said. She blinked back threatened tears, thinking of the care he had determined to give her, even if his son had not. He'd made quite certain even before his death that his Maryland banker would see to the return of his body, and his last business papers, to his home in the West. He'd made certain she'd had money for any immediate needs. Then, of course, the trickery came in, because he'd assured her as well, in the event of something happening to him, she needed only reach Mayfair, and his "people" would help her understand his affairs.

"Well, David, I am beginning to understand!" she murmured aloud. She still missed him. And she still believed that he had meant the best for her.

She selected a chemise, bodice, pantalettes, and one of the two remaining mourning gowns she had purchased, one with a black silk skirt and form-hugging velvet bodice. She donned it quickly, then brushed her hair with a nervous fervor and started for the door. She paused, staring at the bellpull. She didn't need help to get down the stairs. She'd go on her own.

She hurried down and found the foyer empty. She hesitated, then chose the set of doors to the left of the stairway, quietly pushing them open.

Candles blazed in the room. Dozens of them. Lord David Douglas's coffin, draped in black, sat in the center of the room on a long table.

Hawk was seated in a high-backed brown leather chair before the table, his green eyes on the coffin, his long fingers resting on the arms of the chair. Chameleonlike, he appeared incredibly different from the war-painted man she had first met, and yet, when those eyes lifted to hers, she discovered them to be as searing and warlike as ever. He could slide easily into either world, she thought. This was his heritage, and seated in the leather chair, he seemed very much the lord, a power within the white, civilized world. Tonight he was elegant, austere. The perfect nobleman.

His father's son.

"You were told to summon someone to bring you down," he said coldly.

"I didn't need any help to find the way."

His eyes rose to hers. She thought she saw an accusatory expression in them. "But I did not wish to be disturbed. I will spend tonight alone with my father. Dinner awaits you in the dining room. You may retire at your leisure."

She didn't think she'd ever been quite so cleanly dismissed in all her life. She tried to understand his feelings. Surely, he had loved his father. Loved him deeply. And was now grieving for him.

Yet she couldn't forgive him for the way he was treating her.

"You may go straight to hell," she told him icily, and with tremendous dignity, turning as quickly as she had come, headed out of the room. She crossed the foyer, threw open the second set of doors, and entered the dining room. A single place was set at the end of the elegant dining table that might have easily accommodated a party of twelve. Two candles glowed over the fine china dishes, and a crystal wine glass sat beside a bottle of Burgundy.

As she stood there, a woman entered the room from the rear doorway. She was plump and matronly, with sparkling blue eyes and snow-white hair. She spoke with a refreshingly cheerful Irish brogue. "Ah, dearie, there you be! Welcome then to Mayfair! My, but you're a beautiful wee creature! I'm Megan, my lady, Meggie, as the girls do call me. Cook, chief dish washer, and unfortunately, the best excuse for a butler his poor dear departed lordship could find, way out here in the wilds of the frontier!"

"Meggie," Skylar said. "It's a pleasure to meet you."

"Ah, dear, the pleasure is mine! And, I must add, the surprise! None of us had the least notion that Lord Douglas planned on returning with a wife for Hawk, but look at ye, my dear child. What a fine job he's done of it! And lord, but well, we should have seen it coming, thinking back now, and not the least of it, Hawk himself! But I do go on. Sit, child. I've my famous beef and kidney pie, with pastry light as clouds, and the finest wine to give y'a fine welcome home, lass." Meggie pulled out the chair at the end of the table. Skylar thanked her and took it, reflecting that even if Hawk was a monster, the people who shared his home tended to be charming. She'd discovered that she liked Willow, that he was an intelligent and thoughtful man. Jack Logan was polite and little Two Feathers charming. Then there was Sandra. A young, incredibly beautiful and exotic woman, living within his household. He'd told her there were women in his life. She'd told him that he must keep them there. She was certain he fully intended to do so.

"Take your seat. I'll be right back."

Meggie was good to her word, disappearing for less than a few seconds before reappearing with a tray of food. She poured the wine while urging Skylar to dig in. Skylar was aware that the older woman studied her with good-humored interest and curiosity. "'Tis such a hotbed you've come into, though, lass! Like as not, things will get worse as well!"

"What do you mean?" Skylar asked with a frown. The food was delicious. She would certainly not suffer any of the hardships of the frontier here at Mayfair.

Meggie shrugged. "Ah, well, now, we've been here for quite some time, of course—I came here nearly twenty-five years ago to work for Lord David, imagine—but most whites, well, they've just started venturing here in the last year, since Colonel Custer opened the way through the Black Hills, bringing his massive army with him! What will happen now is anyone's guess, what with the government trying to buy what they had promised as sacred land to the Indians and more and more of the Sioux standing like proud men, determined to tolerate no more of the government's treacherous ways!"

"The government has been at war with the Indians as long as I can remember," Skylar said.

"Off and on, yes. But you don't understand until you've been out here a while that the Indians are not one enemy. You can make peace with one band and still have a thousand enemies. You can wage war against them one day and play cards with them the next. You can find yourself under attack by a Hunkpapa Sioux, and have his brother, a Brule, perhaps, plead for your life and rescue you. Ah, well, the hostile bands are keeping west of the hills these days. It's a hotbed indeed, but we've been good and safe here these many years, and so it will continue. The Sioux do keep their promises better than most white men, that I can tell you!"

With a sniff, Meggie shook her head. "Now you go ahead and eat, lass. I'll be back shortly."

Skylar finished her meal, swirling the dark Burgundy in her glass before drinking it down. She rose then quickly, determined to depart before Meggie returned, anxious to do a little exploration on her own. When she exited the dining room and slipped back to the foyer she heard voices coming from the parlor. The door stood ajar. She glanced through it. Several cavalry officers were in the room. Three stood before David's coffin, their heads bowed. A fourth stood with Hawk at the rear of the room, speaking to him in an anxious, heated whisper. The man looked up. His gaze happened to fall exactly where she stood. He broke off, staring at her with a curious, fascinated smile. Hawk, frowning, followed the officer's line of vision. His eyes touched hers with their customary green sizzle. She would have turned and fled had it not been for the military men. She refused to appear to be a coward.

"My wife, Major," Hawk said, lifting a hand. "Do join us, my dear."

She knew he wanted her in there as much as he wanted a rattler. The invitation was merely a show of courtesy. But she lifted her chin and stepped forward, extending a hand to the tall, handsome cavalry officer who took her hand and bent over it to kiss the back of it lightly.

"Lady Douglas!" he murmured.

He was somewhere around her husband's age, well-built, and striking. He had rich dark hair with a reddish tint to it and very deep dark eyes. Like Hawk, he had an intriguingly sculpted face. There was certainly some Indian blood in this man as well. His eyes were frank in their curiosity and his admiration of her. "What a pleasant surprise. We had not heard prior to the night before last that Hawk is now a married man. Your husband so rarely travels into civilization, we'd never have imagined him taking a whi—er, a new wife. That he has acquired such a devastating beauty scarcely seems fair."

"Your comments, my friend, will go straight to the lady's head," Hawk warned.

"They should. If he does not let you know that you more stunning than sunlight, Lady Douglas, he is remiss."

"You are kind, sir."

"What I am is envious!" he said with a laugh, his comments shared with Hawk in such a way that she was certain that the two men had known one another a very long time.

"I hardly imagine, sir, that you ever need envy any man," Skylar told him. "The pleasure of this introduction is mine. I'm afraid I missed your name, Major—"

"Trelawny. Sloan Trelawny," the major supplied.

"Cougar," Hawk interjected dryly.

"Pardon?"

The major had arched a brow at Hawk. Again, it was apparent the men knew one another well.

"Cougar-in-the-Night, to be exact," Hawk said, his eyes tauntingly on the major in return.

"Apparently, he wants you to realize that I am Sioux as well as a member of the United States Cavalry," Sloan Trelawny said, amused. "Just in case you had missed the heritage in my features. Your husband and I grew up together. Our paths seem to keep crossing."

"You're Sioux—and with the cavalry?"

"My dear Lady Douglas, at times the cavalry seems to be peopled with more Indians than the plains themselves. I am with the cavalry, yes."

"But no, he doesn't go shooting his own people," Hawk interjected for him. "Sloan is a scout and liaison."

"How interesting. But don't your own people try to shoot at you upon occasion?"

He shook his head. "Not so far. When I speak, they may not like what I have to say. But they know that the words they hear from me are true. It's my job to battle graft and corruption."

"And the Crows, now and then. Not to mention old friends."

"I'm cut to the quick, Hawk. Now, he's the dangerous one," Sloan said, indicating Hawk. "Ready to go to battle over something like an eagle feather."

"We were four years old at the time," Hawk said dryly.

"What he wants, he goes after."

"I believe that could be said for you as well."

"Ah, but the poor lady is not my wife, therefore she must be warned against you."

"I think she stands duly warned."

"Yes, well"—Sloan lowered his eyes as his lips twitched in a small smile—"again, we were all quite delighted to hear about the marriage."

He was amused, Skylar thought. She wondered why. What had Hawk said to him?

"And again, sir, it's a pleasure to make your acquaintance. You came to pay your last respects to Lord Douglas?"

"Indeed, as well as to speak with the new Lord Douglas," Sloan Trelawny said, glancing at Hawk. Then, changing the subject, he continued. "It's wild country you've come to, Lady Douglas. But among the most beautiful in all the world, I'll warrant."

"Yes, it's very lovely here," she said.

The other three men gathered around them. "Lady Douglas, may I introduce to you Sergeant Walker, Private Hamilton, and Private Stowe." She greeted each man, relieved to see that none of the soldiers were the men who had burst in on the lodge two nights before. Apparently, they had been on some kind of mission, looking for Hawk. And just as apparently, the way that they had found him had caused them to delay their mission. But now these officers were here, at his house.

She realized why Sloan Trelawny appeared to be so very amused.

Every man in the army must have heard why there had been such a delay in contacting Hawk the other night. The thought brought a rush of color to her cheeks, which she was determined to subdue as she pondered the appearance of these men. This was far more than a courtesy call on behalf of the departed Lord Douglas. They definitely wanted Hawk. For what? she wondered.

"Gentlemen, shall I see you out?" Hawk said. "My dear, I'm sure you're anxious to retire after traveling so long and hard. And taking such a curious route to your destination." With his hand on her elbow, he led her from the parlor and saw her to the foot of the stairs. "You can find the way?" he inquired.

"I can," she told him.

"Lady Douglas!" Sloan Trelawny said, tipping his hat to her. A bright light of amusement played in his eyes when they met hers. She determined he was as much of a scoundrel as her husband, and that still, he would be a daring and fierce defender of anyone within his fold.

His men politely bid her goodnight. She smiled pleasantly and started up the stairs. She listened as the men filed out of the front entry way. Hawk was going out with them, she realized.

She didn't go immediately to the master bedroom but hesitated on the landing. When she was certain that Hawk had gone outside, she set out to explore the rooms upstairs. She opened the door opposite her own. She was disappointed to discover a bedroom, probably a guest room, for though it was handsomely furnished, it seemed devoid of personality. She wanted to find the late Lord Douglas's office and try to discover if there were any papers that might have been returned to the house explaining just what her rights were, not as his widow, but as his son's wife.

She tried a second room. Another bedroom. In the dim moonlight she could make out several framed pictures on the mantel. She walked over to take a closer look at them. One was of a slim, handsome man, wearing a kilt and standing in front of a stone wall on which hung a coat-of-arms. The picture beside it was a small painting of a very pretty, light-haired woman. Skylar studied the two and thought that she saw the late Lord David Douglas in both of the faces. The coat-of-arms on the wall was probably that of the Douglas family.

She opened the wardrobe in the room, but it was empty. Pensively, she left the room, closing the door behind her.

She opened another door, then hesitated. She'd come to a library. Bookcases lined three walls. In the moonlight she could make out books on every subject imaginable. Military manuals, almanacs, novels, books on animal husbandry, herbs, sheep, cattle, horses. More military manuals.

As she walked along the shelves, she suddenly froze, hearing a door close nearby. She turned around, realizing the library led into a bedroom. The door was wide open. When she turned, she saw that the girl, Sandra, had come into the room. She hummed as she turned down the sheets on a large, quilt-covered bed there. The girl ran her fingers over the pillow and bedding with a slow, sensual flair.

Skylar backed away, feeling as if she were intruding. She heard the door from the hallway to the bedroom open and close again, and she jumped. Hawk came into the room. He approached the girl, speaking a strange language.

Sioux? Skylar couldn't understand a word of it. Apparently, the girl did because she gripped his hands, speaking earnestly to him in return. Hawk freed his hands and smoothed back her long black hair. His words, unintelligible to Skylar, nonetheless sounded gentle.

The girl spoke in an anguished tone. Hawk took her face between his hands. He bent down and kissed her forehead. Feeling ill, Skylar silently backed out of the library into the hallway. She strode quickly to the master bedroom, slipped inside, and bolted the door behind her.

She leaned against the door, wondering at the tumult of emotions that raced through her. She should be glad. He wouldn't be disturbing her tonight. He kept his own suite of rooms in this house. This was the master bedroom, but not the one he chose to use.

The bathtub was gone, she realized. As was the towel rack. Her trunk was gone as well. Frowning, she moved across the room, opening the wardrobe and the drawers within it. Someone had unpacked her belongings. Hung her dresses, skirts, blouses. Folded her undergarments, set them into the drawers. She turned around. Her brushes, combs, perfumes and toiletries were all arranged on the dressing table.

Had Sandra done this while she had been downstairs? She was startled by her sudden longing to slap the girl. She didn't want Sandra touching her belongings.

She expelled a long breath, hating both Hawk and the girl. Then she plucked up her hairbrush, using it vigorously, taking her anger out on her long blonde tresses, burnishing them to a glow.

This was the master bedroom, but the master did not sleep here. Good. It was all very good for her. She had so much to work out. How to carry out her own desperate plans now that he stood in the way.

She set her brush down and threw open the wardrobe again. She found a nightgown. Soft white flannel with embroidery at the collar and cuffs. She slipped into it, thinking, Tell him the truth? Ask his mercy? Never. He is more ruthless than any heathen on the warpath! He's still convinced I did ill to his father. Imagine trying to explain...

No. And yet, she had to accomplish what she had set out to do. Oh, God, she had to!

Everything had seemed so simple at the beginning.

And now...

Now she was married to a man who despised her. One still convinced that she was a scheming adventuress at the very best. One she could only fight in return. One she would have to learn to get around somehow.

She pulled down the covers to her own bed and lay down. She watched the fire, then closed her eyes, but she could not sleep. Her thoughts kept running rampant in her head.

With a deep, exasperated sigh, she rose at last, thinking that since she had just seen Hawk upstairs and the rest of his household was surely asleep, she might pay her own last respects to Lord Douglas in the parlor. Despite everything that had happened and the way he had tricked her, she still missed him. His death hadn't been the painful shock for her that it had been for Hawk. But she still had a few prayers of her own to say for the man who had apparently been even more of an admirable individual than she had ever known.

Maybe some answers would come to her again with him near.

She slipped out of her room, down the stairs, and into the parlor. She touched the lid of the coffin tenderly. "Well, Lord Douglas, just what do I do now?" she whispered fervently.

"You could begin by telling me exactly what went on between you and my father!"

She spun around, gasping at the sound of the deep, masculine voice behind her.

Hawk was no longer upstairs. His frock coat shed, his dark hair no longer neatly queued but falling free to his shoulders, he stood in the shadows by the mantle. He set down the brandy snifter he'd been holding and crossed his arms over his chest. "Do go on, Lady Douglas," he said. "I am so eager to hear this story."

# CHAPTER 10

She simply wasn't going to let him ridicule her, command her, demand his rights, sleep with other women, and emerge to threaten her anew. Skylar crossed her arms over her chest, facing him.

"I've nothing to tell you," she informed him regally.

"Nothing?" he queried, a dark brow arched high.

"Nothing. You seem to know everything already. I wouldn't dream of trying to correct the assumptions within that arrogant head of yours. If I've disturbed you again, I do apologize. It was not my intention. So if you'll just excuse me..."

She started to move past him, but he caught her wrist. "I don't excuse you. You came down to be by Father's coffin. Saying your prayers? For his soul—or your own?"

"Perhaps I'm praying that a large pit will open up in the earth, and you'll fall into it," she replied sweetly.

He smiled. "That is a given."

She narrowed her eyes, staring at him hard. "Perhaps I pray that Colonel Custer will lead an expedition against you, catch you in your war paint taunting some other hapless victim, and riddle you with bullets!"

To her amazement, he started to laugh. "Sorry, my dear.

"Old Curly may have learned Indian country, but he couldn't trail me even if he had a map in front of him. But do go on. This conversation might become enlightening. For what else do you pray? And just what do your prayers have to do with your relationship with my father? What was that relationship?"

She wrenched her arm free. "I saw an elderly man. Being a mystic, I determined that he was more ill than he would let on, that I should marry him as quickly as possible. I have such powers of persuasion that I not only convinced him to marry me, I also caused his heart to stop by the sheer seduction of my smile. But I'm not a very good mystic, am I? I was unaware that Lord Douglas had a bitter, cruel mixed-race son who liked to dress up in war paint and attack stagecoaches. That is your assumption, isn't it?"

"Have you something else to give me in its stead?" he asked blandly.

"I've told you. I'll give you nothing!" she promised vehemently. She took another chance at getting past him.

He didn't stop her this time, and she raced up the stairway to her room.

Still standing in the parlor, Hawk heard her slam the bedroom doors closed. He was certain that she had thrown the bolt.

He shut his eyes.

Why wouldn't she talk to him?

Worse. Why did it seem that she had gotten so deeply into his blood?

Why did it seem, even now, that his body was wired, hot and burning, that his soul and mind were torn. That he wanted to stay away from her, that he wanted...

The soft flannel gown had hugged her body. The fire had given it the effect of light and shadow as it fell over her form, highlighting curves and movement. Curves he had touched. Movement he knew.

Damn her. He wouldn't be so swayed.

Damn her.

He would.

She was here as his wife.

Skylar furiously wrenched the covers from the bed and was about to slide into it when the bedroom door suddenly burst open with a violent slam. Hawk stood there. She stared blankly from him to the doors and realized that his force had easily broken the flimsy bolt. He had snapped the wood that had surrounded the metal bolt.

His eyes on her, he stepped into the room, drawing the doors closed behind him.

"Can't sleep, Lady Douglas?" he inquired politely.

"I think I will manage just fine now," she informed him.

"We'll see to it. I hadn't meant to be remiss. Were you ready for bed, you needed only say so."

He moved about the room, methodically blowing out candles, turning down the flames on the gas lamps. Only the firelight still glowed when he finished. He sat at the foot of the bed then, pulling off his boots. He stood, pulling his shirt over his head. Skylar remained dead still herself, standing as if frozen, just watching him.

"What do you think you're doing?" she demanded huskily.

"Undressing."

He unbuckled his belt. His pants fell to the floor with a soft thud and he stepped from them, kicking them aside. For a moment he stood facing her. She couldn't keep her eyes from sliding over his body nor, to her own dismay, could she keep from feeling that there was something strangely superb about him. He stood so very tall, broad shouldered, with his flesh burnished copper by the very pale firelight that danced so lightly upon the nighttime shadows. A fierce wave of sensation seemed to encompass her, one she fought to throw off. She crossed her arms firmly over her chest, demanding, "Why?"

"Why? I prefer to sleep naked. I was raised in a tipi, you must realize," he mocked.

Then tremors shot through her because he was so suddenly at her side, sweeping her off her feet, laying her down upon the bed. He was beside her then, his fingers upon the lace and ribbon of her bodice.

"You can't do this!" she lashed out as she tried to catch his wrists.

"But I can. I have, and I will."

"No, you can't—you can't just..."

He released her, rolling over to strike a match from the bedside table and relight one of the candles there. He stared down at her, naked, his flesh glistening, his eyes unfathomable. He looked far more civilized with clothes on, she decided. He didn't touch her as he leaned over her, staring into her eyes.

"Don't you think it's a little late for you to be reneging on the marriage agreement? What's the matter with you?" he demanded.

"The matter with me—I beg your pardon?" she cried, shimmying up to the headboard to put distance between them. "What is not the matter here!"

"The rules were set. You chose not to get an annulment—"

"I chose not to get an annulment? If you wanted one, why didn't you file papers?" she demanded in return.

"You chose not to get an annulment," he repeated, seeming to grow angrier. "You chose to be a wife. Now suddenly—"

"Suddenly! There's nothing sudden here! It's a wretched situation. Let's see," Skylar told him. "Just for starters, I barely know you!"

"You know enough. We got acquainted rather well last night. I know everything I need to know about you."

"There you have it, Lord Douglas!" she exclaimed. "You think you know everything! You're rude, presumptuous—"

"Yes, but I'm also your husband. Married to you. Just as you have willed it that you are my wife. Our agreements have been made." He threw up his hands with impatience, and his tone was harsh. "What do you know of this great western frontier you've come upon? Especially since the war, with the death of so many men back east, women have flocked out here by the scores to husbands they have never before seen to take up the toil and drudgery of eking out an existence on the plains. You'll not have to get a single blister. But I promise you, those husbands have not brought their wives west so that they may sleep apart."

There never seemed to be any arguing with him, she thought rebelliously. She felt the rise of tears coming hot to the backs of her eyes. She fought them, her chin very high, her voice regal.

"Those husbands want wives. They are surely courteous, while you, Lord Douglas, are one wretched, cold bastard!" she hissed to him.

"Not true. Not true at all. Bear in mind, those husbands knew they were acquiring wives, while I am still in shock over your arrival. No, I don't want a wife. I've never lied about that, and neither will I forget the very strange circumstances of your arrival and cast flowers at your feet. Indeed, I did not desire a wife, but I have discovered that I do want the woman I've acquired. Therefore, I am not cold at all, rather, I'm burning. A bastard on fire, if you will."

"Then very recently heated, I think! This isn't even your room. You had no intention of coming here until I had the ill fortune to stumble upon you—"

"And how do you know that this isn't my room?" he demanded, watching her. Then he suddenly smiled. "Ah, you've been exploring. Searching my house. Uninvited. So, you're offended that I didn't have you taken to my room."

She shook her head strenuously. "You're mistaken. I'm offended that you're in mine."

"Or are you offended because you suspect others might have been invited to mine?"

"Not at all, if you'd only the good grace to remain there yourself!"

He started to laugh. "Lady Douglas, you are unique, I do grant you that!"

"And you are a presumptuous bastard, I do swear it. Still assuming I somehow wronged your father. Well, I didn't seduce him into his heart attack. I never slept with him. You surely do know that now for a fact —" She broke off, wanting him gone.

"Tell me what happened."

"I'll never tell you anything! Never!"

"Then it seems that what we share in this bedroom must suffice to make us man and wife."

She cried out in rage and surprise when he moved with ungodly speed, catching hold of her bodice, ripping the white gown cleanly down the center. She tried to slam her hands against his chest, but he was too quick, catching her wrists, staring at her as she stared back at him. He eased his hold on her wrists.

She shook, still meeting his green gaze, making no move.

"How dare you?" she grated out furiously.

He leaned over her, pinching out the light of the candle with his thumb and forefinger. Then his body covered her like a blanket, his fingers winding around her wrists and bringing them to her side, exposing her bare flesh to his. His skin sleek and hot against her own. She felt the pounding of his heart, the ripple and form of muscle.

"You told me if I wanted a wife, I would have a wife. Your words, your promise. Tonight, I want a wife." She was startled by the tension in his features above her in the near darkness. She swallowed hard, twisting her face from his in the darkness. Dreading his touch, anticipating it, yearning for it. What could she possibly do now? Revise at this late moment what she had said before? You may have a wife anytime you want, just as long as you touch no other woman.

Let him know that unbidden jealousy tore at her heart. It made no sense, really, but it was there.

She stared at him again. "Fine. You're right. Take what you want. Any time. But again, I swear, I'll give you nothing. Nothing. Until..."

She broke off, gasping. His lips were on her flesh. His mouth closing over her breast. Subtly stroking, moving, suckling. His hands... on her body. Thrusting between her thighs. His fingers touching, rubbing, parting...

She nearly cried out loud in anguish, but she willed herself to silence.

Just as she willed herself not to move. Not to give. Not to deny, but not to give...

Damn him.

The feel of his flesh, his lips and teeth, the stoke of his tongue. Damn his bold intimacy. Damn him, damn him, damn him. She clenched her teeth together hard. Tossed her head to the side. Felt him, felt sensations so newly awakened, so prepared to come awake again, flesh so tender, to be stroked, caressed, kissed...

Him. On top of her. Filling her. The feel, the friction, the speed, the fever—it was unbearable. She would not give! She'd have back her soul, please God...

In the end, she never made a voluntary move. She never had to. He had the satisfaction of feeling what she could not hide, the constriction that seized her, the trembling that shook her, the liquid heat encompassing him. But that was all. She gave nothing more. Nothing more at all. It didn't seem to bother him. He reached his own climax, his body locked atop hers, once again, and again. He held there a long while, still within her. She refused to open her eyes. She barely breathed.

"How long will you play this game, I wonder?" he queried, studying her face when he withdrew from her at last. She turned her back on him, furious with men in general. They never seemed to understand anything.

"Have it your way then, Lady Douglas," he said at last.

"Would you stop that mockery?" she demanded, still resentful that it seemed she had managed nothing more than to amuse him.

"Which mockery is that, since all seems mockery to you?"

"Lady Douglas."

"You are Lady Douglas. You've been most insistent about informing me of that fact."

"I will never be Lady Douglas to you," she said, wishing she could draw away from him completely. She felt like an injured cat. She wished she could lick her wounds. But she could not. She could turn from him, but it seemed she couldn't escape him completely.

He was silent a long moment. "Skylar," he said. It was the first time she could ever remember his using her given name. She had even wondered at times if he remembered what it was.

He leaned over her shoulder in the shadows. She felt the brush of his ink-black hair against the flesh of her shoulder. "Skylar, you are mistaken. It seems you are Lady Douglas," he told her, adding, "Indeed, you are to me and to everyone else."

He shifted, turning his back on her. She lay in silence, wishing she could sleep. Wishing that she didn't feel both the closeness of his body and the distance that lay between them.

Eventually, she slept. She dreamed. Distorted dreams that her mind couldn't seem to hold on to. Yet sometime during the night, she woke, frightened, and not at all certain as to why she was afraid. She'd been alone, she thought. Alone, and she'd needed help so badly. She sat up, shivering.

"What is it?"

She jumped, startled. She wasn't alone. He remained with her. He lay at her side, his dark head upon a white pillow, his eyes opened, seeing more in the darkness than she, she was certain.

"Nothing," she whispered, swallowing uneasily.

"Come back to sleep." It was more of an impatient command than an invitation, yet somehow...

There was something almost normally domestic about it.

"It's at least another hour until dawn," he informed her.

His long dark fingers fell upon her arm in the moonlight. He pulled her back down. Against him. His arm remained around her. Her back was tucked to his chest. She could feel his chin atop her head, his movement as he smoothed down her hair to keep it from tickling his nose. She could feel the smoothness of the flesh on his chest, the ripples of the muscles beneath. She could feel the hardness of his hips and the bulk of his relaxed sex against her buttocks. For a few seconds she dared not move or breathe. She felt the rhythmic pulse of his heart. Slowly, she felt more at ease. She closed her eyes. Drifted.

She was warm.

And she wasn't alone.

When he awoke, she still slept. He found himself propped on an elbow, regarding her again with a brooding deliberation. How long had she been a part of his life now? Three days? How long since he had actually verified their legal relationship and taken possession of her as a wife? Not quite two days. So why was it that he felt she had seeped inside of him? Why was it he still felt such a keen fury to shake her, make her explain? Take the hostility she held against him like a steel shield and snap it and break it.

He rose quietly, washed, and dressed in the clothing he had shed the night before. Today they were going to bury his father. The father he'd trusted. The father who had saddled him with this impossible, exquisite woman. This woman who had influenced his father's last will and testament, something that still shook him to the core. And hurt. And she'd been there when David had died.

He had not.

He stood over the bed for a moment, remembering the silver fire in her eyes and the flippant tone she'd used when mocking him last night. He smiled, then let fly with a firm whack against the tempting ivory curve of her buttocks. She instantly jumped up with an indignant cry, drawing tangled skeins of golden hair from her face as she looked up at him—ready for warfare.

"Sorry, my love, but it's going to be a very busy day. I'm sure Megan will need help and direction from the mistress of the house. I have no idea how many people may arrive, but the Reverend Mathews is due at half past three."

He turned and left before she could reply. Something struck the door behind him. He smiled, but his smile faded as he walked down the stairs. Willow and Lily had already arrived and were hanging black crepe over the front door and window frames.

He hurried down the steps, greeting Willow, kissing Lily. He was very fond of his cousin's wife. Lily had come west because she'd been a sixteen-year-old girl left with nothing at the war's end. She'd joined with a musical troupe and been part of a revue in Dodge City for many years. Heading farther out west, her company had been waylaid by a band of Cheyenne on the warpath soon after what had become known as the Sand Creek Massacre—the total devastation of a Cheyenne and Arapaho village by the army. Lily had been spared. She'd been taken as a second wife by a Cheyenne warrior who had later been killed. The Cheyenne and the Sioux had often formed alliances in those years. Lily had come to the Oglala, and Willow had become smitten with her. She'd lived an Indian life for many years, but there was little doubt that Willow's decision to live in a lodge house had been influenced by his wife and his love for her.

"Hawk, Dark Mountain has just arrived," Lily told him. "He is in with your father now." She was a small, attractive woman with dark red hair and a smattering of freckles. He squeezed her hand, glancing at Willow. "I'll talk with Dark Mountain."

"I'll see that you're not disturbed," Willow told him.

Hawk nodded and entered the parlor where his father lay. Dark Mountain, his best friend from his boyhood days in the Sioux camp, stood by the coffin. He had apparently opened the lid, and now he closed it again. He was a tall warrior, dressed completely in buckskin, two feathers worn in his hair, symbols of his triumphs in important battles.

"Thank you for coming," Hawk said, speaking in Sioux, which had been his first language.

Dark Mountain nodded gravely and embraced him. "I am the only one who will come from the Crazy Horse people," he told Hawk. "Your father was a great man who will be missed by all. Crazy Horse has said, though, that you will understand that he and his followers cannot come here now."

"Yes, he's right, I do understand," Hawk said. The Crazy Horse people were not a natural family band. They were not Miniconjou, Two Kettles, Oglala, or other—they were defined simply by the fact that they had chosen to follow Crazy Horse and resist the white onslaught. Nor was Crazy Horse a hereditary chief. He was, however, a very brave warrior among the Sioux. When he was a boy, his vision quest had shown him a warrior, facing a rain of bullets and arrows, riding a horse among them, never being hit. As the years passed and he saw the way the white government broke every promise it made to the Sioux, he became that warrior, a man determined to lead his people in battle. He would be a free Indian, not a reservation Indian. More and more young men, women, and even children flocked to him. The seven-foot warrior of the Miniconjou, Touch-the-Clouds, had tried reservation life. He left again to join Crazy Horse. Those bands now moved to the northwest to the final hunting grounds of the Sioux, far from the white settlements, where Sitting Bull had also amassed a large following. No matter how hard the government tried to get them to come in to negotiate the sale of the Black Hills, the Crazy Horse people determined to stay away.

"The army will ask you to visit Crazy Horse and plead with him to come to a meeting near one of the agencies and listen to their arguments. You will come?"

Hawk grinned. "Yes, the army has already asked me. Cougar-in-the-Night has asked me to talk with Crazy Horse. And I will come. I'm anxious to see my grandfather. And my friends."

"Cougar brings the words of the army."

"He brings them honestly."

"He tries. The army has taken him away. Yet he doesn't forget that he grew up among honest people."

"He will not try to influence any man against what he thinks is right or wrong. He will try very hard to explain how the Sioux can best negotiate."

"War may be the best negotiation."

"Each man must decide."

Dark Mountain nodded gravely, then let the matter rest. "You have a new wife, I am told."

"Yes."

"I have a new wife as well."

Hawk smiled, teasing him. "You've not misplaced the old one."

Dark Mountain grinned, shaking his head. "I have taken Little Doe, Blue Raven's sister, for my wife as well. I've a son by her now."

"Your family grows. You're richly blessed."

"You should have married again before now," Dark Mountain told him gravely. "Had you had two wives before...you'd have had solace for the loss of she you loved so much."

Hawk smiled. "It's different in my father's world, you know. A man takes but one wife. At a time, at least."

"Because white men must worry about their belongings," Dark Mountain said with a shake of his head.

Hawk nodded. "Yes, that can be quite true. But then again, wives can cause headaches. One at a time can be enough."

Dark Mountain was grinning. "I've heard tales about your new wife," he said. Hawk arched a brow, though he realized his cousins Blade and Ice Raven must have been talking about the parts they had played for him in the stagecoach attack. "One husband needs all his strength to subdue her. Though for a white woman, she is said to be very beautiful, with hair just like the sun, well worth a battle."

"She does have a fighting spirit," Hawk admitted dryly.

"Well, even if she's much trouble, I am glad you have a wife now. You will not be alone. You've lost much, suffered much. In time, perhaps, Wakan Tanka will bless you with many children. When you come among us, we will do the proper ceremonies. You are a warrior who has graced his heritage. Wakan Tanka will listen. He will give you sons. Sons will help you remain close to your father with less pain because you will give them all that your father was, and in the telling, you will remember. Loss, my friend, is the way of life."

Hawk nodded, smiling. He was truly glad to see Dark Mountain today. Though their paths had greatly diverged since the days when they had been boys, they remained friends, and Hawk felt certain they would remain so no matter how much time passed and no matter how dire relations grew between the hostiles and the white world.

"I'm glad for you, Dark Mountain, that life remains rich and grows richer."

"It grows more dangerous as well, but that is for another time. I will stay with you and your father now. Soon, others will come, and then you will give him up."

Several hours later, Hawk sat at his desk, rubbing his temples.

There was a tapping at the office door. "Come in," he called wearily. He'd already spent an hour with Henry Pierpont, going over his father's will—and the addendum, which he had just received. The document had arrived, duly witnessed, Henry assured him, soon after the news of his father's death. There were no surprises in it other than what he already knew. The fact that Skylar would receive Mayfair and the Sioux lands if he were to make any attempt to negate the marriage. A reading of the will wasn't necessary since he was the sole heir as long as he complied with his father's wishes. His home was by right his wife's home as well.

It was Skylar herself who opened the door. Skylar in black velvet and silk. Despite the somber color of her gown and the severe twist of her golden hair, she looked perhaps more compelling than usual. Black became her, enhancing the glittering color of her hair, the ivory of her skin. The clean sweep of her hair emphasized the classical perfection of her throat and features. Though she had risen when he had awakened her and done quite an admirable job of taking over a household full of strangers, she had equally managed to avoid him throughout the morning and afternoon.

"Yes?"

"The Reverend Mathews has arrived. He's eager that the service be conducted at the graveside before dark."

He nodded. She didn't leave.

"Mr. Pierpont was your father's executor?"

He arched a brow. "Yes?"

She hesitated still. He smiled with no warmth. "I see. You are curious about whether you were mentioned in the will."

She stiffened. He shook his head grimly. "I'm so sorry, my love. It seems my father left you—me. And your place in this house, of course." He stood. "Other than that—well, my love, I was his son. I'm his sole heir." Was it a lie? No, it was the absolute truth because he'd damned well comply with his father's terms. She wasn't going to walk away free with one bit of Douglas property.

"I am quite aware that you're his heir. But I must admit that I was curious if there were any mention of how I am to live."

He arched a brow and extended his hands. "You're to live here. Amply provided for, no?"

"But there are little things—"

"If you should need something, you need only say so. It will be provided for you."

Her lashes lowered. He thought for a moment that she was in distress, and for some absurd reason, he felt a tug at his heart rather than a rise in his temper.

But then he remembered that he was about to bury his father. And she had thought that she had married his father, had become a widow—and an heiress. The tug at his heart faded. With renewed but controlled anger, he walked around his desk, taking her arm.

"Let's go down, shall we?"

The company was very mixed indeed, with agency Indians, soldiers, settlers, sutlers, and their various wives gathered in the parlor. Old Sam Haggerty and Riley, who along with David Douglas had been among the first whites to stake a home in the Dakota wilderness, sat in the front row of chairs that had been set up there.

The Reverend Mathews stood at the head of the coffin. He looked as if he might be a hundred and ten, with a full head of white hair and a face so wrinkled by the sun that it seemed to carry deep grooves. He nodded to Hawk when he saw him enter the parlor with Skylar on his arm. "My friends, we will begin."

He started with the Lord's Prayer and then read from his prayer book. Then he stopped reading and offered a eulogy, extolling David Douglas as a man unique among men, one who recognized all of God's children, one who had made better the lives of all those he'd touched, helping those in distress.

Hawk was surprised to see Skylar listening attentively to every word the Reverend said, seeming to fight back tears. He nearly set an arm around her to comfort her.

But then he remembered that she had just asked him about money. Her inheritance.

He held still, as rigid as an oak.

Willow, Riley, Sam, and Two Feathers carried the coffin through the back door of the parlor onto the rear porch. From there they led the funeral procession to the massive oak that spread over the back lawn. A double tombstone had already been set at the foot of the oak. His mother lay six feet beneath it. Both her white and Sioux names had been chiseled into the stone. She had asked to be buried here, at Mayfair, beneath the oak. And David had asked to be interred at her side.

So it would be.

The Reverend Mathews finished the service, sprinkling dirt upon the coffin after it had been lowered into the earth. The last words were said. Sandra and Megan, huddled together, cried softly. Lily embraced them both, then led them back to the house. People began to drift away from the grave. Hawk remained, Skylar still at his side.

He disengaged her fingers from his arm. "Go in. I'll be along."

She hesitated. She began to speak, awkwardly at first, then more strongly and quickly. "Hawk...he...I want you to know that he died easily. He had known about his illness. He was truly at peace with God and himself. It isn't easy, it can't be easy, but it was a gentle death. I'm sorry, truly...he was a very good man. Please believe that he didn't suffer."

Hawk nodded after a moment. She wasn't telling him much, but she was trying to give him something. "Thank you," he told her quietly. "Now, please, go on in," he urged her, and despite the feeling of warmth her words had evoked within him, his tone was sharper than he had intended.

As he had commanded, she turned and left him.

He stood at the gravesite, realizing oddly enough that Dark Mountain had been the greatest comfort to him today. Death was part of life. It had been a large enough part of his. He'd said goodbye to a mother, a brother, a wife, and a child. Today, he set his father into the earth. He needed sons, Dark Mountain had said. Sons who he could tell about his father. In the telling, he would remember.

He heard a soft whining sound and realized Wolf had come to mourn with him. He hunkered down by the dog and patted him reassuringly. "He's gone, fellow," he said, then rose, speaking to the grave.

"Pa," he said softly, "I hope you knew. I didn't come to you a very good son. I spent years trying to tell myself what you weren't—because you weren't Sioux. Others saw earlier what I didn't. That you were more Sioux than I, you had all the virtues of the Sioux: courage, generosity, wisdom. I did love you. So much. I'm just not at all damned sure what you were doing there at the end, and I wasn't with you. I mean, Pa, who the hell is she? What was going on? How badly were you hurting at the end?" His eyes blurred. The whites said that Indians didn't have any emotions. But the whites didn't understand. Indians felt as deeply and painfully as white people. They just didn't betray their emotions. "I love you, Pa!" he murmured.

He turned from the gravesite and headed back toward the house. Massive amounts of food had been prepared, and he saw people gathered around the buffet tables that had been set out on the porch.

Skylar had done her job well today. He could definitely acknowledge that fact. Willow had told him she had worked with Megan on pastries and bread all morning, up to her elbows in flour. She had arranged the flowers, set out silver, plates, glasses. Greeted strangers.

Now she stood by one of the buffet tables with Sloan Trelawny. She smiled at what he was saying. Well, Sloan could be a wretchedly charming devil. Hell on women. His manner and dark, striking appearance easily seduced them, and it didn't seem to matter that he carried the blood of a Sioux war chief. But he was a loner, never letting anyone get too close to him. He'd changed—become more distant from his old friends sometime after the War of the Southern Rebellion, Hawk thought. Whatever had happened, Sloan hadn't yet decided to share it with him.

Sloan could easily flirt with Skylar and enjoy her company because he would never touch his best friend's wife. Even though he knew that, Hawk couldn't help feeling irritated because she seemed to be enjoying Sloan's company too much. Her eyes were very bright. Her laughter genuine. Talking with Sloan, she was at ease. Absolutely stunning, graceful, dignified, beautiful.

Sloan turned away from her for a moment. Henry Pierpont, looking very much the attorney in a pin-striped suit and starched-collar shirt, approached her, pushing his spectacles up his nose as he handed her an envelope. She frowned. Henry explained something to her. She nodded quickly, smiled, and thanked him.

Then, looking around somewhat furtively, she curled the envelope into her hand.

"That spectacle-wearing little rodent!" Hawk murmured to himself. "What the hell did he just give her?"

Sloan turned back to Skylar, handing her a glass of sherry. Skylar offered him a charming smile and quickly slid the envelope into a pocket in her skirt.

Hawk could tell she liked Sloan. That much was evident. But she eluded him with a few words and a smile, slipping back into the house.

Hawk determined to follow her.

It wasn't so easy. He was waylaid by his guests, some of them commiserating with him on his father's death, others congratulating him on his exquisite new wife.

When he finally reached the parlor, he saw her standing before the fire, staring into it, with tears in her silver eyes. "Skylar!"

She started, looking his way. Her hand slid back into her pocket.

She wasn't going to volunteer any information regarding the envelope. He would most probably get nowhere by demanding she do so.

"Yes?" she said defensively.

"We've a number of guests," he told her.

"Indeed."

"Has something happened?" he asked her politely.

Her lashes swept her cheeks. She lifted her chin, shaking her head. "No. Nothing. Why?"

"I thought I saw Henry give you something."

"Oh...that. It was a wire, but it must have been a mistake. There was nothing on it."

"How curious. May I see it?"

"I burned it. It was blank, so I tossed it into the fire. I...I think I need to make sure that the punch bowl is filled for the ladies."

She moved past him quickly as if she were afraid that he would stop her.

But he didn't lay a hand on her. He watched her as she left, his eyes narrowed thoughtfully.

His time would come.

# CHAPTER 11

Skylar returned to the porch and circulated among the guests. Hawk watched her all the while.

The evening wore on. People ate, drank. Talked over old times, politics—and Indian policy. Hawk didn't participate in the conversation. Even among the soldiers, there could be disagreement. Add the agency Indians and such conversation could be explosive—if not deadly. At several points during the evening his guests very nearly quarreled. Skylar had a knack for stepping in at the right time.

Finally, everyone had gone except for the household, Willow, and Sloan Trelawny. Hawk and his two old friends retired to the downstairs library together, closing the doors on the rest of the world, drinking brandy. It was natural that such close friends should stay with him late that night.

But he was more temperate in his consumption of brandy than he might otherwise have been on such an occasion.

"It's dying," Sloan was saying, swirling his brandy in its snifter. "The way of the plains. When I try to explain that to friends, they don't understand. But I know that you do, Hawk. And it doesn't matter that you grew up among your mother's people or that you rode with Crazy Horse years ago. You see it as clearly as I do."

"Maybe the army will eventually give up," Hawk suggested. "Leave the Sioux their last hunting grounds. There's enough land—"

"There's never enough land; you know that," Sloan said. "But don't think that the whites aren't aware that the Indians are cheated," he added. "There are many who know this is true." He looked at Hawk. "Scandal is about to erupt like wildfire in Washington. Your friend Custer—"

"My friend?" Hawk queried.

Sloan shrugged with a wry grin. Hawk and Custer had been known to clash upon numerous occasions. They'd been at West Point together. They'd ridden into the Civil War together and from that point on, had often taken decidedly different sides on numerous issues.

"Custer is a popular man," Sloan reminded him.

"Even if those in the military know that he is an incredible braggart."

"He's a war hero—there's talk he could run for president. But my point here is that the man has been vociferous in attacks on Indian agents and all the corruption and graft that has occurred out here. I don't think that he wants to take on the entire Grant administration, but being Custer, he may well do so. And still, being a man who says what's on his mind, he's let it be known that he thinks the Indians have been cheated as well."

"He's champing at the bit to lead an expedition against the Sioux," Hawk said heatedly.

"He's a soldier—he needs a war victory. Just as Crazy Horse is a warrior—who needs to make war," Sloan said.

"Custer is too eager to campaign. He doesn't want peace," Hawk argued.

"If you think that you can blame the national sentiment on Custer, Hawk, you are wrong."

"I don't blame the national sentiment on him, just the way he works. He—" He paused, shaking his head. George Armstrong Custer, "Autie" to friends and family, had enjoyed playing pranks at West Point. He'd scalped squirrels on occasion to leave upon Hawk's pillow. Hawk had swallowed down the jest against his Indian pride, but he had seethed and retaliated by taking Custer where it hurt him in return—

making the best shot on a hunting expedition, outriding Custer in a show of military horsemanship. That his marks were better meant little to Custer. He just got by in school, though Hawk had to admit he did so brilliantly. No cadet could receive more than a hundred demerits a term. Custer could receive ninety-nine demerits almost immediately but then manage never to get the final citation. He had his good points. To Custer's credit, despite the fact that war—and death—definitely helped men rise in the military, Custer was never prowar. He was sorry to fight his Southern brothers.

Yet it was during the war that they first clashed. They were both young, daring cavalry commanders. They crossed paths upon occasion. Once, Custer had been so aggravated with Southern Colonel Mosby's raiders in the Shenandoah Valley that he had ordered a number of the captured raiders hanged. As Custer had ordered, the deed was done. Sent to the same stage of fighting, Hawk had been appalled. It was war, Custer said. The Southerners would gladly hang him. It had been wrong, Hawk was convinced. Such brave men, fighting for their states and what they believed to be right, shouldn't have died so. He realized that he and Custer were fundamentally opposed, even though Custer remained fond of reminding him that he was Sioux—and suggesting he refrain from scalping his Confederate enemies.

Over the years, they'd often had occasion to meet again. With time, Hawk began to feel that Custer had remained an overgrown boy. He was ambitious to a fault. He was also honest. His courage could never be questioned, even if his wisdom could. Again to his credit, he never asked a man in his command to do anything he would not do himself. But then, most men found it difficult to ride as hard as Custer did or drive themselves so diligently. Though he fought the Indians with perseverance—and adored his wife, Libby—it was either common knowledge or accepted rumor on the plains that he'd had a Cheyenne child. The baby, however, had supposedly perished from disease as a toddler.

But then, Custer was a man of many contrasts. Again, though he doted on his wife, it was also common knowledge or accepted rumor that she often vied with his beloved hunting dogs for space upon their bed.

None of these things mattered on the battlefield.

"Custer disturbs me," Hawk said at last, "because he is far too eager for glory."

"But he may wind up in political trouble," Sloan told him. "You know, he had President Grant's son arrested on his expedition through the Black Hills. Arrested him for being drunk. Custer might well have been in the right. He's at odds with the administration on other matters. He may well find himself without a command when the campaigns against the Indians begin in earnest. If someone reasonable spearheads these movements, there will be war and blood, but someone may live to tell about it."

"Autie Custer is a hero," Hawk argued. "People love the boy, whatever his failings. I fear him—and fear for him."

"But can there be peace?" Willow said, his very tone suggesting it was not possible. "It will do no good for you to speak with either Crazy Horse or Sitting Bull," Willow told Hawk.

"I know."

"But you plan on speaking with them anyway?"

Hawk nodded gravely. "I'm riding with Sloan."

"You're sure you're willing to take the time now?" Sloan asked him.

Hawk nodded. "I'm sure. I know that I can speak with them if anyone can." He smiled. "It was my vision quest, remember? I'll bring the word of the eagles to the buffalo. It wouldn't be right if I did not because they must hear one another, then weigh their choices. Sloan, what made you think that I might not go?"

Sloan lifted his snifter, indicating the floor above. "We'll have to leave quite soon. Within a week, if at all possible. Were she my new wife, I'm not certain I'd be undertaking any journeys."

"Ah, yes. My wife," Hawk murmured. He lifted his snifter toward Sloan. "To my new wife!"

"Here, here," Willow and Sloan agreed.

Hawk set down his snifter. "Gentlemen, if you will excuse me... Sloan, if you've leave from the army for the night, both guest bedrooms remain empty. Take your pick. Willow, good evening. Thank your wife for the time she has given me and for her generosity in lending her husband to a friend in his time of need."

"Lily is glad to help. Good night, Hawk," Willow said.

Sloan echoed him. "If I stay, I'll be gone early. I've still supplies to gather. And you've still time to change your mind."

"I won't," Hawk said. "I can't."

Hawk left the library behind and quickly climbed the stairs to the master bedroom.

Skylar was asleep. The lights were out, and the fire was low. He was quite certain she wasn't feigning her rest because the hour was so very late. She was in soft blue flannel tonight. Another nightgown that encompassed her from neck to toe. He shook his head. She didn't seem to realize yet that no matter how concealing her gown, it would mean nothing against him if his determination was set. But for the moment, he let her rest.

He silently looked through the wardrobe until he found the black silk skirt she had worn for the funeral. He found the pocket, slipped his fingers inside. He found paper. The wire envelope. And in it...

The wire.

Not burned.

But here. In his fingers now. He carefully opened the paper, wondering if it could give him some clue to his wife.

But the words were cryptic.

"Trouble. Have you legal title? Can manage no more than a few weeks. Help fast. Pray you're well."

The wire wasn't signed. There was no indication of who had sent it.

If the sender had been male or female.

He folded the telegram thoughtfully, sliding it back into the pocket of her skirt. He closed the wardrobe doors and came to stand over his wife once again. She still slept, the picture of angelic chastity in her modest flannel. In silence he stripped down, mechanically folding his clothing, leaving it lying on the trunk.

He slid in beside her, keeping to his side of the bed. For tonight, he'd leave her in peace. He stared at the ceiling, closed his eyes. Heard his heartbeat. It was slow, soft.

She shifted beside him. He felt just the movement of the bed. Then the soft brash of her golden hair against the flesh of his arm. He smoothed it away.

He felt his heartbeat once again, its pace growing faster. Louder. Pounding throughout him.

If he'd meant to leave her alone, he should have retired to his own room.

He could smell her. The scent of her flesh, clean, carrying the subtle, evocative scent of Mayfair's rosewood soap. She'd washed her hair recently as well. It, too, carried a soft, titillating scent. He moved a hand, running it over the golden tendrils curled over the sheets by his side. They were unbelievably soft, silky...he buried his face in them. Closed his eyes again. Leaned back.

His heartbeat shuddered, skipped. Pulsed into his limbs, his loins, his blood, body, sex...

He rolled next to her, lifted her hair, nuzzled his lips against the lobe of her ear, her throat. She didn't awaken, but twisted, her body coming flush against his. He pulled down the sheets, slipped his hand beneath the hem of the chaste flannel gown, drawing it up. He stroked her thigh, drawing incredibly soft, lazy circles against it. She moved against him, a long expulsion of breath escaping through her lips, some slight, sensual sound mingling with it. He brought the movement upward, caressing her hips, belly, ribs. Lower, higher. A feathery touch against her breasts. Between her thighs. She roused but didn't waken. Undulated, pressed against him. Her neck arched. He placed his lips against it, felt her pulse, then...

Fierce impatience seized him. He caught her hips and drew her buttocks hard against his loin. One swift movement and he was within her, satiation of the pulsing hunger within him his one driving goal.

At the invasion of his first thrust, she woke fully. Had she wished to protest, it would have been far too late. But she wouldn't protest. Nor would she allow herself in a fully conscious state the subtle but sensuous movements that had served to so fully rouse him. She buried her face against the bedding. Her fingers fell upon his hands where they steadied her hips, holding her to his will. She didn't try to stop him, she simply dug in, as if she braced herself, and waited.

Not even her stubborn determination to remain unmoved could dampen his fire. Within minutes he rose to a swift, violent climax, ejaculating into her with a shudder that ripped through the length of him. First, the sweet simple warmth of basic satiation filled him. Then the ragged edge of disappointment. He rolled to his back. "Sorry, I didn't mean to wake you. But then, I guess I actually didn't."

She spoke without turning to him. "I told you—"

"I know. You'll give me nothing. Whatever I get, I must take. Perhaps you should be careful. When I set my mind to it, I can take a lot."

"You can't take everything."

He turned on his side, away from her. He felt her shifting in the bed, pulling her nightgown back down.

He wondered then what it was about her that could make him behave so irrationally because her simple movement suddenly sent his temper soaring. He spun on her, drawing a startled gasp. "What in God's name..."

With the same fluid movement, he caught hold of the flannel garment he found so offensive and ripped it with the strength of a madman, not ceasing then, but tearing and pulling despite her ground-out curses and flailing protest. At last the remnants of the gown lay on the floor beside the bed.

"Damn you!" she gasped. "Just what is it that you seem to have against my clothing?"

"It doesn't belong in bed," he told her blandly.

"It was a nightgown!"

"For a schoolmarm. It doesn't belong in bed."

"Lots of women, lots of wives, wear nightgowns!"

"Not my wife."

He fell away from her, turning his back on her, feeling the shame creep over him again. In some things, perhaps, he was justified. Because she was full of secrets. And lies. And because she had made her own choices.

But still...

Why get so worked up about a nightgown? Because it came between them.

Along with what else?

*Trouble. Have you legal title? Can manage no more than a few weeks. Help fast. Pray you're well.*

If he confronted her now, she'd lie. Close more tightly against him. He'd have to find her out. Take what he wanted to know because she'd give him nothing.

He closed his eyes. He needed to sleep.

His eyes flew open again when her fist slammed against his back with surprising strength.

"You son of a bitch!" she hissed, turning away from him once again.

He stiffened, then eased. A smile slowly crept onto his lips. Fine. He'd had no right to rip up her nightgown. She could have the last word. Tonight.

The days that followed his father's burial were busy for Hawk. He would have to spend at least five to ten days away from the ranch if he was going to ride north and find Crazy Horse. The ride was a beautiful one, but he and Sloan meant to take cattle and presents, which meant pack mules and a slow-going route. The idea of leaving his mysterious wife behind did not appeal to him, but the current hostile Indian situation was so severe that it had to take precedence over her personal problems. And she would never actually be alone. Willow, Rabbit, and Jack Logan would be around to keep wary eyes on the new mistress, right along with Megan and Henry Pierpont as well, should she threaten the estate in any way.

So far, she didn't seem to be intent upon doing any such thing, even though the telegram she had received continued to haunt his mind.

She gave no sign of having any interest in anything beyond Mayfair. By day, she was truly the model wife, lending a hand to whatever household tasks were on the calendar, be it candle making, washing, or bread baking. She managed to avoid him throughout most of the day or, perhaps, he managed to avoid her.

By night...

The first night he had come into her room after that of his father's funeral, he had found her cocooned in the covers. But when the lights had been snuffed out, and he'd crawled in beside her, he'd been both pleased and amused to discover that she wore nothing beneath those covers.

"At least you learn quickly and have taken the vow of obedience to heart."

"I'll never be obedient."

"But you've obeyed."

"I'm merely trying to preserve my wardrobe. Though I should insist that you replace what you've destroyed."

"Buy you new outfits?"

"Pay me for them. I can replace them on my own."

"Ah. But then, you don't need a nightgown replaced, do you?"

He waited. When was she going to ask him for the money she apparently needed? Send help. He was certain the words were a plea for financial assistance.

"You are exasperating."

"At this moment, I am distracted. Come here."

"If you want me—"

"Yes, I know. Take what I want. I shall."

"Are you always so wretchedly persistent?"

"Always."

But she was equally as stubborn. Every night, he made love to her. Every night, she held herself aloof. And the dissatisfaction within him grew along with his unease. She filled his thoughts when he was in the midst of payroll checks, haunted him when he rode with Willow, choosing cattle to be taken on his ride to see Crazy Horse. Determined to shake her hold on him, he spent a night in his own room.

Being away from her didn't help. He was not just disappointed or vaguely dissatisfied.

He was in pain. It had been a fool's determination. He was about to leave her. The longing would intensify a hundred-fold.

He'd be damned, of course, if he let her know.

The night before the morning he had planned to leave, he sat in his office, ostensibly going over accounts, in actuality asking himself if he felt safe leaving her. He heard a tap on his door. Sandra stuck her head in, smiling her exotic, catlike smile. "May I come in?"

"Please."

She came to his desk. Her smile faded. "I think that I must tell you about your wife."

"Oh?"

"She found her way to Gold Town today."

"What?" he demanded, startled.

Sandra nodded. "She has studied the maps in your library. She had no problem saddling a horse and slipping away. But I saw her, and I followed her."

He leaned back. Under normal circumstances, he shouldn't have said or done anything that might encourage Sandra to spy on her mistress.

But these weren't normal circumstances. "What did she do?"

"She went to see Mr. Pierpont."

"Ah." He wondered if Skylar had discovered that she would have inherited the house and most of the surrounding property if he had sought an annulment.

"What then?"

"She went to the telegraph office. Then she rode home."

He nodded, tapping his pen against the blotter on his desk. "Thank you," he murmured absently.

Sandra nodded. "Do you want to know what she said?"

He frowned. "In the telegram?"

"No, to Mr. Pierpont."

"You know what she said to him?"

Sandra smiled broadly. "I stood outside his window. She said she had come to find out if she could have some kind of allowance of her own. Mr. Pierpont told her that she had to speak to you. She said that she didn't really need very much. He said that he was truly sorry, but that she still had to speak to you."

"Well, good for old Henry!" Hawk mused. Henry had drawn up the papers for his father to arrange a proxy marriage for him. But at least now Henry seemed to have discovered a new loyalty.

Not that there was actually anything wrong with Skylar's receiving an allowance for her personal expenditures. He just wanted to know what she so obsessively needed the money for. It had something to do with someone back east. A lover? No intimate affair had been consummated, but that didn't mean that she hadn't been involved with someone else.

He looked up at Sandra, smiling. "Thank you again."

"It's important, the information I've given you."

"It may be."

She smiled again. "Then I'm pleased. I won't let her hurt you."

"Sandra—" He hesitated. He was aware that she cared about him. He had found her, orphaned as a girl, on the plain. She'd literally been alone, seated in the middle of a small Sioux camp after a Crow raid that had taken the lives of all the others in the band. His father had gladly taken her in, giving her small jobs at first and seeing that she was tutored in English and history. She had white blood, possibly Oriental as well, and David felt she should learn about a variety of cultures and make her own choice as to which she would like to live in. She had liked Mayfair, and as she grew up, she had taken on housekeeping chores and became a part of the family. She'd loved his father and was equally fond of him, and he returned her affection. He was just uneasy about the way her affection for him seemed to be shifting. "Sandra, she is my wife. She isn't going to—"

"You didn't want her. Your father found her because she's white. You can't trust her."

He hesitated in midbreath.

It was true that he couldn't trust Skylar. It was equally true that...

She was his wife. The wife he hadn't wanted. The wife who obsessed him. And somehow, he'd break down the barriers between them. Find out what had happened in the past. And just what the hell she was up to now.

Find the woman he had touched that first night he'd made love to her...

"Sandra, Skylar is my wife."

Sandra smiled. "But you keep your own bed."

"Many white couples keep separate rooms."

Sandra smiled. "Because most white men tire of their wives."

"Sandra, you're mistaken."

She shook her head, as if she knew a secret truth. "I'll still keep her from hurting you. And I'm glad you keep your own room."

She left before he could say more. He leaned back, lacing his fingers behind his head.

It was growing late.

Sandra might be mistaken about many things, but he did seem to have a serious problem with Skylar regarding the activities she chose to keep hidden from him. He didn't know how to solve that problem, but he couldn't spend much more time now pondering it. He needed to gather a few personal belongings if he was going to ride out tomorrow.

He left the office behind for his own bedroom. He pulled a bedroll from beneath his bed and gathered his razor, strap, and brush from the dresser. He mulled over the information regarding his wife's day, trying to determine just how to handle her. How to approach her.

How to leave her.

He realized he'd been fooling himself. He couldn't leave her.

Just as he reached that conclusion, he was startled by a soft tapping at his door.

He threw it open, amazed.

He wasn't going to have to approach his wife.

She had come to him.

Skylar stood there. She was wearing some kind of a night garment, but one quite different from what she had worn before. This was all silk. Deep blue, very low-cut in front and in back. Where it didn't blatantly hug her body, enhancing every perfect curve, it seemed to shimmer around her. Her hair was down, brushed to a flowing, golden sheen. She appeared elegant and soft. Dignified...and sensual. The gown had been chosen with care. As had her perfume. It was musky and...seductive.

Her smile was charming and hesitant.

The rapid rise and fall of her breasts and her labored breath belied the very lightness of her smile.

He could tell that she was appalled to be here.

But she wanted something. Yes.

He wondered just how far she'd go to get it.

# CHAPTER 12

She hated being here. She wanted to crawl beneath the floor.

It was all the worse because she realized she might be attempting this course of action too late. It seemed he wearied of her at last. He hadn't come near her last night. Had he slept here with someone else who didn't mind that sometimes he slept elsewhere?

Was he perhaps expecting that someone now?

"Yes?" he inquired politely.

"May I...enter this sacred domain?" Skylar asked, wincing as she realized that her query had been half flirtatious and half very dry.

He stepped back mockingly. "Do come in. Indeed. I am stunned by the honor of your visit."

Skylar walked nervously past him, crossing her arms over her chest, then allowing them to fall as she realized it was a defensive gesture, hardly seductive. She forced a smile onto her lips, turning to survey the room as she did so. She extended a hand toward the connecting doorway to the library. "What a wonderful place."

"I'd give you a tour, but it's evident you've taken one on your own."

"I never actually took a tour," she said pleasantly.

"What do you want, Skylar?"

She grated her teeth together beneath her smile. Hating him. This was sheer misery to begin with, but he was making it immeasurably harder.

"I just heard this evening from Megan that you are planning to leave in the morning."

"I am."

Skylar stood at the foot of his bed, curling her fingers around the bedpost. "You hadn't said anything to me," she said very softly.

He studied her for a moment.

Then her heart leapt as he took a few steps toward her. Coming around behind her, he lifted the heavy fall of her hair, placing his lips against her nape, then her shoulder. His breath was warm against her ear as he murmured, "You were concerned. You would have noticed that I was gone."

"Obviously, I would have noticed," she murmured.

He lingered behind her. She couldn't see his face. Her pulse raced, and she prayed that she was doing the right thing. Her pride seemed to be suffering an almost mortal blow, but she couldn't let that matter at the moment. She had to get her hands on some money. And it was true that he was leaving. She'd have to endure one wretched night of giving away everything, but then he'd be gone. And she'd have days in which she could prepare for the next battle.

He moved away from her, striding toward the brandy decanter on a side table near his wardrobe. "May I pour you a drink?"

"Were you going to have one?" she asked in what she hoped was a soft and seductive tone.

"Now that you've chosen to honor me with this visit, of course."

Despite her best efforts, she spoke before she thought. "You're not honored in the least. If you'd wanted to see me, you'd have done so."

He glanced her way briefly as he poured an inch of brandy into each of two snifters. "Perhaps," he agreed, bringing the brandy to her. "But it's quite different to have you here."

She accepted the snifter from him and felt his gaze so intently that for a moment, her eyes fell. She could not meet his. She took a sip of the brandy, then tossed back her head and swallowed it all. It nearly choked her. It was wonderful. It warrmed every part of her body.

"So," he murmured, still very close. "You're concerned that I'm leaving. Why?"

The abrupt question startled her. "I..."

"I mean, frankly, you came this great distance, into the wilderness, land barely known to whites until a little more than a year ago, assuming you'd be on your own, taking charge. Staking claim," he said politely. "You're suddenly afraid?"

"No, I'm..." She pushed away from the bedpost, easing a small distance away from him. She set her brandy glass down, running her fingers idly over the handsome crystal carafe that held the brandy. "Perhaps I hadn't realized quite how hostile the territory can be. The army forts are much farther away than I had imagined."

"There's a company of men who were sent to keep the peace around Gold Town, which isn't that far from here."

"That, of course, is reassuring. It's just that when you're gone..."

"Yes?"

She hadn't heard him move. He was behind her again. He set his own brandy glass down. She realized he had barely taken a sip from it. He took the carafe from her fingers and poured more brandy into her snifter, raising it before her. She took it from his fingers, turning away, lowering her head. "Well, it's quite unnerving."

"How so?"

"I understand you will be going into hostile territory." She gulped down the brandy and once again a flood of warmth and conviction filled her.

"And you're concerned?" he inquired. Once again, he was behind her. The glass was plucked from her hands. She felt his hands on her shoulders.

"Well...naturally."

He turned her around, lifting her chin. "But you said you would gladly see me slain and scalped by my own kind or any other."

She wanted to lower her chin. He wasn't going to allow it.

"We all say things in anger," she murmured.

She saw a slight smile upon his lips. Skylar exhaled and was afraid for a second that she wouldn't be able to catch her breath again. He seemed even more formidable than usual this evening. Taller, his body more tense.

"So you actually are concerned."

"Yes."

"But surely I am a hostile myself in your eyes."

"Your charade when we met was cruel," she told him, forcing the words to be a reproachful whisper and nothing more.

"But it wasn't really a charade. You quickly saw all that I am."

"Perhaps that's true," she murmured. She lifted a hand in a helpless gesture. "I just...I was surprised that you would leave without saying a word. I didn't want you to leave with—with so much hostility between us."

"Ah!" he murmured. He was behind her again, his fingers on her shoulders moving lightly beneath the straps of her silk gown. His husky whisper was warm against her ear. "Then could it be that you missed me last night?"

One of the straps fell from her shoulder. He pressed his lips against her bare flesh. She closed her eyes, stunned by the sensations that such a simple touch could create within her. Something hot and powerful seemed to race through her body. She gritted her teeth together very hard. In all the times that she had fought the arousal his touch created, she had never felt quite so swiftly inundated with desire.

Tonight, when it mattered most that she take the greatest care...

"I..." It was difficult to speak. She had come here to seduce him. To tantalize him, elicit promises from him. But his arms had slipped around her from behind. The searing brush of his mouth moved against her shoulder. His right hand stroked down her side, over her ribs, cupped her breast through the silk, his thumb and forefinger rubbing her nipple erotically through the thin fabric. She began to ache, burn, long...

For more.

"Did you...miss me?" he whispered against her flesh.

"I..."

She had to remember why she had come. "Yes, I did. I will miss you. Must you...go?"

For a moment, he stopped caressing her.

"Yes, I must," he told her.

"If you must leave me..."

"Yes?"

"Would you please make arrangements so that I can be more independent from the household?"

There was silence, just his touch, then a murmur.

"Ummm..."

He agreed, did he?

He shifted the other strap of the gown from her shoulder, pressing his lips once more where his fingers had been. She was vaguely aware of the sultry feel of the silk as it slid down over her breasts and her hips to the floor. Both of his hands were upon her breasts, encircling them, palming them, the touch almost unbearably erotic.

"Of course, my dear, for a woman of such inestimable value!" he whispered very huskily. His hands moved over her, skimming her ribs. Her waist, her hips. His lips continued to move over her bare shoulders. His hands moved lower, his palms pressing upon her mound, his fingers stroking lower against her thighs. She felt his mouth, moving downward, stroke by stroke, his tongue touching upon the vertebrae in her back. Unwittingly she leaned against him, arching like a cat to capture the exquisite feel of him. She'd promised never to give herself to him, and she'd kept that promise. Yet tonight she had a mission, and she was suddenly achingly glad of that mission because she so desperately longed to allow herself to feel, perhaps, to give... Suddenly he turned her within his arms, cupping her chin, raising her face to his. His kiss was fierce, his tongue forcing her lips apart, stroking and ravaging her mouth. He moved back slightly, ripping open his white shirt, then drawing her against him. Fire snaked through her. She rose up on her toes, hesitant, then daring, kissing his throat, tasting the bronze flesh with the tip of her tongue, instinctively discovering the right movements, savoring the heat of his bronzed chest. He wrenched the shirt from his body. She continued to move against his chest, her hair brushing his flesh, her lips, tongue, and teeth teasing it. He threaded his fingers into her hair, lifting her face to his once again, finding her lips, kissing her with hot, open-mouthed passion as he kicked off his boots, then unbuckled his belt urgently with his free hand, dropping his pants. Still holding her to his kiss, he stepped from them. She drew from the heady force of his kiss, gasping and trembling, yet craving more. She touched him, moved against him, exploring each ripple and crease of his muscles, finding an erotic new power in the shudders she sent rippling forcefully through his body. There was a curious sweet pleasure in knowing him, in glorying in him, in realizing how finely honed he was, how perfect in his masculinity. There was that...and then a reckless, spiraling fever, a need that surged in her blood. She wasn't aware of anything but the heat emanating from him, the power of him, her need for him. Everything within her cried out to respond to the least suggestion from him. Instinct alone made her crush herself fully against him, rubbing her breasts and body down the length of his as she slipped to her knees. Her hands cradled the hardness of his buttocks. She nuzzled his thighs, the silk of her hair teasing him with her every movement. His fingers curled into the tendrils. A shudder ripped and tore violently through the length of her as she first tentatively curled her fingers around his sex. Nothing had ever seemed so hot, so vivid, so filled with violent pulsing. His fingers dug with greater pressure into her hair. Crushed her against him. Again, instinct told her what to do. And the sensual fever that ran hotly through her body caused her to do it well.

She was suddenly all but dragged to her feet and thrown upon the bed. He caught her knees and forced them apart. She braced, her eyes closed, expecting the savage thrust of his body. Instead she felt his touch, parting her, opening her. Felt his hair brush her thighs, his fingers probe, caress, discover...

She gasped, tossing and struggling to be freed from his weight. She'd never imagined there could be such a tiny part of her body that created such agonizingly sweet sensations. Yet it was not over. The sensations built slowly, deliberately, until the whole of her body was racked with them, the climax burning throughout her, so sweetly intense that the world seemed to blacken and pale.

And only then did she feel the force of him invade her. The fullness of his body penetrating her. She lay still, stunned at first, unable to move, aware only of the size and force and fullness of him. Then suddenly, it began again. Friction that seduced. That created new fire, ignited her hunger again, the need again, the yearning. The desperate desire to reach that pinnacle again when the light of the fire seemed to burst, and to saturate her body with the deliciousness of it...

His climax was the catalyst to hers. The staggering force of him against her as he rained his seed into her brought the searing sensations within her to a peak. Her nails clawed heedlessly into his shoulders and back. Gasps and sobs were wrenched from her. She was drenched with perspiration, keenly aware of the wetness and sleekness of his body as well, yet once again the sheer intensity of the sensation seemed to create blinding light...and then a fall of gray shadows upon her...

Later, she was aware. Aware that she lay at his side, aware that the bed remained covered, that they both lay naked. The candles had burned down to nothing. They were in his room. She had come here. To do this.

Yet it didn't matter. She was still steeped in the extraordinary sensations she'd experienced. She'd tasted before the possibilities of pleasure she could have at his hands, but she'd never imagined how amazingly exquisite it would be. She wanted to close her eyes and savor the feelings forever, be cocooned within them.

At her side, he shifted. She opened her eyes and found him staring at her.

"Just how much money is it that you want?"

"What?" she managed.

"How much money. I'm assuming it must be a lot, for such a performance."

She stared back at him, shocked. The sweet cocoon around her seemed to shatter like glass.

"The amount will be intriguing. I'm supposedly a wealthy man, but I wonder just how often even I could afford an evening like this."

She closed her eyes quickly again, astonished at the depth of the hurt that filled her, afraid that tears would fall and betray her completely after this devastating humiliation.

Her eyes flew open. She cried and hit him, trying to punch him out of her way. She caught his chin, but he barely seemed to feel the blow.

She nearly rose to her feet, but he grappled her back down, his countenance grim.

"What do you think you're going to do, go running through the halls naked? And what then? Do you think you can race to your room like some kind of princess and shut me out?"

"You are a—"

"You came for money! Admit it."

"I came for money!" she cried out, glaring at him, her eyes shimmering.

"How much, damn you? Let's see how much you think you were worth!"

"Sweet Jesus! Did you treat your last wife so?" she demanded in turn. "Then surely, she most probably died to escape you!"

The fury in his eyes frightened her so that she closed her eyes, nearly crying out. But no blow fell upon her, and she opened her eyes. A chilling dismay swept over her at the way he looked at her. She was the wronged party! She wanted to cry out, but her pride saved her.

"I—I don't understand you!" she choked out, barely able to hold back her tears. "No man leaves his wife with—with nothing."

"Damn you. I'm asking again. How much money do you need?"

"About a hundred dollars," she said warily.

He arched a brow, sinking back on his haunches. "You do value yourself, Lady Douglas!"

She ignored his mockery. "You asked me what I need!"

"For what?" he demanded.

"I..."

"For what?"

"My sister!" she cried out.

"Sister?" he repeated, amazed.

"Yes! My sister," she hissed. "I need to wire money to her for travel expenses. I want to bring her—here."

"You have one sister?"

"Yes."

"Older, younger? What's her name?"

"Two years younger. Sabrina."

"I see." What did he see? She had never been in a more miserable position, trapped, with him settled back on his haunches atop her, her hips caught between the lock of his thighs as he stared down at her, ready to make demands.

"Have you more siblings? Brothers? What of your mother and father? Other family? Will I be bringing scores of citizens westward?" He shrugged with a mocking glint to his eyes. "Such a procession could prove infinitely entertaining, I imagine."

She felt her cheeks redden, and she longed to strike out at him.

"Take care!" he suggested lightly.

"I have one sister," she snapped out, her lashes lowered as she self-consciously crossed her arms over her chest, very aware now of both her nakedness and her vulnerability.

"No other family?"

"My parents are dead. I—" She broke off, fighting her temper and her unease. She stared at him and spoke as softly as she could manage and with all the dignity she could gather under the circumstances. "It is very important to me. Please, I need to bring her out here."

He wouldn't deny her such a thing, would he?

But he shook his head. "A hundred dollars is much more than her journey here is going to cost her."

Skylar lowered her lashes again. "We—we have a few accounts that must be settled."

She looked at him. He seemed to accept that yet still seemed somewhat amazed and puzzled by what he was hearing.

"You needn't think that my sister will be a burden to you. She won't be. She won't bother you. Or get in your way. I swear it—"

He lifted a hand. "Had you wished to bring half a dozen sisters into this house, I wouldn't have been bothered. Fm merely having a difficult time understanding you. All that you want is to send your sister money to come live out here. Have I got this right?" he demanded.

She nodded. It was mostly the truth.

"You little fool. Why didn't you just come right out and ask me? You could have saved yourself...this evening."

"You mean—"

"I'll see that the money is wired first thing in the morning."

"Oh ..." she breathed. "I don't want to trouble you. If you just give me the legal right, I can take care of everything. I don't want to ruin your trip or delay it."

"The trip you're so concerned about me taking, right?" he demanded dryly.

"I understand it's important to you—"

"Yes, it is."

"Then I wouldn't want to interfere."

He watched her gravely, then smiled wryly, but there was little humor in his eyes.

"You're the most incredible little liar."

"Damn you, I'm not lying," she inhaled, fighting back her temper, hating to acknowledge gratitude toward him in any way. "I'm grateful that you'll send for Sabrina, and I don't mean to delay something that's important to you. And speak of incredible liars! How you could ever fault me after the performance you put on when you pretended to attack the stagecoach—well, you've incredible gall!"

"Perhaps. But you'll understand if I find it difficult to trust you. I'll see that the arrangements are made."

She started to speak again, but he interrupted her. "I'll also see to it that you have a reasonable sum of money for personal expenses."

"I don't really want your money," she said uncomfortably. "I just—needed it."

"Women always need money, don't they?"

"Not necessarily. Not usually. I wouldn't have taken anything from you if..."

"If you hadn't felt that you had to?"

She refused to meet his eyes.

"So you really don't want to take anything from me, but earning it in your own mind is different?"

She had gotten what she wanted from him, nonetheless, it didn't seem to calm the tempest within her. At that moment, she wanted to slap him with every ounce of strength in her. But again she controlled her temper. Sabrina wasn't here yet.

She stared up at him furiously. "Have I earned it?"

"A down payment, at the least."

Temperance lost out. She gritted her teeth, striking out, then ruing the action because he had goaded her into it, and far too easily he caught her wrists, bringing them back to her sides.

He arched a taunting brow as he stared down at her; for the moment, she almost wondered which of them he mocked. He spoke somewhat harshly. "A man's wife is entitled to his resources," he said.

Startled by his words and manner, she felt again the tug of wounded pride. "I will be all right on my own," she told him. "Once you've sent for Sabrina, there will be nothing I want, and there really isn't anything I need here at the house."

"Umm. You'd be happy as a lark with me out of it?"

"I didn't say—"

"You didn't need to." He suddenly rose, picking her nightgown up from the floor, offering it to her. "I do, however, insist you dress before going back to your own room."

She took the garment from him. Then she inched back on the bed, realizing that she was shaking as she tried to shimmy quickly back into it. But he wasn't watching her. He was pulling his pants back on.

"You're free to escape," he said lightly. "You've done what you came to do."

She flushed deeply, dismayed to feel that she was being dismissed.

"You can be very cruel," she told him, rising with as much dignity as she could muster.

"Can I? Well, you can be very secretive."

"You're a stranger."

"One you accidentally married for the sole purpose of coming here. And taking over Mayfair."

"Well, then, I suppose, as you have suggested, I will revel in it in the days to come!" she said lightly, turning to leave.

He laughed softly. She was startled by his hand upon her arm, swinging her back to face him. "No, I don't suppose!" he informed her.

"What do you mean? If your trip was so important—"

"It is."

"You mean that you're not going?"

"I'm going."

"Then—"

"My love, you're coming with me."

She stared at him, then gasped, pulling free from his touch. "But you're riding out into the true wilderness for days. You're riding out to spend time among the Sioux. You—"

"Right. You're forgetting something I keep telling you. I met you as a Sioux. There was no charade in that. I am a Sioux. Just as you are Lady Douglas, mistress of Mayfair, you're also wife to Thunder Hawk, warrior of the Oglala Sioux. You've spent some time at Mayfair. Now you'll get to see a bit of the other half of the life you have chosen."

She continued to stare at him, convinced he wasn't serious.

"But—"

He put his hands upon her shoulders, this time prodding her toward the door.

"Go to bed. Get some sleep. We'll have to start early to make the arrangements you want and still give ourselves most of the day to ride into the hills."

"Wait!" she cried, turning back to him, searching his eyes and looking for some hint that he was only teasing her. "I'd prefer to stay here—"

"Yes, I know."

"You're just being cruel again."

"I'm not in the least. I can't leave you here. I don't trust you."

"There's no reason not to trust—"

"Skylar, my mind is made up."

She slammed her bare foot against the floor. "This is America!" she informed him.

He laughed. "That's debatable at the moment! Skylar, go to bed. Get some sleep. You're going with me."

"I refuse—"

"Afraid of Indians?" he taunted lightly.

"Damned wary of them," she countered.

"Umm. But you've already been savaged and waylaid by one. Good heaven! You're married to one. What greater horror could befall you?"

"I'm fond of the hair on my head."

"Actually, I rather enjoy your hair, too."

"You—"

"I assure you. I'll see that you keep it."

"Are you so sure you can keep your own?" she demanded.

"I know where I am riding," he told her. "You can ride with me, or I can bring you along the same way I did when I met your stagecoach."

"Attacked the stagecoach."

He shrugged, his arms crossed over his chest.

Oh, God, she thought with dread. He was serious.

"It's going to be a very early morning," he warned her, his eyes narrowing, "if you want to wire money east."

"You're bribing me!"

He shook his head. "I don't have to bribe you. You're going. That's decided. How you go is up to you, and actually, it doesn't make much difference to me."

She gritted down very hard on her teeth. He was going to send for Sabrina. He was going to give her the hundred dollars. That was what mattered.

"Fine!" she snapped out.

"Fine?" he said skeptically.

"Fine! I just said fine, I'll go."

"You're right," he said very softly. "You will."

"And you are a damned savage!" she hissed.

He laughed softly, suddenly pulling her to him. "You were wonderfully savage yourself tonight, my love!"

She tried to kick him, but he moved swiftly enough to avoid her toes.

"Bastard!" she cried, jerking free from him and striding to the door, which she slammed behind her with such force she was sure its reverberation could be heard throughout the house.

Then she spun and ran toward her own room with all possible speed.

# CHAPTER 13

Everything was going to be all right. Despite the fact that she was far from thrilled by the prospect of riding into completely uncivilized country with Hawk, she should have had the easiest rest she had known since arriving in the Dakota territory. Hawk was going to send for Sabrina first thing in the morning. Jimmy Pike at Pike's Inn would receive the wire and slip word to Sabrina. And she would be free as well.

Maybe it was her relief that brought that last incident rushing back into her dreams.

Dillman. Unchanged. After so many years.

Handsomely dressed in his dark suit, tall and trim. He spent hours each week at his club, boxing, shooting, fencing, perfecting his physique and his image. The ultimate politician.

With the local police in his pocket.

He'd had over a decade then in which to achieve the image. As a young child, Skylar had known only that he'd killed her father. As she'd grown up in what he had made into his own household, she had come to realize many things about the man and his motives. He had seen what her father had possessed, not just in material goods, but in his home and family, and most importantly, his position in the very exclusive strata of Baltimore society. By killing her father, he had won her mother, and when Jill, the granddaughter of a Revolutionary War hero, had accepted and wed him, he was well on his way to achieving all that he desired—power, social prestige, and wealth.

There were times when Skylar could almost be glad that she had grown up in the darkened shadow of war herself. She and Sabrina moved in the proper circles and attended all the right parties. The tension of living in their house was sometimes alleviated by social functions. And though Skylar had actually met several men she had liked and enjoyed, she had been grateful that the pressure to marry young had been taken away simply because so many young men had been killed. Dillman wasn't ready for the girls to marry because his family made such an attractive political platform. Skylar and Sabrina were not ready to leave either their mother or each other.

Jill's death, however, had changed everything.

Skylar had been convinced that despite their loss, she and Sabrina could at last find freedom.

She and Brad Dillman had fought on the upper landing of the stairway. It was rightfully their home, but after their mother had died and been buried, Skylar had wanted only to get away. She had stayed all those years because of her mother, even if Jill had failed to see the evil in Brad Dillman. There were times when Skylar had hated her mother for refusing to see the truth, but then she had realized that Jill had been completely shattered when Skylar's father had been murdered. She had wanted so desperately to believe in Dillman. And Dillman had been good at his chosen role. He had made such a point of being so tender and gentle, taking care of everything for Jill in her sorrow—even dealing with a hurt young child who ignored his goodness and made terrible accusations against him. He had always pretended to be the perfect gentleman to his wife. Jill had always believed that Skylar's love for her own deceased father had allowed her to create terrible fantasies in her mind about Dillman because she simply could not accept him as a stepfather.

It had not just been her love for her mother that had kept her home, refusing the marriage proposals that had come her way. It had been the veiled threats that Dillman had cast out over the years.

Reminders that sad things could suddenly happen to people who appeared to be in the very best of health.

But then Jill had died.

And on the stairway that day, Skylar was finished with any attempt of pretense regarding Dillman.

"Now there's no way for you to stop me from leaving. You can't threaten me with Mother anymore because she's dead, she's free—"

"And she never did believe you, did she?" Brad had taunted. "She'd never have doubted me in a thousand years, Skylar, no matter what you might have tried to tell her! Because she needed me, and she wanted me. And she didn't want to believe those awful lies you tried to tell her, did she? Remember what happened, Skylar, when you tried to convince her that I killed your wonderful father?"

Skylar knew. Everyone had been horrified that she could have accused a man such as Brad Dillman of murder. People had thought that she was distraught. Bereft, insane with grief. Because everyone believed that Brad had tried everything to save her father, everything. He had been there, such a firm, strong support for the family, there for her mother, there for them all...

Her mother had been so upset she'd left the problem of Skylar up to Dillman. As sad as it was, Skylar had to be punished for saying such terrible things. God, had Dillman laughed when they had been alone together. And enjoyed the responsibility of taking a switch to her.

It didn't help to remember the past.

"Dillman, you're the fool. My mother knew about your other women."

"She knew I slept beside her every night, and she was grateful."

"You're despicable. And what you have to say to me doesn't matter in the least anymore. I'm leaving. And I'll get lawyers to settle the estate—"

"The estate? Skylar, you've always been a little girl, trying to play against men. Do you think that I've spent all these years here and failed to see to the estate? Let's see, your mother inherited a fine income from your father. Lord knows, I needed that money! So when your poor father died, I married your mother. I managed the money and the legal affairs. You try to leave, and you'll get nothing."

"Maybe. I'll take my chances and fight you. Surely Mother left provisions in her will for Sabrina and me."

"And maybe she didn't think that she needed to leave provisions for you when she was leaving you in my custody."

"Maybe I don't care. I just need enough to get away from you. And I will somehow take Sabrina—"

"Skylar, Skylar! Still the little fool! Did you think it could possibly be so simple? You're not going anywhere. You're going to stay right here. Sabrina is not yet twenty-one. She is legally in my custody. We're going to continue to be the proper family. I want the whole package, Miss Skylar, just as I have always wanted it, needed it. My constituents like my family image, the United States senator and his two beautiful young daughters. We're a family. We understand the difficulties of a family in this day and age. We know about God and society! You're not going to do anything to jeopardize the career I've worked so hard to build—"

"The career you've murdered for?" she accused him.

He hadn't been more than a few feet away. A handsome, compelling man, one whose charm had served him well throughout the years, one whose charm masked the evil within him, a cruelty that was almost casual in its endeavors.

He'd been a strict stepfather throughout the years, his manner sad and despairing to his associates when he discussed discipline in the home, but he'd seemed to relish the task of finding the proper switches to use against his stepdaughters when they disobeyed. Despite the pleasure he had always found in inflicting pain and the ease with which he doled it out, she still wasn't prepared for the force of the blow that came crashing down against the side of her head, knocking her to the floor. The pain was staggering. It robbed her of breath and of vision and, for seconds, even of consciousness. She awoke, blinking, still in pain. He was on top of her, his one hand clasped around her throat, the other moving over her cheek.

"Your mother really was in love with me, Skylar," he told her coldly. "I was strong. She was weak. Your precious father was weak and naïve—"

"My father was loyal. And honest. And a million other fine things you'd never even recognize—"

"Was. An important word in this conversation. He is now very dead, my dear," Dillman said matter-of-factly. "I've been enduring this petty argument with you for over a decade now, and I'm sick to death of it, Skylar. The rules have changed once again. You know me, I know you. You behave, you learn to keep your mouth shut and obey. You cause me any trouble, and I can reach you. I'll kill you. You try to convince anyone that I'm a danger to you or your sister, and I can promise, you'll wind up in an asylum for the insane—you know that I can do it. You've been fighting all this time, most of your life, Skylar. And when the hell has anyone ever believed you? When have you ever managed to beat me? You can't. Give it up. Because I'll win. And I'll do whatever it takes to see that I do."

"Murder me?"

He shrugged. "If necessary. But it would be such a pity. You're really such a beautiful—if vicious—little creature. I always thought you were a pretty little thing, even as a child, but you know, my dear—and you should know well—that I am not a stupid man. I'd not have made advances to you or your sister while my dear wife lived, but then...I'm in mourning right now, of course, over your mother, but a man can be eased from his sorrows by a woman like you."

She was going to be sick. "I would die first!"

He leaned against her, laughing. "Skylar, you continually miss the point. You have been a thorn in my side forever. You might well die an accidental death, but surely, after all these years, I deserve at least a bit of entertainment from you. You could be quite amusing. I wouldn't think of killing you until after I had discovered what charms you may or may not possess."

"You idiot bastard! I will get away—"

"I'll track you down. And have you locked up."

"I'll—"

"Notice, Skylar, I have you by the throat. I could squeeze my fingers tightly now, and you would pass out. I could do whatever I chose to do. Ah, imagine. Were you to go making accusations against me, I could build a case of dementia against you. Then they'd lock you up. In one of those places. Skylar, have you ever visited such a place? The insane! So pathetic. We must do our Christian duty by them! Yet how horrid to live among them. So many of them hosed down rather than bathed. Poor creatures, crying, screaming into all hours of the night! I, your loving stepparent, would visit. Why, my dear, they've not really rooms in most of those establishments. They've cages and cells. With locks and keys. I could come, and we could play for hours. And no one would ever hear your screams."

"God, you are wretched! But I will get away—"

"Umm. If you should, well, actually, I have always preferred Sabrina. And the poor dear. It's amusing, really. I'm her legal guardian. She'd have to be very, very far away to escape me, wouldn't she, Skylar? How would you ever do it? How would you manage the resources to do it? I'll follow you to hell, girl, and so help me, I'll have it all my way. Are we understood?"

Understood. Oh, God.

And it had gotten worse from there. Or better. If only Sabrina would arrive here quickly now. She could see her sister, standing behind Dillman, trying to tug him away from Skylar. She could see Dillman laughing. Turning on Sabrina. Threatening, promising, touching...

She remembered herself flying into action. She could see it all again, relive it. See Dillman falling, falling, falling, screaming. She could see his legs, twisted, and hear her sister. "Go, you have to go! If he lives, he'll have you hanged, imprisoned, put away—"

"I can't leave you—"

"Skylar, you've got to! You've got to get completely away, disappear! We'd be too visible trying to escape together, and he'd get the law out after both of us. He still has a legal claim on me. He's still my guardian. But I'm safe for the moment! He can't hurt me now. Go! Find us a way out, a new life, Skylar, not a prison sentence!"

"I can't—"

"Then we've got to kill him!"

"No! It would make us what he is! We can't—"

"Then you've got to run. Can't you see, he can't hurt me now."

"I'll get word to you as quickly as possible. Go to Pike's. Jimmy Pike is our only friend."

"Go! My God, go! Get far away before he can send someone for you, before he can come, before—"

Words faded, darkness swirled around her. There were hands, reaching for her, dragging her down, pulling at her. She heard his laughter, felt herself falling, unable to breathe. She saw his face, and felt his touch...

There was a bursting sound as the door to the room swung open. She heard it dimly, far in the back of her mind. Then her name.

"Skylar!"

She fought the web of sleep that wrapped around her. Someone was touching her. Hands, strong hands were upon her. She screamed, her eyes flying open. Darkness seemed heavy all around her. She was being held while shadows hovered in the hallway.

"Skylar!"

Oh, God! She woke fully and exhaled raggedly. It was Hawk. She realized that she was shaking, a fine sheen of perspiration bathed her flesh. He was holding her. Fingers threading through her hair. He wore a crimson smoking jacket, the V top loose. He drew her against the bare flesh of his chest, stilling the trembling that seized her.

"It's all right," he said to the shadows in the doorway. "She was dreaming."

Shadows melted. The door was closed.

"Oh, God!" she breathed.

She swallowed hard, fought the emotions the vividness of the dream had brought home once again. She bit into her bottom lip, preparing for the onslaught of questions he would snap at her now.

But amazingly, he was quiet, fingers running gently through her hair.

"I think the entire house heard you screaming," he said softly at last.

"I'm so sorry."

"It's all right."

She opened her mouth, still seeking an explanation.

But to her amazement, he spoke first again.

"One might have thought I was in the act of scalping you. Are you that afraid of coming with me over the hills?"

"Afraid of the hills?" she repeated. "No, of course not, I'm not—" she broke off, realizing far too late that he had assumed she had been dreaming of an Indian attack! "I—"

He pulled away from her, lifting her chin. The firelight was low, and it was all that illuminated the room. Still, she knew that he saw quite well in the dark, and that he was studying her now. It seemed too late to dissemble now.

"I'm not afraid of going with you."

"Why were you screaming?"

She managed a smile. "I really didn't mean to convince the entire household you were scalping me."

"Then?"

She was startled by the warmth that filled her as his thumb moved over her cheek. She lowered her lashes, shaking her head. "Monsters," she said with a shrug. "I don't really know. It was a nightmare. Dreams are so terrible, but then they fade so quickly. I'm sorry, I didn't mean to disturb everyone."

"And you're not afraid? Of riding with me?"

She shook her head again, sighed, and admitted, "No—I'm not afraid."

"You just don't want to come."

"I—" She paused, trying to study his features in turn. But he gave nothing away. His eyes seemed almost as dark as his countenance in the shadows. Yet his very austerity seemed to offer her a strange sense of security now. His force and body heat offered a strange comfort.

Her lashes swept her cheeks. "Lord Douglas, I do strive to be a good wife. If you wish company on a journey, then I would most obediently oblige you."

"Ah! At least until the wire is sent, Lady Douglas?"

She glanced up at him, but he laughed softly, drawing her against him. "You really need to sleep, Skylar. Morning will come quickly. It probably would help if you'd tell me the truth about that dream."

"I—I told you—"

"Monsters. Umm. It's amazing, Skylar. I seem to be able to force almost anything from you—except the truth."

"You don't want to believe the truth."

"Want to tell me about the dream?"

"I told you—"

"What? You told me what, Skylar?"

"It's—gone. I don't remember the dream."

There was a strange disappointment in his eyes as he looked at her then. "Never mind, Skylar. Whatever—or whoever—those monsters are, I promise, you're safe. They'll not get by me."

He drew her closer, moving his fingers through her hair, over her cheek. "Skylar, try to sleep. I'll be here. Nothing will hurt you. No one can hurt you."

But she sat up, looking at him in the shadows. He was a man of so many contrasts. With his ruggedly hewn bronze features and straight ebony hair, he might have appeared strangely out of place at Mayfair. Yet he did not. He looked very much like his father as well, wore the smoking jacket with complete ease, lay upon the handsomely carved bed with natural comfort. Likewise, his temper could flare so quickly, his violence surge, yet in startling moments, he could betray a gentle touch of tenderness.

"I swear to you, I never hurt your father," she told him. "I didn't hasten his death in any way."

He sighed softly, reached for her, and drew her down to the covers against him once again. Her cheek lay against his bare chest. She was grateful for the warmth. Glad to lie against him.

He stroked tendrils of hair from her forehead. She thought that he would not reply. That he did not believe her.

"Skylar, you've got to sleep. You'll be sorry if you don't, I'm telling you."

"Do you believe me?"

"I'm not sure that I want to believe you now," he said softly.

"Why not?"

He hesitated. "Then I'd have to apologize for attacking your stagecoach, wouldn't I?"

She smiled and closed her eyes.

"Yes."

"But then again, maybe not. You were out here to lay claim to my property, hmm?"

"Have I managed to claim any?"

"You might be surprised," he murmured. "Go to sleep, Skylar."

She lay with her cheek against his heart and listened to its beat.

And slept.

---

IT WAS EARLY when he awakened her, ridiculously early.

She'd fallen into a deep, restful sleep, so she was especially irritated when the covers were wrenched from her and she heard, "Up, Lady Douglas. Thirty minutes, and we're on our way."

She grabbed the covers, dragging them back over her head.

Once again, they were wrenched away. She still didn't bother to open her eyes. "I can't!" she murmured. "You'll have to go without me."

Then she felt a stinging swat on her backside. Indignantly, she leaped up to a sitting position, staring at her tormentor.

Hawk was dressed in dark buff buckskin, his jacket and boots fringed. His head was bare, his black hair falling loosely to his shoulders.

"Lady Douglas," he told her, his impatience held in check with mock gallantry, "your mule awaits."

"Mule?" she gasped.

"Thirty minutes. I left you a mug of coffee by the water ewer. Get going."

"If you're serious about a mule, it had best keep waiting!" she warned.

"Thirty minutes. The mule may be patient. I am not."

She rose and washed quickly, then dressed in what she hoped would be an appropriate outfit for a ride into wild country—cotton shift, petticoat, and calico dress—and good riding boots. The sun could be very bright by day, but the nights could be cold, so she brought her hooded wool cloak. She created a blanket roll with a second dress and underclothing and then hurried down the stairs with a few minutes to spare.

Meggie was at the front door, shaking her head. "Riding off at the crack of the dawn, and not a decent breakfast into a one of you!" she said unhappily.

Hawk walked in from the porch, an empty mug in his hands. Meggie glanced his way, shaking her head. "Ye've not even fed the lass, Lord Douglas!"

He arched a brow, looking from Meggie to Skylar. "I'm not setting out to starve my wife, Meggie. We've just got a busy morning ahead of us. We're already leaving hours later than I had intended. Besides, we've had your fine coffee, Meg, and I packed your biscuits in our bags." He handed her his empty mug and touched her cheek affectionately. "I do trust you, of course, to hold down the fort in my absence. We'll be gone one to two weeks, I believe." He winked, looking at Skylar once again. "Skylar is sending for her sister today, Meggie. I can't imagine that a lone woman might come all this way west before we return, but then she is Skylar's sister, so I assume anything is possible, don't you think, my love?" he queried Skylar.

She ignored him. "My sister's name is Sabrina Connor," she told Meggie. "And I imagine that she can make it out here in a week, assuming she can manage connecting train schedules and a decent stagecoach ride north from the railhead."

"It took you two weeks," Hawk commented quietly, for her hearing alone.

"I had a few things to attend to along the way."

"Really? What things?"

"Personal affairs," she told him.

"Umm," he murmured, his dissatisfaction with her reply obvious. "Eventually, Skylar, you will answer my questions."

"Eventually, I may."

"At the moment," he said irritably, "it seems like it's taking me two weeks to leave my own damned house."

Meggie, unaware of the tension between them, shook her head with concern. "The stagecoach coming north from the railroad usually stops overnight on the road and then takes the passengers into Gold Town," she reminded Hawk worriedly.

"She'll find Henry then. I'll instruct him to make arrangements for her to stay in town at the Miner's Well until he can arrange for someone to bring her out here," Hawk said.

Meggie nodded. "Make sure Henry knows to watch out for a young lady."

"We will. Well, then, we'll be on our way." He smiled at Meggie and led Skylar out the front door. Sloan, dressed in buckskin as well, was mounted on a large bay. Willow was at his side. Ten head of cattle grazed there in front of the elegant Mayfair, waiting to be driven forth with them.

Something cold touched Skylar's hand. She looked down to see that Wolf had come over to her. She scratched his head.

"The roan gelding, named Nutmeg, is your choice, right?" Hawk said from behind her. "It is the mount you chose to ride into Gold Town behind my back?"

"It wasn't behind your back," Skylar said.

"It wasn't with my permission."

"I'm rather old to ask permission."

"That's debatable, and beside the point out here."

"The roan gelding is fine."

"Good morning, Lady Douglas!" Sloan called to her. Willow nodded to her. "I understand you're taking a side trip into town this morning."

Hawk nudged her down the steps and toward her horse. He set her up on the roan. She smiled at Sloan. "I hope I'm not inconveniencing you too greatly."

He shook his head. "I enjoy being in and near the Black Hills. And every brief moment of peace and freedom that is left us!"

She wasn't quite sure what he meant, but he had moved his horse forward, closer to the house. "Goodbye, Meggie. Thanks for the coffee!" he called.

Poor Meggie still looked so distraught.

"Hawk—Lord Douglas—"

"Yes, Meggie, I'm absolutely certain that I should be taking my wife!" Hawk told her. "We'll be back in no time." He waved, whistled to Wolf, then trotted his horse along the path, circling around the cattle to get them moving ahead as well. Willow joined him in the effort, and their small party was quickly moving out of the yard. Skylar rode behind with Sloan, turning to wave goodbye to Meggie as they departed.

They had ridden some time in silence when Skylar drew her horse closer to Sloan's to talk. "Sloan, what did you mean by what you said earlier?"

"About what?"

"Peace and freedom."

He shrugged, then glanced her way. "Not long ago there was nothing here."

She smiled. "I know something about history. Not long ago, the Sioux weren't here. They were farther east."

"Ah, but they were forced out quickly by the whites, and even more quickly, they became some of the best bow and pony Indians ever."

"You're part of the cavalry," she reminded him.

Once again, he glanced wryly her way. "Hawk and I have often led parallel lives. But my circumstances were different from his. My grandfather's name was Granger Tremayne. He was a full general, a hero of the Mexican War. When the army moved west, his family moved west. My mother was with a small army escort moving from fort to fort when an Oglala war party happened upon them. She was sixteen years old when she was taken. My father was the brave who took her. He was young himself at the time, and when I was a boy, I remember that they had a very close relationship. My mother remained a feisty and opinionated soul, but my father had his image and his pride to maintain, so sparks frequently flew. Like Hawk, I was Sioux as I grew up."

"Sioux then, cavalry later."

"My grandfather was a full general, remember?" he said, smiling. He shrugged. "My father was killed in a skirmish with the Crow. He had asked Tall Man, an important warrior of our society, to see that my mother and I were returned to her people in the event that something happened to him. Tall Man returned us to the whites at the fort. I was ten. I was sent to school. I grew up with other army children. I traveled back east. I was sent to West Point. That's what happens to the grandson of a general, regardless of if he is a product of an Indian attack."

"It still seems that you are more Sioux," she said.

He smiled. "Because I look Indian."

"Because of the things you say."

"Maybe I am more Sioux."

"Why do you stay with the cavalry?"

"Ah, well, that way I know what is going on. And I can do my very best to relay it to my Indian brothers. Agency Sioux have gone out to try to talk Crazy Horse into coming to one of the agencies to discuss the sale of the Black Hills. I'm the cavalry's messenger, bringing the same request."

"Can you convince Crazy Horse?"

He shook his head. "I know Crazy Horse. He will not come. But he won't resent me for asking."

"What happens if you're with troops that are attacked?"

"When I'm attacked, I fight."

"Even if you're with the Sioux when the cavalry attacks?"

"Lady Douglas, you ask very personal questions."

"I'm sorry, I didn't mean—"

"Now, what about you? What are you doing out here?"

She stared at him, her mouth half open. Then she started to laugh.

She glanced up and realized that Hawk had reined in just ahead of her and was staring. To her surprise, he said something to Sloan in the Sioux language. Sloan nodded.

"Skylar, come this way," Hawk commanded.

She narrowed her eyes, not liking the tone of his voice. Sloan, at her side, lowered his. "You're heading into Gold Town. We're moving on through with the cattle."

She rode around to catch up with Hawk. He didn't speak to her, but nudged Tor into a hard canter. She followed behind him.

The entire ride into town was kept at a hard, brisk pace. She was weary when they arrived, stiff when he lifted her down. He barely set her upon the ground before heading for the office of Henry Pierpont, attorney-at-law.

Inside, Hawk spoke to the law clerk and ushered her past the young man. Henry greeted them both with surprise and pleasure, asking what he could do for them.

"I need to send a wire to my bank in Maryland with instructions to pass another wire through to a young lady in that city. Wire first to Harley Gander at my bank, and please see to it that a hundred dollars is sent as soon as possible to..." He glanced at Skylar, one brow arched. "To a Miss Sabrina Connor. My wife will give you the address."

Skylar shook her head, addressing Henry. "Any correspondence, from the service here and from the Maryland bank, should address Miss Sabrina Connor through Jim Pike, Pike's Inn, Baltimore."

"As you wish," Henry said. "I'll get my assistant busy on the papers immediately. I'll need your signature, Hawk. It'll just be a minute."

He left the room.

"Why can't you send this money straight to your sister?" Hawk demanded.

"Mr. Pike will be certain that Sabrina gets the money."

"Pike's Inn—it's where my father died, right?"

"Yes."

"Where we were—married?"

"Yes."

"I should remember it well!" he mocked.

"I'm really sorry that all of this has so inconvenienced you!" she hissed. "You've got to remember, I didn't even know that you existed!"

"And I didn't know about you. What an amazing marriage!"

"Again, I'm sorry," Skylar grated. His temper this morning was such that she might have imagined the few moments of gentleness he had offered her last night. She wasn't going to lose her own temper, though.

He was right. She was coming to know her husband very well, and though she knew he definitely had his honor, she didn't want to light a match to his very volatile temper until this transaction was completed.

When Henry returned to the room, he cleared his throat uncomfortably. "Hawk, er..."

"Ah, there was another matter you wished to discuss," Hawk said.

"Yes," Henry murmured.

Men. They seemed to have a private way of communicating

without words, Skylar thought somewhat resentfully. Her husband was instantly upon his feet. "Let me see that my wife is comfortably settled over a meal, and I will return to discuss this matter with you."

"I'm really quite all right," Skylar said. She smiled sweetly. "It would distress me so, milord husband, to dine without you."

"Indeed?" Hawk countered dryly. "I'm afraid it would distress me to think of your being bored and taxed by matters that are not your concern. Come, my dear."

The words were politely spoken, but his grip upon her arm to help her rise was so determined that she nearly cried out. "You can thank Henry now for his speed and competence in wiring the money. Few men can attend to such matters with such swift discretion."

She smiled. "Thank you, Henry."

"My absolute pleasure," he assured her.

"Come, my love," Hawk urged.

The inn was directly across the road from Henry's office. Despite her curiosity and unease regarding what matter might have Henry seeking to speak with Hawk alone, Skylar was impressed to see that the inn was a place so handsomely furnished that she could easily imagine she was back east.

Hawk deposited her at a table, ordered her meal despite her assurances that she was quite capable of doing so herself, and then left her. Quickly.

Skylar was starving by the time her dinner arrived, but unease continued to plague her. Just what might Henry be telling Hawk?

---

HENRY WAS WAITING for Hawk when he returned, but before Henry could explain his business, Hawk said, "While we're at this, Henry, I want some inquiries made."

"Regarding?"

"My wife."

"Ah, yes, of course. I'll see that I have a full dossier on Lady Douglas as soon as possible. If she, er, is—Lady Douglas."

Hawk's brow shot up. "You mean we're not married? Aren't you the one who assured me the lady is my wife?"

Henry nodded his head strenuously. "You're legally married, no matter what. Your marriage license very definitely states your name, and it is your signature and agreement upon proxy." He inhaled and exhaled. "Yesterday, I was visited by a very strange young man. He was a rugged fellow with an ungodly accent. He insisted upon seeing me, then demanded that I understand him completely before so much as contemplating repeating his words." Henry paused, then added, "I very nearly threw him out of here."

"Henry, what are you trying to say?"

Henry reached into his pocket, then offered a gold and ruby ring to Hawk.

Hawk felt a strange sensation of cold ripping into him. He knew the ring very well. It was an insignia ring. It had been in the Douglas family for centuries.

His brother had worn it. Always. It should have been buried with his remains.

"I was to give you the ring, then tell you that your complete discretion was absolutely necessary."

"My discretion?" Hawk whispered. "My brother died an agonizing death! What is this cruel joke?"

"I was begged to ask that you use discretion—"

"It is his ring," Hawk murmured. "I saw him buried. There was an inquest. I nearly throttled half a town, determined to know the truth." He rolled the ring in his fingers. It was the Douglas ring David had always worn. He stared at Henry. "What if...if my brother might be alive...how can I not search for him with all my strength and effort—"

Henry was shaking his head. "Your brother most probably is not alive. I'd say the factors here indicate a hoax. But if it isn't a hoax, if any of this is true, Hawk, David was apparently set up. And I would assume there are a few discoveries he is anxious to make on his own before he lets it be known that he is not long dead and buried. Anyway Hawk, this strange fellow suggested to me that David—if he is alive—is well aware of your concerns and the difficulties here. He would not have you jeopardize negotiations with your people on his behalf. But..."

"But what?" Hawk demanded. "Sweet Jesus, what, Henry?"

Henry shrugged. "This strange little man said if there is any way possible—and here is where things become stranger and stranger—the man who demanded the ring be given to you would like to meet you 'on the night of the Moon Maiden at the Druid Stone.'"

Hawk felt as if the blood had been drained from his body. It seemed that for long moments, he could not breathe.

"This can't be a hoax," Hawk said.

"This means something to you?" Henry asked.

Hawk nodded. The Druid Stone stood on a cliff by Greyfriar Castle, the stronghold of their particular branch of the Douglas family. The night of the Moon Maiden fell upon the first full moon after All Hallows' Eve, this year, in the middle of November. Curious timing—he would have weeks in which to carry his messages to Crazy Horse and enough time left to take a train east and board a ship for Scotland and reach his father's ancestral homes in plenty of time for the date required. If David was alive, he would have planned so carefully and courteously.

He didn't dare hope. He was still coming to terms with the pain of his father's death.

Henry cleared his throat. "You realize, if David is alive, he inherits—"

"I would gladly give anything and everything I own for my brother's life," Hawk said simply.

Henry smiled. "Well, nothing so dire as that would be the case. Your father's previous will would fall back into effect, with David inheriting all Scottish lands and titles while the American properties remain yours."

"You're sure the wife remains mine?"

Henry nodded emphatically. "Oh, quite sure. Unless you annul the marriage. Then, if by some miracle David is alive, David would retain the title, but your young lady would take your lands. It does get rather complex. And again, Hawk, the chances of your brother actually being alive are so slim!"

"I'll have to find out though, Henry, won't I?"

"Think carefully," Henry warned him. "Others from your Scottish hills and cliffs and vales may well know what words to use to trick you. If David and you both perish, there are numerous distant relatives waiting to take over not only your Scottish lands and titles—but now all your American wealth as well. This may be a malicious trick."

"Again, I'll most certainly have to find out, won't I?"

"What about your business here with your mother's people?"

"I have time," Hawk said quietly. He stood. "Not a great deal of it, but I do have time."

"Don't get your hopes up, Hawk. It's so incredibly unlikely that David could be alive. You saw him buried. I suspect some impostor means to get his hands on Douglas land through you. Don't be tricked. You have too much business here—and a new wife."

"Oh, don't worry, Henry. I intend to see to my business here—and, of course, to my new wife. But I do believe that I will meet this man, impostor or no, on the night of the Moon Maiden at the Druid Stone."

Skylar had long finished eating when Hawk returned. To her relief, he didn't seem to have learned any damning information about her. He sat opposite her, appearing preoccupied, then looked at his pocket watch while he drained the shot of whiskey that he'd ordered the minute he had sat down. "Let's go," he told her curtly. "I've a few more words for Henry."

Skylar didn't realize just how late it had become until they walked back across the street to Henry's office.

Hawk told Henry very briefly that they were heading west over the hills for an indeterminate time and that Hawk would inform him when they returned. If Sabrina Connor should arrive before they made it back, Henry should see to her overnight accommodations at the inn and then her ride out to Mayfair.

"It will be my pleasure," Henry assured them.

Minutes later they were out on the street again. Hawk walked quickly ahead of her. He waited impatiently at the horses, ready to boost her into her saddle.

Skylar refused to mount so quickly. "What took you so long at Henry's?" she asked.

"Nothing that concerns you. Ah! Is that a sigh of relief I'm hearing?"

"You're hearing nothing that concerns you," she replied sweetly.

"But you do concern me. Henry has assured me that we are most legally bound together. It's so curious. Did you marry for the title or the money?"

She longed to hit him. His voice was so strange, so taunting. "Neither," she informed him. "But you've no desire to see anything other than what you've chosen, so you can take your title and your money and go to hell. Except—"

"Except?"

He never would understand. She'd married to escape. And now, no matter how hateful he was being, she owed him.

She lifted her chin. "Thank you," she said, her tone cool, controlled, as distant and dignified as she could possibly make it.

He made a sound of impatience, apparently no longer interested in the fight. "A man is obligated to help his wife's kin."

"But you didn't want a wife, much less her kin. Although you may actually find you like your sister-in-law better than your wife."

"Skylar, I don't dislike you."

"You don't even trust me alone in your house."

"I don't trust you—that doesn't mean I dislike you."

"Well, you can't possibly like someone you don't trust."

He put his hands on his hips and looked straight in her eyes. "Well, you can't possibly trust someone who doesn't tell the truth!"

She was suddenly sorry that she had started this—so much for a simple thank-you to this man. His mood was foul. She'd leave him to it.

"I haven't lied to you."

"You haven't told me anything."

She lifted her own hands in a gesture of impatience. "There's nothing to tell you—"

"I imagine there is."

"Look, I was trying to say thank you—"

"The truth would be a nice thank-you."

"I told you—"

"Tell me what you told my father that made him choose you for this marriage."

What was he accusing her of now? "Go to hell," she told him

evenly. "I'm sorry that you don't like anything about this." She started walking by him. She could mount a horse by herself.

Except that he wouldn't let her. Even as she passed him, he caught hold of her around the waist, lifting her with ease, and setting her firmly upon Nutmeg. His hands lingered upon her as he looked up at her.

"I like the nights," he drawled.

She felt herself blushing. "What a pity, then, that we couldn't stay home. That we're now on a trail into Sioux country with one full-blooded Oglala, another mixed race, and ten cows! And we just won't be able to have a half second alone."

He started to laugh, mounting up on Tor beside her.

"Lady Douglas, surely, you've heard! Where there is a will, there is a way. My dear, just where do you think little Indians come from?"

"You're impossible. You can't begin to think that we'll have a moment's privacy—"

"I imagine we'll have quite a bit of privacy, actually," he assured her. "There is no more beautiful country than that which surrounds the Black Hills, and I'd be greatly remiss if I did not see to it that you enjoyed the absolute glory of nature all around us."

"What an incredible man! You're ever so good to me!" she exclaimed sarcastically.

He walked Tor around her roan, facing her. "Well, Lady Douglas, I didn't want a wife, but I acquired one. And once something is in my possession...well, I do my best."

"Thank the Lord. In your possession, I just know that I'll be completely safe."

"Thank the Lord, indeed. I can promise you safety, my love, because I'd kill any man, red or white, who tries to take what is mine."

The intensity of his words sent a shiver of unease shooting within her. He wasn't a man to be crossed.

Well, she didn't intend to cross him.

"Aren't you in a hurry to get moving?" she demanded.

He shook his head slowly, a satyr's smile curving into his lips. "Not anymore."

"What?" she demanded.

"Not anymore."

"You've been as impatient as a prowling cat all day and now—"

He pointed to the sky. "The sun will be setting soon. We'll have to catch up with Willow and Sloan tomorrow."

"But—but—they'll be waiting. They'll be worried. They'll be expecting us, they'll—"

"I told Sloan that if we ran into darkness, we'd catch up with him tomorrow. They'll wait."

"But then—"

"We'll take a room at the inn."

"Tonight?"

His smile deepened. "Obviously, my dear."

"But—"

"Imagine! All that privacy!" he drawled with relish. "Hmm. Privacy and a wife who should be damned grateful at the moment. Oh, I should really, really like this night!"

# CHAPTER 14

"You should be hanged," Skylar muttered.

He arched a brow, looking at her with mock despair. "Whatever happened to 'Thank you, Lord Douglas, my dear husband?'"

"You know, Hawk, you have a nasty way of taking advantage of things."

"I intend to take advantage of things quite pleasantly, actually."

She groaned.

His eyes were green fire as he laughed up at her. "You were trying to say thank you properly, weren't you?"

She groaned again, allowing her face to fall against the roan's mane. He laughed.

"Come on. I'll leave you at the inn, then take the horses over to the livery stable."

Hawk came into the inn with her briefly. He apparently knew the round, very proper proprietress, Mrs. Smith-Soames, well enough because the woman was quick to assure him that she had the best room in the house available and that every amenity would be afforded them.

Skylar was left in the foyer with a cup of tea while Hawk's "customary requirements" were seen to. Hawk took the horses over to the stables. By the time Skylar had finished her tea, a maid appeared to tell her that her room was ready. She followed the girl, who was wearing a black dress and a perfectly starched white apron and cap, up the stairs to the end of the hallway. Double doors opened on a sumptuous room. A huge four-poster bed was against the far wall, a fireplace spanned half the opposing wall, and the largest hip tub Skylar had seen in her entire life, made of copper and wood, sat in front of the fire, steam rising from it in great waves.

"Lavender soap, Lady Douglas," the young maid said, setting a purple bar down upon a huge pair of bath sheets. "And sandalwood here, for Lord Douglas, of course."

"Lovely," Skylar murmured.

The maid moved across the room. "Mrs. Smith-Soames has sent up her finest champagne, ma'am. It's here, with glasses, and some chocolates, all with her fondest wishes for the happiness of your marriage."

"My marriage...oh, yes."

The maid smiled. She was a rosy-cheeked girl with a few traces of a British accent remaining. "If you need anything at all, there's a bellpull by the bed."

"Thank you so much."

The girl left her. Skylar restlessly moved about the room. She'd dressed for a night in the wilderness, and now suddenly she was standing on a handsome Persian carpet. Nothing had been what she had imagined since she had come here.

Did it matter? Her all-important wire was soaring across the country even as she stood there. Jim Pike would receive word tonight. He was so wonderful and kind a man, he would immediately find a way to reach Sabrina, who would be waiting, hoping...

By tomorrow, she could pick up her money and be on her way.

Skylar exhaled, moving thoughtfully across the room to the windows, opening the heavy velvet drapes that fell over them. She thought about Hawk and felt a strange quivering in her abdomen. She was somewhat alarmed to realize that she wasn't dismayed about being here. She wasn't dismayed about him. She was anxious...

Excited.

No, no, no, no, no, no, no...

Yes.

She frowned, realizing that she could see another establishment just across the yard. She could dimly hear the sounds of laughter and music coming from it. A window on her own level was open. A brunette in nothing but a corset and in the altogether was leaning out the window, laughing delightedly, calling out to a man below. A man who had just stepped out of the saloon next door to the inn and was now lighting a slim cheroot.

Skylar looked down. Her heart skipped a beat. Blood rushed to her face. The man was Hawk. He was staring back up at the whore, smiling, saying something in return.

The woman suddenly stared across the way at Skylar. She laughed harder.

Skylar let the drapes fall. She turned away from the window, incredulous. How long had he been gone? Had he been with the woman? Did he really think that he could just waltz from one woman to the next, from a whore to a wife? A wife he didn't want. Good God, when she'd been threatened with being forced away, it hadn't mattered what she had said to him. She'd told him that he could have whatever woman he desired, hadn't she?

But good Lord, she hadn't meant it! Well, perhaps she had at the time, but then she'd never imagined a marriage as intimate as the one they were sharing.

He could move quickly when he chose. Damned quickly. The door opened, and he walked in. He'd cast away the cheroot somewhere and entered, closing the door with a shove of a booted foot, folding his arms across his chest, his head cocked, green eyes on fire as he stared at her.

"Spying?"

"Spying!" she gasped out incredulously.

"Watching? I hadn't imagined you as the voyeuristic type, my love, but then, if there is a different entertainment that might amuse you..."

"It would amuse me to see you hanged and scalped!" she hissed. She wanted to walk out. He barred the door.

"What happened to 'thank you?'"

"I already said it."

"I thought you meant to show it."

"You shouldn't think."

"You shouldn't talk."

"It seems to me you've found appreciation elsewhere."

He arched a brow very high, then strode across the room to her. She looked for a way to avoid him. There was none. She backed herself to the window, then there was nowhere else to go. He kept coming. If the window hadn't been closed, she might have fallen right out of it. His hands fell upon her shoulders.

"Do you immediately think the worst of every man?" he demanded. "Or is it only me?"

She gritted down hard on her teeth. She shouldn't be goading him. He'd seemed in a strange mood since he'd left his private meeting with Henry Pierpont, yet she didn't think he'd learned anything about her. Still, he seemed dangerously tense. And still, she couldn't seem to control her own tongue. "I just saw you talking to a naked whore," she told him matter-of-factly.

"She wasn't exactly naked."

"She wasn't exactly dressed."

"Did you care?"

"Perhaps we are in the age of an industrial revolution, but I do not care to be part of an assembly line!" Skylar assured him.

He shook his head, laughing suddenly. "You want to be believed all the time, taken at face value! I don't know a damned thing about you or what really went on between you and my father, but you tell me that you cared for him, and I am simply to believe it. Well, my dear wife, I took our horses to the stable, I talked with old Jeff Healey, and I passed by the Ten-Penny Saloon to come here. You are now free to believe me, or not, as you choose."

"What if I choose not to?"

"It will make no difference to me."

She stared back at him, wondering in what way it would make no difference. Would he stay with her anyway—or would he choose to spend the night elsewhere?

Did the threat matter? She did believe what he was saying.

She simply wasn't convinced he cared enough about her or her feelings to lie.

"Do you know the naked whore leaning out the window?" she asked politely.

"I do," he acknowledged. Her lashes swept her cheeks. He emitted a sound of impatience. "I haven't been a married man that long, you know."

Her lashes fell again. He set his knuckles beneath her chin, lifting it, forcing her eyes to fall upon his once again. "I stabled the horses, I returned here. I'm going to go downstairs and ask Mrs. Smith-Soames to awaken us at the crack of dawn tomorrow morning. When I come back, I really would like not so much a proper thank-you but a bloody truce if nothing else."

"And if..."

"And if what?"

"If I'm not obliging?" she whispered.

He smiled. "That remains to be seen, doesn't it?"

He turned and strode away, leaving Skylar to stare after him. She bit into her lower lip, watching the door close in his wake.

For several seconds she stood very still. Then she suddenly began to kick off her boots, hopping about as she tugged off pantalettes and hose. She cast off her clothing, paused, folded it neatly. She didn't want it to appear that she had been panicked or rushed. She wanted him to think that the truce she had decided to grant him had been a careful decision.

Not a mad scurry of uncertainty!

She piled her hair on top of her head, securing it in a knot. Then she plunged into the tub with a washcloth and the lavender soap. She heard the door open and made a careful display of raising one of her legs and slowly, sensuously washing it.

To her amazement, she suddenly heard a very feminine clearing of the throat. She dropped her leg back into the water and turned around to stare at the young maid who had come back into the room carrying a tray.

The girl was blushing slightly. "I'm so sorry, Lady Douglas. Lord Douglas suggested I bring up a tray now in case you two get hungry later. I knocked, but you didn't hear me. I thought perhaps you had left the room as well. I didn't mean to interrupt you."

"You—didn't interrupt me," Skylar murmured, feeling very foolish. The girl scurried into the room, set the tray on a table, and scurried out.

So much for attempting to become something of a siren, Skylar thought. Maybe he had gone back across the way. To the half-naked, bosomy brunette.

"Truce?"

Her eyes flew open. Hawk was back.

He smiled, hunkering down beside her.

"I like you wet, you know," he told her. "It brings back fond memories of our first meeting. Is this a truce?" he demanded.

She nodded, then suddenly stretched out her wet arms, wrapping them around him. "I'm taking you at face value," she said quickly, earnestly. Then she felt the urge to back away from what she was beginning.

"Yes?"

"I'm—believing what you say to me." There could be no backing away now.

He nodded. "Yes?" There was the slightest trace of wry amusement in his voice.

"I just...I just want you to believe in me, too."

He nodded. He picked her up, wet and dripping, held her close to him, heedless of the soaking he was getting from her.

"Hawk?" she murmured insistently.

"I slay all monsters," he said.

"Promise?"

"I promise."

"No matter what they appear to be?"

"What do you mean?"

She shook her head. "Just...if I ever ask, give me the same in return."

"Skylar—"

"I swear, I believe what you say. Believe me in return."

He didn't reply. It didn't matter at the moment. He carried her to the bed, laid her atop it on her stomach. He kissed the entire length of her back, her nape...each little bone, the small of her back, her buttocks, the backs of her knees, of her thighs...

The clean sheets were cool beneath her. The feel of his flesh was fire. The touch of his lips a simmer that brought the blood racing throughout her body. Firelight crackled, the night air was sweet. She was drowning in sensation, sensual comfort...desire.

The firelight flickered. She came atop him, glowing almost as copper as he in the low-burning light.

He stroked her cheek, her collarbone, the valley of her breasts.

"I just have to find a way to be thanked more often," he murmured.

She smiled. His fingers threaded through the hair at her nape, and she rolled with him. It was their last night in civilization. A reprieve. She allowed the lure of sensation to sweep her into the sweetness of the night.

Morning always came too soon.

---

Senator Brad Dillman sat in his chair before the fire, staring at the flames. Night had come, but he wanted no other fight within the room. A blanket lay over his legs. He was warm and comfortable. And waiting.

Sabrina had been out, which meant something was going on.

They were sisters, but they were as different as night and day. Skylar could never control her temper. Sabrina could hide her every thought from the world. She could play any role asked of her, and at the moment, she was playing the role of dutiful daughter. At first, Sabrina had obviously been afraid that he'd call the police, report Skylar. Perhaps even have Pinkertons hunt her down. But now...

Now, she was simply...dutiful.

And waiting. He was damned well aware of it.

He shook his head. Fool girls, they could plot, and they could plan, and they could even run. But they couldn't run far enough or fast enough.

He heard the door closing downstairs. Very quietly. Sabrina was going out again.

He quickly rolled his wheelchair to the window and saw that Sabrina was indeed hurrying from the house. Furtively, of course. He didn't allow her to go out alone after dark.

But he certainly intended to let her go this time.

He spun his chair around and rolled quickly down the hallway to Sabrina's room. He quickly looked over his shoulder. She might well suspect that he would come here, even though she had been very careful not to make him suspicious.

Skylar had always proven to be trouble. He should have gotten rid of her when she was a child. The idea of killing a child had never disturbed him. General Sherman himself had said it best in reference to the Indian problem when the soldiers killed little ones by accident or design—nits make lice. However, with all the accusations she had thrown his way, it had always seemed best to appear the martyred stepfather. Now she had somehow made good an escape. He'd had his aides go through every train, ship, and stage schedule available, and they had found no trace of a Connor traveling, or even of a single female. He didn't know what she had managed, but one thing was certain—she would send for Sabrina. And when Sabrina went to her...

Well, now she wasn't a child anymore. But she still hadn't discovered what she was up against.

He'd find her.

And when he did...

She'd be easier to kill than her honorable damned father.

Where to look...

He smiled suddenly. High. If she'd had correspondence, she would have hidden it high. Where a crippled man couldn't find it.

He started to laugh.

Thirty minutes later, he was making his own plans for travel.

And though it was late, he was a senator. He had no difficulty summoning an aide and explaining that it was necessary his telegram get out that night. He was a part of the government of the United States, a lawmaker. If there was anything he could do to help his country in the current Sioux situation, he naturally had to become involved, no matter what personal dangers it might entail.

He slept very well that night.

Better than he had slept in a long, long time.

As he drifted into slumber, he imagined proving his power to her, taking his revenge.

He'd find her.

Oh, God, yes! He'd find her. And now he was close, so very damned close...

Bless her! She couldn't begin to imagine how damned close!

---

HAWK DIDN'T SEEM to require very much sleep. When Skylar awoke, he was up, bathed and dressed, sipping coffee. Late last night, they'd drunk the champagne and eaten the fruit, cheese, and bread on their elegant platter. Skylar still felt exhausted.

Hawk, apparently, did not.

She saw that he was losing patience waiting for her to rise. He was coming toward her. She remembered the less than dignified rap she'd received upon her person the morning before and rolled swiftly away before he could manage a repeat.

"Ah, you are awake."

"Is it really morning?"

"It was really morning when we actually went to sleep. Now it is really, really morning, and we have to get moving."

"Yes," she said. But she rolled again, closing her eyes. A big mistake. That less than gentle pat upon the rear came upon her, resounding in the quiet of the morning.

"Must you do that?" she demanded irately, springing up, clutching the pillow to her chest.

"Well, it does work."

"Well, I imagine one day it will work equally as well on you."

"I'm not terribly afraid of such a consequence, since it seems I'm the earlier riser. And I want to start on the way. Sloan and Willow will be anxious if we don't catch up with them soon."

"Now, why would they be worried when they might surely realize you spent a night in civilization?"

Something changed within his eyes. They glittered with a hard light once again when they had actually gazed at her with something akin to gentle amusement if not tenderness. In the pink filtering early morning light, his hair was very sleek and very black, his stance hard, his features chiseled. He appeared very much the Sioux, and one ready to do battle at the moment.

"We are leaving civilization now," he said, his tone harsh. He came to her, his fingers threading through her hair. "At long last, into the heart of enemy territory!"

"Are these people your enemies?"

"They are yours, aren't they?"

She lifted her chin, staring at him. "Do you immediately think the worst of every full-blooded white? Or is it just me?" she demanded.

He smiled slightly, as if he might almost appreciate the humor of his words.

"Things will change," he assured her. "They will change. I don't know where you've come from, other than that my father found you in Baltimore." He plucked up one of her hands. "But you've never known much hardship."

"Do you think the only hardship is to be found in the wilderness?" she demanded heatedly.

He arched a brow at her. "Want to tell me about it?"

"I can live with your hardships," she informed him coolly.

"Ah. Well, then, though I greatly appreciate your present lack of apparel, I'm afraid I must suggest that you put clothing on. I'll be in the dining room—I admit to liking morning coffee served to me with cream and breakfast. If you make it down soon enough, I'll even let you have breakfast as well."

"You are truly the finest of husbands."

"Take it while you can," he warned her. "Trust me, in Sioux country, things will change."

"Is that a threat?"

"Absolutely."

He left the room. Skylar was capable of being very quick—and she knew him well enough to take his threats to heart. The road might well be full of hardships, and she was certain she was as prepared for them as she boasted.

In fifteen minutes, she was downstairs with him in perfect repair, even her hair combed and simply tied back at her nape by a scarf. She thought that he might offer a glance of approval. H offered her eggs if she could finish them in another fifteen minutes. She gave him a smile in return, ordered eggs, bacon, ham, biscuits, and grits. She managed to eat somewhat daintily—and finish the entire plate within the time he had allotted her.

"Let's move. I want to catch up with Willow and Sloan before nightfall."

"Don't you have to go for the horses?"

"They're waiting outside."

"Our bill—"

"Is on account. May we leave?"

They rose to leave the Miner's Well, assuring Mrs. Smith-Soames on their way out that their accommodations had been excellent. Skylar was certain that the woman was still talking to them when Hawk drew her outside, nearly throwing her atop her roan.

"Come on," he said.

"Damn you, Hawk!" she grated to him. "You're in the most terrible hurry in the world until you decide to stop. You were rude to that poor woman—"

"I wasn't rude. I was on my way."

Dear God, but he was different by morning. Games were over. Playtime was done. She was furious. She wanted to protest his behavior anew. Now he was like the warrior, the stranger who had abducted her from the stagecoach. His mood and manner were wild.

He could hold her, and she could feel so close to him. So secure.

She could believe that he could keep all monsters at bay.

But now...

She didn't know him. He was different. He was a different breed.

Before she could offer another protest, though, he gave the roan a slap on the rump and they were suddenly racing out of the raw, tiny village of Gold Town as fast as they had come into it.

She looked back and shivered.

Aware that it was the last of civilization she might see for a very long time.

She was entering a savage land...

With a savage man.

Her husband.

# CHAPTER 15

By early afternoon, they caught up with Willow and Sloan.

They didn't pause long for any greetings but spent the rest of the day riding very hard.

In addition to the horses and the cattle, there was a mule in their traveling party that carried all the equipment they needed to camp out in the hills.

Skylar became acquainted with the stubborn creature not too long after sunset when Hawk and Sloan agreed to stop for the night. They were both familiar with the region, knew right where to find a beautiful, bubbling little brook with flatlands right around it sheltered by low-dipping trees.

Skylar was amazed when at last they stopped. She had ridden all her life and was a good rider, and she had never thought of herself as a person lacking in stamina, but she was so sore she was afraid she'd fall when she dismounted from Nutmeg. Thank God, for the absolute salvation of her pride, she didn't do so. In fact, none of the men even seemed to notice her discomfort, they were apparently so accustomed to such hard rides themselves. "We'll see to the cattle for the night," Hawk said, looking down at her from Tor's high back. "Perhaps you could get some coffee started."

She nodded. He'd made the suggestion politely enough. The brook was clearly in her view, and Willow, bless him, was starting to make a small fire.

"The coffee pot—?" she asked.

"Oh, in the pack. On Skeffington," Hawk said, gesturing toward the mule before moving on.

And thus she met Skeffington. As soon as she approached him, he turned. "Stand still!" she commanded the creature. She came around again. Skeffington moved in another half circle. "If you'd stand still, you'd be happier. I'd get those packs off your back, and you wouldn't have to carry them anymore!"

Skeffington apparently didn't care. He moved again.

"Skeffington, we have to make coffee."

The mule lowered his head and let out a loud bray. He'd been left untethered, and he suddenly started walking off, straight toward the water.

"Don't you walk off on me!" Skylar said, running after him. But Skeffington was already in the water. "Get out of there!" Skeffington ignored her. He was drinking. She swore and removed her shoes and hose, lifted her skirts, and went after him.

The water was icy. She stepped on little rocks. Her hem was quickly soaked.

"I wonder what mule meat tastes like!" she muttered fiercely.

She reached Skeffington and caught hold of his lead rope.

"Come on. You're not going to enjoy a drink or anything else until you learn to behave!" she threatened.

She tugged on the lead rope. Skeffington bucked his back legs and tugged in return. She redoubled her efforts.

"Hey! How's that coffee coming?"

She looked back at the left bank of the brook. Hawk was standing there. As she turned to him, Skeffington suddenly decided to come along. He did so with such an abrupt force that she was sent spinning forward, falling into the icy water.

As Skylar stumbled up, she was shivering wildly. As she found her footing, she saw that Skeffington was standing docilely on the bank, right next to Hawk. Wolf ran around the mule, barking excitedly, wagging his tail.

Hawk wasn't exactly laughing—his smirk was worse.

"Come out of there!" he told Skylar. "That water is cold."

Dripping, well aware that the water was damned cold, she walked from the brook. She passed by Skeffington.

"What about the coffee?" Hawk asked.

"Make your own damned coffee!" she retorted. She made her way to Willow's fire, hunching down before it, trying to warm her hands. A moment later Hawk was at her side, setting the coffee pot atop the blaze, then throwing a blanket around her shoulders.

She stood, allowing the blanket to fall.

"You know, you're as stubborn as that mule," he told her.

"You knew I'd have trouble."

"I know that you are an incredibly resourceful young woman," he told her. He rose, picking up the blanket. "I have more clothes for you. You don't need to freeze."

She arched a brow at him. "You—brought clothes for me?"

He shrugged. "I didn't know how well prepared you might be for this kind of ride."

"Thank you. I can prepare on my own."

"If you insist upon freezing, freeze!"

He left her. She heard him then with Willow and Sloan, back by the brook. She glanced toward the roan and her blanket roll where she carried her own change of clothes.

Not about to undress too close to the men, Skylar led the roan about a hundred yards down water from them. She paused there, looking around. The barest vestiges of natural light remained, softly glowing upon the landscape. It had to be one of the prettiest places she had ever seen. Here, where she stood, an outcropping of rocks rose high to her left, with the brook bubbling just to the side of it. Wildflowers grew around the rocks and trees in profusion, their colors a soft palette in the twilight. The night was cool but beautiful, the air incredibly fresh. She could immediately understand why this place was so important to the Sioux people. It did seem like a holy land, shrouded in natural beauty.

The roan suddenly hedged back on her, much as the mule had done, neighing, snorting restlessly.

"Not you, too!" she warned the horse. "So far, you've been an angel. No acting up on me now."

She glanced around, a feeling of unease settling over her. She felt as if she were being watched. No wonder the poor horse had been so skittish. "It's nothing, nothing at all." She lowered her voice. "Just another trick being played upon me, probably."

She sensed movement behind her, as if the rocks were coming alive. She spun around, still cold and shivering, feeling the dampness of her clothing more fully now with such a keen sense of discomfort stealing into her as well.

She wasn't alone.

Four braves had slipped down in silence and now stood on the ground, creating a semicircle around her. Despite the coolness of the night, they were dressed in moccasins, leggings, breechclouts, and paint. Their chests were bare, other than the designs sketched upon them in shades of yellow, black, blue, and red.

More of Hawk's friends! she thought, her anger simmering hotly. He didn't dislike her...hah! He didn't believe a word she had said about never hurting his father, and even if he had sent for Sabrina, he was still furious over discovering himself married. He meant to torment her until the end of her days. First the stupid mule and the icy water. Now this.

Well, she wasn't going to fall for any of it anymore.

One of them, the brave in the middle with several feathers plaited into his long hair, raised a knife to her, then his free hand, indicating that she should come to him.

"Oh, no. I don't think so!"

He frowned angrily, brandishing the knife again.

"You can stop it right now. You're not frightening me in the least. I've done this once already."

The men looked at one another, then all four painted faces stared back at her.

She walked up to the one closest to her on the right, a fellow with one feather stuck into his head of waist-length ink-black hair. He, too, lifted a knife to her threateningly. She struck out with her palm, hitting his arm with such force that she sent his knife clattering down to the rocks. "I said I've had enough of this! I've had this game played on me once before. I'm not afraid, and I'm not doing it again! You should all be ashamed of yourselves. Just what do you think you're doing?"

They had been quiet, almost uncannily so. Now the fellow toward the center with the most feathers started laughing at the brave whose knife she had knocked away. The other two joined in, coming behind him in a taunting circle.

"Fellows," Skylar said. "This is enough. You were great. You looked wonderful. But I've had it. Now..."

She broke off with a startled scream. The single-feathered warrior she had struck was now coming toward her, plucking up his knife and walking with menace. "You take it any farther, and I'll press charges, whether you're a friend of Hawk's or not!" she warned. "I won't be responsible for what I do to you. You could wind up hurt yourself."

Her threats didn't seem to carry much weight. The warrior kept coming toward her. "Stop it—I mean it, now!" An arm snaked out for her, dark fingers encircling her wrist and wrenching her forward. She let out a loud shriek, slamming her free fist against the brave's face while kicking him in the shin. The others continued laughing as the brave wrenched her forward, then dragged her back toward the center of their group.

"Let me go, I mean it!" she cried out.

Then she heard her name called. The sound of pounding hooves against the earth.

Hawk, bareback on Tor, burst into the clearing. He cried out words she didn't understand. He leaped down from Tor, pulling his own knife from a sheath at his calf as he faced the party of four, speaking again in an Indian language.

"I've told them to stop it," Skylar said. "I've told them that enough is enough, that the joke isn't funny—"

"It isn't a joke," Hawk said.

"But they're your friends—"

"Not even my acquaintances."

"But—"

"They're not Sioux, Skylar. They're Crow!"

"Crow?" she repeated.

She was wrenched around then by the Indian with the knife. Hawk came flying across the ground, tackling the Crow brave who held her. Freed from his touch, Skylar instantly backed up against the rocks. There were four Crow Indians. And Hawk. Where were Willow and Sloan?

The two men on the ground rolled furiously in the dirt. She heard a thudding sound. Both men were dead still. Then the Crow, who had been on top, slid into the dust, blood staining his bare chest. Hawk leaped to his feet. Even as he did so, Skylar let out a warning shriek. Two of the remaining braves rushed him then, their knives raised high, aiming to take his life.

She leaped to her own feet, searching the area frantically for a weapon. She found a heavy rock and lifted it, then threw it hard at one of the braves Hawk had pushed away from himself. She'd aimed for his head, but the rock hit him in the shoulder. He let out a bellow of pain, then struggled to his feet with fortitude, staring at her. He no longer seemed interested in the fight between Hawk and the other Crow. He lunged toward her.

She turned to run but tripped over the body of the dead Crow warrior. She landed next to him, staring into his open, glassy eyes. She shrieked out again in terror, trying to rise to her feet. The brave behind her caught her around her waist. She struggled wildly, kicking, flailing, screaming.

Nevertheless, she was dragged away.

The fourth warrior had apparently gone for the Crow ponies. Skylar suddenly found herself thrown atop one, with the Crow leaping up behind her. While Hawk continued in hand-to-hand combat with the Crow on the ground, the other two warriors began to ride, with her draped over one of their horses and her roan being led along. They paused long enough to try to steal Tor as well, but Tor would have none of it. He reared with such violence that the Crows quickly abandoned their attempt to take him.

Skylar screamed again as loudly as she could manage. She'd been so determined to put some distance between herself and the men! Now there was no one to help her. Hawk would be murdered, and she would be...

Crow.

She struggled to rise, but the Crow were excellent horsemen. The pony she'd been tossed upon was moving at reckless speed in the twilight, running ridiculously hard over land that was rocky, uneven, rising, falling.

Her head slapped against the horse's haunches. She tried to brace herself. She could see the ground moving, dust flying up from it. If she fell, she'd die.

What of Hawk? If he died, she realized, she'd be heartbroken. How insane! This had been his fault. Her fault, too. She'd left the camp. Because of the stupid mule incident. His fault. He taunted her constantly. His fault. Because she couldn't quite manage to tell him the truth. He'd never given her the benefit of the doubt. But he had been ready in an instant to risk his own life for hers.

Tears suddenly flooded her eyes. Was he dead? He had to be, or he'd be coming for her now. How did she know that he wasn't?

As they approached a high outcropping of rocks, the Indians reined in their horses. She heard voices, a number of them, excited voices. She was dragged down from the pony. There were more warriors here. She tried to count them. The two who had taken her and five more men. They encircled her and spun her around to face each of them. They were mocking her. tormenting her, she thought.

Yet she wasn't as terrified as she should have been. She had known this fear once before. And strangely enough, she was now more worried about what might have happened to Hawk than about anything that could befall her.

One brave thrust her toward another, and then another. She'd had enough. The next time she landed in a pair of arms, she kicked the brave in the shins with all her strength. He howled, raising a hand to strike her down.

It didn't fall.

A warrior whose face was painted black across the eyes suddenly grasped her. She struggled as he pulled her arms behind her back, tying her wrists securely. He issued a few harsh commands to the others, then dragged her behind the outcropping of rocks before thrusting her down. Though she could see a great deal around her, the rocks would conceal her from anyone coming from the east. She stared up at him belligerently. He made a sitting motion with his hands. She realized that she was to remain where she was. For the time being.

She leaned against the rock, closing her eyes.

How long did she have?

She opened her eyes. The last of the daylight had gone. Night had come. A full moon was rising, casting its glow over the beauty of the landscape.

She looked around her. The Crows were not far from her, on the flat stretch of plain on the westward side of the rock and cliff formation. They sat around a small open fire upon which two spitted rabbits roasted.

One lone warrior stood closer to the rock, a rifle in his hands. She strained to see what it was. It appeared to be a very old Enfield, a weapon she knew well because it had been in heavy use during the Civil War. It wasn't a repeater, but she had heard that soldiers good in the use of the rifle had managed to get off several shots in a minute during the war. It wouldn't compare with a six-shooter, she thought.

She wondered if he was waiting for his friend to return—or if he was prepared for an attack.

She sighed, closing her eyes again. She couldn't just sit there. She had to plan. Something. Anything. How could she plan? She was numb with fear and pain and worry.

She had to plan. Things could become much worse. These Indians might well decide to kill her. Torture her. Scalp her. At the very least, she'd be scraping buffalo hides for the rest of her days for the men who might very well have killed her husband.

Don't think that way! she warned herself.

She forced herself to watch the braves again. The two who had abducted her, it seemed, were acting out what had happened. The Crow who seemed to be the leader of their party asked questions. There seemed to be laughter, then sorrow as well, and then amazement. The leader with the painted face suddenly turned and stared at

Skylar thoughtfully. He smiled in a way that brought a new terror into her heart.

She had to escape. There was no reason she could not. She was not tied to the rock. Her wrists were merely tied together. If she could just free them...

Never. He had tied her with some kind of rawhide. It was very tight, chafing. Perhaps if she worked the strip of leather against the rock...

She did so. It was slow going, painfully tedious, but she concentrated very hard on her work.

She realized suddenly that someone was near her. She went dead still, slowly looking up.

He had come over by her, the one who seemed to be the leader of the war party. He hunkered down in front of her, a piece of the rabbit in his hand. He brought it near to her lips. Skylar stared at him and at the meat and shook her head. She thought that he might insist on her eating, but he did not. He smiled and shrugged, standing. He watched her curiously, then looked to the others, shook his head, and started to laugh again. When he walked away, she had the uneasy feeling that he would be back.

Hours crept by. The warriors continued to talk and laugh.

And wait.

Skylar kept working away at the rawhide bonds that held her.

She was very thirsty, but no one offered her water. Her shoulders and arms cramped painfully. She glanced toward the warriors, who were illuminated by the firelight, and saw that they all seemed very involved in their conversation. She inched forward, getting into position, rising on her bare feet. The earth was studded with pebbles, gravel, and stone. She wished she'd never shed her shoes to go after the stupid mule. Then she felt hysterical laughter bubbling inside her once again. She wished Hawk had never seen fit to leave her with the damned mule. She wished she'd never been so determined to be away from him. She wished that he was alive. Oh, God, she wished so badly that he was alive.

She wished that she would live as well...

The Crows still talked, bragging, she thought, of their own

exploits, laughing at the expense of the man she had struck, then mourning his loss as well.

She started to tiptoe away, heading for another rise of rocks back toward an easterly trail, praying that there might be somewhere in the formation of the rock and hill where she could hide. She had barely gone five feet when she became aware of movement.

The Crows.

The man with the black-painted face leaped before her, laughing still. He didn't seem to want to hurt her, though. He seemed far too amused by her.

When she looked over her shoulder, she could make out two of the other braves behind her.

She didn't want them to touch her.

She turned around and went back to the rock. One of the Braves stopped on his way back to the fire, crouching over her, touching her cheek. The man with the black-painted face spoke to him. He shook his head in disgust but left Skylar alone.

She leaned back against the rock in misery. The warrior with the black-painted face stood before her, holding what looked like a drinking gourd. Keeping her eyes on his, she accepted the water. So far, they had not harmed her. Hawk had not come riding over hill and plain to save her, but neither had the man he fought reappeared to join his war party. She couldn't fall prey to despair. She had to have hope. She had to live and escape these warriors. She needed water to live, and that was that.

The brave pulled the water gourd from her lips, tossing it aside. For another few minutes, he studied her. Then, to her horror and amazement, he suddenly grabbed her bare ankles, jerking her so that she was drawn down to lie flat on her back in the dirt.

She started to shriek. He clamped a suffocating hand hard over her mouth. With her hands still caught in the rawhide bands behind her back, she was almost powerless to struggle. His weight and form were between her legs, his hands were upon her, ripping her pantalettes. She tried desperately to twist and squirm, since there was no denying the man's intentions at this point. She could barely breathe. The pressure he put against her mouth was great. When she tried to rise, his weight merely pushed her back down. She could barely even kick or thrash, he had pushed her thighs so far apart.

His hand slipped. She bit into his fingers with a fury that drew blood and a curse. She saw his face lowering furiously before hers. He raged at her in his own tongue, still keeping his voice low. She inhaled to scream again, hoping that she might create trouble among the men, cause them to fight each other and forget her. She never managed to scream. The side of his hand clouted her head. She fell back, dazed, only very dimly aware that she was nearly stripped of her pantalettes.

Then quite suddenly, she saw a flash of silver. She stared at a knife. And that knife was set at the throat of the Crow on top of her. She looked up at a hard, bronzed, merciless face.

"Hawk..." She could barely form his name. No matter. Something inside of her gave rise to a staggering happiness. He lived.

And even as the simple joy of that thought filled her, her attacker was wrenched from atop her. The Crow faced Hawk, whipping out a knife of his own from a sheath at his hip. For a moment the knives glittered in the glow of the moonlight. Then there was no contest. Hawk moved like lightning. Again, his knife flashed. The Crow still held his high. The knife remained high in the air. The Crow fell forward, onto Hawk.

Hawk had given his combatant a chance. His ancient and traditional enemy slipped down the length of his body and fell dead at Skylar's feet.

It all happened so quickly. So quietly.

Hawk reached out for her, aware that her hands were bound behind her back. He plucked her up by both shoulders, spinning her around so he could cut the rawhide bonds with his knife. He paused for a just a split second.

"You'd nearly worked through them," he said, surprised.

Her knees were wobbly. She was afraid she wouldn't be able to stand, afraid that tears of relief would suddenly spill from her eyes. But he spun her back around again, staring at her, assessing her quickly and gravely.

"Are you alright?"

She nodded. "You came just in time."

"I've been here."

"What?" She almost shrieked the word before his hand clamped down over her mouth.

"I had to wait for a few of them to drift off!" he whispered in return. "I know that I'm just supposed to up and die for you, but it wouldn't have done you any good if I would have walked right in and been shot by the guard."

"All he has is an Enfield!"

"Enfields can kill! Believe me, I've seen a few men downed by Enfields!" he told her. "Skylar, we have to argue later. We've got to get out of here now."

He started walking, pulling her along. She stepped upon a particularly sharp rock, and despite her will to be silent, she cried out softly. He turned back, staring at her. "I'm sorry!" she hissed. "It hurt."

"What are you doing barefoot?"

"I was after your stupid mule, remember?"

Something suddenly whistled by her ear. A knife stabbed the earth by their feet.

"Sweet Jesus!" Skylar breathed. She gritted down on her teeth when Hawk pulled his Colt from the holster at his hips, quickly firing off several rounds. The reverberations were deafening. A cry in the night assured her that at least one of the Crow war party had been hit.

She gasped when he swept her up, carrying her then as he hurried away from the rocks. She swallowed hard as he stepped over the body of the Crow guard who had been carrying the Enfield.

"Duck!" she suddenly heard.

Sloan was before them, falling to his knees. Hawk went instantly downward to a hunching position. An arrow flew past them, slamming into a tree beyond. Sloan, still on his knees, fired off several shots. Skylar heard a shriek of pain. Hawk spun around, his Colt raised, just in time to stop the warrior who was about to pitch his entire weight against him. The man went down in absolute silence. Another warrior followed behind him, tomahawk raised. Hawk fired again. The second warrior fell upon the other.

Skylar closed her eyes tightly, biting back a wave of purely hysterical screams. God, the death and mayhem seemed to be all around her.

"Do we finish it?" Sloan asked.

"Do we have a choice?" Hawk queried in return.

Still clinging to Hawk, Skylar began to shake. She raised herself against him, grabbing his shoulders. "Let's go, let's just go—"

"Skylar, they'll come after us. All the way," Hawk told her.

"There can just be two men left alive. They—"

"Skylar, these Crow are very far from home. They were pushed from these lands a long time ago. They're on a war party. They've come for something. They may not be alone. There could be many more warriors who might join up with them. Perhaps they've come to raid the whites—to most Indians, there is far more profit in stealing from white settlements than there is in raiding other tribes."

"Let's just go—" she insisted again, but Sloan cut her off.

"Skylar, you don't understand. You humiliated that warrior who accosted you by the brook. You struck him. That was like a woman counting coup against a brave. He's dead, but sometimes humiliation is worse than death. Don't you understand? They might come after you until they've found a way to take you."

Her agreement or disagreement didn't matter anymore. Arrows suddenly began to land again, so near them that her skirt was shot through and pinned to the ground. Despite herself she screamed, only to find Hawk pressing her down to the ground and rising over her. He didn't get off a shot. One of the Crows threw himself against Hawk and then went rolling into the dust and earth.

"Stay down!" she heard Sloan command when she would have risen. The second surviving warrior came catapulting over her, striking Sloan. All four men were now engaged in life-and-death battles, rolling in the earth around her.

She couldn't stay down any longer. She jumped to her feet, then dove back to the earth for Hawk's Colt. How many shots remained? She had no idea. The gun seemed hot and heavy in her hand. She tried to aim it. She looked over at Hawk and one brave, Sloan and the other. They all twisted and rolled so frequently and so fast she was afraid to fire. She might kill one of them.

Hawk was suddenly on his feet, along with the one brave. They circled one another. Skylar raised the Colt. Just as the brave went rushing for Hawk, she fired.

She heard Hawk cursing. The brave was slumped against him. She shook, thinking she had killed the brave. Hawk pushed the man from him. He fell on his back, and she saw that he had been stabbed in the heart.

Hawk was clasping his arm. She saw him staring at her, but it was too dark to read his expression.

"I shot—"

"Me!" he announced. "Get down!" he suddenly commanded.

She did as she was told. She saw her husband's bloodied knife go whipping past her, just in time to prevent the last surviving Crow from bringing a rock crashing down on Sloan's head. Sloan, too, had been prepared. The Crow died with one knife in his back, another through his heart. Staring at him with horror, Skylar dropped the Colt and backed away, her hands upon her face as she fought the waves of blackness engulfing her.

"Uh-hmm!"

She drew her hands from her face. Hawk was coming toward her, one hand clasped over his arm. "Did you miss the man trying to kill me—or was your aim just a little off and you hit my arm instead of my heart?"

She rushed toward him, feeling absolutely hysterical at this point. She slammed both fists against his chest. "Oh, God, oh, God, how can you..."

"Hey! Shh...shh...it's all right, I was teasing. I think. Skylar, it's all right."

She buried her face against his chest. "It's not all right. There are dead men everywhere."

He lifted her chin. "Did you want us to be the dead men?"

She shook her head. "No!" Suddenly, no words would come. Shaking she threw herself against him again. Over his shoulder, she could see Sloan collecting their knives from the body of the Crow brave.

"Oh, God," she whispered again. "Can we go? Can we just go now, please?"

"Not quite yet," Sloan said. He had come to stand behind Hawk. He touched her cheek, offering her a dry smile.

"But—"

"We haven't scalped them yet," he told her.

"What?" she cried.

"Skylar, he's teasing you," Hawk assured her.

"Of course. Neither Hawk nor I have scalped an enemy in almost twenty years."

Hawk disengaged himself from her. "Skylar, we're going to bury them."

She looked at him uncertainly. "Indians don't—get buried, do they?"

Sloan cast Hawk a glance. "Sometimes. Most Plains Indians scaffold their dead, but occasionally, the dead are buried in shallow graves near cliffs. Not that that particularly matters at the moment. We don't want what happened here to be obvious to other warriors who might be meeting up with this war party."

"Oh," she murmured.

"Think you can watch the horses?" Hawk asked her.

She nodded. She didn't think that the horses were going anywhere; Hawk and Sloan just wanted to keep her busy.

She started to walk with Hawk again and winced, her feet in desperate pain by then. He picked her up again, telling Sloan briefly that he'd leave her with the horses and be right back. He carried her to a cove of trees just fifty feet down a slope. Among the trees stood Tor, Sloan's horse and her own roan. He set her down atop the gelding. She stared down at him.

"You got the horse back from the Crow?" she said.

He patted the roan's neck. "Nutmeg is a fine animal," he told her. "Important to me."

"You got the horse back before you came for me?" she whispered.

A smile twitched at his lips. "We didn't know how many braves there were here. And we didn't want to be followed. The Indian ponies are scattered ahead of us. We'll take them to my grandfather's band along with the cattle."

"You rescued the horse before you rescued me?" she repeated.

Again, he laughed. "At least I didn't shoot you."

"Oh!" She was about to ask after his wound, but it was still too galling that the horse had mattered more than her.

"You went for the horse!" she repeated.

He shrugged. "Among the Sioux, one man's family may pay a husband with a horse if one of their kind steals that man's wife. Both are actually property."

"I should have aimed better!" she warned him.

But he still smiled. He stood very close to her, his fingers moving very gently over her injured foot. "Sloan went for your horse and the Crow ponies," he told her. "I came straight for you. I watched, and I waited. I told you before, my love, that I'd kill any man, red or white, who threatened to take what was mine."

She felt very warm suddenly, still shaken by the events. His voice had been very intense. She wanted him closer, yet she was suddenly so afraid in a different way that she wanted to back off as well.

"So," she murmured lightly, "did you kill them for me, or for the horse?"

He reached up, touching her cheek. The moonlight caught his eyes, and they glittered strangely against the rugged lines of his handsome features.

"Both, my love," he murmured. "Both."

He turned and left her, ready to join Sloan for their burial detail.

# CHAPTER 16

When they rejoined Willow, he had moved their camp farther northwest and alongside a different little stream. The eight Crow ponies they'd taken were tethered with their own, and the cattle were gathered in a makeshift corral.

The coffee was perking away. They had Meggie's biscuits, along with a few waterfowl Willow had snared. Skylar also took a huge sip from the bottle of brandy Hawk had handed her. When they had finished eating, Willow on watch all the while, she realized that Hawk was staring at her, smiling slightly.

"Smudge on your nose," he told her.

She lowered her lashes, biting her lip. Smudge everywhere, she thought. Her clothing was torn and dusty.

"Stream's just about thirty feet down that way," Sloan said.

"Want to wash up?" Hawk asked her.

She nodded, rising.

"Want some fresh clothes?" he asked her.

"I brought my own," she told him.

"Ah," he murmured, nodding. She thought that he was smiling again. She pointed to her blanket bundle, lying now near a tree next to her roan's saddle.

"Allow me," Hawk said, going for the bundle. He took her arm. Sloan, nibbling at a blade of grass, lay back against his own saddle, smiling slightly as they left.

When they reached the stream, Skylar knelt down, sliding her fingers into it. She shivered. The water was cold.

Hawk was behind her. "You don't have to douse yourself in it," he told her, handing her the bar of sweet-scented soap he'd taken from her bundle.

She shook her head strenuously. "I do!" She could still feel the touch of too many hands upon her. Maybe he couldn't understand that. Maybe he could.

She stood, stripping quickly in the cool night, and plunged into the water. Gasping and shivering, she scrubbed herself with the soap. Hawk waited beside the stream with a blanket. When she couldn't stand it anymore, she rose.

He clasped her with the blanket, wrapping it around her and pulling her close to him. Despite the warmth and the comfort he offered her, she was shivering wildly.

"There were so many dead men!"

He sighed, running his fingers over her hair. "We are warrior societies," he told her. "Crow boys grow up knowing that they will fight, that they might meet death in battle or on raids. They are a very brave enemy. Sioux children are also taught that they must fight their enemies. Neither are they afraid of death."

"They are harsh societies."

"It can be a harsh world, Skylar. I entered a white war where brothers fought brothers, fathers might have faced their own sons. Can our battles on the plains be any more harsh?"

She fell silent, then whispered, "I was so afraid."

"It's over."

"The one with the black-painted face. He might have—"

"He wouldn't have. Skylar, I was there. Yes, I was watching, taking care. Assessing their strength and trying to give Sloan time to get the ponies. But I was there. No matter when he might have tried to touch you, he couldn't have done so. He was doomed by his very interest.

Come on, let me help you get dressed. Sloan will take second watch, but I must take third. We need to get some sleep."

She was still cold, but she managed to stop shivering long enough to let him help her slip into the new chemise, pantalettes, and dress. He noticed the red rings chafed into her wrists by the ropes. He pressed his lips against the pulse at one of her wrists and then at the other. "Do they hurt?"

She shook her head, pulling her hands back. "What about you—where I shot you?"

He smiled, shaking his head. "Flesh wound. You barely grazed me."

"Let me see it."

He sighed, pulling back the ripped flap of his shirt. She had just grazed him, but there was still a nasty gash on his arm.

"It doesn't look good—"

"I washed it out with whiskey. It's fine."

"At least bandage it up!" she said, reaching into her blanket bundle for a cotton handkerchief. She soaked the material in the cold water before binding it around his arm. She didn't meet his eyes as she went about the task. She was afraid he would try to stop her.

She tied the cotton securely around his arm and then started to turn back toward their camp, hoping that Willow had retrieved her shoes for her. She suddenly felt Hawk's hand upon her shoulder, drawing her back around.

"Was it different?" he demanded.

She shook her head, at a loss.

"I don't know what you mean."

His tone remained somewhat harsh. "Was it different? You were hauled off by a brave before. Attacked."

She tried to pull her arm free. He wouldn't let her go. She couldn't meet his eyes.

"Yes!"

"Yes?"

"Yes, it was different."

"How?"

"Some—how. It was always different. You were different. Then you were speaking. And you—"

"I what?"

She looked up at him at last. "You gave me a choice," she said.

He shook his head. "But it wasn't really a choice for you, was it? You were staying here, no matter what. Because you weren't going back."

"But that was my choice. You—you were my choice!" she said, and she tried to wrench free from him once again. But he wasn't letting her go.

He swept her up. She struggled briefly against his hold, then met his eyes. She ceased to struggle.

"Feet still hurt?" he asked.

She nodded.

"We'll hurry home then. My aunts will have salves to heal them."

We'll hurry home...

He said nothing more as he carried her back to camp. He laid out their blankets by their saddles. He rested his head upon the seat of his. His chest was her pillow. He wrapped his arms around her protectively. He smoothed back her hair. His touch was almost...

Tender.

She was exhausted. And despite the trauma she'd suffered earlier in the night, she began to drift.

We'll hurry home...

Home.

Home to him was still among the Sioux.

She wondered a little bit wistfully if home to him would ever mean her.

She was riding with Sloan the following day when he suddenly turned and told her, "There are good things about the Plains way of life as well, you know."

Startled, she looked at him.

"Few people make better parents than the Sioux," he continued, gazing her way. "They are generous to a fault, finding the only good in collecting material possessions to be in the act of giving them away. We cherish the wisdom of our aged and take the greatest care of them."

"We care for our aging people!" she protested.

He looked at her.

"Most of us do," she said.

He smiled.

"You said 'we,' you know," she told him. "A cavalry officer who considers himself one with the Sioux."

He shrugged. "Striped like a zebra. What can I say? I'm telling you this because you seemed so appalled last night. Glad to be rescued—yet almost as horrified by your rescuers as you were by your kidnappers."

"That's not true at all," she protested. "I just—Sloan, I've just never seen such bloodshed."

"I'm afraid there will be a great deal more of it on the plains," he said matter-of-factly. "Bad things happen."

"I didn't say that I've never seen bad things happen," she murmured. "Sometimes I think that I've seen the worst. Just not so much...blood."

He glanced back at her again sharply. "So life in the East was wretched, eh?"

She smiled slowly. "We were talking about the West."

"But we can talk about the East. How did you and Hawk wind up married? I hadn't heard a word about it. And suddenly, a bride appears. A stunning beauty, at that, like a princess out of a fairy tale."

"Hawk hasn't told you?"

With a devilish grin he leaned toward her. "There were rumors, you know. Tales about a woman arriving claiming to be Lady Douglas yet seeming to have no idea that there was a Lord Douglas, or at least a live one. Now, one could think that you might have been an impoverished beauty, cast upon hard times, seeking whatever fortune the wind might blow her way."

"I see. You think, too, that I somehow took advantage of Lord David Douglas?"

"Not in the least," Sloan said, and she was surprised to realize that he was speaking honestly. "David might have been ill, and we might not have realized it. He was a man of great strength. If he chose not to reveal a weakness to others, then no one would know about it. But he was no fool. No young woman, no matter how lovely, could have taken advantage of him."

"Thank you."

"I didn't mean to be insulting."

"I really meant 'thank you.' I didn't take advantage of him, nor did I ever try to."

"Agreed."

"Between us."

"Ah! You think your husband assumes otherwise."

"I know so."

Sloan was quiet for a minute. "He loved his father, you know. In a way you may not even be able to understand. Hawk judged David wrongly for a very long time. When a man has done that, he owes a great deal to the man he has misjudged. In David's final years, they were very close. If he judges you harshly, it's most probably because of the pain he feels himself. Then again..."

"What?"

"Well, what is your story, Lady Douglas?"

She smiled because he could so charming. He was a hard man, almost ruthless at times, yet he could be so kind when the occasion demanded it.

And damned persistent and cunning when he chose as well.

"Long and complicated," she said simply. "Let it suffice to say for the moment that I meant Lord Douglas no harm, that he was my dear friend, and that I cared for him deeply." She felt herself blushing. "Not in that way," she amended.

Sloan laughed. "I imagine David took one look at you and knew that you'd be just right for his son."

"But I'm not, am I?"

Sloan reined in his horse suddenly, facing her squarely.

"More right than you may ever realize. You haven't passed out on us once yet, have you?"

"Well, once."

"And when was that?"

"When Hawk told me that he was Lord Douglas."

Sloan laughed, then laughed harder. He nudged his horse, cantering on ahead of her. When he had gone, she rode a few steps in puzzlement until she realized that Hawk had come from behind to ride with her.

Sloan, apparently, meant to keep his laughter to himself.

"Well," Hawk commented, moving Tor along next to Nutmeg, "at least you seem to get along well enough with my friends. Enjoying the ride?"

There was a slight edge to his voice. For the moment, she decided she'd enjoy it. She smiled. "It's very beautiful here."

"Wakan Tanka lives here."

"The Great Mystery?"

He nodded.

"Do you believe that? You gave your father a Christian burial."

He shrugged. "My father was a Christian."

"And you?"

"Among the whites, I'm a Christian. I believe in a power greater than man. You may call him God or Wakan Tanka. And all men are his creatures, no matter what their color may be. When you see this kind of beauty on earth, then you must believe in a god. Do you?"

She nodded. "Definitely. And in all the powers of good—and evil."

"Heaven and hell?" he inquired.

She nodded.

"Evil spirits?"

"Evil," she told him softly, "lies in and is created within the hearts of men."

"Red men?"

"Perhaps—if they are the same as white men."

"Imagine," he murmured to her. "Something we agree upon."

She smiled, then laughed. It was amazing, but the fear and terror of last night seemed so very far away.

"Of course, among the Sioux, Wakan Tanka is the Great Mystery. But the Sioux have many gods, and they are all very colorful."

"Are they?"

He nodded gravely. "There are four superior gods beneath Wakan Tanka. They are Inyan, the Rock; Maka, the Earth; Skan, the Sky; and Wi, the Sun. They all have very special responsibilities. Beneath them are four more gods, associate gods, because they all associate with one above them. Wi's associate is Hanwi, the Moon. Tate, the Wind, is associate to Skan, the Sky. Whope is the associate of the Maka, the Earth. Whope is the daughter of the Sun and the Moon and is known as the Beautiful One. Wakinyan, the Winged, who cries out like thunder and has eyes like lightning, is the associate of Inyan, the Rock. Make sense?"

"I suppose...what a world!" Skylar exclaimed, gesturing at the clear blue big sky and the magnificent land.

"Many Sioux feel that they have the world. The sky, the sun, the earth, the beauty of the land around them."

"The land they are losing?"

He nodded gravely.

"What will happen?" she asked him.

"The government has determined that the American people must have the Black Hills."

"And?"

"They will have them."

"But if an agreement can be reached—"

"There have been dozens of agreements. None has ever been worth the paper it was written upon. Yes, the Indians have committed atrocities upon the whites, and indeed, the whites have practiced tremendous cruelty as well. One wonders if any man's god is looking down at all of this. Personally, I think that a time has come when there will be a great deal more tragedy before another 'agreement' is reached."

"So then—"

"So then I'm here with Sloan because we always try for peace, the least possible bloodshed. It's the best that anyone can do."

He smiled ruefully at her and nudged Tor's ribs with his heels and started riding hard, cantering ahead of the cattle to ride alongside Sloan.

That night, when they stopped to make camp, Skylar took it upon herself to tie Skeffington securely to a tree. The mule still twisted and wiggled to elude her, but Skylar was determined she'd not be gotten the best of by a mule again. She had Skeffington's packs down and the coffee perking before the men returned from caring for the cattle for the night. No one, however, seemed to expect her to know how to cook over an open fire. It seemed to be Willow's task to prepare their meal, but Skylar had never minded cooking, and she made herself available to Willow to help in any way she could. They hadn't hunted that evening, so they warmed some of the food Meggie had packed for them. Ham, beans, and corn muffins, warm against the coolness of the night.

Yet even as they ate, and even if it appeared that they were all relaxed, Skylar was aware that either Sloan or Hawk was standing at all times, that they were both well-armed with their Colt repeaters and knives, and that, though they didn't seem to expect an attack, they intended to be prepared should one come their way.

"Do you think there are more Crow near us?" Skylar asked Hawk, trying not to sound nervous.

"Not now," he said, shaking his head and taking a seat beside her while Sloan rose and leaned against a tree as he stared out at the night sky. "We're very close to the Crazy Horse people."

"How do you know?" she asked.

"The trail."

"The trail?"

He smiled. "Men have hunted through here. Many men. I don't know what those Crows were up to, coming so far east. But this would be a very dangerous place for any Crow right now, so close to a large Sioux encampment of warriors."

She shook her head. "I'm sorry, but it's all still so confusing. Some of you get along, some of you don't. The Crazy Horse people hate the whites so much that they won't go to the agencies to talk, but both of you, with white blood, can go to the Crazy Horse people!"

Hawk glanced up at Sloan and shrugged in a way that assured Skylar that both men believed there were things she just would never understand—she wasn't one of them. But Hawk tried to explain.

"Each man is an individual among the Sioux. He has his own path to follow. No man can tell another man what his path is."

"So anyone can do what he wants to do at any given time?" she asked.

Hawk shook his head. "Most of the time, men and women desire to live up to certain mores that rule our society. There are four great virtues we strive to achieve: bravery, fortitude, generosity, and wisdom."

"Naturally," Willow offered, "they are virtues which helped us to survive through the years."

"Naturally, a warrior must be brave. He must defend his home, be a great hunter, and take many coup against the enemy," Hawk said.

"Coup?" Skylar murmured.

"Coup—unfortunately, taking coup has sometimes hurt us in warfare," Sloan said. "Coup is what you took against that Crow yesterday."

"What?" Skylar demanded.

"You struck him," Hawk said. "In battle, it is a braver deed to come close to the enemy and strike him than it is to shoot him down from a great distance. Very often, in battle, the Sioux are determined to count coup, and so they come close and strike their enemies, but in so doing, fail to eliminate some of their numbers."

"Whereas white soldiers know damned well they can be killed by tomahawks, rifles, and arrows and are determined to kill the enemy who are carrying those weapons with all possible speed," Sloan continued. "In our system, officers must achieve great victories in order to rise through the ranks."

"Or beyond. If the rumors are true, Autie Custer is trying for one great victory over the Sioux so that he can run for president of the United States, become the Great White Father, and keep his promises to his Crow scouts and others," Hawk said, his voice carrying a definite note of irritation.

"A Sioux doesn't need to seek a great victory. He needs to lead a continually brave life," Sloan said. "Taking coup is part of the bravery of battle. And last night against the Crows, you, a woman, struck a warrior. They were still talking about it when we arrived on the scene. It was a great humiliation for the warrior."

"But it made you a greater prize of battle," Hawk murmured, throwing a stick onto the fire.

"Any warrior can instigate a war party," Willow said. "And those who choose to follow him may do so."

"If a man chooses not to follow a war party, then that is his prerogative," Sloan said.

"However," Willow continued, "during important movements, hunts, or major battles, the akicitas must control the young braves who might jeopardize the party by seeking to break early and count coup or rush the buffalo for the first kill."

"The akicitas?"

Hawk looked to Willow and Sloan, then lifted his hands. "Indian police."

"Who change with the wind."

"I'm lost again."

"They are chosen from the warrior societies, but the head men choose warriors from different societies so that no man may have too much control over others."

Skylar smiled. "It all sounds very democratic."

"It is a free society," Hawk said softly, "and that is often the best of it, and the worst of it."

"What do you mean?"

"He means," Sloan said, "that in the army, the generals give the orders and privates obey without question. No one chief can command hundreds of braves if the braves do not choose to follow him."

"The people who have banded together with Crazy Horse have done so because they have chosen to do so," Hawk said. "And when we visit there, although we have chosen to enter the white world, we don't visit there as whites."

"So what am I?" Skylar demanded.

Hawk lifted his hands and looked to Sloan as if he were again seeking the proper explanation. Then he stared at her and shrugged. "Property," he said complacently.

"You're not serious—"

"You will own the tipi," Sloan assured her, grinning.

"She'll have to make it first," Hawk reminded him. "And she'll have to remember as well that women have their place. They serve their men, then dine themselves."

"Oh?" she said.

"You may need to be careful. Wife-stealing does take place, though it is a shame upon those who indulge, unless, of course, a man is so powerful that the warriors around him are willing to let their wives go."

"There have been such occasions," Willow said.

"But sad ones as well!" Sloan commented. "Think of what it cost Crazy Horse when he fell in love and ran away with No Water's woman."

"Of course, he failed to pay No Water for the woman," Willow reminded them.

"Crazy Horse was shot in the face, and his family was shamed. Thankfully," Sloan said, "his family did not seek retaliation for the shooting."

"And neither was Black Shawl harmed," Hawk reflected, smiling at Skylar. "She could have had the tip of her nose sliced off—it would have been her husband's right."

Skylar had had enough. She stood, angry with the lot of them. Hawk had been almost charming himself that afternoon. But no more. He, Sloan, and Willow might well be telling her the absolute truth, but in the telling, they were very definitely taunting her.

She tossed the rest of her coffee into the fire, dropped her camp cup, and started off on a walk toward the water.

"Skylar!" she heard Hawk call sharply.

She ignored his call, bristling as she hurriedly walked along the trail, pulling her cloak around her. The moon remained round, lighting the path well. Only the trees around her were shrouded in shadow. Not far ahead, she could see the glowing patterns of moonlight dazzling and rippling upon the stream by which they camped. The sky itself as well as the landscape seemed to be reflected there.

It isn't my world! she thought furiously. Damn him! She'd done her best, she was here. She'd come with him into uncivilized country. She'd been abducted by enemy hostiles. She'd even made the damned coffee.

She kicked the earth furiously.

She was still paying.

She reached the water's edge and squatted, scooping up a handful of the cool, clear water with which to bathe her face. Her touch broke the soft rippling reflection, sending small waves shooting out against the night-darkened stream. She cooled her cheeks again, wondering why she was so angry when they had all probably been speaking the truth. It was the way they had spoken it. So mockingly. No matter what price she paid, it didn't seem that Hawk could forgive her. Right now, she hated him because of it.

And she hated herself for caring.

The rippling waves she had created began to ebb. A huge, dark shadow suddenly appeared on the water. She watched the shadow in honor, panic rising within her. The Crow. The Crow were back again...

She leaped up, a scream of terror forming in her throat.

She'd walked away again! God help her, couldn't she learn to be angry and stay where she would be safe?

She spun around, ready to lash out, scream—run.

"Skylar!"

Her scream faded. Relief filled her with such force that she trembled with it.

Hawk stood behind her, his shoulders broadened by his cross-armed, irritated stance.

"What?" she demanded, trying hard not to gasp or to betray how very afraid she had been. She kept her distance.

She saw that he was trying to control his temper, grinding his teeth, relaxing his jaw once again.

"You can't keep walking off."

"There was little reason to stay," she replied.

He lifted his hands. "There are certain things which are true in Sioux society. I cannot tell you differently."

"I'm afraid I know nothing about making a tipi."

"We'll be staying in my grandfather's home." He stretched out a hand to her. "Come back to camp."

She didn't accept his hand. "I'm glad I'm not a Sioux," she told him coolly.

Again, she watched him struggle to control his temper. He dropped his hand and spoke with impatience. "Again, you fail to understand. We are all people. A Sioux wife is sought by her husband, cherished by him. Though mores may be different in different human societies, emotions remain the same. A wife cares for her husband and children. In return, she is defended. And loved. And her children will love her, and when she is widowed, her family will care for her, her husband's friends will give to her and honor her in his name. She is free to laugh, to excel in her arts, to seek to love and be loved. Know pride. She has little need for deception or cunning."

"Unlike a white woman," Skylar commented.

He said nothing.

"Unlike me."

He continued to stare at her. She fought the tears that threatened to roll down her cheeks. She gritted down on her teeth, realizing with a flash of insight that she had actually hurt him first. She had attacked what he was. He had attacked in return. She wasn't up to the battle.

"I shouldn't have forced you to come," he said.

"But you did."

"You have a talent for goading my temper."

"You have a talent for goading mine."

"You chose to come west."

"Yes, but I—" she began, yet broke off quickly, not at all certain of exactly what she had been about to say.

"But you didn't choose me," he finished.

It wasn't what she meant at all, but she couldn't seem to find the words to say so. Even when it seemed that peace between them was within reach, she somehow seemed to lose grasp of it. His fault as much as her own, her heart cried out.

"You're the one who doesn't want a wife," she reminded him lightly.

"But I've got one. And this is my life. Which you have chosen to join, since I did give you the opportunity to go back." Again, he stretched his hand out to her, palm upward. "Let's go back to camp."

She hesitated.

"Damn you!" he swore. "I offer you what I can."

"And maybe it is not enough."

"And maybe you'll have to give more to get more."

"What could I possibly have left to give?" she cried out passionately.

He arched a brow, startled. "The truth," he said simply.

"I haven't lied—"

"And you haven't given."

"You're wrong! I have given. I have given more than I had ever imagined I was capable of giving. There's nothing—"

"There's something. But I don't think even the Crows could torture it out of you." He lost patience and grabbed her hand, starting back along the trail toward their camp.

"The Crows!" she hissed. "You're probably far better at torture!"

"We do like to think ourselves superior to our enemies," he retorted.

"And am I your enemy?"

"You're my wife."

"But unwanted. So surely, there are times when you must forget that fact!"

He stopped walking so suddenly that she plowed into his back. The buckskin of his shirt smelled good. The feel of his strength, his warmth against her was still somehow reassuring in the wilderness despite the hostility of the words passing between them.

She stepped back, looking up at him, meeting his eyes, as he turned to her.

"Not for a second, my love. Not for a single second. And let me warn you. There'd best not be a single second you forget it either."

"Is my nose at peril?" she demanded.

He arched a jet-black brow. "Your nose? How ridiculous." He caught her hand, drawing her suddenly hard against him as he stared down at her. "Now, come along," he told her again. Then he smiled, a menacing glitter in his green eyes.

"Squaw!"

# CHAPTER 17

They reached the camp of the Crazy Horse people during the late afternoon of the following day.

For many hours before they had actually come upon the camp, Skylar had felt as if there were the slightest change in the breeze, as if the trees could see. Sloan assured her that they had been watched for a long while. Before they actually reached the camp, a warrior rode up to their party. He frightened Skylar because at first, to her, he looked just like the men in the Crow war party. Hawk seemed impatient that she could not see the differences in paint and manner of the Crow and Sioux, but Sloan assured her that men who had ridden with cavalry for years did not always learn the fine distinctions between many of the Plains tribes.

It seemed to Skylar that there were hundreds of tipis, lodges as Hawk called them, stretched out along the river. There would be hundreds of Sioux here. Indians. More than she had seen in all her life. She didn't want Hawk to know that she was afraid of his people.

But she was.

The warrior who had ridden out to meet them was his cousin, Willow's brother, Ice Raven. As they entered the camp, children gathered around them, scampering beside the horses, laughing all the while. Women, working by their tipis, cooking over fires, sewing hides, paused, looking up with the same avid curiosity. Men and women called out. Hawk, Sloan, and Willow responded. They stopped before a large tipi in the center of the camp. Hawk dismounted from Tor. Willow and Sloan followed suit, greeting the tall, straight man with long, iron-gray hair who stood there. He was old, Skylar thought. Very old, yet he appeared to be in good health. He was proud and dignified, captivating in his stance.

Hawk, Willow, and Sloan all greeted him the same way, taking his lower arms as he grasped theirs in return. Children, women, and some of the braves gathered around behind them. Hawk called out to some of the older boys, and they came over and took the cattle and ponies from their party. Skylar suddenly felt the old man's eyes on her. She returned his gaze, at a loss for what to do.

But by then, Hawk was beside her, lifting her from Nutmeg, speaking to the elderly man as he did so. He nodded gravely, watching her, then indicating the flap opening to the tipi. For the moment, Hawk's arm was around Skylar's waist. She hoped he would stay with her for a while.

"I have to go. You must stay with my grandfather while I'm gone."

"That's your grandfather?" she whispered.

"Yes."

"He's—fierce."

"He won't hurt you."

"I didn't say he would. I just...I don't speak any Sioux. Do you have to go now?"

Hawk laughed. "Now you're suddenly eager for my company?"

She flushed. "I—"

"You don't need to be afraid."

"I'm not."

"You'll do fine."

Hawk's grandfather stepped aside, and Hawk ushered Skylar into the tipi. He wasn't going to come in with her, she realized. He was determined to leave her to her own resources with his fierce-looking grandfather remaining at the entrance to the tipi. She straightened, still afraid despite herself. She was startled at first by the size of the tipi. Then she was further alarmed to realize that there were people inside it.

Indians.

An old woman with white hair sat near the center of the tipi. She sat not cross-legged but with her limbs folded beneath her. She sewed fine turquoise embroidery into bleached-white buckskin. It would be a beautiful garment, Skylar thought. A robe of some sort or perhaps a dress like the ones most of the women were wearing. The old woman looked up at her. She nodded as if she had expected Skylar and was not alarmed or even disturbed by her presence.

Besides the old woman, there were children in the tipi.

There was a girl of perhaps eleven or twelve, a boy of maybe eight, and four very little children—one a baby in a cradle board, two toddlers, one a bit bigger. She wasn't even sure of the gender of the little ones, but as she stood there, the twelve-year-old girl offered a tentative smile, and the little ones, except for the babe in the cradle board, started coming toward her.

The girl's smile encouraged her. She ducked down, ready to greet the children.

They literally crawled on top of her. She laughed, falling back on the ground. One of the toddlers laughed with delight then as well, and the others joined in. She plucked up the erring fellow who had toppled her, setting him down at her side. The girl came to her then, smiling tentatively again, and speaking in her own language but making a drinking motion Skylar couldn't fail to understand.

"Water, yes, please," Skylar said.

Hawk's grandfather entered the tipi. He watched her, his eyes dark and fathomless, his face deeply lined by time and the elements. She drank the water offered to her from a gourd and thanked the girl and then Hawk's grandfather. One of the babies found a tortoiseshell comb in her skirt pocket. She drew her eyes from those grave ones of the old brave and showed the child what the comb did, laughing as she drew it through the babe's dark hair, then offered it to the little one. The child watched her with enormous, almond-shaped dark eyes. Beautiful eyes, in a face filled with wonder. Skylar bit her lower lip suddenly, remembering accounts she had heard of Indian babes being killed when the soldiers had triumphed over the bands. It had seemed so distant then, so real now. The children were beautiful.

No one had a right to slaughter innocents. Cherubs like these. Little ones who smiled, laughed, gurgled, reached out to be touched, expected love. She shivered suddenly. She looked up at the old Indian brave. And as he looked down at her, she felt that he knew what she was thinking. She couldn't talk to him. She didn't know a word of his language. But he seemed to understand her thoughts. He smiled, and somehow, they communicated.

And she wasn't so afraid.

The old woman spoke very quietly to the man. He shrugged, then looked at Skylar again.

"Deer Woman would ask if you are you hungry if she could. She does not speak your language and so cannot."

"No, I'm—" She broke off, startled. Hawk's grandfather spoke English quite well. Regaining her composure, she wondered if it would be rude not to accept something to eat. "Perhaps, I'm a little hungry. Only if it is no problem..."

Her voice trailed as he turned back to the white-haired woman. She rose, setting her work aside, and left the tipi. She returned with a bowl filled with meat in a thick juice. Skylar thanked her and tasted the meat, hoping that she would find it good and that she wouldn't embarrass herself further by choking it down—or worse, being sick.

The food was delicious. She arranged her legs beneath her the same way she had seen the white-haired woman do as she ate, aware that the children continued to play with her comb as she did so.

Hawk's grandfather sat before his fire, gazing at her.

"Your feet are hurt," he said.

"Just a little sore."

"Deer Woman has salve for them."

Skylar straightened her legs so Deer Woman could reach her feet. As the woman gently tended to them, Hawk's grandfather continued to speak to her.

"You came from the East?"

"Yes."

"Married to Hawk?"

"Yes."

"How?"

"I—I met Hawk's father there."

The old warrior nodded as if her explanation made perfect sense to him when no one else had ever really understood it. "David found you for Hawk."

"I—yes," she said simply.

The old man smiled.

"What do you think of us?"

The blunt question threw her. "I...I don't know yet. I have just come here. I know so little and I'm trying to learn so fast. I think the children are beautiful."

"Good. I am their great-grandfather. Four of the children belong to Pretty Bird, Hawk's cousin, sister to Blade, Ice Raven, and Willow. Two belong to their brother Red Fox, who died in battle."

"I'm so sorry."

"Thank you. So what do you think of us?"

"I think...I think that I still have a great deal to learn. I know that Sioux must be brave, strong, generous, and wise. I hope that you'll be —generous with me. I—" She broke off again. "What do you think of me?" she asked him.

He was a great deal like his grandson—noncommittal. "I have much to learn," he said.

She smiled, lowering her lashes, nodding and accepting his words.

"What do you want me to think of you?" he asked.

"I—I want you to like me," she admitted.

"Because of Hawk?"

She looked at him, hesitated, then nodded.

He smiled and told her, "My English is good. My grandson and my son-in-law taught me to speak English. I do not share the fact that I speak it often."

"I will never tell anyone," Skylar promised.

He nodded sagely, then shook his old head as if in disgust. "I'm glad that you wish to learn. The whites, they are so quick to judge us. They think of us all as one out here on the plains. They talk of us being savages. You cannot imagine the things that have been done." He lifted a hand, indicating the slim, immaculate white-haired woman with her neatly tied braids. "Deer Woman lived among our allies, the Northern Cheyenne. They are a people who call themselves the Human Beings, a fine people."

She smiled. "Naturally, they are a fine people. They are your allies."

"Yes. Good people. Our allies." He had a wonderful smile. A strange wisdom. He could laugh at himself while speaking the truth with all seriousness. "The whites often say that the Sioux are the most warlike tribe on the plains. We didn't seek war with them. There were things that we were promised. Certain lands that were to be ours until the grass no longer grew, the wind no longer drifted and bellowed over the plains, the sky was no longer blue. Cheyenne camped along the Washita at peace. The women worked with their awls, and the men cleaned their hunting rifles. The winter snows were on the ground. Children played, babies cried. The white soldiers' bugles started to call. Their horses were racing through the snow, dozens and dozens of them. They pounded into the village, shooting, clubbing, setting fire to tipis. They didn't care if they shot warriors, ancients, children, women, babies. Deer Woman's daughter was killed with one child in her womb, one in her arms. The blood spilled over the snow in great pools. If we are savage, then what are whites? Deer Woman was left for dead herself. There were few survivors. So you see, granddaughter, we are all many things, and I am glad that you have eyes to see beyond what one sees first."

"Thank you," she murmured.

The old woman, Deer Woman, finished with Skylar's feet and looked at her. She went away for a moment and then returned and hunched down before her, pressing the beautiful garment she had been working on into Skylar's hands and talking to her. Skylar looked at her, listening. The woman spoke kindly, but Skylar had no idea of what she was saying.

Hawk's grandfather interpreted for her.

"Deer Woman says you must take the dress."

"Oh! It's beautiful. But I couldn't accept it—"

"You must accept it. You have brought us ponies and cattle. The ponies are survival, the cattle are a feast. You will wear the dress and accept the other presents the woman have made for you."

"The women?"

She heard a giggling. There were a number of women at the entrance to the tipi. They had been there, peeking in, watching her, she realized.

The pretty girl who had kept the children occupied while she ate rose, laughing. She drew Skylar to her feet and led her out of the tipi.

The women touched her, spinning her around. For a moment, there were so many of them, reaching for her hair, her gown, that she felt a rise of panic. She'd heard what Sioux women could do when torturing prisoners or stripping the bodies of dead enemies.

But these women were giggling, not hurting her. Perhaps, somewhere in the village, there would be those who might despise her for what she was. But these women offered her no malice. They were curious. She wished desperately that she could speak with them, know them, know their lives.

Suddenly, her arms were caught, and she was led forward.

And shown her present.

She gasped, amazed, touched. She thanked them profusely. And she was certain that they understood.

---

BECAUSE THEY WERE SIOUX—SIOUX who were also wasi-chus, white—and because they had just come from their other world, Hawk and Sloan, who was called Cougar-in-the-Night among his father's people, spent several hours engaging in the purification rite of the sweat bath, inipi. They atoned there for whatever wrongs they might have committed and cleansed themselves of outside forces.

When they were done, they dressed in breechclouts, leggings, and moccasins, and prepared for their official visit to Crazy Horse.

Crazy Horse awaited them with He Dog, one of his closest friends and supporters. They all greeted one another as old friends, with restrained pleasure, as was the Sioux way.

Because they had come to speak, Hawk and Sloan sat on either side of Crazy Horse. Willow, Ice Raven, and Blade joined the circle as well. First, Crazy Horse lit his pipe, which he shared with the others in the spiritual way. After they smoked, Crazy Horse's wife, Black Shawl, and her mother, who lived in the tipi as well, served the guests food, well-prepared buffalo meat which was sweet and rich. Only when they had finished and complimented their host on his hospitality did it become time to talk. And it was Crazy Horse who began.

"I know why you have come. Sioux have come from the agencies as well. Men from Red Cloud, who once fought the whites so vigorously, now tell me that we can never best their numbers."

"Red Cloud has been in Washington, and yes, he has seen that the whites are incredibly numerous," Hawk said.

"The white settlers are a wave, a great wave, spilling over the country," Sloan said.

"Throughout my life, we have gone through one treaty with the whites to the next. We have told them where they must not build their railroads, then we have watched as their railroad builders have come anyway, protected by the white soldiers. We have often asked before attacking why they are where they have promised that they will not be. The Black Hills are Sa Papa. The whites were not to be there. Cougar-in-the-Night—your army was to keep the whites out of the Black Hills."

"My army despairs. They attempt to stop the settlers. But there is gold in the Black Hills. When white men get gold fever, they can't be stopped."

"Red Cloud's opinion is that the Black Hills are already lost," Hawk told him.

Crazy Horse waved a hand in the air. He looked from Sloan to Hawk. "You live at the base of Indian lands. Your father, the man we called the white Sioux, lived there in peace. He made use of the gold he found only where he knew he did not trespass on holy land. Why can't the rest of the whites understand this? We've listened when they speak. 'The railroad must be here.' They bring their railroad. We've watched them, we've waited. Nothing is ever enough. They always demand more. They claim that they are at peace and raid Indian villages. Where will it end?"

"It won't end," Hawk told him truthfully.

Crazy Horse smiled. "You came to ask me to come in and listen to the whites' words about buying the Hills."

"Yes."

"Are you asking me?"

"I'm asking you."

"But you know I'm not coming."

"Yes, I know."

"So, the invitation is given and refused. Cougar, you know as well that this is true. You can return to your army with the assurance that you have done all you could do. I will not see the whites. I will not agree to sell the Black Hills. Perhaps the whites swarm over them. It is not with my agreement. I promise no safety to the whites there. Or here. The white man has asked for war. I try to keep my distance from him. When he steps on me, then I must throw him from my back. That is the way that it is."

"Perhaps bloodshed can still be avoided," Hawk said.

Crazy Horse stared straight at Sloan. "The army wishes us all dead."

Sloan shook his head. "Not the army," he said. "But yes, there are men, some of them generals, who want the Indians gone. They cannot kill the agency Indians because there will be a terrible outcry among Americans back east if they hear that peaceful Indians are being murdered at the agencies."

"And will that matter?"

"Yes," Sloan said, "Because among the whites...well, among the whites, the Americans, men who want power must be granted some of it by the people around them. To become really great chiefs, they must be elected by the people. To some people, a great victory against the Sioux would enhance a man's favor. But equally, Crazy Horse, there are gentle people among the whites. Many people, like those who said that black men should not be slaves, who don't believe that any human being, living at peace, should be murdered."

"So you think I should try for peace and forget what the whites have done to me and my people?" Crazy Horse demanded.

Sloan shook his head again. "No." He stared at Crazy Horse. "I hate what has been done. I am disgusted by the slaughter that has befallen so many of our Plains brethren. Crazy Horse must fight if attacked. With Sitting Bull, Gall, and others, you are the backbone of our people. Maybe the time will come when the Sioux will be so outnumbered there is no more choice. Now I know that to hold against the whites is the only choice you can make."

Crazy Horse smiled at Hawk. "He is not a white man."

"In his way, he is. The words we bring to you are important, but those we bring back from you are equally so. Cougar will tell the army that Crazy Horse is strong, that many Sioux—and allies!—stand with him. And it is hoped that the army generals will tell the white fathers that they cannot steal the hills as they have stolen so much else. Yes, the whites swarm there now. But perhaps the Sioux will benefit because a line will be drawn and a price will be paid."

Crazy Horse shrugged. "The army will ride against us, but that time has yet to come. When it does, we will make a stand. Hawk, you have brought your new wife?"

He nodded, taken aback by the abruptness of the question. Crazy Horse seemed intrigued, but Hawk was aware that his old friend meant as well that they were done discussing the business of the Black Hills and the council the whites—and Red Cloud—had been so anxious for Crazy Horse to attend.

"I have."

"She came here willingly?"

Well, willingly wasn't quite right, but he hadn't actually dragged her either. He'd threatened to, of course.

They'd bargained. But he wasn't accustomed to lying in Sioux life, and neither was he ready to speak the truth.

He frowned instead. "We had trouble coming here. A party of Crow warriors attacked. They were very far east. I don't remember the last time I saw Crow so deep into Sioux land. They seized my wife. We followed and seized her back."

"And the Crow warriors?"

"Are dead."

"I'd heard you brought Crow ponies."

"Yes."

Crazy Horse glanced at He Dog. "I don't understand this either, why the Crow would attack a white woman on our hunting grounds, and when she was so close to her own people. The Crow tend to become scouts for the whites—against us. It's very strange to me." He shrugged. "There was an incident, though. Some young Oglala bucks rode out to raid a Crow camp not long back. They stole a number of ponies and the daughter of a Crow war chief. The girl wanted to be stolen. She is now the wife of Stands-Against-Darkness. But perhaps Crow warriors are riding in revenge. They cannot attack our camp here. There are too many of us. But you must take extra care when you ride back. Perhaps you had best gather more braves to ride with you when you leave here."

"Cougar, Willow, and I are accustomed to taking care of ourselves."

"But you are riding with your wife. Her hair alone, I understand, might be considered a great prize to any man. You are white—and Sioux. You are Thunder Hawk, a brave who took many coup against them, even as a young mixed blood. Sometimes, though, that blood can tell. You cannot see danger as clearly as perhaps you should. Your wife would be a very great prize to a Crow."

Hawk inclined his head. "Crazy Horse, you grow richer in wisdom each year."

"His wife counted coup on her own against the Crow," Sloan said. "She fought them, struck them."

Crazy Horse arched a brow at Hawk. "It's good that you killed them all. Is she that fierce? A brave woman. One who fights to protect her home and children. Bravery is as commendable in a woman as in a man."

"Oh, she is brave. She's very fierce!" Willow said, a smile tugging at his lips. Hawk noted that his cousin refused to look at him, but he did refrain from telling Crazy Horse that Skylar had fought him with just as much vehemence as she used against the Crow.

He forced a smile to his lips. "She's a dove," he said. "An absolute dove."

Crazy Horse smiled. "I have learned not to steal wives. I am happy with Black Shawl. I wish you happiness. You, too, have suffered the losses of many loved ones. I am glad of your wife—even if she is white.

And your children...they will be so white." He said the words very sadly. "I am anxious to see your wife."

Hospitality was very important. Though Hawk had his own home in the white world, here, among the Sioux, his grandfather's home was considered his as well.

"Will you eat with us tomorrow?" he asked Crazy Horse. Crazy Horse would want to see not just what his wife looked like, but he would want to judge her "wifely" attributes as well. He wouldn't expect her to be an expert tipi maker or skinner, but he would certainly expect her to make a good meal. Skylar was a good cook. She had made a delicious soup the night he had discovered they were married. He just wondered what her reaction would be when he told her they were having Crazy Horse to dinner. And that she was to serve but not eat with them.

Skylar would be receptive, he determined. She had to be. And if not... He remembered the gut-wrenching feeling he'd experienced when the Crows had taken her, the agony of watching her touched by another, fear, fury. Longing. Hurting. Wanting. He hadn't wanted a wife. Truth. He didn't want one now. Lie. He wanted his wife. He was tantalized, captivated by his wife. Holding something...and still not knowing what he held. She had sworn she never meant to hurt his father, and he believed her, believed her to such an extent that he was sorrier than he could ever say for whatever fear and humiliation he had caused her in the certainty that she had. Yet, God! He wanted something from her, something he couldn't shake, drag, or demand. He wanted to understand her, wanted to know what was driving her, what made her ready to cast her fate to the absolute horror of himself. He could still see her face when she had looked up at the Crow who had attacked her. She had looked at him the very same way.

Because he was Sioux. That fact hardened his heart each time he found himself too enamored of the perfect beauty of her face, the softness of her hair tangled against him, the silk of her skin against his own...

If the Crows had taken her, he would have spent his life killing Crows. Every last one. Until he perished himself. He didn't want to shake her, strangle her. Beat her. Hurt her.

Hmm.

Bribery remained.

He smiled. "I'm very anxious for my friend Crazy Horse to see my wife. You will come?" Even if Skylar proved to be difficult, they'd be in his grandfather's home, with his grandfather's wife, to help.

"I will come," Crazy Horse said. "We've known you would come, of course. Many of the women have wanted to make you especially welcome here, should you bring a wife. They have made a special tipi for your wife. I'm sure that they have shown it to her by now and that she will await you there."

"A special tipi of her own," Hawk said and smiled. He inclined his head. "How very generous."

Crazy Horse inclined his head in turn, offering Hawk a shrugging smile. "It is our way."

"It's our way," he said.

"No wife yet for you?" Crazy Horse asked Sloan.

"There are too many women for a Cougar-in-the-Night," Willow teased.

Sloan shrugged, his dark eyes inscrutable. "Ah, well, wives and women! They are like the sun, eh? Beautiful, dazzling...burning. One must always take care. No wife for me, Crazy Horse."

"And no children," Crazy Horse noted sagely.

Sloan smiled ruefully. "You're right, my friend."

They rose then, bidding one another good night, all of the guests leaving Crazy Horse's home.

Night had come. The air was crisp and cool, stars dotted what appeared to be a never-ending velvet and ebony sky. It was stunning country, cloaked in a beautiful night.

As they stood just outside Crazy Horse's home, Ice Raven pointed in the direction of the newly made tipi the women had given to Skylar. "Sleep well, cousin!" Ice Raven told him. He clapped him on the back, turned, and started toward his sister's. His brothers followed him.

"Hmm. Nice place. Just a bit different from Mayfair, but then, it is completely hers. I did tell her that the tipi was the wife's property, didn't I? How convenient. You'll get to be alone when you tell her you're having Crazy Horse to dinner!" Sloan told him, smiling.

"Every single god out there will do something evil to you, Sloan!" Hawk muttered.

"It's a hell of a night. A hell of a night! Because just think of it. You've given her one hell of a time," Sloan said.

"I haven't really had much choice," Hawk muttered.

"You bet!" Sloan said. He was still laughing, Hawk thought, but then Sloan suddenly sobered, shaking his head to the sky above them. "Actually, I envy you the night!" he said lightly. "Good night, Hawk."

He turned and followed Hawk's cousins.

Fires blazed outside tipis. Smoke rose into the night sky. The breeze just stirred the dirt on the ground, and the stars burst down on the river.

Hawk hesitated just a moment longer.

Then headed for his wife's new home.

# CHAPTER 18

It was an extremely handsome tipi. The women had done an exceptional job with it. It had been sewn from bleached-white buffalo hides, and someone with great artistic skills had painted his life upon it, his days as a child, his participation in the Sun Dance, his coups against the Crows. Scenes depicted his departure with his father, his "white" war against his own people, his marriage and loss, his years at Mayfair—his arriving home to his grandfather with a new wife. It had all been very beautifully done.

Yet standing in the center of the tipi, having studied the pictographs, he felt a moment's sharp dread and a simmer of defensive anger—he was alone. She wasn't there. She had run somewhere.

But then his eyes adjusted to the hazy firelight, and he saw that against the wall of the lodge there appeared to a long bundle. It was a sleeping robe, and someone slept within it. His wife. The hour had grown very late, though he had not realized it. He had spent a long time in the sweat bath, and a far longer time with Crazy Horse than he had realized.

He approached the sleeping robe—warning himself that he couldn't just assume that the body was Skylar's—she might have disappeared, and an old friend might have found her way in here. But when he knelt down, he saw the stream of blonde hair flowing over the buffalo robe and he sat back on his calves with relief. As he did so, she stirred, turning within the robe restlessly, trying to kick it aside. It was warm within the lodge. A fire burned in the center—set there by someone who had known what he or she was doing—and she was dressed in doeskin as well, a beautiful dress, expertly embroidered and cut. As he studied the garment, surely from the talented hands of Deer Woman, her eyes suddenly fluttered and opened.

She stared at him, her eyes widening. For a moment he thought that she was going to scream, and he belatedly realized how he was dressed himself, still in breechclout, leggings, moccasins, and no more.

"It's me, Skylar," he said quietly.

She nodded, staring at him, still struggling to awaken.

"You survived the day, so I see."

She nodded again, still studying him.

"And my grandfather."

"Your grandfather was very kind."

"He is a great man. A wise one." He waited, curious as to what she would tell him. "And his English is much better than he is ever willing to allow others to know, so I'm sure you had no difficulty understanding him."

"I had no difficulty understanding him."

"And no one scalped you."

She shook her head. "But I have seen..."

"What?"

She shrugged. "I have seen a number of white scalps tied to poles in front of tipis."

"It might surprise you to discover that certain men in the cavalry collect Indian scalps."

"No," she informed him. "Very little surprises me anymore."

He offered her a dry smile. "You do have your own home in the West now, you know. The tipi is yours. If we were to divorce one another, it would remain yours."

"Does one easily obtain a divorce?"

"Very easily."

"And not so among the whites!"

He shook his head, staring into her eyes, and wondering what thoughts really played within her mind. Tonight she seemed strangely vulnerable. Perhaps it was the golden flow of her blonde hair over the doeskin of the dress. Perhaps it was the shadowy light within the lodge. Perhaps it was even the fact that he had caught her asleep, that she hadn't had time to gather all her defenses against him. He knew that he was going to touch her. Knew that he wanted her that night, that he would have her. And in the same breath of hunger, of rising passion, he knew that he wanted to hold her as well, throughout the night. Cherish her.

Protect her. From whatever it was that she had needed to escape. From the fears she would not admit. The past that had driven her here.

"No. Divorce is extremely difficult among whites."

"Yet you are among the Sioux."

He laughed softly. "Yes. A Sioux would never conceive of obtaining a wife unseen, that words on paper could make a woman a man's wife."

"The Sioux would surely Have a point," Skylar murmured.

"Perhaps," he murmured, amused. "But then, a Sioux can acquire a wife just as strangely."

"How so?"

"If a man's brother dies in battle, he is obligated to take on his brother's wife. Or wives."

"And if he already has a tipi full of his own?"

"The tipi gets fuller. Of course, both parties must find it a satisfactory agreement, and a wife may thank her brother-in-law, applaud his sense of responsibility, and choose to go along on her own. As sometimes happens."

She was watching him very gravely.

He leaned down on the ground next to her, stretched out on his side, and propped himself up on an elbow. "Had you and your sister been Sioux, I'd be acquiring a second wife right now." He wondered if she might betray a sliver of jealousy. Her silver-gray eyes continued to study him quite seriously without the least hint of inner turmoil.

"I did tell you that you might like Sabrina."

"If you say so, I'm convinced that I will."

"Are you considering more than one wife?" she asked politely.

"I didn't want one, remember?"

"But now we are among the Sioux. Since you are burdened with one you don't want, you might be considering taking on a second wife you do want."

"And you would share the tipi?"

She smiled sweetly. "Never. I would be long gone, Lord Douglas."

"What if I chose not to let you go?"

"We're in Sioux country. You'd have to let me go."

"I beg your pardon?"

She flashed him a quick smile. "I am learning Sioux ways. A very great warrior is too important a man to be bothered by a woman. A Sioux leader as respected as yourself would have to allow his wife to leave if she chose to do so. Your pride would surely dictate that you not be disturbed by the comings or goings of someone so inconsequential as a wife."

He grinned, watching her, shaking his head. "Perhaps that is the Sioux way. But don't forget, my love, that men are men—red or white—and that passion and jealousy are human traits. Dangerous, combustible traits. And on this you may rest assured. In my mixed-blood way of thinking, white or Sioux, wives can be troublesome. I cannot imagine more than one—at a time."

Her lashes swept her cheeks. She was still smiling. Then she suddenly stared at him with a pained curiosity.

"You had a Sioux wife and she died. What—happened?" she asked him.

He sighed, unwilling to dredge up the memories now. "Smallpox."

"I'm so very sorry."

"It was a long time ago."

"Still, you seem to be in pain. I am truly sorry."

"And I told you," he said, wondering why he was growing so irritated, "it was a long time ago." Yet the last time he had lain in a tipi with a woman, it had been with Sea-of-Stars. She had been learning to speak English because she'd been aware that he was a different man with property in the white man's world, and she had wanted to be all things to him. She hadn't wanted to visit Mayfair until her English was fluent, but she'd happily listened to him talk about his home, his father's property in Scotland, anything that interested him.

"I could take a walk," Skylar suggested. "Perhaps you'd like to be left alone."

"What?" he demanded, startled.

Sea-of-Stars was gone. He had loved her for her gentleness. Yet he suddenly realized that he'd never felt as passionate about any woman as he felt about Skylar. The two women could not have been more different. Sea-of-Stars had been as dark as Skylar was fair. Sea-of-Stars had believed that whatever he said was right, whereas Skylar would fight tooth and nail for her right to have her own opinion. He had indeed loved Sea-of-Stars. He had suffered her loss and the loss of their baby greatly. For a long time, he had dwelled in bitterness and somewhat relieved the pain of his grief by casting himself into the current conflict between the Sioux and the US government. Sea-of-Stars had been part of a different time. Life itself had seemed shaded in pastels and comfortable earth tones, the colors of the grass and the trees, the hills and the sky. Now life itself seemed much more vivid, the color of blood, and the crimson flow of the tide that was destined to run around them. Likewise, it seemed, his emotions regarding Skylar were equally vivid. From the moment he had first seen her, she had both angered and aroused him, and each of those strong emotions had only intensified since then.

Skylar stood, the white buckskin dress with its beautiful embroidery hanging in soft fringes to her calves. Her feet were bare. Her hair was tousled. The firelight played upon all the vivid colors that were here: gold, silver—even white. Shades of crimson and sunset were cast upon her. The night was cool, yet a certain warmth was captured within the tipi. He rose to stand before her, a brow arched.

"The tipi is yours," he told her.

She flushed with a half-smile. "Yes, but I can be generous, living among the Sioux."

"There are some matters of generosity I haven't quite learned myself."

She arched a brow.

"If you were to walk from here, where would you go?"

"I...walking!" she said simply. "Perhaps to your grandfather's, perhaps to see Willow or Sloan."

"I think not. I could not dream of being generous with a wife."

Her eyes narrowed sharply. "Generous in what way?"

"My friends and family must find their own women."

"Don't you dare be wretched," she warned him. "I'm out here at the very ends of—"

"Civilization?" he queried.

"Amid hostiles, and you're the worst of them!" she assured him.

"Want to lose a nose?" he taunted.

"Want to lose something worse?" she countered quickly.

He laughed aloud, arching a brow high once again.

"I'm trying to be decent," she assured him. "I believe you're feeling the pain of your past tonight. I'm trying not to intrude on your memories. I didn't mean to come into your life, hurt you worse—"

"You didn't mean to come into my life—or have me in yours."

"You twist everything!" she accused him. "I was trying to leave you alone—"

"But I don't want to be alone." He wasn't quite sure what it was in his tone or perhaps even in the way that he looked at her, but he somehow disturbed or startled her.

She took a step backward, tripped over the sleeping robe, and landed hard on her back and buttocks upon the hide-strewn ground. Not one to lose an advantage, he quickly pounced on top of her, straddling her hips. The buckskin dress had slid upward when she fell so that his thighs embraced bare flesh. The soft brush of her blonde triangle teased against his own flesh made bare by the briefness of his breechclout. A shudder ripped through her, yet she stared up at him quite defiantly as he smiled, threading his fingers through hers before pressing her hands to the earth by her side. He leaned low, his lips just inches from hers as he asked her politely, "Now, just what was it you intended for me to lose?"

"You think you've got me down, don't you?" she queried.

He looked at his position and hers. Shifted slightly. Felt the rub of her flesh, her softness.

"Quite frankly—yes."

"Your time will come."

"I'm planning on it," he assured her.

She shook her head and sighed with exasperation, but her eyes were bright, filled with laughter as well as irritation as she tried to ignore the sensuous fire that was being stoked between them. "I was truly just trying to give you time to think—"

"I don't want to think."

"Ah! That's right!" she murmured, staring defiantly into his eyes. "You like—" She hesitated, swallowing. Every ounce of sensation within him must have been vividly clear to her at that moment. "—the nights," she finished a little breathlessly. Then added, "Even in a tipi."

"Especially in a tipi. I love the scent of the earth. The feel of the night. The fire so close that you lie right beside it, feel its heat on your flesh..."

Flesh...God, he could feel her flesh!

"Isn't...isn't there some sort of a taboo against such things while you're in the midst of important male discussions?" Skylar queried sweetly. She shifted slightly. The dress rose higher.

"Though there are many things I find exceptionally admirable about my mother's people, I am also quite glad at times to be white. Sioux braves believe that intimacy with their wives weakens them when they are about to go into battle. Before they leave on a war party, they abstain from sex and go through various purification rights. Often, when I'm among my Oglala brethren, I try to do as they do."

"Do you?"

He smiled at her, moving his hand from hers to draw a strand of hair from her face. "Ah, don't sound so anxious, my love! You see, a meeting is quite different. There is no war party being planned for the moment. And if there were...the white half of me just wouldn't feel the need for abstinence."

"No?" she whispered.

"No." With his free hand he removed the breechclout and tossed it away.

He was probably lucky it didn't land in the fire.

Didn't matter at the moment.

She mattered.

He shifted his position, thrusting his knees between her thighs, lowering his face very slowly to hers, meeting the silver glitter in her eyes all the while. His mouth touched hers. He ran his hand down the length of her thigh, from her knee to her buttocks, shoving the buckskin dress still higher, caressing the soft, firm flesh of her derriere, lifting her. He thumbed the soft petals of her sex, teasing, stroking, parting. Thrusting. Finding the perfect place.

He had ceased kissing her. Her eyes were closed, her lips parted. Her breath came in ragged bursts. She tossed and writhed, set her hands upon his shoulders to push him away, to stop the seductive movement of his fingers. Her eyes opened, and he smiled, as pleased as a wildcat with its prey. He shoved her knees higher, shifted his weight once again, and thrust within her with the fullness of his sex, sinking until she had taken him completely inside her, holding there as their eyes locked, and smiling once again before beginning a slow, torturous movement, building, blinding, becoming thunder, hammering in his ears, throughout him. His body quickened, stretched, reached, and seemed to...explode.

Long moments later, when his heartbeat and breathing had slowed to something of a normal rate, he rose from her side, stripping off his moccasins and leggings, and tugging gently upon the garment she had smoothed back down over her hips. "That dress is really beautiful," he said, running his finger over her cheek, then down upon the embroidery at the bodice. "Deer Woman's work?"

"Yes," Skylar said.

He leaned close to her. "I'm glad that you accepted the present so graciously. But you needn't wear a dress into a sleeping robe." He smiled, thinking that the Sioux sleeping robe, a huge blanket that swept around the body bringing comfort and warmth, was a wonderful invention. Two in a robe was incredibly intimate. He caught her about the waist, lifting her, drawing the gown carefully over her head and folding it before setting it aside. She sat, watching him gravely, at long last seemingly comfortable with him in her nakedness. The low-crackling firelight played upon her shoulders and breasts, bathing them in the soft crimson fire. Her hair was touched by it, too, her breasts, half-shadowed by the dance of the fire, peeked out from swirls and waves of golden hair. Silver eyes studied him gravely from the classical perfection of her ivory features, so out of place among the Sioux, yet so strangely in tune with the setting.

"It's quite amazing," she told him.

"What's that?"

"Your tender care of that beaded dress!"

He reached out, drawing her down beside him. She offered a token resistance, sighed with impatience, and allowed him to press her back down against the soft hides and furs that made their bed.

"Deer Woman worked very hard on that gown."

"What if a good, honest, hard-working maiden aunt had worked very hard on the black gown you so quickly destroyed the day we met?"

"Had there been a good, honest, hard-working maiden aunt to make you such a gown, she'd have never allowed you to take off into the wild, wicked, uncivilized West without her."

"Someone worked long and hard over that gown."

"Did you want me to rip this one off you?"

"No, of course not, Deer Woman worked very hard—"

"I rest my point. No maiden aunt."

"No, no maiden aunt."

"Just a sister?" he queried. Angled at her side, he stared at her face, watching her hesitate in response to the question.

"Just a sister," she said.

He watched anew as the fire rippled within the tipi, touching the walls, the pictographs there, touching Skylar, splashing their curious red-gold display of color upon her body. It was certainly warm enough in their snug home here, but she shivered. He set his hand upon her hip, drawing her more tightly against him, casting a leg over hers to offer greater body warmth. He could have drawn one of the large, fur-trimmed sleeping robes around them. He chose not to. The flickering flame that cast waves of light and shadow and color upon her form fascinated him.

"Just a sister," he repeated. "Did you and she spring from the earth? No parents?"

"My father died a very long time ago. My mother more recently. Not long before your father's death."

He was quiet a moment, but his curiosity about her past was piqued once again.

"I'm sorry. It must have been very painful for you."

"You—you can't imagine."

"But I can."

She turned to him suddenly, intense, passionate. "I swear to you, I did nothing to hurt your father. He knew that my situation was painful. He just wanted to help. I believed with my whole heart that he needed me, that I could help him."

"Skylar, I want to know about your past."

She looked away, shaking her head. "My father died a long time ago, my mother more recently. I have my sister. We needed a new life. I never meant to hurt anyone."

"That's not my question at the moment—"

"I have nothing more to tell you."

"Damn you, Skylar—"

"There is nothing more to tell! There's nothing more anyone needs to know if you just believe that I never meant to hurt your father, that I cared for him. I swear—"

"Skylar, stop it. I believe you."

She searched out his eyes, not seeming to trust his words. Her own were huge, silver orbs, almost magical in the night. He tried to focus on them. They were like mercury, fascinating. Just as the delicate beauty of her face was captivating. But the night and firelight had their own compelling magic. His eyes fell, focusing on her breasts.

She began speaking again, hesitantly, then quickly. "I'm sorry as well that you had no idea...that you were forced into this without even knowledge of it. I—"

"Skylar, stop."

"But I—"

"Skylar, it's all right."

"Is it?"

"Skylar, I am completely resigned—"

"Ah, yes. You like the nights."

He managed to focus on her eyes, arching a brow. "Indeed!" he whispered huskily. "I like the nights!" In a fluid movement, he brushed the fall of her hair from her breast, his palm sliding over the nipple before he brushed it with his tongue and teeth, sucked it with his mouth. She shuddered, her fingers digging into his hair. Passion, satiation, and desire were so strange. He had just made love to her. With vehemence, hunger, and energy. Touched a shattering peak. Drifted from it. He should have been satisfied. But the slightest movement of her flesh beneath him seemed to awaken him. The simple scent of her, the taste of her aroused him anew. The least shift of the silk of her hair against his flesh...

He moved his caress down the length of her body, but her fingers tugged tightly into his hair, drawing him up. She came to her knees, meeting him thus before the fire. She captured his face between her palms, found his lips, kissed him. Her tongue skimmed over his lips, slipped between them, sent wildly lapping flames down to a pit deep within his loins, sent those flames shooting out into his limbs, his sex.

He crushed her against him. Again, every little touch, brush, caress, seemed magnified. He ached for her lips to fall against his shoulders. They did. He hungered to feel her wrap her fingers around him. She did. He threaded his fingers through her hair, drew back her head, kissed and caressed her throat, her breasts, the valley between them, the expanse of abdomen below them. Fire played. Their flesh grew slick and glistened with the rise of heat and desire. He lowered her. Licked her, stroked her. Aroused her, awoke her. Shuddered violently with the vivid feel of her fingers, her hands upon him in return. Her lips, teeth, tongue, rhythm, caress. He met the misted, shimmering silver of her eyes.

"I like the nights," he whispered softly. Then lowering his lips against her ear, he told her what it was he liked about the night, each word erotically graphic, bringing a fresh crimson glow to her cheeks and the ivory silk of her supple form. He turned her, kissed her nape, her shoulders, her spine. This vertebra, the next...the next. She trembled, whispered unintelligible things in return. His arms swept around her, drawing her against him, impaling her with the one movement.

The fire glowed. They whispered, cried out. Stars rode the night sky.

Climax burst upon them, shattering, dazzling like the stars.

Beyond the soft crimson glow that danced in light and shadow in the tipi, the moon began to hide her face as the sun sent its first slim rays peeking out from the eastern horizon. They slept.

Skylar woke again very slowly. She was exhausted, bone weary. Sore. Yet she felt delicious. Cherished. The Sioux cherished their wives, he had told her. Last night, he had made her feel that way.

She opened her eyes fully, then realized that Hawk was awake at her side. The fire had died, but the sun's light was so strong beyond the tipi walls that even though the flapped doorway was closed, there was plenty of light within. She couldn't help noticing how the muscle rippled cleanly within the lines of his handsomely developed chest and shoulders, along the flat line of his abdomen...hips, thighs. He was beautifully formed and perfectly honed. She was coming to know him so well. The feel of his face, his hair. His mouth. What she feared and resented, she now longed for. He angered her so quickly but compelled her so completely...it was so dangerous!

He was her husband, she reminded herself, and the thought made her tremble.

A husband who hadn't wanted a wife.

He was staring at her, she realized. She prayed he wasn't reading her thoughts. He drew a line down the length of her cheek with his thumb, drew another across her lower lip.

"It's late, isn't it?" she asked.

"In the morning, yes."

He still watched her very intently. Then he smiled. A satyr's smile. She understood its meaning almost instantly, but by then, she was drawn against him. He was atop her and all too quickly eliciting a response from her, so easily did she surrender to his desire.

And her own.

Afterward, as he lay beside her, Skylar closed her eyes, succumbing to exhaustion. She could have slept so easily then. She'd never felt so sated in all her life. So filled, so a part of another, and oddly, glad of it. So very much that was wrong lay between them. Yet the distance that stretched between their hearts and minds seemed to be shortening. She'd never imagined such an intrusion as this man in her life. Yet he was her life. Waking, sleeping, and in between. He was her life.

She opened her eyes, only to find him staring at her intently once again. Something about his gaze caused her to ask, “What is it?”

He shrugged, smiling slightly. “Nothing, my love. I just discovered something new, that is all.”

“And what is it that you’ve discovered?”

“I like the days as well,” he told her. Then he rolled away from her and rose, drawing up one of the massive robes from the ground and slipping into it. He left the tipi, and she smiled, hugging her arms tightly around her chest as she closed her eyes once again.

Indeed.

She liked the days, too.

# CHAPTER 19

Skylar had slid back into the doeskin when she heard a soft call coming from outside the tipi. It was Little Rabbit, one of Hawk's cousin Pretty Bird's daughters. Little Rabbit peeked into the tipi, smiling shyly. She made motions with her hands to show Skylar she meant to take her to wash her face.

Skylar smiled and went along with her.

They walked some distance from the camp, downriver, until they came to a place where a number of the women, both old and young, were bathing. They had lain their clothing upon the shore and slipped into the water. They laughed, splashing one another, and called out to her in words she could not understand. She felt somewhat shy herself about stripping completely before such a large group, but she found herself surrounded. The dress was pulled over her head, and she was being led into the water.

The cold water was shocking. She would have leaped from it had she been allowed. As it was, she found herself in the middle of a massive water fight, studied by many of the giggling women.

The Sioux women came in all sizes and shapes, slim and plump, short and tall, young and old. Many of them were very pretty, but one woman stood out, Skylar noted. Not only was she exceptionally well-shaped, but she had unusually beautiful eyes, which slanted slightly upward, and she continually carried the curve of a secret smile about her lips. Her every movement was sensual. Someone said something to the woman, and she laughed, looking over to the embankment. A man was standing there, in the shadows hidden by the brush, so Skylar couldn't see who he was. The sensual Sioux woman made no move to duck beneath the water. Instead, she cupped it in her hands, sluicing it down over her body. None of the women seemed concerned about the situation. It must not have seemed unusual to them.

In time, the women came out of the water, found their clothing, and dried their hair in the sun. Skylar saw the exceptionally built young Sioux woman slip off into the bushes. She watched her, then thought no more of it. She wished she knew where Hawk had gone. She hadn't imagined that he would disappear so early and not come back. He was perfectly at home. He was home. She wasn't exactly suffering, but she couldn't speak with these women, and she didn't have the least idea of how she was supposed to spend the day.

Hawk's little cousin provided her with a comb that had been carved out of bone.

And she prayed that it wasn't human bone.

She worked on her hair, then saw that the women were beginning to drift back to camp. She followed along, but halfway back, noticed that she had dropped her comb. She fell behind the others to search the ground for it, then realized that she had taken a turn from the water as she had done so. She had turned into an area where little alcoves jutted from the hills, almost like caves. She couldn't be lost, she assured herself. She hadn't come that far. Then she heard a woman's laughter. She followed the sound into one of the grass-carpeted alcoves, surrounded by berry bushes. There stood the sloe-eyed beauty from the stream. She hadn't bothered to dry herself. Her doeskin dress, so soft it might have been cotton, was molded to her body. She talked to the warrior in front of her, a man dressed in leggings, breech-clout, moccasins, and no more. She laughed softly again, doing most of the speaking, and though the language was Sioux, Skylar was well aware that her words were both sultry and seductive. She started to back away, hoping to disappear without being seen. But then she heard the man's reply. Again, she didn't know the words.

She did know the voice.

Hawk's.

She was completely unprepared to discover him where he was and with whom. She didn't think, she reacted, and her reaction was frightening. She felt as if she had been knifed cleanly through the lungs, and the pain was staggering, as if she could no longer breathe.

And she felt like a fool.

Believe him, take him at face value. Well, he constantly admitted to his past. The past kept catching up with them now. And this woman seemed a very determined piece of his past.

Furious, Skylar turned and stumbled from the alcove. She walked straight into a bramble and was almost blinded. She spun around, the bramble catching her hair. As she tugged to free the wayward strands from the bushes, another set of hands came in to help her.

"Stand still."

Hawk.

She wrenched at her hair, trying to free it from the bush and his grasp.

"Let go of me."

"Skylar, stop it, stand still—"

"Get your hands off me!"

"Skylar, I'm warning you—"

She was free. She'd left half her hair in the bush, but she was free. She spun around, hands on her hips, meeting his gaze and hoping she wouldn't burst into tears. Just when she had thought that...

That what? she mocked herself. He had fallen madly in love with her? That despite the circumstances of their marriage and everything he had said about other women, he had come to long for only her? A whore in town was perhaps easily forgotten. Perhaps he had intended on meeting an Indian lover here all the time. But what difference could that make? He had told her he wouldn't allow her to really mean anything in his life when she had insisted that she wouldn't go back. Why did she care?

"You had no right to drag me here. None. You could have ridden here on your own without humiliating me, you could—"

"Shut up, Skylar."

She inhaled instead. He looked wickedly dangerous. Half naked like any pagan on the plain, sun-bronzed, lean and muscular. She hated it—hated it! She wanted to be reasonable, but jealousy and pain were overwhelming her. She fought it as best she could. "You could have just left me alone, you mixed-race bastard. You could have left me at Mayfair and come here and done—done whatever you chose to do without causing me—"

"Skylar!" His green eyes narrowed sharply; his voice lowered. "I'm warning you, lower your voice."

"Don't you dare warn me about anything—" she began, then gasped. She hadn't chosen to be silent. She simply gave up speaking because all the air that had been in her lungs had been swept out of them when he'd wrenched her up and thrown her over his shoulder. She tried to push up against his back. She slid—his body had somehow been subtly greased. She slid down against his flesh, but managed to inhale again, growing worried despite her anger as he walked long and furiously down a path through the brush that fronted the river.

"Let me down now! You can't get away with this—"

"You're going to stop me?" he demanded, suddenly setting her upon her feet.

"Yes, I'll stop you!" she challenged.

But as she stumbled and tried to catch her balance, his hands were on her again, pulling off Deer Woman's elegant doeskin dress. She swore, striking him, fighting to retrieve the garment. But she was lifted again, and then she had the sensation of sailing. She cursed him as she flew through the air, only to cry out as she landed in the icy cool river once again.

She sputtered to the surface, but he was there. Instead of admitting defeat, she flew at him again, but his chest was now wet and slick, and her blows seemed to be deflected even as they fell. He caught her arms. "I don't begin to understand you. I don't even know what the hell this is about, but you will not do this here."

"You don't know what it's about? And I will not do what here?" she demanded. Then she cried out because his fingers had tightened to such an extent that her arms were in real pain. He didn't seem to notice.

"Hawk! Damn you, please!"

"We're going back to the camp. Where you are going to be a good wife. No one expects you to really understand a woman's work, but you are going to cook a delicious meal for your husband and a number of his peers."

"Oh, am I?"

"You are."

"What peers?"

"Crazy Horse is joining me to eat this afternoon."

"Crazy Horse is coming to dinner?" she repeated, astonished.

"And it had best be a damned good one!"

She tried to jerk free. He held her fast.

"You're out of your mind. I'm not—"

"You are."

"Since it seems you are in pursuit of another woman, get a second wife for the entertaining you plan on doing. Your white wife is leaving."

"What?"

"You heard me!"

"My white wife is about to be throttled or drowned. And if you humiliate me any further—"

"If I humiliate you!"

"You risk our lives if you risk my reputation here. I'll tie you to a lodge pole and take a buggy whip to you before I let that happen."

It was an idle threat. He'd never dare carry it out. Or would he?

"Let me go!" she demanded.

To her surprise, he shoved her from him. She landed some distance from him in the water. She quickly scurried across the shallow river to the other side, emerging naked upon the grassy embankment.

She stood, flipped her soaking hair around, and started walking.

"You're walking back naked, my love!" he called back to her.

"Well, you are the one who just removed my clothing."

"You needed to cool off."

"Fine. I'm cool. And I don't give a damn! Morality seems completely lost here."

"Morality is higher here than anywhere you know, Lady Douglas. Now get your sweet little butt back here and listen to me before—"

He was still talking, but she suddenly stood dead still. She was looking across the river again, near where where she had found Hawk. The buxom Indian maid remained in the general area, but now she was back in the water, her doeskin dress once again lying upon the branches of a tree. Her back was to Skylar as she laughed softly, talking with a brave in the water, splashing him. Skylar saw the brave, leaned back upon the embankment, scantily clad in breechclout and buckskins he didn't seem to mind wetting any more than Hawk had minded. From the rear, from the side, he looked very, very much like Hawk. He lifted his dark head, his eyes focusing on Skylar, a brow rising.

It wasn't actually a warrior. It was Sloan. Casual, muscled, bronzed, and yes, so very much like Hawk in that strange way they shared as mixed blood.

A smile of amusement flicked across his features, and she realized that she was standing there stark naked. But even as she made that realization, the breath was knocked out of her again as she was swept up firmly from behind. Hawk. His hold a vise once again, his body slick, wet—and burning. He was angry with her. Nothing new. He was more than angry. He was furious and disappointed.

The Indian maid turned, smiled, and waved—bountiful breasts bouncing in the water. She waved to both of them, Skylar thought. With a gnawing in the pit of her stomach, she realized that Hawk had probably come to the river with Sloan. He might have just been talking to the girl who was obviously close with Sloan.

Then again, she obviously might be close with everyone.

Hawk lifted a hand in turn to the girl and a very amused Sloan and hissed in her ear. "You ever take off naked again, Lady Douglas, and I promise you'll spend a night lashed to a lodge pole!"

They were going back downriver again. She shivered in his arms, chilled by both the cold and his manner. For once, she thought that she had been wrong. Oh, God. She'd been hurt. She'd been jealous.

She'd behaved ridiculously. Why? Why had she allowed herself to care so much that she could behave so badly? What was it about him that had seeped into her system, making her want him, making her care?

She felt like a total fool. She didn't know how to apologize, and then again, he hadn't behaved so very well himself. After everything else, he didn't really deserve an apology.

"Hawk!" she cried out, gasping as she hit the cold water once more. He ignored her, dragging her across the river until they stood in the sun once again, and he had picked up her dress. "You're the one who stripped the damn thing off! Now you're half killing me to get it back on. You had best make up your mind!"

"And you—!" he retorted, fingers threaded into her hair, tilting her head back so that she was forced to meet his eyes. "You had better be the best damned Sioux wife you'd ever want to imagine!"

He held her hair too tightly. Tears burned behind her lashes. "Damn you—"

"No, Skylar, this time, you've got no right! And you don't know the least thing about fair play, about carrying out a bargain—"

"Fair play!" she gasped.

"You wanted money, you wanted it your way, sent to your exact specifications. I did exactly what you wanted. But those little things don't mean a hell of a lot to you, do they?"

He released her so suddenly that she would have fallen had there not been a tree branch conveniently within reach as she stumbled back. It didn't matter. She was chastely dressed once again, and he was walking away.

Shaking, she closed her eyes—regrouping whatever pride, strength, and dignity she could muster.

What really bothered her now was that he had seemed so disgusted with her lack of...commitment? Fairness? She had to admit that he had sent the telegram exactly to her specifications. Thankfully, as well, there was a great deal of Douglas money in eastern banks. She had gotten precisely what she had asked him for. And wasn't that all that really mattered to her?

Skylar squared her shoulders and started back to the camp. She couldn't be the absolutely perfect Sioux wife— she was going to need some help.

But she did believe in fair play, and she did owe Hawk. And Crazy Horse was coming to dinner.

When she reached the camp, she saw that people were watching a group of braves prepare to ride out of camp. Some of the men were adding touches of paint to their ponies and faces before mounting up. Hawk and Sloan were among the group. Neither seemed to notice her.

One brave, however, seeing her, suddenly broke from the group and came striding toward her. He wore a red jagged slash of color down his face and no more. The color partially hid a scar on his face, but neither the paint nor the scar diminished the fact that he was a striking warrior with strong chiseled features. Arms crossed over his chest, he surveyed her without apology. Skylar didn't think she'd ever seen a more menacing warrior, but she determined to stand her ground and returned his perusal. Yet even as she stared at the warrior, Hawk, chest naked but unpainted, strode to her side, pulling her in front of him as they both faced the man. "Crazy Horse," he said, then switched to Sioux for a moment. She heard her own name spoken before Hawk returned to English, telling her, "Skylar, this is an introduction— acknowledge it!"

She longed to elbow her husband directly in the ribs. She controlled her temper, refrained from doing so, and nodded gravely to the impressive warrior before her. He smiled. He became completely different in that moment—a man like any other man. She smiled in return.

He said something to Hawk in Sioux. Hawk stepped by her, and the two men strode back to their party, swinging up with swift agility onto their horses. Crazy Horse suddenly lifted his rifle into the air, letting out a frightening cry. Skylar nearly jumped at the sound of it but managed not to do so. Sloan raised a hand to her. He had quite a smile of his own, she thought. For a man who could be so intense and determined, the charm and the sensuality in his grin were startling. She flushed slightly, remembering that she had sauntered naked in front of one of her husband's closest friends, yet it was with a certain encouraging friendliness that he smiled to her now. Sloan was willing to do something Hawk was not. Accept her without terms.

As she watched, Sloan reached over, touching Hawk's bare bronze arm. He spoke, and Hawk nodded, but Hawk's back remained toward Skylar. He knew she was there. He wasn't going to acknowledge her now as he rode away.

And he did not. He rode on ahead with the party, right behind Crazy Horse.

Sloan, however, rode back toward her for a moment. "Where are you going?" she asked him worriedly.

"Hunting."

She nodded, glad to hear that they weren't going on a raid. She glanced over Sloan's bronze, barely clad body to the single feather in his hair. "If you run into army troops, they're likely to shoot you and Hawk."

Sloan nodded with a slight shrug. "We won't be running into any troops. Not today. We're heading west."

"Crow country?"

"Probably not that far."

She approached Sloan's horse, frowning. "You're only hunting to make sure there are no more Crow parties in the area, aren't you?"

"We're hunting because the season is still good. And maybe we're looking for a few Crow."

"Be careful, Sloan. Make him be careful, too, please."

"We both know what we're doing, Skylar."

"Generals with every skill in the world and years of experience can be shot out of their saddles."

"Skylar, we'll be careful. By the way, what's for dinner?"

The wicked gleam in his eye assured her he was well aware there might be controversy within her tipi.

"Something quite unbelievable," she assured him sweetly. Then she started, moving back, because from where she had stood, Sloan's horse had blocked her view of the trail from the camp—and the fact that Hawk had ridden back along it. He moved his horse alongside Sloan's, talking to his friend. "Are you joining us, or do you intend to flirt with my wife all day?"

Sloan refused to take offense. “I’d probably rather flirt with your wife. Actually, I was just asking about dinner.”

Hawk lifted a brow as he gazed down at Skylar.

“She’s assured me that the meal will be unbelievable,” Sloan said pleasantly.

“You came back to ask about dinner?” he demanded of Sloan.

“I’m hungry,” Sloan said simply. Hawk gazed at him through narrowed eyes. “And quite curious to discover your wife’s cooking talents. And besides, I thought she did deserve an explanation of where we were going.”

“Hunting,” Hawk said.

“And looking for Crows,” Skylar accused him.

Now Hawk was glaring at Sloan. Sloan lifted a hand. “I told her we know what we’re doing—”

“And I told him that the most experienced man can get himself killed.”

“I’m not going to get myself killed—if I’m the one you’re worried about. And you needn’t fear for yourself. My grandfather knows that in case something happens to me, you’re to be returned to Mayfair.”

“I’m not worried about getting back,” she told him.

“Then I guess we’re all just worrying about dinner,” Sloan interjected.

Hawk made no effort to hide his exasperation. He leaned toward Skylar, saying, “Lodge pole!” Then he kneed Tor and cantered off down the trail.

“Lodge pole?” Sloan demanded.

Skylar shrugged. “Is there any recourse Sioux women have against their husbands?”

“Divorce,” Sloan said cheerfully.

“Can’t she tie him to a lodge pole and take out her frustrations on him?”

Sloan laughed softly. “I’m afraid you’ve little hope of ever doing that. If he were to beat you too severely, your relatives could certainly protest and endanger his respect within the community. But you haven’t any relatives here. Skylar...”

“Yes?”

"Has he really hurt you so badly?"

She flushed uncomfortably. "No, he scared me halfway to death at first, but he's never hurt me, it's just that..."

"This meal with Crazy Horse is important to him."

"And I intend to be a proper wife."

Sloan smiled. "It's too bad the three of us aren't full-blooded Sioux. I could steal you away, leaving several good ponies as payment."

"It appears to me," Skylar said shrewdly, "that you are quite busy enough without a wife."

"What? Ah...Earth Woman."

"Is that her name? How fitting."

"Ouch. You do have claws."

"Well, I thought...never mind."

"Watch those thoughts. Sioux men and women are like other men and women. Within the framework of society, some are simply better people than others. But morality is high here—"

"When a man isn't wife-stealing."

"Wife-stealing brings about a stigma."

"Wife-beating."

"Very few men beat their wives. And you tell me, are white men always kind and gentle with their wives?"

Her heart seemed to harden as she looked at him. She shook her head. "You're right. White men can be monsters." She inhaled. "Don't you dare let him enjoy the day, Sloan. But you needn't worry. I do intend to be the perfect wife."

Sloan smiled. With a wave, he rode off to join his hunting party.

They rode for several hours on the trail of an elk herd. Hawk used the time to talk with Crazy Horse and his cousins, finding it important to keep communication between them as open and complete as possible. But after a while he found himself drawn back to Sloan, and they rode at the rear of the party.

"Tension in paradise?" Sloan drawled.

"You caused the tension this morning," Hawk informed him.

Sloan raised a brow.

"She thought I was the man waiting for Earth Woman."

"Why didn't you just tell her the truth?"

"If she was going to be so quick to assume that I'd do such a thing, she didn't deserve the truth."

"Ah."

"And I've never been able to get the truth out of her."

"She lies?" Sloan queried, startled.

Hawk shook his head. "Not exactly. It's just so damned frustrating not to know anything—"

"She's on the run," Sloan said simply.

"You think she's wanted by the law?" Hawk demanded incredulously.

Sloan shook his head. He shrugged. "She was a little upset, asking me if Sioux women had some recourse against their husbands."

"Really?"

"Well, did you threaten to beat her at a lodge pole?"

Hawk shrugged. "She wasn't really threatened."

"Maybe she's not quite so sure of you—or herself—as you might think."

"What are you talking about?"

Sloan shook his head. "I don't know exactly—she's not my wife. I can't threaten to beat things out of her."

Hawk exhaled with impatience. Sloan put up a hand to stop him before he could talk.

"She told me that you had never really hurt her—"

"Damn it, Sloan, that you would need to ask—"

"But someone did hurt her, Hawk. Someone who still scares her now. Someone in her past. Maybe she ran from a husband—"

"I'm her husband."

"Hawk, I'm just telling you—"

"She was never married before."

"How can you—"

"Unless she was married to a damned eunuch."

"Oh. Well, there's someone out there she's running from. Maybe an abusive father, brother, uncle—who knows? She said that she knew white men could be monsters."

"Monsters?" Hawk said.

"Yes."

"Monsters?"

"Yes! Monsters."

Hawk frowned, remembering the way she had awakened, screaming, from her dream. She'd refused to describe the nightmare that had plagued her.

Except that it had contained...

Monsters.

"What? Is that some kind of a clue?" Sloan demanded.

Hawk shrugged. "I don't know. I will know soon enough. I've asked Henry to find out about her past for me. And she's going to have a real monster in her life tonight if she's rude to Crazy Horse. Me. I damn well guarantee you a monster!"

Sloan shrugged, then pointed ahead of them. "I think that our hunting party ahead may be on to something!"

"A party of Crow?"

"No, I think we'd have heard a war cry by now, were that the case. Though I just don't get it. I didn't understand the other night at all, and I can't believe there are more Crows in the area. They'd have to be half insane. What in hell would they be up to, riding in this region?"

"I don't know," Hawk said. It bothered Sloan, it bothered him, but why, he couldn't quite say. "It seems like a strange time. A damned strange time," Hawk muttered.

Sloan glanced at him sharply. "Why? What more?"

Hawk looked quickly to his friend in turn. "A strange man approached Henry Pierpont. He had a Douglas ring—one that should have been buried with my brother. And I was asked to go to the Highlands—to a place we call the Druid Stone—on the night of the Moon Maiden."

Sloan stared at him incredulously for a moment, then carefully lowered his eyes, composing his features. Hawk knew that he intended to weigh his words, to keep his friend from what might be false hope. "How could David be alive? You buried him yourself."

"I buried a burned corpse, of that I am certain."

Sloan shook his head. "Someone suddenly appearing. Saying that David might be alive? It sounds like a hoax. You shouldn't get your hopes up, my friend."

"How can I not go?"

"Because life is grave here. Have you thought that someone may want you dead now? Your brother has been gone more than five years, now your father as well. If you are killed, there is a clean sweep, and the title and rights to your Scottish estates may be very dear to someone else."

"Indeed, I've thought of all the angles."

"Including your wife, I imagine!" Sloan smiled suddenly. "Poor thing—after all this, she may not be Lady Douglas."

Hawk nodded grimly. "Would it matter to her, do you think?"

"Would it matter to you that you were not Lord Douglas?"

"You know that it would not."

"Nor do I think that it would matter to your wife. Hmm. Interesting. Is she your wife? If David proved to be alive? A Sioux warrior first, a bloody Highlander next. The poor woman could be sorry she ever heard the name Douglas."

"She is my wife. Henry guaranteed me of that legality. Imagine poor David back from the grave—with a wild creature for a wife! Nay, the lady is mine. And I wish I dared believe we were not Lord and Lady Douglas. Still, Sloan, I wonder what she will think when she discovers that I may well whisk her back from Indian territory to drag her across the seas."

"Hawk, I think you judge her too harshly. But then, I am afforded the luxury of my distance while watching you fall in love with the lady, so it is far easier for me to be generous."

Hawk offered him an irritated scowl. "It's best she's becoming accustomed to the tipi, don't you think?"

Sloan smiled, then sobered. "You can think of leaving here now—"

"I won't leave while we're in the midst of negotiations. But I admit, I am anxious to discover the truth."

"You'd think that something going on here would tie in some way."

Hawk arched a brow. "What do you mean?"

"I don't know...your mysterious new wife. Crow acting strange. And someone claiming that your brother is alive, after all these years."

"I can't imagine a connection between Scotland and the Badlands."

"Nor Crow and your wife."

"Scotland will wait. The Crow situation—especially as it now involves my wife—will not."

"The Crow have always been our enemies, but they are an enemy we recognize. An enemy who is brave, who battles in our ways. We respect a warrior, they respect a warrior. I don't know what it is about this that doesn't seem right at all," Sloan said.

"It was an absurd place for such a party to be," Hawk mused. "Still...why the hell does it bother me so much?"

"Why the hell?" Sloan agreed. "The men are all dead," he reminded Hawk.

Sloan was right. The Crow who had attacked Skylar were dead. The incident was over. Hawk looked at Sloan, then let out a sudden bird cry to the others ahead of them in the party, though a Crow might well recognize it as a false cry anyway.

But from up ahead, Crazy Horse called back softly. Sloan had been right. Crazy Horse and the others ahead had not come upon a party of their enemies. They had happened on the family of elks they had followed.

Hawk drew an arrow from the quiver at his back for his bow. He glanced at Sloan, who likewise had taken along his bow and arrows for the hunt.

With somewhat sheepish shrugs, they kneed their horses as they had done as boys.

They let out loud, whooping cries and raced after their prey like the wind.

The hunt was on.

# CHAPTER 20

Deer Woman arrived at Skylar's tipi moments after the men had ridden off to hunt. She tapped on the layer of skins just as politely as a neighbor in town might knock at the front door. She brought a large quantity of buffalo meat, all manner of berries, and sweet corn, which she had probably acquired from a trader. Little Rabbit, who accompanied her, carried water and a heavy kettle for cooking. Skylar thanked them both. When it appeared that Deer Woman meant to do all the work for her, Skylar shook her head, encouraging the woman and the girl to sit. Even though she was aware that neither of them understood her, she chattered away, keeping her voice friendly and light. "I've never minded cooking, but of course I've been rather lucky in that respect. We weren't incredibly wealthy, but we always had help. Servants, not slaves. We were never actually Southern, even though some of my relatives live in Virginia and fought for the Confederacy. Maryland, where we lived, was a true border state, neighbor spying on neighbor. And worse. But that was a long time ago now. My sister and I always loved to play in the kitchen. Not too long ago, our mother took ill. We loved her very much, so we'd do anything to help her—and looking after her probably kept our minds off him. But I think he's paid by now for what he did to us. God, I'm not even sure if he's alive or dead. No, he has to be alive; that's why it's so important to get Sabrina here quickly. Away from him. It's all happening now, so I am in Hawk's debt, you see. And I'm also feeling just a little bit foolish for having attacked Hawk when I really had no reason to. It's a strange bargain that he and I made."

Deer Woman looked at Little Rabbit. Little Rabbit looked back at Deer Woman. It was obvious they were slightly afraid that their beloved Thunder Hawk had taken on not just a white woman but a crazy one.

But Skylar kept busy as she talked. The women had also brought loose tea and coffee in their bags, and she made tea for them, lacing it with sugar cubes she had brought from Mayfair. Deer Woman appeared very skeptical when Skylar tried to get her to drink but Little Rabbit was adventurous and inquisitive. She tasted the tea and then smiled, encouraging Deer Woman to do the same. Skylar was happy to see her Sioux friends enjoying the new treat of sugary tea.

The three of them wound up giggling and laughing. Soon, other women in the band began to arrive. Skylar kept making more tea. Eventually, Earth Woman arrived. Skylar knew that she stiffened when the woman smilingly joined them. She tried not to get upset because Earth Woman seemed very happy to join the gathering. She had brought Skylar a second dress, one in a darker shade of doeskin, with exquisite quillwork. Skylar knew that she had to accept the garment, but she was learning Sioux ways as well. She kept talking, even though the women couldn't understand her, and she gave away every piece of clothing she had brought with her. The women giggled and laughed over her pantalettes, enjoyed her corsets, adored her hosiery. It was a strange party, and all the while that it took place, she worked on the dinner she would serve when the men returned. And despite her determination to work alone, she had help. Crazy Horse's people were a hunting band. She understood that much. They were not like the agency Indians who had become farmers. But even when they were at odds with the government, it seemed, they had ways to trade. The list of ingredients for her stew had grown. In addition to the salt and pepper she had taken from her own saddlebags, and the buffalo meat, corn, berries, and potatoes Deer Woman had brought, she also had onions, which some of the other women had given her. By the time the women began to leave, returning to their tipis to make sure that they had food for their own returning warriors, the stew bubbling in her cauldron was giving off a mouthwatering aroma.

Earth Woman hovered behind, not leaving with the others. When they were alone and Skylar turned to look at her, the beautiful Indian woman smiled. "I made you mad this morning, no?"

The woman spoke English. Skylar wondered with a sinking sensation of dismay just what she had said throughout the afternoon. She tried to assure herself that anything she might not want repeated had been said before Earth Woman had arrived.

"You didn't make me mad," Skylar said now, carefully choosing her words. "I was—upset. Because—"

"Because you thought your husband kept a Sioux woman."

She tossed her hair back. "Upset, mad. My English is only so good. They are one and the same. I am not Sioux, I am Cheyenne. I was very young, with my first husband, when my band was massacred along Sand Creek. I was not much older, with my second husband traveling with Black Kettle, who also survived Sand Creek, when the Son-of-the-Morning-Star, Long Knife, Custer, came and murdered all the women and children along the Washita. Neither my husband nor Black Kettle survived that time. My third husband was crippled in a battle with the Crow. He was taken prisoner by the Americans, and I learned my English at Fort Abraham Lincoln while he fought to live. But he, too, died. Now I am here, living with Crazy Horse. My husband's brothers hunt for me. The Sioux are a strict people, virtuous. But I am a human being who has suffered greatly, and I have earned the respect of the people here who know that I was good and loyal to a dying man. I will not take another husband. I am afraid that the spirits have put something in me that might make any such brave man die. Cougar-in-the-Night desires no wife, so we are friends. Your husband is my friend as well."

Friend, Skylar thought. Did the woman sleep with all her friends? Jealousy stabbed her, but she realized that she liked and admired Earth Woman just as it seemed the Sioux of Crazy Horse's camp and their Cheyenne allies did. Earth Woman was a female living in a male-dominated society who had created her own place within it. She was definitely a renegade in her way, not at all ashamed of her own sensuality in a place where chastity was as important among the women as ferocity in battle was among the men.

"Good friends?" she heard herself croak out.

Earth Woman smiled. Her ink-dark lashes swept her beautiful cheeks. "I am not young. Many years ago, when Sea-of-Stars had died and I was lonely and broken as well, we were very good friends. That was long ago. Don't be mad at me."

"I'm not mad. I was—hurt. I was even—afraid."

Earth Woman smiled. She came toward Skylar and hugged her. "The Sioux do not show much emotion. But you are white, and I am Cheyenne. You are welcome here. And do not be afraid of me. Your husband has no desire for me. He very much desires you. You must see that."

"Does he?"

Earth Woman rolled her eyes.

"Most human beings are not so blind!" she said, laughing, and departed quickly. Even then, there was a natural sway to her hips as she left the tipi.

Skylar hoped that her husband desired her. Because if he didn't, Earth Woman was definitely worthy competition.

They came back with several elk. Sloan had taken down two, and Hawk had slain the same. Neither of them needed the food, so their kills were delivered to the poor of the tribe—two widows with children who had no brothers or brothers-in-law left to help them, and two very old warriors with very old wives. Hawk had just finished with the courteous routine of giving his kill away when he saw that Crazy Horse had gone to his tipi.

"Oh, hell!" he swore softly in English.

Sloan, at his side, spun around.

"Finish here, will you?" Hawk asked quickly. He turned with a last smile for the old woman who was going on and on thanking him and raced for his own tipi.

He jerked up the flap, blinking as his eyes adjusted to the firelight within.

Crazy Horse was seated, awaiting him.

To Hawk's amazement, his pipe and tobacco awaited him in the center of the tipi, laid out so that he could share a smoke with his guests. The aroma drifting throughout the habitat was delicious. Skylar was standing near the rear of the tipi, as far back as she could manage without bending. She met his eyes as he entered. There wasn't anything particularly humble in her gaze.

In fact, she looked rather amused.

But she lifted her hand, indicating where he should rightfully take his place as host. He narrowed his eyes at her, in warning, hoping that she had no tricks up her sleeve.

Soon after he entered, Sloan arrived, then Willow, Ice Raven, and Blade. Crazy Horse's friend He Dog arrived as well, and the tipi was quite full.

They smoked, and they drank brandy that Hawk had brought from Mayfair. Skylar served them the liquor, and she served them stew in wooden bowls. She never looked directly at any of the men—except at Hawk once.

And still there was that glint of amusement in her eyes, which made him a bit uneasy, but...

She was beautiful, graceful, so very quick to serve—and most mercifully, silent. She couldn't have been more charming and subdued.

Which was why he was so startled when her revenge befell him.

He noted that He Dog was behaving strangely at first, gulping down brandy as if it were water. Crazy Horse, who had appeared to savor Skylar's stew, was suddenly doing the same. Skylar was quick to serve more and more brandy, but it never seemed enough. His guests stopped eating and kept drinking.

Hawk took a bite from his own stew bowl. Skylar really was an excellent cook, the stew was very good, but...

Hot. Burning. There was enough pepper in it to season half the buffalo kill in the West.

Crazy Horse was wheezing. He Dog was coughing. Even Sloan was choking. Hawk grabbed his own brandy—guzzling it. He set his stew bowl down and rose, staring at Skylar.

She stared back blankly. With complete innocence. He excused himself to his company striding toward the back of the tipi where she was standing. His mouth, his throat, his eyes, nose, and body all still seemed to be burning from the pepper. None of his guests said a word, of course. Crazy Horse was being courteous, assuming Hawk's wife could do no better.

"Lady Douglas," Hawk said, keeping his voice low so that he could not be heard by those among his company who understood English. He opened his mouth to continue. He was afraid to talk, afraid to move, so furious that he was afraid he would hurt her. He reached to the ground, picking up a large skin gourd and shoving it into her hands.

"Water!" he ground out.

Her brows shot up. "What is the matter with you? I've done everything—"

"In the world to humiliate me. Get water, now!"

Her lips pursed, her eyes burned silver. She started to shove the gourd back. "Get your own damned water—" she began.

But never finished. He caught her wrist, twisting it around with such speed and determination that he had forcefully pressed her before him and was on his way out of the tipi with her. He excused himself to his guests, explaining that his wife wasn't as familiar with the use of her Mayfair seasonings in different surroundings as she was at her customary home.

"This time, Lord-Wretched-Manhandling-Douglas, I have had it!" she cried out, still propelled forward as they left the tipi. She cried out, swearing at him, as his rush toward the river caused him to press harder upon her arm. "I spent the entire day trying to entertain squaws who spoke no English, I welcomed one of your ex-mistresses into the tipi—since it seems you and Sloan apparently never minded sharing before. I worked the entire day and now—"

"You worked the entire day!" he exploded, shoving her forward and free from his grasp. "You plotted the entire day, is what you did!"

They'd come to the same alcove in the trees by the river where Sloan had been with Earth Woman that day. Night had brought a definite chill to the air, and Skylar was shivering. "Plotted! I beat the meat, seasoned it—"

"Enough to kill a herd of buffalo!"

"I did not!" she snapped back indignantly.

"You almost ended the entire Sioux problem all by yourself, choking to death half the leaders of the resistance!"

"I did not!" she repeated, appalled, her indignation growing, along with her tremors.

"I hope you're freezing," he told her, "Because I'd like to shake you until every bone in your body rattles, slap your perfect little derriere. String you up—"

"Me!" she shrieked, suddenly approaching him. "You ungrateful, swaggering egotist! How dare you!"

She came before him. Directly before him. She suddenly slammed both fists against his naked chest with a power that hurt.

"You get your own damned water and kiss your own damned butt! I've had it!"

She slammed her fists against him again and turned imperiously on her heels to walk off. Incredulous, he watched her for a moment. Then it seemed that his fury ignited, sending him tearing after her, not knowing what he was doing, but damned determined she wasn't going to just walk away. He caught her by the hair. She shrieked. He grabbed hold of her shoulders, spinning her around. He was down upon a knee, not really intending to drag her over it, but she tripped and fell there and was shrieking like a wild cat before he made a conscious move. "Don't you dare, don't you dare—" she cried.

He dared. Her doeskin dress had been dragged up her body. His hand fell upon naked flesh.

She bit his knee.

To free himself of her teeth he shoved her down to the ground, then pounced hard upon her. She was inhaling and exhaling in a rapid fury, her eyes silver daggers, her fingers clawing at him. He caught her hands, then found himself staring at her, realizing in dismay that he wasn't just furious, he was aroused. More than aroused. He was in agony.

"Bastard!" she hissed. Yet her fingers unclenched. She was reaching for him still, touching his shoulders, fingers digging into them, but not to draw blood. Tears stung her eyes. She brushed them away. His lips fell upon hers, and she responded wildly, her mouth crushing his in return.

Their lips parted. "I'm going to kill you," she promised him.

"Only when I finish with you," he responded.

"You'll be on your knees to apologize," she told him. Her hands moved over his throat, his chest, hungrily. Her hands. Oh, God. Fingers running up his thighs. Beneath the breechclout. Stroking, rubbing, caressing...

He caught her hands. Pressed her back hard into the earth. The stars above them danced madly in the heavens. She thrashed, undulated, strained against him. The stars erupted. He climaxed in a wave of passion, need, fury, and confusion, crushing her against him and feeling the same response within her as she jerked with each little after-climax that seized her body, bringing them both back down to the dirt on the forest floor in the cool night by the river.

She stared up at him, her eyes misted. He felt like an ass. A fool. Still angry, and yet...

He heard a rustling behind him. Close.

Damn her! He should have heard it before!

With lightning-quick reflexes, he instinctively leaped to his feet, drawing her dress down the length of her body as he did so. He felt her halfway rising behind him as he swiftly scanned the brush and the night-shadows surrounding them.

She inhaled sharply, looking past his shoulder. He turned to her quickly, just as she began to scream out a warning. It was too late. Even as she cried out, the end of a war club struck him at the back of his head, and he knew no more.

Her scream was abruptly cut short as suffocating fingers clamped over her nose and mouth. Skylar had seen that the brave coming out of the darkness wasn't alone. The other came from behind her. She struggled insanely, trying to free herself, trying to see Hawk. Darkness and shadows seemed to be closing in around her. Her attackers didn't seem to care in the least that they might suffocate her. The world was spinning, turning black, stars were dotting the blackness...

No! She couldn't lose her senses. Hawk!

She twisted. Saw her husband's body, fallen on the earth. She bit into the fingers pressing so brutally against her mouth. The grip upon her slipped. She let out a long, shrill scream.

Another hand clamped down upon her, more brutal, more punishing. She was vaguely aware of the face atop hers. Dark-eyed, dark-skinned, a scar running atop the forehead. "Another sound, I slit your throat."

English. He was speaking English. He looked like a Crow. Or did he? Something about him was subtly different. She hadn't been here long enough to learn the different ways of dress and manner and adornment between the tribes.

The fellow holding her so tightly dragged her to her feet. She threw an elbow back into his ribs with all the force within her. He gasped. For an instant, he released his hold. She flew forward, trying to reach Hawk. She nearly touched him but was drawn back before she could do so, drawn back by a hand around her throat. Yet even as she gasped and choked, seeing stars again, she thought that she saw Hawk's chest move. She thought that he breathed.

Someone snapped out an order in an Indian language. Not Sioux! she thought. Not Sioux.

She was dragged back, unable to breathe. She saw stars. She heard the man whisper in English again. "A sound, and I take my knife where my arm wraps around your throat. I slice the vein where I see it pulsing now. Watch the blood flow down your breast..."

She was certain they meant to kill her anyway—but they weren't taking chances on her now. There were a number of men, how many, she wasn't sure. Four...five...six.

The man's left hand slipped from her throat as they reached his horse. He kept his right pinned firmly over her mouth. Another man was there to help him get her quickly up on his horse. Within seconds, they were racing away from the camp.

They slowed after twenty minutes of nearly breakneck speed. One of the other men came up by them as they rode. She didn't understand his words, but she saw his movements and realized the fellow was saying that she needed to be tied. The other disagreed, looking back.

They were in a hurry. A desperate hurry. As well they should be.

When someone within the camp realized that Hawk had been attacked, that she...

Oh, God, would anyone come after her? Any of the men who assumed that she had peppered their meals to humiliate her husband? And if Hawk lay dead, did any of it matter? Would she ever be rid of the terrible pain in her heart?

The Sioux warriors would come, she thought. They would come because they were warriors, because they were proud, because they wouldn't let such an insult go unavenged. They would come because...

They had to!

Oh, God, they had to. This could not happen. Not now. She was desperate to live if Hawk lived. If they had killed Hawk, then...

She didn't dare think.

She abhorred the smell of the man holding her so cruelly as they rode. She despised the sound of his voice, the look in his eyes. He meant to kill her, she was convinced. Somehow, she knew these men were...evil.

Monsters.

# CHAPTER 21

Hawk awoke with a groan. Crazy Horse was hunkered down at his side, his long fingers moving over Hawk's skull. His head throbbed with pain, but he sat up to discover that he remained in the little forest alcove, and he was now surrounded by his friends.

"Where is she?"

"Gone. Sloan and the others went for the horses. We'll start after them."

"Who?"

"Crow."

"Crow. Here in your camp?"

"Dead Crow. They will be dead Crow, very soon, I vow it," Crazy Horse said. "Can you ride? We will go for your woman. There is no shame in your not coming when your head is battered. Strange, they didn't make sure you were dead. They didn't take your scalp."

"They didn't take the time," Hawk commented, coming carefully to his feet. Crazy Horse steadied him when he would have staggered. He was completely perplexed and worried sick. It was his fear, far more than the pounding in his head, that was making him feel nauseated. "Damn, what the bloody hell is going on here?" he swore.

"The horses," Crazy Horse said.

Sloan, He Dog, Willow, Blade, and Ice Raven were mounted, along with a dozen warriors who had joined them as they bridled their horses. Sloan led Tor for Hawk while He Dog led Crazy Horse's mount.

"You're sure you can ride?" Crazy Horse began, but Hawk had already swung himself atop Tor's back, a fistful of mane in his hand. Crazy Horse leaped atop his own mount, and they started out, Blade leading. He had already tracked the enemy across the river, a futile attempt to lose trackers who knew the Black Hills as well as the Sioux.

They rode fast across the river, picked up the trail again, and galloped hard across the terrain toward an outcropping of hills and brush. Willow raised a hand. Blade leaped down from his horse when the trail seemed to split. Hawk started to follow. Sloan caught his arm.

"What the hell happened?"

"Damned if I know. This is insane behavior—"

"On your part, too," Sloan said gruffly. "You can usually hear a twig snap in the next territory. If you hadn't been so damned busy manhandling your wife—"

"I wasn't manhandling my wife!" Hawk exploded, amazed to realize that he was in such a blind fury he was ready to tear into the one man who was not only a solid friend but an associate who knew the world of red-and-white he lived in as he knew it himself.

Sloan arched a brow. "I wasn't manhandling my wife," Hawk repeated more quietly. "I was simply—completely involved with her." He groaned. "Damn it, Sloan—" he began, then he shook his head, squared his shoulders, and hurried toward Willow, hunkering down close to the ground to study the tracks with him in the pale glow of moonlight. "To the left," he said.

Willow nodded. The trail of hoofprints had split, but they were deeper to the left. They'd gamble that meant there was a horse in that party bearing the weight of two riders.

They leaped back on their horses. "We'll get her," Sloan assured him. "We're breathing down their necks now."

"I don't know how long I was out—" Hawk began.

"Not long," Sloan assured him.

"How do you know?" Hawk demanded.

Sloan glanced at Crazy Horse. Crazy Horse shrugged. "I went to find you. Cougar-in-the-Night suspected your wife knows how to cook better than she did. He left when you did and came back with Earth Woman. Earth Woman dumped the spices into the food. I was looking for you when I heard a woman screaming."

Hawk thought that he would die if something happened to Skylar. Go mad, bury himself in ashes, tear his hair out. It was his fault. He never should have let down his guard. He had survived the war and every danger on the plains by never letting down his guard. She'd seeped into his blood. And it was dangerous.

Because in discovering that he needed her, he was going to lose her. He couldn't. Wouldn't.

Damn, by every concept of heaven and hell, he wouldn't lose her now. He'd kill every Crow in the West if that was what it took to get back.

"Ahead!" Crazy Horse cried suddenly. "Just ahead! Listen!"

---

THEY KEPT UP A BRISK PACE. The Indian riding with Skylar had held her tightly at the beginning of the ride, but then his hold had begun to ease somewhat. She tried to wriggle from it. If she could test his hold, she could perhaps break free when the right time came.

The right time...

What would that be? she asked herself hysterically.

When they rode through a wooded area. When she could run into brush. When she could escape...

She couldn't escape.

The Indians had split their party. Two of them had gone down one trail, while three remained with her and the man who held her now. Still, four altogether against her. If she leaped down, they'd come after her. They were far from the Sioux camp now...

One of the other Indians rode up close to the man riding with her. He indicated the path behind him. He spoke in his own language.

Skylar realized that someone was following them. "Help! Help me!" she shrieked.

A dirty hand fell upon her mouth. "Damn it, I'd just as well kill you sooner than later, bitch!" he hissed to her.

His vise upon her mouth was so tight that she had to lean back against him to keep her neck from breaking. The pain was unbearable. She grasped his leg to steady herself and felt the sheath at his calf.

Then the steel within it.

She drew the knife from the sheath and slammed it into his leg with all her strength.

He let out a bone-chilling scream, cursing her. Promising her a slow, agonizing death.

But he instinctively let go of her to grasp his thigh.

And she was free.

She leaped down from the horse, shrieking again as her ankle twisted. She didn't care, couldn't care. The others in the war party were staring at her with murderous fury.

Shouting to one another.

Racing toward her.

She turned and ran into the brush, hobbling with amazing speed, the bloody knife still clutched desperately in her hand.

---

THEY HEARD A CRY FOR HELP, then a shriek from a very feminine, well-recognized voice.

Then a masculine voice crying out in pain, cursing.

"Come!" Hawk shouted, kneeing Tor so that he and his horse leaped forward as one. He burst onto the narrow trail through the trees to discover Skylar racing down a path that ran parallel with his own. Three warriors on horseback were trying to corner her and trap her.

One of the nearly naked Crow, still cursing, was bearing down on her quickly. Hawk didn't think. He drew his knife from the sheath at his calf and hurled it swiftly through the air. He must have hit the Crow's heart dead on, for the man fell from his horse without a whimper.

He thundered through the trees, weaving perfectly on Tor. He didn't fear his other enemies. His own people would be protecting his back as he retrieved his wife. He rode up behind Skylar, who still ran. She heard Tor and turned back, her golden hair flying in the night, her flawless features wild as she looked up at him, silver eyes still defiant, nonetheless.

She gasped his name, her hand flying to her throat as she ceased running, stumbled, stood still. He swept her up, cradling her against his body, running his hands over and over her, touching her face, her lips, trembling as he did so.

"Oh, God, oh, God, you came, I was so afraid you were dead, I was so afraid—" she sobbed.

"Shhh...shhh..."

He held her more tightly against him. A knife was clasped tightly in her fingers. He had to pry her fingers free from it.

She surely felt the terrible thunder of his heart, the rampant shaking within him. He gave a slight twist to the reins, urging Tor to take them back to the trail, assuring Skylar softly all the while that she was all right.

Their Crow enemies lay dead on the ground, stretched out next to one another. The man Hawk had killed with the knife to the heart also sported a bloody leg—Skylar's attack, Hawk was certain.

Sloan and Willow stood by the bodies, shaking their heads and speaking softly to one another.

"What is it?" Hawk demanded.

"I don't know. It's just so strange. This one..." Sloan said, striking a match against his boot to better illuminate the body and indicating the man Hawk had killed himself, "He's dressed like a Crow, painted like a Crow. But I don't think he is a Crow."

"What do you think he is?" Hawk demanded. He was going to jump down to study the dead brave himself, but Skylar clung to him so tightly he didn't want to rip himself away from her. Besides which, he knew and trusted Sloan's opinion.

"He's a mixed race. And I think he's half Arikara."

Crazy Horse spoke up. "The Arikara have been known to be our enemies as well. This man, though...he pretends to be what he is not. It is very strange."

Sloan spoke again, slowly. "I agree. I think I've seen him before."

"Where?" Hawk asked.

"Hanging around Fort Abraham Lincoln. Trying to get a job as an Indian scout."

"So he didn't get work with the white army, and he started to run with the Crows," Crazy Horse said. "What does that mean?" He spat down on the body.

"I don't know," Sloan said. "Any ideas?" he asked Hawk.

Two of the Sioux warriors with them had leaped down from their horses.

They were going to take the scalps, Hawk realized. A woman had been abducted from their very camp, and they had taken a war party out in the night to bring her back. The scalps were theirs. And these were no-good warriors, sneaking into a camp, attacking a brave from the back, abducting a lone female. They would be maimed so that they would not play so foolishly in the afterlife.

He needed to move on with Skylar and ponder the problem of these strange "Crow" attacks later.

She was silent as they rode and still. She didn't even wince as she heard the tremolos and cries go out as the Sioux took the Crow's scalps.

He nuzzled the top of her head. "Are you alright?" he asked her very softly.

Her hair was as soft as silk against his chest as she nodded.

She wasn't all right. She was as strong as steel. She would defend herself to the death, he knew, but even steel could be bent.

"Thank God!" he murmured, urging Tor in a steady walk along the trail. He drew the backs of his fingers over her cheeks. "You've got to be all right tonight. I don't want you to miss the sight of me on my knees when I know you'll enjoy it so much."

She jerked slightly away from him and turned around to look at him. Her face was smudged. The beautiful doeskin dress was a mess. She had put up quite a fight. He drew a line over one of the smudges on her face, smiling.

"Earth Woman admitted to the pepper."

Her eyes widened. "Why, that—bitch!" she exclaimed.

He smiled. "I'm sorry."

"Not good enough."

"Really sorry."

"Still not good enough."

"Then you'll just have to wait a bit," he said gruffly. "But then, you owe me an apology as well."

"I owe you—"

"For this morning. I was never with Earth Woman." When she said nothing, he prompted, "Well?"

"I'm sorry, too."

"You didn't believe in me."

"You certainly didn't believe in me regarding the pepper!"

"I already promised you a better apology, but I think life will go a little bit more smoothly if we both start believing in each other. What do you say?"

She nodded.

He nudged Tor to a quicker gait. The others rode behind them now. When they returned to the camp by the river, though the hour was late, other warriors, old men, young men, women, and children rushed out to greet them. Squaws took the scalps.

The camp came alive with activity.

But Hawk evaded it, leaving Sloan to make any apologies for him. He carried his wife into their tipi and set her down, studying her from head to toe for injury as he had done once before.

"I'm all right," she insisted. "Well, my ankle is a bit sore because I tripped and bit my lip when that Crow warrior clamped his hand down on my mouth, but—"

"No one hurt you."

She frowned suddenly. "Hawk, one man spoke English."

"Sloan said he was a mixed blood he'd seen around one of the army forts," Hawk said.

"He said he'd just as soon kill me sooner than later if I didn't shut up, but one of the others shouted at him, and he shut up. Are such attacks common?"

"Yes and no. The Crow and the Sioux have been enemies forever. We have fought forever, we take coup upon one another, steal horses...

but this...this is the strangest damned thing I've ever seen, even if you do have spectacular hair."

"Do I?" she inquired, almost smiling. Hawk breathed a sigh of relief. She was going to be all right.

"I'm waiting to see you on your knees," she told him.

She was definitely going to be all right, he thought as he went down upon a knee. "I'm sorry. I am really, truly, honestly sorry. I kneel humbly before you in apology. Will that suffice?"

"With a little more pure humility in your voice it won't be half bad."

"I'm humble."

"The hell you are."

"But I really am sorry. You did work hard all day, and you did intend to appear to be a perfect Sioux wife."

"I always pay my debts."

"Your debts? Ah. Your sister, right?"

"Yes."

"Well, it seems you've found monsters here, but apparently, you've known a few monsters in the past. I wouldn't want her under attack by any monsters either. But then, perhaps you'd like to tell me a little bit more about the monsters in your past?"

Skylar shook her head. "Not tonight, please. The past, please God, is behind me," she said softly. She wasn't about to give him anything more. And tonight it didn't matter. Nothing else mattered. Right now, it was too good just to hold her.

"Am I forgiven?" he asked her.

She nodded, then shivered fiercely. "I have to forgive you. You came for me again. You were alive. You saved my life."

"They wouldn't have killed you."

"I think that they did mean to kill me. Eventually."

Hawk stood, shaking his head. "You're safe," he said huskily. "And very beautiful. Maybe you're not so safe. I'm shaking, needing to hold you again."

"I'm a mess, covered with dirt."

"You're very beautiful, and I can understand why any man would want to ravish you."

"I think you've already done some ravishing tonight."

"I thought you were doing the ravishing there."

She smiled. A real smile, sweet and warm. She shrugged.

"I was so afraid that you were dead. And at the same time, I couldn't believe that you could have possibly been killed."

"If I'd been killed, you know, Mayfair would have been yours. And you would have been the widowed Lady Douglas."

"I never wanted to take anything from your father—or you," she told him. "And I—"

"What?"

She shrugged. "I don't want to be the widowed Lady Douglas."

He smiled, nodding his head. "Do you know what?"

"What?"

"I'm actually rather glad to have a wife."

"Are you?"

"Very much so at times like this."

There was a definite insinuation in his voice. "I was frightened by what happened tonight," she reminded him, "but you were injured. Your head—"

"I had a headache, but it's gone. Now that I have dutifully groveled, I could perhaps use a little gentle care myself."

"Hawk, they knocked you out. You were hurt—"

"Nothing that you can't make better."

"But—"

"Lady Douglas!" he groaned. "Must I state it plainly? You'll not get me on my knees again, I'm not in any pain, and I want my wife. Come here, woman," he demanded with a wry grin.

Skylar lowered her head, a half-smile playing upon her lips. She looked up at him. "I know that we're in Sioux country, but could you possibly come here, man? Meet me in the middle?"

He arched a brow. "Hmm. What an invitation."

Skylar took a step forward. She reached down for the hem of the buckskin dress and drew the garment over her head, tossing it carefully aside. She was smudged with dirt and dust, just as he was, but he just didn't give a damn right now. Passion simmered slowly. Provocatively. He needed to hold her now. Touch her.

Shivering just slightly, she stared at him, waiting.

"What an invitation!" he repeated in a husky whisper.

Her smile deepened. Her eyes glittered, and she cocked her head just slightly.

"Want to bet I can't get you on your knees again?" she teased him.

But then she gasped because he had moved so quickly, sweeping her up. Then she was on the ground, lying upon a bed of furs, his body on top of hers. What remained of the red blaze from the cooking fire warmed them, just as the silver fire that exuded from her eyes seared into him, building new heat, slow, simmering warmth. Everything slow, everything savored, so careful...

So tender.

She did get him on his knees again.

And magically, a night that had begun in fear and bloodshed and fury became...

Eden.

# CHAPTER 22

They stayed among the Crazy Horse people for three more days, then they prepared to depart. They would head south to the site where the meeting between the representatives of the American government and the Sioux was scheduled to take place. It would take them two days to ride there. They would be traveling southeast, from Montana back to Dakota territory.

When they were ready to leave, Skylar bid a fond farewell to Hawk's family and to the other people she had come to know during her visit. When they mounted their horses, she was surprised to see that Blade and Ice Raven would be accompanying them.

It was ironic, she thought, that she would be riding with all four of the warriors who had attacked her stagecoach and convinced her that she was about to be slaughtered and scalped just a matter of a few weeks earlier. Sloan made their number five. He and Hawk still wore the clothing they had donned each day during their visit to the camp: breechclouts, leggings, moccasins, little else. If it weren't for her hair, Skylar thought, she would fit right in with them. She had become so involved in Sioux generosity that she had given away all the clothing she had brought with her and now wore nothing more than doeskin herself.

Crazy Horse came out to bid them all farewell. What the men said, Skylar had no idea. They seemed to be parting in complete friendship, but for some reason, the words spoken between them made her uneasy. She smiled at Crazy Horse and waved goodbye to him. He smiled in return and raised his hand in farewell as well. She was glad that he seemed to like her, for she had to admit that she liked him, even though he was extremely warlike and might go to battle against the whites at any given time. He was still a man of integrity, one who had been backed against a rock time and time again. He didn't intend to be an agency Indian, a drunkard, or a layabout. His way was free and steeped in tradition. She couldn't blame him for being ready to fight for his own existence.

Earth Woman, who had apologized about the pepper and decided to become Skylar's friend after the attack, bade her a warm farewell—one that seemed sincere. But then Hawk had told Skylar that both Crazy Horse and Sloan had severely chastised her—the incident had made them all vulnerable to the attack.

The children ran alongside them as they rode from the camp by the river. The men tossed down keepsakes to the children, Sloan providing whistles he had carved and cavalry buttons, Hawk, Ice Raven, and Blade dropping some of their arrows.

When they reached the more heavily wooded countryside, Skylar urged Nutmeg up closer to Tor. "Why are your cousins coming with us? I thought they had decided they wanted to stay away from the white community, with the Crazy Horse people."

Hawk shrugged without saying anything for a moment, then he told her, "No one understands why parties of Crow Indians and others keep appearing to wrest you away."

Skylar frowned. "I don't mean to tread upon your feelings, but it is natural for many of the Indian bands in the West to attack whites."

Hawk smiled wryly, shaking his head. "The attacks were just a bit too strange. You thought so yourself. Remember? You told me one of the men spoke English. Sloan had seen one of them before."

"Is that so unusual?"

"Maybe not. It's just that..."

"What?"

"Something seems not quite right."

Skylar sighed softly. "Hawk, lots of things just aren't right at all."

"Beyond the obvious," Hawk told her. He cocked his head toward her, a wry half-smile curved into his features. "Skylar, I don't tend to be a superstitious man—perhaps I'm too grounded in my father's white world—but having you abducted twice in less than a week seems a bit on the strange side. Even among warring Indians. To be less than careful would be entirely foolish. Between us, Sloan, Willow, Ice Raven, Blade, and myself, of course, we're quite a powerful group."

"I do believe you." Skylar smiled. "So Ice Raven and Blade came along to protect me?"

"They won't come to the conference on the Black Hills. They'll turn back when we near the site."

"That makes it all the nicer that they are willing to come so far."

"We do our best to protect our women."

"Wives," Skylar murmured.

"What?"

She looked at him innocently. "Wives. In the plural."

He grinned. "Such jealousy warms my heart, Lady Douglas."

"I'm not jealous in the least."

He reined in suddenly, catching hold of Nutmeg's reins to pull her back as well. "I can be a very jealous soul myself, my lady. Thank God you hadn't had much of a past when you came to me. But then, there's so much about your past that I don't know! Should I be jealous, worried?"

"I can't imagine you worried," she told him.

"Ah, jealous, then."

"That from the man who might not have chosen a multitude of wives at one time, but most certainly entertained a score of lovers!"

"But my past is an open book."

"Umm. I get to read it every time I stumble upon it."

He laughed softly. "Well, there is nothing anyone can do to change the past."

"Only the present—and the future," Skylar added.

"Umm," he murmured. He was looking at her intently, and she was tempted to start blurting out explanations. But the bonds that held them together still seemed too fragile and tenuous. How could she explain that she would have done anything in the world—to escape the man who had killed her father?

The respected man who had killed her father.

She saw that he was still looking at her probingly. She pointed to her right, where the sun was just falling behind a mound of emerald-green grass, dotted with purple wildflowers. "My God, have you ever seen such a sunset!" she exclaimed.

His gaze moved in the direction in which she pointed. She kneed her roan and glanced back at him. "Race you to it!" she challenged, and took off, flying across the field.

She knew she was not nearly as good a rider as Hawk. The Indians of the Western Plains tribes seemed to be the most spectacular horsemen she had ever witnessed in action. But she was a good rider, and she could certainly try to outrace him.

The only problem was that he raced on Tor.

Nutmeg tired as she dipped down into the valley. She slowed her gait. He came behind her on Tor. Before she could catch her own breath, he had leaped from Tor and caught her about the waist, bringing them both down into the rich green grass. They rolled in it, laughing. Then Hawk rose, drawing her to her feet. "The others will be right behind us. Seems like a good place to camp for the night, though. What do you think?"

She looked around, then shook her head. "No water."

He smiled. "Smell the air."

"The air?"

"The water is down at the bottom of that hill."

She stared at him doubtfully, then started to run down the hill to the next rise.

A brook gently trickled by beneath her.

Sloan, Willow, Ice Raven, and Blade came riding up and dismounted from their horses.

Hawk started to unpack with Willow.

Sloan rode over to Skylar. "Did he really smell water?" Skylar demanded.

"Of course," Sloan told her.

He lifted his horse's saddle from the animal. "Then, of course, we camped here a few times before, so he probably knew the creek was right down there anyway."

He winked at her and walked away.

That night, they slept in a circle in a copse of trees. Two men remained on guard throughout the hours of darkness.

It was a peaceful night. Skylar slept beside Hawk. Slept with her head upon his chest.

He rested his hands upon her shoulders, her hair.

But even when his watch was over, he stayed awake through most of the night.

Watching.

He sensed a strange danger. Sensed a warning in the call of the night birds. Felt it burn within his blood.

But he couldn't see it.

The hours passed. The night was uneventful. Morning came, and they prepared to ride again.

Though they traveled light, it took them two days of riding in a southeasterly direction to reach the agreed-upon site for the conference.

The morning before the meeting was to take place, they came upon a temporary camp for some of the white commissioners, army personnel, journalists, and the sutlers who were bound to follow such a group.

Before they neared the white camp, Ice Raven and Blade departed. Skylar wanted to thank them, perhaps hug them goodbye. But the Sioux were not demonstrative, and she had learned that wives were seldom direct with the male relatives of their husbands, and so she simply said goodbye and thank you, and waved when the two of them left.

"Hawk! Major! Willow!" A soldier called as they neared the camp. He hurried out to meet them, a young man with red hair, freckles, and a lieutenant's insignia upon his uniform. He wore a broad grin. "Why, you two look more like redskins than redskins!" he exclaimed. "And Willow, well..."

"Well, I'm Willow, eh?" Willow said.

Skylar was surprised that neither her husband, Willow, nor Sloan seemed to take offense. Sloan looked at Hawk. Hawk shrugged.

"It's the boy's red hair," Hawk said. "He wishes he had the skin to match it."

"Irish," Sloan said sadly with a shake of his head.

"Irish is just fine," Hawk said, "if you can mix it with Sioux."

"An Irish Sioux!"

"It's happened upon occasion," Sloan warned.

The young man grinned, but then his grin froze as he gazed at Skylar. "Oh, my God! Is this gorgeous creature such a mixed blood? I'd have never imagined—"

"Danby, this is my wife, Lady Douglas, recently come west from Baltimore," Hawk said.

His jaw dropped. "Oh, God! Now I've sworn—I'm sorry, Hawk, I—"

"Skylar, meet Lieutenant Danby Dixon. Danby, Lady Douglas," Sloan interrupted.

"Skylar, please," she told the lieutenant, smiling down at him. "It's a pleasure to meet you, sir. And thank you very much for finding me gorgeous."

The lieutenant smiled sheepishly up at Skylar, "Good day to you, Lady Douglas—Skylar!" He gaped at her a second longer, then seemed to come to his senses. He lowered his voice quickly. "Hawk, Major, Willow, I think it's a hard time to be Sioux, indeed. Why, it seems to me folks in Washington must be blind. They can't keep a promise to save a life, and that's a sad fact. They're tense as rabbits about this conference. The general is just about gnawing on his own hat, awaiting your report, Major. Though what anyone is meeting about, I don't know. The folks from Washington want the Black Hills burst wide open. And it's happening!"

They neared a cluster of tents where Skylar saw officials in civilian dress, military men in uniform, and Indian scouts in their mixture of Plains dress and army issue. Suddenly a young woman with long pigtails came hurrying forward. "Bless me!" she exclaimed, staring at Skylar. She pressed her hand to her heart. "Bless me!" she repeated.

"Minister's wife, Sarah," Danby said, making the introduction as if it were a warning.

Skylar realized that it was her doeskin dress the woman was staring at in horror. She had forgotten her apparel until now. How foolish. There weren't many women at the camp, but those she saw were respectably dressed, in petticoats and skirts that had been somewhat modified for prairie conditions, but they were all quite feminine and fashionable, nonetheless.

"You poor, poor dear!" she exclaimed. "Lord Douglas, has this darling creature been a prisoner among the Sioux? Have you brought her back to the bosom of her own people? Does she speak English?"

"Quite well, Sarah. This is my wife, Skylar."

Sarah's jaw dropped, much as Danby's had done. "There was a rumor from up your way that you had married, Hawk, but—oh, God, I am sorry. Lady Douglas. Er, Lady Douglas..." she broke off, extremely uncomfortable. "Lady Douglas, the sutler has some lovely gowns, if you're interested."

Skylar glanced at Hawk, amused.

He smiled in return. "I imagine my wife is quite interested. Skylar, I assure you, you'll be fairly safe in Sarah's company."

"Lord Douglas, you can be very bad!" Sarah chastised him.

"Bad can be good upon occasion, Sarah," Sloan assured her.

Poor Sarah flushed crimson. "Danby, can you please escort these men to the general? He'll get them into some civilized clothing, and perhaps they'll learn to mind their manners and quit taunting a naïve little spirit like me!"

Hawk laughed. "Don't let her fool you, Skylar. She's a tigress."

"Danby!" Sarah cried. "Will you please!"

"Major, Lord Douglas, please follow me."

Danby seemed happy enough with his task as escort. "Lady Douglas, if you wish to accompany Sarah, I'll care for your horse."

Skylar thanked him. She slipped down from Nutmeg, well aware that Sarah was staring at her. Sarah suddenly regained her own manners. "I'm so sorry. Your hair is just so—"

"Blonde?" Skylar suggested.

"For that outfit!" Sarah gasped.

"I'm afraid I gave my 'civilized' clothing away," Skylar told her, emphasizing the word "civilized."

Sarah didn't notice. She shuddered. "You've just come from the East? And been cast among the heathens!"

"My husband is half heathen."

Sarah crossed herself. "Hush now! We've worked hard to bring him into the proper fold."

"Oh!" Skylar said. She hurried along with Sarah, who could walk very briskly. She felt the eyes of soldiers, civilians, and the scattered women here and there upon her. She straightened her shoulders, wondering with more than a trace of amusement how many of them thought that she had been a prisoner of the Sioux, recently released by Hawk, Sloan, and Willow.

Then she felt guilty, well aware that many people here had had friends and family slaughtered by the Indians. She had found it very easy to take the Sioux side in this battle, perhaps because she had seen the Sioux side of it for the first time.

War was tragic for both sides, she reminded herself.

In a matter of moments, Sarah had her to the sutler, and in a matter-of-fact way, had quickly managed to go through every single one of the man's garments, bargained outrageously for everything Skylar could possibly need, and managed to get it all folded and in a basket.

"The general will make arrangements for your tent tonight," Sarah assured Skylar. "For now, you must come with me. David—my husband—is out among the men. You can wash and divest yourself of that dreadful garment—"

"This dreadful garment is a cherished gift," Skylar said firmly.

"Oh." Sarah didn't exactly say the word. Her mouth rounded into it. She stared at Skylar. Then she started walking again. "Well. Well. One day, we'll reach the Indians. David says so. Then they won't be heathens any longer, and they'll learn that they can't do murder and that they must settle down to white ways. You can just...change your clothing. Fold up your, er, gift, and pack it for home."

Sarah hurried on. Skylar followed her, considering the woman a rather pompous but well-meaning creature.

Two hours later, she had washed. Her flesh carried the scent of Sarah's lavender soap, and she wore a dress of calico cotton, silk stockings, and leather shoes. David, young like his wife—just as pompous, Skylar thought, but just as well meaning—had come back to the large tent he had set up at the campsite. Hawk, Sloan, Willow, the general, and many of his aides had come to the minister's, and Skylar sipped sherry while she listened to the men worry about the question before them. She realized that the soldiers among them seemed to realize that the treaties thus far made with the Sioux had been nothing more than promises made to be broken, and that half of them were sick about what duty required them to do.

A serious, middle-aged captain named Clark was especially interested in querying Hawk, Sloan, and Willow.

"Is it definite, then, that none of the Crazy Horse people will come?"

"It is definite that Crazy Horse will not attend," Sloan told him politely.

The captain seemed deeply depressed. "I see trouble ahead. Great trouble."

"The whites just don't want to see how far they're pushing the Sioux," Hawk said.

"The whites! The whites!" Captain Clark exclaimed unhappily. "We group them all together as savages. I suppose it is only fair that they group us together in return. I find our policies appalling! But if we wind up in battle, no brave will stop to ask me if I approve of American policy before he takes my scalp."

"He wouldn't understand that you weren't part of it," Skylar said quietly. "The only reason he will go into battle against you is because he chooses to do so. He assumes you have made a similar choice."

She had spoken so softly. She realized that despite that, everyone in the tent was staring at her. Her husband in particular. He smiled at her and set down the glass of sherry he had been drinking. He turned to the general and the minister and his wife.

"We've had a long ride. If I understand correctly, you've accommodations for me and my wife?"

"Of course, Lord Douglas! Danby will be glad to escort you to your tent."

Skylar said her goodnights, thanking Sarah. She paused by Sloan. He smiled and very elegantly and properly kissed the back of her hand.

Danby, talking away, brought them to their tent.

It was fairly large, with a decent enough camp bed. It was closely surrounded by many other tents. Hawk sighed softly, removing the white shirt he had donned since she had seen him before the party, tossing it over the back of a folding camp chair.

He sighed. "I guess we'd better get some sleep," he said.

Skylar nodded, stripping down to her chemise. She climbed into the small cot. He doused the lamp on the crude table in the center of the tent, getting in beside her. He scooped an arm around her, holding her close.

"Comfortable?" he asked her.

"Yes."

He was silent a minute. "You know, you've actually done quite well in a house, a tipi, and a tent."

"I'm so glad you think I can handle 'hardship' competently."

He laughed softly. "I'm very..."

"Yes?"

"Proud of you," he said.

She smiled. "Thank you."

His arm tightened around her.

"We've no..."

"Privacy?" he finished for her. He must have felt both her comfort —and her discomfort.

"No privacy."

"We need some sleep anyway," he said politely. His hand moved very gently through her hair. "Good night...wife."

She smiled and closed her eyes.

He didn't close his. Somewhere in the night, very late in the night, he noted a shadow.

The fire just outside the tent had burned low. Perhaps he imagined the shadow.

No. No matter how low the light might be, the canvas of the military tent was light and thin, reflecting any form of shadow.

And someone was moving just beyond their tent. Lifting the flap.

He leaped up in a silent flash, prepared this time, ready to follow...

"Hawk?"

She whispered his name, frightened, only half awake, clinging to him.

The shadow was gone.

"Hawk, what is it?"

"Nothing. Nothing, Skylar. I'm so sorry I woke you. Just a—a dream," he said. He smoothed her hair.

She lay back again, her cheek against his chest. So trustingly. He stared at the canvas ceiling, entirely frustrated.

"Monsters," she murmured, falling back asleep. Her fingers moved over the bare flesh of his chest. He bit back a groan.

They'd be home soon. Back to Mayfair. He'd be in complete control there. She'd be safe from Crow attacks.

He wondered why he had the feeling that monsters just might follow them anyway.

The actual meeting was to take place some distance from where they had camped.

The site had been chosen by two of the major Indian reservations, so that all traveled the same distance and none of the major chiefs would be insulted.

Seated upon Nutmeg, at a place somewhat back from where the action was to take place, Skylar watched as the meeting formed. She had seen the Indians, of course. Seen them all day. Walking and riding along the hills above the valley, some sitting as if they, too, had come to observe and awaited the spectacle of the day.

But then, as the United States commissioners and their army guard along with their Indian scouts set out and waited before their command tent, the warriors began to arrive in earnest.

The sun was high in the sky. It was noon.

They came out of the hills, and though they frightened her, they were a fantastic display. Their ponies raced, churning up dirt and dust and earth and grass. They galloped, reared, cantered, the first chief leading his men, perhaps a party of two hundred, down a sloping hill.

They whooped and cried out. Their voices rose in a tremolo. They burst down upon the waiting commissioners, circling them in a dramatic, awesome, terrifying display. They took their places before the commissioners. Their chief dismounted from his horse and came forward, taking his place.

Then the next group rode down from the hills. Then the next, and the next. The riders were magnificent. Some more heavily clothed, some nearly naked. They wore feathers in their long dark hair, some with one or a few feathers, some with beautiful bedecked, long, glorious bonnets. They were incredibly disciplined in their display. And when they had all congregated before the commissioners, there were thousands of them.

They called out, shouted, raised their weapons, shook their fists.

"Think we may have trouble?" Hawk asked Sloan.

Sloan shrugged, his dark eyes slanting toward Skylar. He smiled. Shook his head.

"Not even two hundred whites. Thousands of Indians. Why would there be trouble?" she asked sweetly.

Hawk looked out over the assembly. "They know what will happen if they slaughter these commissioners and the army officers."

"A lot of innocent men will die," Skylar murmured.

"The whole army would come after them, with the complete blessing of every citizen in the United States. So far, there are still those back home who frown on the wholesale slaughter of native peoples in the pursuit of Manifest Destiny," Hawk said coolly.

"Red Cloud is getting ready to speak," Sloan said.

A warrior, dark and leathered from his life in the sun, yet with a strong, dignified bearing, stood before them all. Yet before he could begin to speak, it seemed that the crowd of Indians began to undulate, breaking apart, giving way. Skylar heard a screech rising high on the wind. She turned from Red Cloud to see that another man was racing into the crowd. She thought that she knew him. He was the one they had called Little-Big-Man—he had been one of the warriors who had ridden with her husband against the Crow when they had rescued her that night. He was completely naked upon his pony except for a small breechclout and the war bonnet he wore, created of feathers, streaming like a banner in the wind as he burst his way through the Indians, past Red Cloud, to the open space before the commissioners. He carried a rifle and lifted it high, shouting.

"What's he saying?" Skylar asked anxiously. She could see that the Indians were growing restless. A low sound was building among the warriors as they talked among themselves.

They didn't answer her. Hawk, Sloan, and Willow had grown very tense as they listened. Now they mounted their horses and flanked her.

"What—?"

Willow, at her husband's side, gave her the answer. "He says that he has come to kill the white men who are stealing Indian lands."

Skylar clamped her hand over her mouth, silencing a scream, as she saw the warrior take aim at one of the white commissioners. But he never fired a shot. Young-Man-Afraid, a warrior who had joined with the agency Indians, rode through the crowd with a small group of his Indian police behind him. He spoke very quickly, disarming Little-Big-Man before the indignant warrior could fire at anyone.

"Thank God!" Skylar breathed.

"Trouble," Sloan said softly.

"But—"

Hawk had suddenly turned in the saddle to Willow. "Stay with Skylar," he said.

And raced into the grouping of Indians, Sloan quickly following behind him. Yet even as they rode, cries, tremolos, and shouts were rising among the Indians. The sounds were menacing.

Thousands of Indians.

Only a couple hundred whites.

The Sioux were raising their weapons. The shouts were growing more furious.

Hawk burst in among them, calling out.

"What is he saying?" Skylar cried worriedly.

Willow looked at her, not wanting to tell her.

"Willow!"

"He's telling them that they must not murder the whites gathered here. If they do, the whites will come by the tens of thousands and slaughter them all in turn. They mustn't let violence happen today."

"Will they listen?" Skylar demanded.

"I hope so," Willow said.

Sloan was in the midst of the agitated Indians as well. Young-Man-Afraid shouted to them, crying out.

"I should get you out of here, back to where we camped," Willow said.

"But—"

"Skylar, don't make him worry about you in the midst of this!" Willow said.

She nodded to his wisdom. She turned her horse and started to ride. But then she heard a thudding sound. Willow gasped out. She turned back and saw him clutching his head. "Ride!" he commanded her, then toppled down to the ground. Just behind him, Skylar could see a mounted Indian—and on the ground the heavy rock he'd cast at Willow.

She didn't know what kind of Indian he was, but he was dressed in splendid regalia, with all manner of paint on his face. He let out a cry and started toward her.

She kneed Nutmeg, well aware that there was so much cacophony around her that no one would notice a single Indian chasing after a single rider. Yet she realized she would be best off racing toward the fray, rather than away from it. She circled Nutmeg, with the rider close behind her.

"Help me!" she cried out, but the din around her was too loud.

She remained on the outskirts of the crowd. The Indian suddenly leaped from his horse, bringing her down to the ground. She lashed out at him, shrieking. His fingers closed around her throat. She didn't know if he was trying to silence her...

Or kill her.

She heard the sudden whip through the air of a knife.

The Indian stared at her, falling toward her. She pushed his body from her person, scrambling her feet in a desperate rush to avoid his blood. She looked behind her, from where the knife had come.

Sarah stood there. Blessed Sarah. Skylar had had no right to mock the woman—she'd seen the trouble and gone for Hawk regardless of the melee around them. Hawk stood at her side. Hawk had hurled the knife. And now he walked past her to kneel down and study the brave on the ground.

"Who is he?" Skylar demanded.

"Elk-Who-Runs. A Sioux from the Red Cloud agency."

"A Sioux?" she whispered.

He looked up at her, his green eyes veiled. When he spoke, his words were deep and brittle. "Yes, an agency Sioux. This will not sit well today."

"I've never, never seen anything like this!" Sarah exclaimed. "Never. In the midst of something so important as this council, a warrior trying to take down a woman!"

"Sarah, this isn't over," Hawk said. "Will you go with Skylar back to the camp? Some of the soldiers will escort you." They were ringed now by a number of men who saluted their agreement.

Sarah nodded. She came forward, taking Skylar's arm. The dead Indian remained on the ground. Hawk remained kneeling by his side.

Skylar was hurt and humiliated. She'd never seen Hawk so cold, and she didn't begin to understand him. But she went along with Sarah, awkwardly smiling a thank-you to their impromptu guard. "I think you just saved my life," Skylar told Sarah. "Thank you.so much."

Sarah nodded in simple acknowledgment, not terribly impressed with herself. "I saw what happened—I was amazed. I sent David to Willow and went for Hawk. Come on, let's get Willow ourselves now and go back to camp."

"Willow is—"

"Hurt with a terrible headache and a gash against his temple. His pride is wounded to the core. Let's go."

"Oh, God, I'm afraid to leave!" Skylar said, turning back. Hawk was gone—the dead man was gone. The Indians were still shouting, moving about on their horses in a menacing way.

A Sioux was dead. A man who had attacked her.

"The men are still in danger—"

"The men will do their jobs. Our job is to let them do theirs."

And to worry, Skylar thought. Worry sick...

Yet as Sarah urged her away, it seemed...seemed...that the situation was coming under control. Young-Man-Afraid was speaking again. He was surrounded by his police, Hawk, Sloan, and others who were desperately urging peace.

"Why would a Sioux have attacked me?" Skylar whispered.

Sarah sighed. "Dressing up in buckskin doesn't make you Sioux. Please, Skylar, please come on."

Skylar remounted Nutmeg and rode with Sarah.

She was in her own tent, curled up in the camp bed when Hawk finally came back. She'd waited and waited and half dozed. When he came in, she forgot how cold he had been to her before. She leaped up and threw herself into his arms.

"My God, you're back! I was so frightened—"

"What the hell is going on?"

He was shaking, she realized. His voice was harsh, furious.

She pulled back from him. "I was worried—"

"You were attacked again! Willow was struck, injured. And you were nearly throttled."

"Perhaps I shouldn't have been where I was."

"Skylar, what the hell is going on?"

"I don't know what you mean!"

"What have you done? What were you running from when you met my father?"

She pulled away from him completely. "Not the Crows, I can assure you!"

"That man was Sioux!"

"I did nothing to any Indians. You attacked me, as a matter of fact. Add that to the number of attacks I've suffered in the Dakota territory!"

He was suddenly on top of her, shaking her. "You could have been killed."

"You could have been killed!" she retorted. "We could all have been killed. It was an explosive situation!"

"And it's still a damned explosive situation!" he assured her.

"Hawk, shush! The entire camp can hear—"

He lifted her by her upper arms, throwing her back down upon the cot. "You could have been killed. And I was nearly helpless to do a damned thing about it. If Sarah hadn't come for me ... Tomorrow—tomorrow we head back to Mayfair, and so help me, Skylar, so help me! You're going to tell me what's going on!"

"I don't know what's going on!"

His fingers squeezed her arms painfully. His features were dark, constricted, his eyes gleaming with a furious green fire. He looked as if he longed to throttle her himself.

"Damn you, Skylar!" he hissed.

His hold upon her eased. Then he rose, swearing heatedly.

He walked out of the tent.

Skylar tossed. Turned. Lay awake. Tossed and turned again. Where was he? Why wasn't he coming back? Why did he think she could possibly have an explanation for the strange behavior of Indians?

At last, in exhaustion and misery, she dozed. Then she slept deeply.

No monsters troubled her dreams.

No monsters. Her dreams were sweet. She felt his touch. Featherlight. Erotic. Sensual.

His fingers...along her thighs. Palms, cradling her breasts. His lips upon her bare nape. Lower. His hands again, smoothing around her hips. Pressing downward. Stroking. His lips lower against her back. Lower. His touch, turning her. His lips. The fiery hot liquid stroke of his tongue...

She moaned. Writhed. Awoke...

He was no dream.

She remembered to be angry. Too late. He had taken his time seducing her from sleep. He took his passion quickly. She couldn't deny her response.

But when it was done...

She turned her back on him.

She simply didn't have the answers he was demanding.

And he...

He was refusing to believe.

"You can't do this!" she choked out to him.

He was quiet a moment. "I did do this."

"You can't do this to me!"

"Skylar, you do not know what you have done to me," he told her.

And he turned his back on her.

The next morning, the army doctor said that Willow could travel. He'd have a bump on his head for a few weeks from the rock that had knocked him senseless from his horse, but other than that, he seemed fine.

With very little conversation between them, Skylar and Hawk started home with Willow and Sloan.

The meeting had yielded what they had feared it would.

Nothing.

# CHAPTER 23

Sloan knew that he would have been welcome at Mayfair, but his mood was too volatile for him to feel comfortable in the company of friends.

He was due back in the next few days at Fort Abraham Lincoln, but he was glad as well that he wasn't due tonight—the Sioux half of him was warring away in his soul. There were too many army commanders he would like to scalp at the moment.

He rode into Gold Town alone, taking a room at the Miner's Well. Like most of the town, it offered whatever might be desired. The respectable wives, daughters, sisters, aunts, cousins, and lovers of army personnel and prospectors might take rooms here and find them clean and neat. There was a huge, warm dining room where home-cooked meals were served. Baths were available in room, there was a pleasant downstairs library, and the plump, matronly Mrs. Smith-Soames was available to direct nice young ladies around town.

For those of a more adventuresome nature, the Ten-Penny Saloon sat just out back, the work yards of each establishment being next door to one another, with side doors and servants' entrances facing one another. Though all the food served in Mrs. Smithe-Soames' dining room was excellent, food and liquor could be ordered from the Ten-

Penny at off-hours and discreetly brought in by the side entrance to appease the hunger of late-arriving guests.

Other hungers could be appeased as well from the Ten-Penny. Even more discreetly so. An order merely needed to be placed at the saloon, and a soft tap would come upon a man's door. It was all quite smoothly arranged. As they were located in Gold Town, the saloon and the inn catered to whatever tastes their clientele might have nurtured, be they the most chaste—or the most decadent.

Sloan had never been much of a drinker—he was far too aware of the way whiskey had been used by the red man across the continent, and too often, how it had taken a great warrior, set him upon agency land, and eaten into both his soul and his guts, leaving him a sad creature to wallow in the mud of uselessness. Not that whites couldn't become pathetic drunks as well. They could, quite easily. But the Indians just seemed to have more strikes against them to begin with.

Returning from the travesty at the Red Cloud agency had left him feeling not just volatile but depressed as well, with a slow simmering anger within him that threatened to become explosive. It didn't help to remind himself that though it had actually been tradition that had sent him to West Point, it had been his choice to remain in the cavalry in the West. He'd spent four years going to war against his classmates, instructors, and friends, and now he was taking part in a crusade to annihilate his own people, and it didn't matter that he tried to stand against the tide, to bring some honor and justice to the Sioux. He was a candle against the wind, a flame burning bright, yet unable to illuminate any paths that could take his people out of the way of the onslaught of the storm.

After he bathed and changed his clothes, he decided a few drinks seemed to be in order before retiring. Once he got some rest, he hoped he'd regain the control that allowed him to slip between worlds and remain true to them both.

With the dust of the trail bathed away and himself decked in civilian attire, he took a walk across the yard to the Ten-Penny.

Joe, the short, round barkeep, supplied him with a bottle of his best whiskey, just in from Tennessee. Sloan shuddered as he swallowed the first shot. The second one went down more slowly.

Dusk had come. Darkness was settling over the town. In a few hours, he thought, the place would be crawling with miners and travelers and the unattached menfolk in the area who were looking for a good time. For the moment, a few wizened old prospectors played a game of cards, cackling now and then at an exceptionally good hand.

He was on his third shot of the whiskey when Loralee, proprietress of the establishment along with Peg-Leg Jack Cleat, came to quietly stand beside him.

"You look plum tuckered, hon," she said softly. He glanced over at her, smiling wryly. She was a very attractive woman, probably nearing fifty, but capable of being every bit as sensual as the youngest of her girls. Her blonde hair was turning gray, but she had a beautiful face, soft amber eyes, handsome bone structure. Her waist was minuscule, her breasts, more than bountiful. She had a nice way about her as well. She was a shrewd businesswoman, charmingly pleasant, and strangely enough, incredibly sincere. "Plum tuckered, and mad as a hornet," she continued.

He offered her a half-smile, lifting his shot glass to her, then pouring her a shot of whiskey as Joe set a glass down for his boss.

"Just tired out, Loralee," he told her.

A ripple of rueful amusement passed over her features as she returned his smile. "Wish I could make it better for you. But I can't. I make it a rule never to fall for the men I bed, and you're nearly lethal when you choose to smile."

He laughed. "Thanks. That sounds like a compliment."

"It is."

"Lots of women aren't fond of Indian blood."

"Lots of women are."

He raised his eyebrows in an offhand acknowledgment. He should have just told Loralee that the world was a wicked, wearying place—and the hell with falling in love. He'd done it once, only once. She'd proclaimed undying devotion.

But then her father had spoken. Warned her that she might never know when Sloan's red blood might tell, when the savagery in him might break loose, despite his mother's impeccable family lines. The girl's father had offered an alternative and suggested she marry an all-white boy from Nebraska who was destined to follow his own father's footsteps into the United States Congress. No telling where that boy might go. Undying devotion had died upon the hearth of undying ambition.

The worst part was, he still saw her now and again. Life did play its tricks. Her congressman had become stout and bald—and lost a lot of teeth. She'd gotten what she wanted along the political trail, but not at home. On those rare occasions when their paths crossed now, she tried to rekindle the past. Maybe she had never realized how much she had hurt him. It didn't matter. He hadn't stopped enjoying women—he'd only ceased to trust them.

"Want to talk?" Loralee asked him.

His smile deepened; he shook his head. "Loralee, I'm feeling as restless as a caged tiger at the moment. I'm not good company for anyone."

"We've just taken in the prettiest little piece of baggage you ever did see, straight from the East. A beauty. She'd be just what you need tonight."

For a moment, he reflected on the offer. He thought of Hawk—and his new wife. The two of them had been at odds—naturally. He knew all about the way Hawk had acquired his wife, knew how she must feel about Hawk's tricks and how Hawk felt just because his deceased father had done all the arranging without telling him. Yet he suddenly felt a stab of envy. Sparks flew between Hawk and his wife, yet they made a blaze that burned with a curious warmth. Skylar was a most unusual woman.

He felt any desire he might have summoned for a whore—any whore, even the most beautiful and talented one in the world—wither away.

"Loralee," he said, and kissed the woman on the forehead. "I think not tonight. I'm going to take my whiskey, slink into my room, and drink myself into pleasant oblivion."

"Sloan, I just may surprise you now—"

"Loralee."

"It's on me, tonight. You're a good man, Sloan."

"And a weary, angry one this evening. Break the girl in in a gentler way, Loralee!"

He picked up the bottle, dropped coins on the bar, and left the saloon.

He walked across the small yard in between the saloon and Mrs. Smith-Soames's proper establishment, looking up at the velvety night sky. Damn, he did need some sleep.

He didn't see anyone as he entered the inn by the side door. He climbed the stairs to his room, closed the door behind him, and leaned against it. Nice enough place. A big hearth with a big fire. A handsome set of library chairs before it. A desk to one side, dressing table to the other. A huge bed. It must have cost a fortune to have the thing hauled out here from the East.

Sloan gazed at his bottle of whiskey. Half gone, and the rough edges of his temper remained. When it was all gone, he just might sleep.

A few minutes later, and he sat before the fire, broodingly watching the swirl of dark amber liquid he had poured into one of the two snifters he had found in his room. He studied the color of the swirling whiskey before each swallow.

"To the wrong life!" he murmured aloud, lifting the glass snifter and watching the firelight play upon it. Glittering gold and amber. The rough edges were beginning to blur.

What in God's name had he ever thought that he could do? As a half-breed, he lived not so much in treacherous times as wretched ones. There would be no real truce now, and if so, what would it matter? The Indians would be pushed back again and again.

He rubbed his forehead. He was a madman, trying to make some kind of difference for the Sioux by serving in a white man's army where the general consensus was that it was all right to murder Indian children because "nits made lice" and Indians were "savages" while the white men were "civilized."

He was in this frame of mind when his door suddenly opened and closed. Frowning, his fingers instantly falling upon the Colt sidearm he had placed on the occasional table next to the chair, he stared at his unbidden visitor.

He hadn't lit any of the lamps within the room. The brocade drapes at the windows had been shut. There was only the light from the fire, which cast a warm orange glow and many shadows over the room. The flickering firelight only served to enhance the exquisite and stunning beauty of the woman who had entered.

All right, he thought, so he was, finally, fairly drunk. Maybe she wasn't so beautiful. She was blurred. As softened as the rough edges of fate that had been ripping at his soul.

She stood stiffly with her back pressed against the door, her eyes at first closed as if she were listening for something out in the hallway. Her hair was glorious—dark and waving with a touch of gold and crimson fire down her back, over her shoulders. Her face, framed by the thick tendrils, was an ivory oval, cheekbones high, mouth generous and defined. Her beautifully arched brows added to the regal perfection of her face. Her skin looked smooth and flawless.

Her eyes suddenly flicked open. Sloan could hear the murmur of voices in the hall. It appeared that those voices had alarmed her, and he realized that she must be Loralee's new "beauty," just in from the East. Perhaps it was the first time she had been sent over to the inn, and the appearance of others in the hall had disturbed her.

He'd never seen a woman arrive from Loralee's in quite the fashion this one did.

Even whores usually dressed to come across the yard.

She was wearing an elegant white robe with chaste and virginal white lace at the collars and cuffs. She hadn't quite tied the garment though, and it hung open to reveal white hose, pantalettes, and corset, the latter laced through with blue satin ribbon. Even taking into consideration the effect of a corset, she had to be the most incredibly curved female he had ever seen, elegantly slim, but endowed with ripe, voluptuous breasts and enticingly rounded hips. He might be deep into the bottle, but this girl was still extraordinary. He found himself standing. He had told Loralee not to send her new beauty. Loralee had apparently done so anyway, undoubtedly thinking she knew damned well what could lighten his mood.

He opened his mouth to tell the woman harshly to go away. To his own surprise, the words died on his lips. He might be drunk, but only a dead man wouldn't be aroused by this creature.

She was staring at him, as if she had just noticed he was in the room. It was a strange gaze she gave him. One something akin to alarm. He wondered if Loralee had warned her he was half Sioux. But any whore coming west would have to realize much of her clientele would have mixed blood. Her gaze moved swiftly from his face to the opening of his white civilian shirt, down to his black boots.

He wasn't sure why, but a sudden warmth suffused him. Lust. Straight and simple, he mocked himself. She was something, all right. She'd make a mint. All a man needed to do was stare at her. Half the deprived fellows coming out of the hills would explode before ever setting a hand upon her.

"Come in," he said. Was his voice slurring roughly? What if someone had been coming in to rob him? Would he have swept that Colt from the table and taken aim quickly enough?

He smiled wryly at himself. He'd wanted the world a little bit blurry. It was damnably so. Was the girl real? He'd have to get closer to find out.

"Wh—what?" she whispered. Her hand was on the door.

"Come in," he repeated, rising from the chair.

She continued to stare at him.

He shrugged and took a long sip of the whiskey. What in the hell was she doing? This was Gold Town. People were shy. Whores weren't shy. Miners weren't often in the mood for a simpering belle. Business was done here, short and simple.

"To be honest, I don't want you here, but you've come. So, either get out or get in and quit clinging to the door."

He took three long strides toward her. "If you don't want to be here, get the hell out. And if you're going to stay, come into the room and away from the damned door!"

She looked as if she might flee at that moment. He could still hear the voices in the hallway.

"Are you going?" he demanded.

"Now?" She seemed appalled at the thought. Maybe she was afraid that Loralee would be furious if she didn't prove her worth. Whatever, he definitely wasn't in the mood for any games.

"Yes, now! Damn you, I just said that I didn't want you here. But you are here. But if you don't want to be here, get out! Is that clear? Just get out!"

"No!" She shook her head wildly.

He caught her arm, mindless of the slight cringe she made, and drew her past him. He set his hand upon the door bolt and slammed it, then set his hands upon his hips as he faced her. "You needn't look so damned panicked. You're not going to be seen with me. No one can get in here."

"No one can get in," she said.

"Of course not."

He tried to curtail his impatience. But hell, this was one strange whore, and he'd already told Loralee that his mood was wretched.

She was still staring at him, and the way that she did so was irritating.

Insulting.

He almost wished that she had gone.

But staring back at her didn't calm the cyclone brewing within him. The heat of his very basic lust was growing. Maybe Loralee had been right, had known exactly what he needed. Whiskey to blur the edges. Some good, fast sex to burn off the fever and passion rolling like the wind within him. Standing closer to her in the flickering firelight, he was made ever more aware of her startling beauty. The girl should have been pouring tea in an aristocrat's dining room, not whoring in a dust-covered mining town. But people made their choices. The clothing she wore was obviously very expensive. Apparently, she had rich tastes. Lucky for her, she was probably going to do damned well out here.

His gaze rested on her throat, the ivory whiteness of it, a pulse beating against it. His gaze lowered. His insides quickened. Her breasts were all but spilling over the corset.

He didn't want her to go.

Yet still...

She was looking at him with that same trace of alarm in her eyes.

He approached her again, grabbing her hand. Long fingers. Manicured nails. An elegant hand. He drew it to him. Opened a button on his shirt and placed her hand against his chest. "Do you have a problem with Indians?" he demanded.

She jerked her hand free. "Are you an Indian?"

His brows shot up, and he looked at her incredulously. "Do I look Norwegian?" he asked slowly.

She extended a hand, indicating the cavalry jacket he had thrown across the foot of the bed. "I—thought you were an officer."

"I wonder about that myself," he murmured. He stared at her again. "I ask you once more, do you have a problem with—"

He broke off. She wasn't listening to him. Again, she seemed to be paying attention to whatever was going on in the hallway.

The hell with it. He'd drunk too much. The right thing at the time. Now it seemed that war drums were pounding in his head, coursing through his body. Loud, hammering, demanding. Sheer forgetfulness was at hand, appeasement for the thunder pulsing through him.

Unbuttoning his shirt, he took a step, closing the gap between them. Caught her face between his two hands. Brought his mouth down hard upon hers. She tasted like mint. Her lips were rich, provocative. He wanted more of them. He drove his tongue between her lips, drawing her hard against him. Her breasts rose, lush and tempting, against his chest, which was bared now. Again he felt the rise of an almost overwhelming desire, stronger than anger, irritation, impatience, bitterness. The deeper he kissed her, the stronger his desire became.

Her hands were on his chest, pushing free. He groaned deeply, unwilling at first to let her go, his desire suddenly so strong that he was tempted to throw her down upon the bed with the brutal force firing its way into his being. He made himself free her. "Damn you, go!" he shouted, shoving her toward the door. She reached it. Her fingers fumbled at the bolt. He thrust past her, opening the bolt.

He heard the voices again. A man speaking. "If I can find the younger girl first—"

He heard no more because she had spun in his arms, slipping beneath the one to stand in the center of the room again. He stared at her, baffled, as she stared back at him. Her eyes huge. Her lips damp, slightly swollen, very provocative. Her robe all the way open. Her breasts heaving with each gulp of air she took.

He fought for control. "Woman, if you don't want to be here, go!" he exploded with impatience.

She focused on him, really focused on him. "I—" she began, then broke off, and apparently came to some decision. For a moment, her lashes covered her eyes. "I'm sorry. I—I'm afraid you're right. I was just—thrown. You are an Indian. Part Indian."

He nodded, his eyes narrowing. "And you are free to leave."

"I—I don't want to go. May I have a drink, please?"

He was about to explode in a dozen pieces, and she looked as if she were expecting finger sandwiches. "Did you want me to order tea?" he inquired in a long drawl.

"Tea. Yes, that would be—" She seemed to catch the incredulous expression on his face. "No!" she exclaimed. "Not tea. I—"

"I have whiskey. From Loralee's."

"That would be—fine."

Perplexed, Sloan poured his visitor a snifter of whiskey. She accepted it, smiled flirtatiously, and walked over to the fireplace. The red glow rose around, casting a very soft crimson sheen over her elegant white robe and lace undergarments. She sipped the whiskey and then gagged.

"Listen," he said. "It's quite apparent you're having problems tonight. But I'll be damned if this is the way I'm going to spend the evening. I can take you back—"

"I'm fine," she protested. She offered him a smile. She had beautiful white teeth. She moved with a quick, supple grace. She walked toward the door again, swallowing more whiskey. This time, she didn't choke. She shuddered. Then she swallowed the rest of the whiskey in the snifter. She hesitated by the door. Once again, he didn't seem to have her full attention. He brought the bottle to her. Poured out another few fingers of whiskey into her glass. That would be about it. He'd almost done in the rest of the bottle himself.

"Thank you," she said briefly.

"Cheers." He clinked his glass to hers. She nodded, jerked her head back. Swallowed. All of it. Three shots of straight whiskey in just about three minutes. Saloon girls were good. They could cost their clientele by drinking down half a fellow's bottle themselves.

This one didn't seem to have much experience drinking as of yet. And he wasn't going to pass out himself. He'd be damned if he'd have her doing so at this point. He took the glass from her.

"I think that's enough."

"No, I, umm..." She stared at him, moistened her lips, seemed to be searching. She started to take a step back, away from him. She faltered slightly, smiled. "I think I need another drink."

"You're weaving."

"I'm—fine."

"You're trying to drink too much."

"I'm not. Besides, you're—"

"Drunk?" he inquired. "Halfway there. Actually, almost just right at the moment. All the edges are nice and fuzzy, but I'm not going to fail you in any way—or let you earn your keep too cheaply. And you're not going to pretend I'm not Indian."

"What?"

"I said you're not going to pretend—"

She swayed suddenly, nearly falling, reaching out for something with which to steady herself. He caught her. She stared up into his eyes.

"Dizzy," she said.

"No more whiskey. You won't be worth ten cents."

She laughed. The sound was a little hysterical. "Depends on who is considering my worth."

"Me." He looked down into her eyes. "I guess," he murmured huskily, "you can pretend I'm whatever the hell you want me to be, hmm?" He didn't remember wanting a woman so much. With such a fever. Such a demand. Now.

He lifted her off the floor. Her eyes closed. Her head hung back. The slightest smile played on her lips. He laid her down, wondering for a moment if she had passed out.

No. She was still smiling. "Dizzy," she murmured. "I feel like I'm floating..."

"Floating. Umm. That's just what I'm dying to do, too. Hell, yes."

He pulled the satin ribbon on her corset. The garment fell loose. Another ribbon held her pantalettes. He tugged at it, then jerked the lacy garment down from her hips. The robe clung to her shoulders, but the rest of her lay naked beneath it. She was enough to rob him completely of breath.

No matter how beautiful she was, she was a whore. Loralee's new addition to the glamourless settlement of Gold Town. Loralee had been right. All the tempest, anger, and passion in him was now directed on one object—this girl. He unbuckled his belt and his trousers. Released his swollen sex. There was no time for play. He caught her ankles, drew her down. Caught her knees, parted them. Her eyes opened wide...

Energy and need pulsed through him wildly. He lay on top of her, his weight and length keeping her legs spread when she tightened them around him.

"Wh—" she began to say.

He barely heard her. He threaded the fingers of his left hand through her hair, pinning her head to the pillow as he hungrily found her mouth, his tongue thrusting into it. His other hand slid along the length of her thigh, into the soft auburn down. He parted her with his touch, plowed into her with the full force of his body. The fever of his hunger had seized him with such startling force and fury that he swept into her again and again before he realized what he was encountering.

She didn't scream, whimper, or cry out. She didn't move.

The most merciful thing about the entire fiasco was that he'd been at such an all-consuming stage of desire that once he'd realized her total inexperience, he'd quickly allowed himself to climax, constricting, shuddering into her again and again—but then withdrawing immediately to rise above her and stare down at her. Her eyes were closed. Her face was white.

He felt...

Duped. Used. Betrayed. Angry. With her. With himself. He'd been drinking, yes, hell yes, but was that any excuse for this?

Excuse? She'd come over as a whore. He was the one who had been taken...

She was the one trembling, biting into her lower lip, refusing to meet his eyes.

He caught her chin between his thumb and forefinger. "Look at me!" he snapped.

Her eyes opened, glittering with tears and fury.

"Was Loralee aware that you hadn't the faintest idea of what you were doing?"

"What?"

He started to rise. "I don't like surprises. You were one hell of a surprise when you arrived, and you were one hell of a surprise just now. I don't know what she thought she was doing, sending you over here, but it sure as hell is time for you to go back—"

"God, no, not now!" she gasped out. Her lashes fluttered over her eyes. "Not...now." Her voice trembled, quivered. She sounded as if she could slip into hysterical laughter at any given second. He gritted down hard on his teeth. She was probably afraid Loralee would fire her. Maybe she had lied to Loralee. But damn...

She was shaking. Her eyes remained closed. "Sweet Jesus, don't throw me out of here now after—after that!" she gasped.

He raised an eyebrow. After that. Her attitude was going to have to improve quite a bit if she thought she was going to make a living out here.

"Please, I can't go now!"

Sighing, he rose, shed his clothing, and lay down beside her. She jumped when he touched her, drawing her against his naked body.

"What is it about your English I'm not understanding?" he demanded irritably. "Didn't you just ask to stay?"

She nodded. "Yes!"

Her hair smelled delicious. Her body was hot, so perfectly curved, flushed against his. He was tempted to touch her. Explore. She shuddered as if with a sob. He shook his head, willing himself to dampen his growing ardor. He knew enough about women to be damned aware she'd be hurting right now. He made do with holding her and letting her sleep.

But he could make do no longer when the morning came.

She had tossed and turned. So had he. Her breasts—those which he considered to be so incredibly perfect, high, rounded, and beautiful—were directly in front of his face. Too tempting to be ignored.

Every whore had to start somewhere—he'd just never had one start with him before—and he felt both the temptation and the obligation to make her realize that her chosen profession could be damned enjoyable. He meant to wake her slowly. Very slowly. He set out to do so.

He touched her lightly with his fingers, his lips, his teeth, his tongue. As he moved against her, he shook his head, incredulous. By morning's light, she was more stunning still. Her flesh was erotically soft, her breasts so firm, her nipples large and pink, swelling, hardening to his elusive touch. Her belly was flat, her throat was long, her legs were wickedly long, curved, beautiful, the down between them was a dark and tempting fire.

She whimpered slightly, rousing. Slowly. Her body arched and writhed, easily manipulated to his desire, each supple rock and undulation arousing new hungers within him. She moaned, twisted. Writhed to the intrusive stroke of his tongue, dug her fingers into his shoulders, his hair.

She woke fully with a shuddering gasp, just as he rose over her. Her blue eyes were wide open. "Oh, God—no! I've got to go—"

"No, I don't think so. All through the night, and you're going to leave now?"

"Not on your life!" he promised her softly.

This time, she did cry out softly, her teeth clamping lightly into his shoulder. He moved very slowly, letting her take him all before stroking into her again, holding, moving, holding, moving again. Her fingers gripped his back.

"I can't..." she whispered.

"You will," he promised. She tossed. He kissed her throat, her breasts. Moved. Rocked. Hungered. Rose higher. Her fists slammed against his chest.

"Can't, can't..." She inhaled on a ragged sob. She seemed to jackknife into a paralyzing constriction, gasping, shaking. He smiled to himself and let the floodgates within him free. Mindless moments of thundering rhythm racked him until he climaxed explosively within her. He fell to her side, then rolled upon an elbow to look into her eyes, laughing. "You can't, my dear, but you just did."

To his amazement, there were now tears in her eyes. "Bastard!" she cried, slamming her hands against his chest. "You bastard!"

He caught her hands firmly. "I don't care how perfect you look. You're never going to make a living at this, behaving the way you do. For one thing, your typical miner is going to want you to arouse him, not the other way around."

"Oh!" she shrieked, wrenching her hands free. She leaped up, hugging her mussed, once elegant white robe around her. He came up on an elbow, watching, puzzled, as she tugged at the bolt. He rose, walking around the bed to the door. Her eyes met his. Swept up and down the length of his naked body. Focused in panic on the bolt again.

He pulled it for her and stepped back. "Come again," he said politely, and opened the door.

"Never! Never in this life, you arrogant oaf!" she charged.

And she was gone.

He shook his head. Strangest damned whore he had ever come across. She'd never make it.

Yet even as he turned away from the door, she was haunting him. And to his amazement...

Her image remained within his mind. His bloodstream. His being. And he wanted her again.

Impatient with himself, realizing that he had the thud of a hangover beginning to pound in his head, he went over to the room's pitcher and basin, and started to wash and dress.

# CHAPTER 24

Meggie made their homecoming warm.

Meggie—and little else.

Skylar wasn't sure just what had snapped within Hawk, but he kept his distance from her. Upon their return, he left her with Meggie and retired to his own room.

He didn't visit hers.

She woke listlessly the next morning, looking about at the beauty that surrounded her. Mayfair was very fine. She had returned to comfort and luxury.

She still loved Mayfair, but everything had changed. Her surroundings didn't matter. She had discovered that comfort was more than crisp, clean sheets. Comfort lived in the soul. It was the warmth exuding from the body of...

The man she had accidentally married.

And then fallen in love with. Not because of the circumstances but despite them.

She rose, determined to find him. She didn't know what answers she could give him about the attacks. She didn't have a long-lost relative who had killed half the Crow Nation. She wasn't related to anyone responsible for massacres. She didn't even have a distant cousin who might have dishonored a Crow maiden.

But she could make every attempt to tell him what she had been running from. He might not believe her. The bond between them was incredibly delicate and fragile. He might think her as insane as Dillman had told her he could convince people she had become. He might not understand. But they had both made mistakes. Half of them through miscommunication. She hadn't expected a living, healthy, vital husband when she had come west, but she had discovered that she wanted him. And she wanted her marriage to work. It was time to put some trust into the relationship that had grown between them.

She rose, washed and dressed quickly, and wondered with a growing excitement if Sabrina might nearly be here. Sabrina would be able to corroborate a lot of what Skylar meant to tell Hawk. But she was actually just as glad that Sabrina hadn't arrived yet. This was something she wanted to do on her own.

Skylar walked to Hawk's room. She tapped firmly. He didn't reply. She realized then that it was late in the morning, that he had probably been awake for hours.

She started along the upstairs hall toward the stairway and then froze.

She heard voices. Several voices. Meggie's voice.

And one male voice in particular. One she knew all too well.

Dillman. Here. Here, in her foyer, in his wheelchair, two young aides—or guards?—flanking him.

Her breath caught as panic invaded her. She'd been an idiot. An absolute idiot, a fool. She should have found a way to create a false identity for Sabrina. She should have told Hawk the truth long ago. Dillman had always been smart. He'd found out about the telegrams. Easy enough for a senator. He'd followed Sabrina. And now...

Sabrina was coming here.

She gasped, inhaling raggedly, realizing she had ceased to breathe altogether.

"Senator Dillman, how do you do? Welcome to Mayfair."

It was Hawk. He was striding into the foyer from the downstairs library. His hair tied back, he was dressed in white shirt, dark, form-hugging breeches, and high boots, ready for a day of work at Mayfair.

"Lord Douglas! I was acquainted with your good father, you know. Casually, I'm afraid to admit. He was a visionary. An extraordinary man. I am heartily sorry regarding his passing."

"Thank you, sir."

"Lord Douglas, Thomas Henley and Bo Dykes. My assistants."

"A pleasure, gentlemen. Won't you come in? Meggie will see to coffee and breakfast. I must admit, however, Senator, that I'm surprised to see you at this late date. I'm afraid the council with the Sioux leaders did not go as the government might have wished, and I'm afraid that I don't agree with the stance the government is taking with the Sioux."

"Precisely the point, my dear sir!" Dillman said. "I'm here to learn what I can from you! I can't agree either with the tone being taken by the generals in the field—kill them all, let God sort them out, and the like! Any man with half a brain—and not fanatical abolitionists!—can take a look at the history between the white man and the Indian and see where we have been at fault."

"That's quite an unusual view, Senator—and an unpopular one," Hawk replied. He frowned suddenly, pausing as they neared the door to the dining room. "Meggie," he said softly, "would you ask Lady Douglas to come down? I'll have Sandra bring the men coffee."

"Of course, Lord Douglas."

Skylar watched Meggie coming up the stairs. The woman immediately appeared concerned. "Lady Douglas! You're ill! Poor dear, my God, you're as white as a sheet. I'll—I'll get Lord Douglas right away!"

Before Skylar could say a word, Meggie was heading back down the stairs. Skylar watched her, glad that she hadn't had a chance to deny the possibility that she might be ill.

She backed away from the staircase. She didn't want anyone coming back into the foyer and looking up by chance. She looked back. The door to Hawk's library stood open. She fled behind it. Oh, God, she'd wanted to tell him the truth.

Now it might be too late.

The truth was sitting downstairs in her dining room.

---

AFTER HE HAD EATEN breakfast in the quiet respectability of Mrs. Smith-Soames's dining room, Sloan decided to pay a visit to Loralee. He walked across to the Ten-Penny Saloon. There was a group of men—very drunk men—seated around one of the gaming tables. Sloan ignored them at first, going up to the bar. He asked Joe for coffee and inquired if Loralee was up and about yet. Joe said he'd see about Loralee.

Sloan sipped his coffee. As he did so, he became aware of the men at the gaming table. One was Ralph Marks, a miner who couldn't seem to strike things quite right. He'd tried gambling, he'd tried scouting. He was a man of about forty, once probably handsome enough, and built like a young ox. But years of drink were catching up with him. He was more rotund than powerful, with a permanent gin blossom reddening his cheeks. The man at his side, sometimes his partner, sometimes not, was a mixed-blood Cherokee named Horse McGee. Horse wasn't given to drink, but he was prone to devious behavior. He was suspected of having been involved in a few stagecoach robberies to the south of Gold Town. Two of the other men were Crows. Both had worked for the army on and off, trailing Sioux warriors. Sioux and Crow were enemies. Sloan couldn't think badly of a man for remaining an enemy when the tradition of violence between the two tribes was an old one. Rounding out the group was Abel Mc-Cord—retired US Army. It was said that he wanted to be in politics in the territory and that he wasn't fool enough to kiss political rump out here, but he made sure he kissed it back in Washington, DC.

Curious group, Sloan thought.

More curious because they were so damned drunk. And talking a bit loudly, as if they weren't even aware he was in the room.

"I still don't rightly get where this gold is coming from," Horse grumbled.

"I tell you," Abel said excitedly, "there is gold, lots of it, being paid by a guy from back east."

"Abel, you know what's going on here," Running Jack, one of the Crows, said.

"I know the money is big, and that it is coming from back east, and that when I can prove I've got the one white woman, dead or alive, all I've got to do is leave word here at the Ten-Penny for a Mr. Smith."

Running Jack groaned.

"Between us, surely, we can get the damned girl!" Abel exclaimed.

Running Jack shook his head. "I know of a dozen men who died going after her. You're forgetting. This woman is married to Hawk Douglas."

Abel didn't seem to hear him. "Both women are worth five hundred dollars. All in gold. He don't care what you do to either of them, and he'd just as soon get the blonde one dead."

It was enough. Sloan set down his coffee and moved behind Abel in a wink. He had a patch of Abel's hair in one hand while he held his knife to Abel's throat with the other. "Five hundred dollars isn't any good to a dead man. And that's about what you are."

"Who the hell—why, Sloan! Sloan, it's you—think about it, five hundred dollars for a pair of women—"

"Abel, shut up, you damned fool!" Horse said, glancing at Abel with disgust and at Sloan with a certain edge of fear. "You're talking to a man who grew up Oglala with Hawk."

Sloan drew the knife more tightly against Abel's throat.

"I don't know nothing more than what you've heard, Sloan—"

"How do you know what I've heard?"

"Why, why—do something, you bloody cowards! There's one bloody mixed-blood behind me, and you're just sitting there like a pack of laying hens!"

"Abel," Sloan said pleasantly, "these boys aren't going to move. Horse there knows I could knife you both before anyone had time to spit. Now maybe I couldn't kill all five, but who wants to chance being one of those I will take down with me?"

No one moved.

Sloan pressed the knife against Abel's throat so tightly that a thin thread of blood appeared against his flesh. "Now, Abel. Either you or Mark knows who the 'he' behind all this is. Start talking."

"You can't kill him! You're a major in the damned army."

"I am. And I'm a damned mixed-blood Sioux as well. And you just ask either of your two Crow comrades there. No one knows how to torture and kill quite like a Sioux. Abel, you better damned well tell me what you know."

---

WHEN HAWK CAME up the stairs, Skylar was nowhere in sight. Puzzled, he remained on the landing, listening. Was this some new trick? Was she aware that a senator was in the house, that they had guests? Was she determined to show him that she could be every bit as distant as he could when she chose?

Damn her, she didn't understand. She just didn't understand how she had tied him up in knots. How it seemed that danger awaited her at every corner, and he couldn't begin to fight it because he couldn't begin to recognize it. He hadn't wanted her in his life, hadn't trusted her an inch.

And now he quite simply couldn't imagine life without her. He hadn't the least idea when he had begun falling in love with her. Nor had he ever imagined that his feelings would grow so deep, so passionate, so nearly desperate. He'd never thought that he could look into silver eyes...

And forget to be wary.

Now he didn't dare go near her. Not until she came to him. Believe, she had said.

She had to do some of the believing.

He heard a sound from his bedroom library. He strode there quickly, pushing open the door to see her standing by the globe. She was definitely pale.

"Are you ill?"

"No—I've got to talk with you."

"Skylar, we have company downstairs. A senator from back east. If you're hoping to get even with me in some way—"

"No, no, he's not a senator from back east—"

"Skylar, I assure you that he is. He's served several terms."

"He is a senator. But he's more. You can't trust him. He's—it's him!" she said breathlessly.

"Skylar, I—"

She rushed at him suddenly, coming up on her toes, taking his face between her hands. "He's come for me. Not for me. Oh, God, I'm not making any sense. I'm of legal age. He can't do anything to me. But he wants to hurt me." She gasped suddenly. "I should have known. He wants me dead. He's always wanted me dead. He needs her, but if I were to perish in the West—"

"Skylar, Skylar!" Hawk exclaimed, catching her hands and holding them tightly. "Skylar, he who? What are you talking about?"

"Dillman."

"Dillman!" Hawk exclaimed incredulously.

"He's the one. I'm sure of it. I don't know how, but I know that he sent the Crows—"

"Skylar! The man is a crippled United States senator from Maryland! I'd heard he'd suffered some kind of an accident, and he's still in a wheelchair. He's probably in a wheelchair permanently. He can't command renegade Crows. He can't hurt you."

She wrenched her hands free from his. "You're wrong! He can hurt me. He's been hurting me. The truth! You always wanted the truth. Well, I've given you the truth now, but I was right. I knew that you wouldn't believe me.

"Believe what, Skylar? Why would a senator want to hurt you? I don't understand—"

"He killed my father!"

"Skylar, slow down!" he exclaimed. He'd never seen her like this. Never. Even when he had burst into the stagecoach and dragged her to the cabin. She seemed more frightened now than she had been of the Crow. "Skylar, you've got to—"

"Sabrina!" she gasped suddenly. "Oh, my God, if he's got her—he can't have her. No, he came here because he hasn't quite gotten his hands on her yet. He knows that she'll come to me. He knows somehow that I'm here—"

"Skylar, he's come because of the Black Hills."

"No!" She wrenched free of him, pushing past him. "I've got to go. I've got to find out if she's reached Gold Town, if Henry has heard from her—"

"Skylar—"

"You can't begin to understand what he can do!" she exclaimed, pausing just briefly to stare back at him. She shook her head. "He is the worst kind of monster because most men never see his evil!"

"Skylar, wait. Keep talking to me. I have to understand what is going on, what has happened." She didn't seem to hear him. In a blur of soft color, she was gone. "Skylar, damn you, stop! Listen to me—"

She wasn't stopping.

He tore after her.

She was swift, graceful, and as fast as a cougar. She was down the stairs by the time he reached the top of the landing. She moved silently, looking into the dining room before she quickly let herself out the front door. She was just seconds ahead of his descent to the ground floor.

"Lord Douglas!"

He paused.

Senator Dillman had rolled himself back into the foyer. He was a man possessing a certain dignified charm. He had a rueful smile that made him seem trustworthy, one with the common man. Level eyes, a square jaw. A voice that quietly filled space and seemed to command it.

"Senator Dillman, you'll have to excuse me—"

"You've married my girl, eh, sir?"

"I beg your pardon?"

Dillman sighed deeply, looking down. "She didn't tell you anything about herself? She ran away, you know." He looked around, assuring himself no one else was within hearing distance. "She's my stepdaughter. She pushed me down the stairs and ran away."

"What?" Hawk snapped out, all courtesy forgotten in his astonishment.

Dillman inhaled. "Your father was a fine man, a very fine man. I'm sure you're one and the same. I'm so sorry to tell you this, but the girl has been filled with delusions since she was a child. Her father was killed during the war. I was with him. I didn't die. She blamed me. I tried. All those years since, God knows I tried! But I married her mother, you see. She couldn't forgive me for living when her own true father was dead."

"I'm afraid I don't know what you're talking about."

"Skylar, Lord Douglas. Your wife." He shook his head sorrowfully. "Sir, I am ever so sorry. She's gone completely mad. Her mother's death sent her over the brink, I believe. I wanted to get doctors for her. The best money could buy. I tried to keep my patience with her, but we quarreled, and she has tremendous strength, tremendous strength! She sent me flying down the stairs, but she is my stepdaughter, my dear departed Jill's beloved flesh and blood. I couldn't call the police. But I knew that I had to find her. Help her."

Hawk crossed his arms over his chest, staring at the man. He had felt the lull of the man's voice, his persuasion. It was easy to understand why he was such a successful politician. He was so convincing.

"She's afraid of you," he said bluntly. "Why?"

"Why? God alone knows, Lord Douglas! Have you been listening, sir? The girl is delusional, poor, poor creature!"

The worst kind of monster, Skylar had told him.

"I'm perplexed. Why did you follow her here?"

"I have business here, my good man. But yes, I did need to find her. She is my stepdaughter. I care for her welfare. And for yours. Before Almighty God, sir, I do swear to you that the girl put me in this chair!"

She had told him she needed to talk to him. Now he needed to talk to her. He couldn't forget the look on her face, and he still couldn't understand her terror and despair. Dillman was in a wheelchair. What kind of a threat could he be?

"My wife has shown no signs of delusion. Or of violence," he added, even if it was a bit of lie. She'd only been violent when she'd been under attack.

Could Dillman possibly have been responsible for those attacks? How had he maneuvered renegades to his will?

"Then I'm glad for you, Lord Douglas. Yet still anxious to see my stepdaughter. You wouldn't deny me the right to see her? Why, Lord Douglas, you are, in fact, my stepson-in-law!"

"Indeed," Hawk murmured.

"I imagine that her sister is on her way here, attempting to be with her. Poor Sabrina! She is well aware of how dearly her sister needs help. We even believe she might be at risk of taking her own life. Still, I can't let Sabrina cast away her life! No, the child is still under my guardianship, and I intend to do the very best I can for her, in memory of my dear, dear wife!"

Damn, Dillman was good. So convincing that he was as hypnotic as a rattler. He could almost be believed except that...

David Douglas had been no fool. Hawk realized with sudden clarity that his father had stumbled upon Skylar when she had been in a desperate situation. David had certainly been captivated by Skylar. She must have shown a tremendous strength under adversity.

He killed my father, she had said. Dillman told it a different way. The war—Skylar would have been young at the time. But still...

He didn't know what had happened. He didn't know the truth of the matter. But he was determined to discover it.

"Excuse me. Please do make yourself comfortable with your companions in my absence."

He exited the house quickly, looking anxiously about the yard. He hurried toward the stables. He nearly collided with Willow, who had been hurrying toward the house.

"Where's Skylar?" Hawk demanded quickly.

"She came out here, completely ignored me, bridled Nutmeg, and took off—hell-bent. I was coming for you, wondering if I should have been going straight after her instead."

"I'll go straight after her. She's expecting her sister to have either arrived in Gold Town and will be heading here. She's trying to reach her. Willow, I need you to go back to the house and give Senator Dillman my excuses. Tell him he's welcome to stay as long as he wishes. In fact, have Meggie do her best to keep him there."

"I'll see to it, Hawk."

In seconds, Hawk was mounted on Tor.

Seconds too late.

---

SKYLAR HAD SCARCELY left Douglas property when the attack came.

They'd been waiting for her.

Too late she realized her mistake. She damned herself, realizing that again she had underestimated Dillman.

They came from the copse of trees to the west of the property line. This time, there were eight riders. They were all dressed in war paint, though even as she lay against Nutmeg's neck to turn her horse and urge her to speed back toward Mayfair, she saw that they weren't all Indians. Dillman had called upon the dregs of the army, so it seemed. And probably prospectors, too. Men who had come for gold and hadn't managed to strike it. Dillman promised them gold without digging. All they needed to do was kill one woman.

And make the murder look like an Indian attack.

Even as she rode back to Mayfair, she realized the men had stationed themselves behind her. As she tried to race back, she was circled.

She had so foolishly run. It had been time to meet Dillman face-to-face, with Hawk. He hadn't denied her. He had merely been stunned. Because she had made no attempt to explain any of it before. Because she had never imagined that Dillman could break in upon her life here. She had felt...

Safe.

She was Hawk's wife.

But she had run away from Hawk.

And now...

She tried to move Nutmeg to the left. A rider, his face painted black, was there. She forced the horse to rear. Nutmeg pounded down to the right.

Then one of the men, laughing, leaped from his own horse to hers, dragging her down from Nutmeg.

Down, down, down...

Monsters had come.

# CHAPTER 25

Hawk hadn't ridden more than five minutes before he saw a familiar figure racing toward him.

Sloan.

He continued forward until they met; both men reined in hard. "Did you come in from Gold Town? Did you pass Skylar?" Hawk demanded.

"Skylar's gone?" Sloan demanded in turn.

"She just rode toward town—"

"She isn't on the way to town. I would have seen her. Hawk, you have to listen to me. I overheard a conversation at the Ten-Penny. There's been a bounty out on your wife. Huge money, payable in gold, for Skylar. Dead or alive. That weasel Abel was passing the word on it. There was money, and power, behind the offer."

"Dillman!" Hawk muttered. "Dillman is in my house right now. He was trying to tell me Skylar is insane, that he was crippled because of her."

"He might be crippled, but he has the dregs of the territory out to find her."

"Did you see signs of a struggle anywhere—"

"I wasn't looking. I was trying to reach you."

"Let's look now. Time, Sloan, time might mean everything."

They kneed their mounts, rocketing mercilessly out along the trail once again. As they rode, they could see a wagon coming in the distance. Hawk slowed his horse, nearing Sloan. "It's Henry's wagon. He must have Skylar's sister with him. That's why Skylar lit out of the house so wildly—she was afraid of Dillman getting his hands on her sister."

"We'll send him back to town."

Hawk shook his head. "We'll send him to the cabin."

But even as they rode closer to the approaching wagon, riders burst out from the westward edge of the forest. Shots were fired. The wagon started careening wildly.

"The whole damned world has gone mad!" Hawk exclaimed. He was unarmed, except for the knife he wore in his ankle sheath.

Sloan pulled his Colt Army pistol from his holster. He fired off several shots, taking careful aim at the half dozen painted men shrieking toward the wagon. The attackers, looking to the north, hadn't seen them observe the assault.

Hawk saw that Henry was no coward. He rose behind the reins of his small flatbed wagon, firing off his shotgun. Then he was hit in the shoulder. He fell back against the seat. The woman beside him, her face hidden by a wide-brimmed hat, shrieked, bending over poor Henry.

Sloan picked off two of the attackers with his Colt while they thundered down upon the wagon. Bullets sizzled by their ears in turn. Hawk would have been hit straight in the heart, but he had learned how to ride as a Sioux. When the bullet came, his body was on Tor's side, and the lead ball of death hurtled on by him. He straightened and came upon one of the dressed-up white men in time to leap from Tor's back and hurtle his opponent to the ground before the man could get off a shot. His wife's life was at stake. His own life, now, too. He reached his knife in seconds.

He killed the man with merciful speed, then stole his pistol. It was out of date, but it had three shots left. He spun just as he heard a rustling behind him, shooting another painted white man who would have attacked him. He rose, just in time to see Sloan leaping atop the step of the wagon to kill the last of the attackers, a man now bent over the woman, trying to wrest her from the wagon. Sloan wrenched the fellow up to a stand with a grip upon his shoulder, then felled him with a blow against his neck. The man silently catapulted from the wagon.

The woman kept shrieking.

"Stop it!" Sloan shouted, holding her back taut to his chest, grappling her arms to her sides and twisting her around so that she faced Hawk. "Hawk, this isn't—"

"Hawk! You're Hawk! Oh, my God, get this man—"

"Sabrina?" Hawk said. She was striking. Auburn hair now wild and tangled around a beautiful face. Her features were something like Skylar's, but her coloring was completely different. Her figure was an hourglass form. Together, the sisters were like a perfect pair of fairy-tale princesses, Rose Red and Rose White, perhaps.

"Hawk, this woman—"

"Lord Douglas, this man—"

"She isn't Sabrina, Hawk, she's—"

"I am Sabrina Connor!" the woman exclaimed.

"She's not! She's—"

"Who the bloody hell is this wretched bastard?" she hissed.

Hawk's brows shot up. "Sabrina Connor, a very good friend and associate, Major Sloan Trelawney. Sloan, my sister-in-law, Sabrina Connor."

Sabrina Connor had something of her sister's fighting spirit about her as well. She stamped hard upon Sloan's booted foot.

"Will you let go of me, please, Major?"

Sloan grated out, "I still don't believe—"

"Wait!" Hawk said, putting up a hand when it looked as if both would begin arguing again. "Riders coming again, from the south. Sabrina, see if Henry is breathing.Sloan—toss me Henry's gun."

He ducked down, taking aim at the half-score of riders now coming toward them. Sloan sank down as well, his Colt leveled upon his arm.

They came into view. Dillman's two aides first. Then two other men, white men, strangers to the territory. They had a look about them. Professional gunfighters, Hawk thought.

Behind them rode Dillman.

With Skylar seated before him on his mount.

For a crippled man, he was riding damned well.

"Are you going to shoot, Lord Douglas?" Dillman called out. "It wouldn't be a very good idea. I'd kill her before you could even pray to hit me."

Hawk stood, shoving the pistol through his belt loop. The group remained perhaps twenty-five feet away from him. He met Skylar's eyes. He could see them clearly at this distance. They were filled with misery and more. A wealth of sorrow that she had involved him in this. Love. Aching. She didn't move, but he could see it all there. So much that he had missed for so long. She wanted to come to him...

She sat dead still. Staring at him with those silver eyes. They misted. "Hawk, I'm so sorry—" she began.

"I nearly had to kill her to get here, Douglas. Or do they call you Hawk, Lord of the Plains? She thought she could keep you safe if she bargained well enough with herself. But then, I'm a gambling man. I've always been a gambling man. If this territory wasn't filled with idiots, she might be dead now, and you might be a grieving young widower. I hate to be forced to show my hand. If you'd agreed that she was mentally unbalanced, I'd have been happy to take her back east and leave you a free man. Unfortunately, this territory is filled with incompetent fools."

"Not everyone would have been fooled, no matter what your offers of gold might have accomplished. You wanted to escalate the Indian problems in the West, didn't you, Dillman?"

Dillman shrugged. "I don't give a damn about the Indians. They don't need me to escalate their problems. Let's just say that I meant to use a situation already well underway. Sabrina! How nice to see you. What a pity you hadn't the good sense to figure out where a decent future awaited you!"

"What a pity I didn't have the damned good sense to realize what a lying pathetic fake you were! You're riding damned well for a cripple, Dillman."

"Indeed, I am. I have a will of steel, girl, and of course, I had your capable, tender care—until recently. Ah, well. Is the driver dead?"

"No," Sabrina said. "But he needs medical attention—"

"See if he's blacked out. It might do well to leave the attorney, since he must have been struck by these painted fools on the ground here before they let themselves be killed by a pair of half-breeds."

"Dillman, just what the hell do you think you're going to get away with?" Hawk demanded.

"This is Lord Douglas," Sloan spoke out, "And I am a US Army major, not a drunken prospector or desperate agency Indian."

Dillman smiled, showing them the knife that he'd been pressing against Skylar's side. It was tipped with blood. Hawk almost made a move. Thought better of it. Dillman was trying to goad him.

"Don't let him get away with this!" Skylar suddenly cried out. "Hawk, whatever happens to me, shoot the bastard! Don't let him bring you and Sloan and Sabrina down, too!" She broke off with an involuntary shriek of pain. Hawk took a step forward. Sloan leaped down from the wagon, catching his shoulders.

"We can take them all if we just wait for the right moment!" Sloan said, switching to the Sioux language.

Sloan was right.

"What do you want?" Hawk demanded.

"You have a cabin in the woods, I understand. Let's go there. I take your weapons, of course, gentlemen. Major, Lord Douglas, mount your horses, please. And keep your distance from one another at all times. The big fellows here with the feral eyes are George and Macy. Between them, they've logged well over a hundred kills. In fact, they're wanted for murder in several places, but I can take care of that for them." He brought the point of his knife up to Skylar's throat. "Well, gentlemen—do we ride?"

The man he had called Macy dismounted from his horse and seized Sloan's and Hawk's weapons. He didn't seem to realize Hawk carried a knife at his calf. One small point in their favor.

Hawk turned to help Sabrina Connor down from the wagon.

"Sabrina, dear, you ride with Macy," Dillman said.

"I'd rather be dragged," Sabrina replied.

"That can be arranged," Dillman assured her.

"Get on the damned horse with him!" Sloan snapped to her.

Sabrina had little choice. Macy was large and powerful and could handle the weapons and Sabrina quite easily.

Hawk and Sloan mounted their horses. Henry was left behind. Dillman ordered his men to collect the bodies of the white men who'd dressed and painted themselves as Indians for the attack on the wagon. They were thrown over the haunches of their mounts to follow along with the group heading for the cabin—to be disposed of at a better place and time, so it seemed. Dillman would want to leave no evidence of white involvement in an Indian raid.

Hawk moved ahead on Tor. He met Skylar's silver gaze once again. He had a chance to speak to her very softly, very briefly as he passed by her.

"I slay all monsters!" he promised.

"What?" Dillman snapped.

"I said you're a damned monster!" he grated.

Dillman smiled. "A damned good monster!" he agreed. He laughed aloud then, enjoying his own joke.

They began to ride to the cabin.

---

WILLOW WAS JUST ABOUT to mount his own horse. The senator had been joined at the house by two other men who spoke with him briefly before helping him from the house. They had all been polite and courteous to Lord Douglas's household. They had made Willow damned suspicious. Now neither Hawk nor Skylar had returned, and Dillman had been gone nearly an hour, and he was growing worried.

Just as he mounted his horse, he heard his name. He looked to see a number of men coming toward him. He was stunned to see his brothers riding toward him, leading a horse-drawn wagon. He never mounted his horse. He hurried toward them.

"Henry Pierpont's inside, shot through beneath the shoulder," Ice Raven told him.

"He's going to make it," Blade said, "but he'll need some care right away."

"We'll get him inside to Meggie—"

"Call the women to get him in," Ice Raven said. "Willow, he came to, raving a little when we found him. Someone just staged an Indian attack on him. He was bringing Skylar's sister out to Mayfair. They were having a nice ride when they were suddenly attacked by painted bucks."

"An Indian raid—" Willow began incredulously.

"There might have been Indians involved, but it wasn't an Indian attack. Henry said that they didn't know he had come to after Hawk and Sloan came upon them and killed the supposed Indians. More men came. Threatening to kill Skylar. They took Hawk, Sloan, Skylar, and her sister."

"Where?" Willow demanded.

"To Hawk's cabin in the woods."

"How many of them?"

"Henry didn't know," Blade supplied. "Several. And he thinks some of them are hired killers."

"I'll call the women to come for Henry," Willow said. "Three full-blooded Sioux. I imagine we can stage an Indian attack of our own."

Ice Raven nodded. "As long as we don't have to go through the paint thing again," he told his brother.

Willow smiled grimly. "No paint. No bows and arrows. Guns, and we shoot to kill. And if it's that Dillman who staged this thing, I want his scalp."

"Hawk just might want that one."

"Hawk will want his heart on a platter," Willow said. He started toward the house, then paused briefly. "What brought you two out here now?"

Ice Raven looked at Blade, then back to Willow. "Crazy Horse had a vision. He cannot come to the whites. He asked that we come see about Hawk."

"Ah," Willow said.

He was Sioux. He was not about to question the wisdom and truth of a vision.

Skylar felt as if she moved within a dream. As if nothing were real. A numbness seemed to have settled over her; the mistakes she had made in the past seemed to play over and over again in her mind. The years of living with Dillman. Of knowing he had killed her father. Slept with her mother. Laughed because there was nothing she could do.

She had escaped him. She had hurt him and escaped him, but she hadn't killed him. Because she didn't want to be him. Now she was paying for her mercy not only with her own life but with the lives of her sister, her husband, and a man who was surely one of the best friends she would ever have.

Dillman wasn't letting up his hold on her. It didn't matter. His knife was biting into the flesh at her side now and then, but at the moment, he was just scratching her. Just enough to let her know how badly he could hurt her. She was certain he wouldn't enjoy the kill half so much as he did the anticipation of it.

Sabrina rode near her. Another mistake. She had never emphasized how important it was that Sabrina never use her own name. But she was certain that nothing she could have done would have mattered. Dillman was a man with connections. He could have discovered the contents of their telegrams no matter what. And now Sabrina was with her.

She couldn't even touch her sister, hold her, hug her, one last time.

She gritted her teeth together, furious with herself, glad of the next prick Dillman gave her with the knife. She was going to feel, and she was going to fight. She had fought before and lost. She was still breathing. She was going to keep fighting him.

Ahead of her suddenly was the cabin in the woods. Now, of course, memories flooded back to her in earnest. Fresh, sweet memories. Ah, but she hadn't found the events so sweet when they had occurred! She had assumed herself under attack by the strangest of Indians. She'd been afraid of so much, fighting so much, disbelieving so much—and she'd been so damned determined to stay out here, no matter what! He'd held her here for the first time. Touched her here. Made love to her here. Made her his wife here. The cabin meant so much to her. Dillman couldn't know that.

He meant to burn it down, she suspected.

"All right, gentlemen—and ladies," Dillman drawled. Skylar could feel his breath on her neck. "Into the cabin, if you will."

Hawk stared at Dillman, his features set in the chiseled-rock expression that gave nothing away. He dismounted from his horse but didn't head for the cabin. He approached Dillman. "I want Skylar. Now."

"Step into the cabin, let Macy tie your hands, and she is yours."

"I'll step into the cabin. No one ties me until she is mine. Dillman, admit it—you want to make it look as if Sioux, angry about my and Sloan's relationships with the whites, came in here and wiped us out. Or perhaps we're supposed to die as if the Crow were carrying out a vendetta against me. Either way, if you have to shoot me in the heart, it won't look good. And no one is tying me until Skylar is with me. Macy there may be one good gunfighter. But I'll bet he can also take one good look at me and know he's got trouble on his hands if I choose to make it happen."

Dillman shrugged. "Sabrina, it's too bad. I hadn't intended you to be a part of this, to have to die, but you've involved yourself. You, in the cabin along with the major there, Lord Redman, you right behind him. Then Skylar follows."

Dillman's men had already dismounted, Skylar saw. They carried large saddlebags, which two of men now started to open. She saw that they contained bows and arrows.

"Brad, are you having us killed by Crow or Sioux?" she asked him.

She felt the knife digging at her.

"Sioux," he said flatly after a minute. "I thought it was a nice touch."

"I'm not going in there," Sabrina said stubbornly.

Skylar glanced at her sister, then at Hawk, still standing in front of her. His expression gave away so little, but he suddenly smiled slightly to her. He inclined his head just a little to the east.

"Remember when we first came here, Skylar?" he said.

She stared at him blankly. She'd certainly never thought of him as being a sentimental man. Wild, passionate, hot-tempered, occasionally startlingly tender...

But not sentimental.

"Yes..."

"Remember how we came to be here?"

She frowned.

"Lord Douglas, this is touching, really," Brad Dillman said impatiently, "but unless you want to watch her blood flow quickly, it's time to move."

"Yes, move into the cabin," Hawk said.

"I'm not going!" Sabrina repeated stubbornly.

Skylar kept looking at Hawk. How they had come to be here that day...

An Indian attack. He had dressed up. With Willow, Ice Raven, and Blade...

Willow!

Was he out there somewhere? Did Hawk know it? Had he heard the call of a dove in the air and known that it was not a dove?

Perhaps she didn't understand him quickly enough. Sloan did. He strode for Sabrina and dragged her down from Macy's mount. "We're going in."

"I'm not, I—"

"Keep quiet!" Sloan insisted, his arms about her waist, Sabrina hanging from his hip as he strode for the cabin door, throwing it open.

"Let me go, you oaf! Skylar!"

As if Skylar could help her in any way!

"The damned army is doing us in, Skylar!" Sabrina shrieked.

Hawk ignored the frantic cries Sabrina let out. He stared up at Dillman. "I'll walk to the cabin door. Then I want Skylar released to me. Understood?"

"I can't see any harm in you fools dying in one another's arms," Dillman said pleasantly.

Hawk started for the cabin. Skylar saw that Macy and George were keeping their guns trained on her and the others while Dillman's "aides" were getting ready to light arrows on fire and shoot them into the cabin.

Hawk stepped through the cabin door. He turned to face them, standing in the doorway.

"Let Skylar go!"

Dillman shoved her. Prepared for his action, Skylar clung to the horse's neck as she fell downward, keeping herself from plummeting to the ground. She had a strange feeling that this was all or nothing now. If she had a chance to live, she wouldn't be able to make the most of it with a sprained ankle or a broken wrist.

She started walking toward the cabin. Macy remained right behind her, a gun trained on her back. Skylar kept her eyes on Hawk's. He met hers in return, the green fire in them encouraging her all the way.

She reached him. He put his hands on her shoulders, drew her very close against him, cradling her head. He might have been whispering love words.

"When I let you go now, get down. Flat on the ground, understand?"

"But they'll shoot you—"

"Skylar, love, honor, and obey right now, please? I love you, Skylar."

"Oh, God—I love you. I love you so much. I—" He started to twist her around. He did so with such speed and energy that it hadn't really been necessary for him to tell her to get down; she all but fell on the floor. And in those few seconds, he had gone for a knife. A knife sheathed in buckskin against the boots at his calf.

It flew with staggering speed and landed straight in Macy's heart. For a few seconds, the giant of a killer stood there, about to reach for the knife, absolutely stunned to realize that he was mortally injured.

And even as he fell, Hawk let out a tremolo before jumping before the fallen man, going flat himself to grasp Macy's weapon, a repeating rifle, before rolling into the brush.

Bullets were suddenly flying everywhere. Skylar let out a screech, covering her head. A burning arrow sizzled into a beam directly over her.

Sloan was above her, trying to draw her from the line of fire. She heard war cries screeching all around her. Sioux cries, the terrifying sound they let out before bearing down on their enemies.

"Get in!" Sloan commanded her. She saw that he'd found a rifle by the hearth. As he dragged her in, he thrust it toward Sabrina. "Get shells, load it!"

"I'll shoot you!" Sabrina retorted, but she had the rifle in her hands and was digging into a wooden box of ammunition even as she spoke.

Another shot tore into the cabin. Sabrina screeched and shoved the rifle at Sloan. He took it. Skylar looked up, gasping. A half dozen arrows had made it into the cabin. Smoke was billowing all around them.

It was going to burn.

"We've got to get out," Sloan shouted.

Skylar came to her feet. Sabrina balked. "We'll be shot. We can't go—"

"Damn it, we've got to get out!" Sloan repeated. Skylar was stunned when he grabbed her sister furiously by the arm, dragging her up.

Skylar shrieked, seeing that George had leaped into the burning cabin. His rifle was aimed at Sloan.

A shot exploded. Sloan didn't go down. George did.

Skylar saw Hawk standing behind him. She let out a glad cry, starting to race toward him. But even as she did, she saw Dillman directly behind her husband. He was raising his rifle.

"No!" she shrieked.

Hawk fell and rolled with lightning-quick reflexes. Dillman's first shot went off, hitting the wall. He didn't seem to realize that the cabin was burning, that fiery timber was beginning to fall everywhere. He started for Skylar, taking aim with his rifle once again.

"Bastard!" she shrieked. He was going to kill her. It had come to this. She was going to die. But he wasn't going to get away with it. Hawk would kill him. And at long last, everyone would know the truth about Brad Dillman.

Despite the gun, she leaped for him. She slammed against him just as the gun fired. They went down to the ground together.

She felt no pain.

Dillman was screaming.

Skylar, dazed by the fall and the swirl of smoke she continued to breathe, realized dimly that Brad Dillman's rifle had misfired. Perhaps it had gotten too hot. Perhaps he'd had faulty cartridges. But the weapon had failed to discharge properly. She was alive, and he was screeching in pain. Because there was a knife in his chest. Hawk had thrown it to keep Dillman from shooting Skylar. And as he had fallen, the knife had been pressed further and further into his body...

Skylar hadn't the sense at that moment to scramble to her feet. She just stared at Dillman. He was really dying. He was in great pain.

He stared at her. "I should have killed you with your old man. Nits make lice." He started to laugh. He choked on his own blood.

She was suddenly wrenched up in strong arms. Hawk's arms. He carried her out of the cabin.

Macy was dead on the ground where he had fallen. The two aides had been hit by rifle fire.

Willow, Ice Raven, and Blade were mounted before the cabin, waiting, watching the fire.

Sabrina was on her knees, smudged, sooty, trying to breathe. Sloan, in similar condition, stood by her side. Skylar realized he had pulled her sister from the flames.

She realized that somehow, they had all known that she and Hawk would come from the blaze as well.

Just as they had somehow known that they were needed.

"Thank you," Hawk said simply.

Willow shrugged. "We wanted to play Indian with you once again."

"But how—"

"Crazy Horse had a vision," Ice Raven told him.

"And Henry Pierpont told us where they were taking you."

Hawk smiled. "Ah."

Skylar felt his eyes touch down upon her. "Let's go home," he said. She nodded. She leaned more closely against him.

"All the monsters are slain!" she agreed softly.

It had probably been the most horrible day of her life.

She had never felt better.

Skylar convinced Ice Raven and Blade to stay with them just one night. She understood their need to be free Indians, but she was so grateful to them both, and they were her relatives through Hawk, and she wanted them to know that she would always be there for them as well.

At Mayfair, though she was somewhat bruised and battered herself, her energy level seemed astounding. She arranged with Meggie, Sandra, and the others to get all the guests to rooms, prepare baths, find clothing, and arrange a meal. She and Hawk were both delighted to discover that Meggie had proclaimed Henry much better than anyone might have imagined. The bullet had traveled cleanly through him. He was going to have to stay in bed for a few days, but he was just incredibly proud of himself, and he didn't mind being bedridden because Sandra was doting on him.

Sandra, in turn, informed them that she found lawyers to be wonderful men.

They had a fine dinner that evening, Skylar and Hawk, Sloan, Sabrina, Willow, Ice Raven, and Blade. They'd sent for the military, determined to tell the entire story to the general and see to it that the truth about Dillman was made public for the world to know. Skylar was especially happy to feel that at long last justice had been done for her father.

It was very late when Hawk and Skylar were at last free to retire.

To her room.

Their room. She felt it now, as soon as they entered together. As soon as he closed the door. As soon as he cupped her face in both his hands and kissed her lips. Warmly. Fully. Passionately.

They fell upon the bed together. Kissing. Struggling somewhat in their haste to remove one another's clothes.

"Are you alright? Truly? I know he drew blood today—" Hawk began.

"I'm not hurt."

"I wouldn't hurt you further—"

"I'm not hurt! I'm alive, I'm well—we've got to build another cabin."

"I thought you hated the cabin."

"I loved the cabin."

"It burned."

"With my past!" Skylar breathed, finally undoing the last button of his shirt, meeting his eyes, and pressing her lips against his chest.

"I'll be happy to build another cabin. I thought you hated it because I...well, I rather forced you that night—"

She shook her head solemnly. Then smiled with a silver glitter in her eyes. "I had dreams of you ravishing me there again."

He groaned. "I'll build quickly," he promised. His lips found hers again.

"How strange. How sad, though. Sloan and Sabrina don't seem to get on well at all."

"Maybe they just haven't had a chance to get to know one another," Hawk suggested.

"Maybe. Oh, well...Hawk, we won't let the Sioux take any blame for what happened today. I mean, truly, there's no way that they can be involved, right? Ice Raven kept telling me that it wouldn't matter, that it would put an end to things—"

"There will be no blame upon the Sioux for Dillman's evil. You needn't worry," Hawk said, triumphant as he tugged her pantalettes from her. With them both naked at last, he bounded atop her, the fullness of his flesh rubbing against hers. He sighed with both contentment and growing ardor.

"Hawk, what will happen?" she asked suddenly, both her hands in his dark hair.

"Now? I'm going to kiss and lick you all over. You're going to writhe in ecstasy and ask me to be with you forever."

"No, no—"

"Yes, yes!"

"With the Sioux, I mean."

He sobered, lightly kissing her forehead and her lips. "I don't know. The future will be painful. That I can see. Will you be with me, all the way through it?"

"All the way. Forever."

"Even though you entered the West through a Sioux attack?"

"Especially because I entered the West through a Sioux attack," she assured him softly.

He hesitated suddenly, strangely. "Even if we have to take a trip away?"

"A trip, away?"

"Even if I'm not—Lord Douglas?"

"What?" she gasped, leaping away from him, her eyes filled with alarm. "You—you mean after all this, you're not Andrew Douglas. We're not married—"

He smiled ruefully, shaking his head, catching her hand, and drawing her back against him. "Come here, wench!"

"Now wait—"

"We are really, truly, absolutely, irrevocably wed."

"Then—"

"Then truthfully, we may not be Lord and Lady Douglas. In fact, I pray that we are not."

She stared at him blankly. "Hawk—"

"Skylar, I had a brother who died in Scotland years ago. Or so we thought. I've recently had a communication from someone supposedly in his employ."

"Recently?"

"At Henry's office, the day we went into Gold Town."

"Oh! And all this time I thought Henry might have found out things about me to tell you!"

Hawk had to smile again. He shook his head. "No, my love, you made me discover all that I know about you the hard way."

She was frowning. "Hawk, I'd hate for you to hope that your brother was alive if someone was playing a cruel trick for jest or gain. How can you think—"

"This fellow had a family heirloom—a ring my brother David always wore—to give me, and I was asked to meet a man at a particular place on Douglas property. Yes, this could be a wretched hoax. It most probably is. But Skylar, I loved my brother. I have to find out."

"We have to find out."

"I've already dragged you through Sioux country—"

"I shall gladly be dragged through Scotland."

"Even to give up the title?" he queried lightly.

She smiled slowly, pressed her lips to his, whispered against them. "I'm Hawk's wife. Nothing else means anything."

He kissed her passionately in turn. Lifted his lips just slightly from hers. "I never wanted a wife and now...oh, God, am I grateful to my father! Skylar, I love you. I cannot remember life without you, and I never want life without you again."

"Oh, God, that's lovely."

"That's all you have to say?"

She shook her head. "I love you. Oh, God, I love you. I—I—" She shook her head again, slightly embarrassed by the emotion overwhelming her. "I adore you!" she whispered. "Don't you even begin to think about going anywhere without me in the future—into Sioux country, across the sea, into hell itself."

He groaned, holding her. "I'll never leave you."

"Perhaps we can leave Sloan and Sabrina to look after things here."

"Perhaps we can."

"Perhaps..."

"Perhaps..."

"Oh, God, who cares right now! Hawk, I love you so much. Whatever lies in the days ahead, we'll meet together. Tonight, I'm just so grateful. What was that you were saying before we got sidetracked about the immediate future?"

"I was saying...never mind. It's much easier to just show you," he whispered, his green eyes afire with passion, promise, and love.

She felt his touch...

Lips, hands, upon her. Fiercely demanding, hot, tender, caressing, encompassing.

And she knew.

They would weather all the fires and storms that lay ahead of them with one another, believing in one another.

Man and wife.

A damned strange marriage, she thought.

And a damned fine one...

And then...she thought no more. She was far too busy being ravished by a mixed-race and doing her absolute very best to prove her love to him in turn.

Ah...did she like the nights!

# A LOOK AT BOOK TWO

## NO OTHER WOMAN

***Savage Thunder* meets *Outlander* in this storm-swept tale of vengeance, desire, and forbidden love in the wilds of the Scottish Highlands.**

Lady Shawna MacGinnis cannot outrun the night that haunts her. In a desperate act of loyalty to her clan, she seduced David Douglas of Castle Rock—and led him straight into a deadly betrayal. Now, tormented by dreams and drowning in guilt, she's certain his blood is on her hands.

But David is not dead.

Forged by betrayal and hardened by years spent among his brother's people—the Sioux warriors of America's West—he returns to Scotland a different man. Colder. Sharper. And determined to reclaim his title, expose those who deceived him, and make Shawna pay—with her pride, her body, and her heart.

Yet in the shadows of vengeance, something dangerous stirs. Desire. Longing. And the echo of a bond neither time nor treachery could break.

*One woman holds the key to his fury... and his redemption.*

***AVAILABLE MARCH 2026***

# ABOUT THE AUTHOR

*New York Times* and *USA Today* bestselling author, Heather Graham, majored in theater arts at the University of South Florida. After a stint of several years in dinner theater, backup vocals, and bartending, she stayed home after the birth of her third child and began to write. Her first book was with Dell, and since then, she has written over two hundred novels and novellas including category, suspense, historical romance, vampire fiction, time travel, occult, sci-fi, young adult, and Christmas family fare.

She is pleased to have been published in approximately twenty-five languages. She has written over 200 novels and has 60 million books in print. Heather has been honored with awards from booksellers and writers' organizations for excellence in her work, and she is the proud to be a recipient of the Silver Bullet from Thriller Writers and was awarded the prestigious Thriller Master Award in 2016. She is also a recipient of the Lifetime Achievement Award from RWA. Heather has had books selected for the Doubleday Book Club and the Literary Guild, and has been quoted, interviewed, or featured in such publications as The Nation, Redbook, Mystery Book Club, People and USA Today and appeared on many newscasts including Today, Entertainment Tonight and local television.

Heather loves travel and anything that has to do with the water, and is a certified scuba diver. She also loves ballroom dancing. Each year she hosts a Vampire Ball and Dinner theater raising money for the Pediatric Aids Society and in 2006 she hosted the first Writers for New Orleans Workshop to benefit the stricken Gulf Region. She is also the founder of "The Slush Pile Players," presenting something that's "almost like entertainment" for various conferences and benefits. Married since high school graduation and the mother of five, her greatest love in life remains her family, but she also believes her career has been an incredible gift, and she is grateful every day to be doing something that she loves so very much for a living.

Printed in Dunstable, United Kingdom

82297181R00211